Praise for *Death, Deceit & Some Smooth Jazz*!

"Claudia Mair Burney's stories explore the challenge of following Christ in a sin-sick world. Don't let the zany humor fool you—this novel also has depth. Jazz and Bell confront the consequences of other people's evil choices while coming to terms with their own temptations and mistakes. From giddy slapstick to wrenching heartache to the troubling and honest portrayal of modern life, this story challenged me at every turn."

Sharon Hinck—author of *Renovating Becky Miller* and *The Restorer*

"You know it's good when you skip meals to keep reading—and by the time I finished Burney's latest book, I needed a really big dinner! Thank you, Claudia, for a hilarious, nail-biting, sexy, and un-put-downable story. Your flair for language and engaging characters make every page delicious."

Alison Strobel Morrow—author of *Violette Between*

"Amanda Bell Brown rides again! With a fabulous, flawed, and wonderfully funny cast of characters, Claudia Mair Burney's *Death, Deceit & Some Smooth Jazz* is a delicious indulgence."

Kimberly Stuart—author of *Balancing Act* and *Bottom Line*

"Better than chocolate! A rich, satisfying read (with a few nuts) that will melt your heart and make you crave the next Claudia Mair Burney novel!"

Ginger Garrett—author of *Chosen* (2006 Christian Book Award nominee) and *Dark Hour*

"Claudia Mair Burney continues to be an amazing and powerful writing force. With *Death, Deceit & Some Smooth Jazz*, Burney gives new meaning to 4-F: Funny, Fast, Fresh, and Fantastic."

Stanice Anderson—inspirational speaker, author of *I Say a Prayer For Me: One Woman's Life of Faith and Triumph*

"With her vivid and magnetic style, Claudia Mair Burney combines humor, romance, and the unexpected into an authentic mystery. An undoubtedly intriguing story!"

Mata Elliott—author of *Forgivin' Ain't Forgettin'*

"Claudia Mair Burney pushes all the boundaries in this smart, sassy, romantic mystery. Don't let the title fool you. *Death, Deceit & Some Smooth Jazz* is a whole lot of fun!"

Cynthia Hickey—author of *Pursued by Evil*

Death, Deceit & some smooth jazz

an amanda bell brown mystery

Claudia Mair Burney

HOWARD BOOKS
A DIVISION OF SIMON & SCHUSTER
New York   London   Toronto   Sydney

Our purpose at Howard Books is to:
• *Increase faith* in the hearts of growing Christians
• *Inspire holiness* in the lives of believers
• *Instill hope* in the hearts of struggling people everywhere
Because He's coming again!

Published by Howard Books, a division of Simon & Schuster, Inc.
1230 Avenue of the Americas, New York, NY 10020
www.howardpublishing.com

Death, Deceit & Some Smooth Jazz © 2008 Claudia Mair Burney

Library of Congress Control Number: 2007038951

ISBN-13: 978-1-4165-5191-1

-

10 9 8 7 6 5 4 3 2 1

HOWARD and colophon are registered trademarks of Simon & Schuster, Inc.

Manufactured in the United States of America

For information regarding special discounts for bulk purchases, please contact: Simon & Schuster Special Sales at 1-800-456-6798 or business@simonandschuster.com.

Edited by Lissa Halls Johnson
Cover design by Terry Dugan Design
Interior design by Davina Mock-Maniscalco

This novel is a work of fiction. Names, characters, places, and incidents either are the product of the author's imagination or are used fictitiously. Any resemblance to actual events, locales, organizations, or persons, living or dead, is entirely coincidental and beyond the intent of either the author or publisher.

Scripture quotations marked NIV are taken from the Holy Bible, New International Version. Copyright © 1973, 1978, 1984 by International Bible Society. Used by permission of Zondervan. All rights reserved. Scripture quotations marked KJV are taken from the Holy Bible, Authorized King James Version. Scripture quotations marked *The Message* are taken from *The Message*. Copyright © 1993, 1994, 1995, 1996, 2000, 2001, 2002. Used by permission of NavPress Publishing Group. All rights reserved. Scripture quotations marked NKJV are taken from the New King James Version. Copyright © 1982 by Thomas Nelson, Inc. Used by permission. All rights reserved.

For Ken—
my husband, my Jazz, my complicated melody

acknowledgments

Glory to the Father, and to the Son, and to the Holy Spirit, now and ever, and unto ages of ages, AMEN!

I'm grateful for every opportunity I have to tell a story. My husband, Ken, and my children, Kenny, Lumumba, Bianca, Abeje, Kamau, Nia Grace, and Aziza are generous in sharing me with the world. They fend for themselves while I lock myself in my bedroom, writing. Thanks, family, for helping me make my dreams come true.

I'm grateful to my mother, Latrecia, and all of my brothers and sisters. You all are always in my heart, and frequently in my stories.

Mom Burney, you've helped so much; we couldn't have made it without your support.

Thank you to my writer pals who keep me going: Mary, Lisa, Heather, Alison, Lori, Paula, Dee, Sharon, Kim, Ginger, and Bethany.

Thanks, church family at Saint Raphael of Brooklyn Orthodox Christian Mission, for hanging in there with me.

Archbishop Nathaniel, Father Leo, and Robert, your generous gifts made it possible for me to buy a new computer and finish this book! I pray my favorite prayer for you: May the Lord have mercy on you. Thank you, thank you, thank you!

I'm deeply grateful to Lissa for dancing this dance with me, once again. You make my work shine!

Many thanks to the team at Howard Books/Simon & Schuster, especially Philis, John, and Chrys. It's been great working with you.

I have the best agent in the whole wide world. He's a beast, but a gentle one. Thanks, Chip, for everything.

Thanks, Sergeant Mike Logghe of the Ann Arbor Police, for procedural information. If I got it wrong I take all the blame.

And for my many friends, you're in my heart if not on this list.

Thank you, reader, for another chance. Grace to you all.

Mair

September 12, 2007

The heart is deceitful above all things,
and desperately wicked: who can know it?

—Jeremiah 17:9 KJV

chapter
one

I HAD TO GIVE UP JAZZ. Not the music; the man.

Now I had Amos, and we were going to "bond." I stood in the middle of my living room holding him. I'd put on my favorite pajamas—the midnight blue pair Carly had gotten for me from Victoria's Secret. They were modest, even if they did have the VS logo on the breast pocket. Cut in the style of men's pajamas and a size too big, they had the effect of looking charmingly baggy on me. I didn't even need a robe with them. Perfect for bonding with the one you love. I could tell Amos liked them.

Amos is my new sugar glider.

I know, nobody knows what a sugar glider is. When the woman at the pet store first mentioned one, I thought she was talking about a kitchen accessory. I hadn't wanted to let her in on my woeful ignorance of household utensils, so I told her a sugar glider sounded intriguing. And intriguing he was.

When she led me over to his cage, I first noticed his peepers. He had big, black, round eyes that reminded me of my pastor and ex-boyfriend Rocky's "I can make you do anything with these" puppy eyes. Don't judge me. Not for that. Having a pastor who is your ex-boyfriend sounds a lot worse than it is. Besides, I've got plenty of *real* issues for you to choose from.

Amos was roughly the size of a Beanie Baby and looked like a cross between a tiny gray squirrel, a skunk, and a kangaroo—with the face of a bat. Kinda.

I never would have gotten a pet if my mentor and spiritual father, Dr. Mason May, hadn't recommended it. I'd gone to see him earlier that day, whining endlessly about being manless, being childless, having endometriosis, and about my grief over my eggs, which were aging faster than my mother said *I* was. I got frustrated while venting to Dr. May and threatened to have an intra-uterine insemination procedure done with some stranger-donor's little soldiers. But Dr. May—Pop, as I called him—stopped me right there and told me I should pray about the matter some more and buy a pet. That's how I ended up at the exotic pet store near my house, feeling guilty about my baby lust and purchasing something that looked like one of the Crocodile Hunter's furry friends. And we had to bond.

How pathetic am I?

Amos didn't seem very prickly. A little standoffish, yes, but nothing that should have stood in the way of us getting cozy with each other. My initial mistake: I should have put together his cage first. But no, being a psychologist, I wanted to get straight to the attachment process. That's important. I reached into his little Exotic Petz cardboard box—the kind with the round peepholes—and picked him up. I could feel him freeze, and I do know body language. I figured it was just nerves bothering him, so I pressed on with the bonding process. Amos didn't complain.

We crossed to my couch. Jazz once described my apartment

as "shabby chic meets Africa." Fair enough, I suppose. The ambience I'd created with my eccentric flea-market finds gave my home a comfy, livable feel. I'd often paint my treasures in hues with whimsical-sounding names like old lace, seafoam, and dusty rose. The walls were a sunny buttercup—I'd called it ocher just months ago, but that was when I'd felt more earthy and African-inspired. Something had happened in my soul, and I'd begun to feel more romantic and feminine. I think it was falling in love with Jazz. Since then I'd given away most of the masks that used to dot the walls and most of my Nigerian baskets. I was trying to make room for Addie Lee Brown paintings and sculptures. But I'd kept a few wood pieces I loved, and I still had all of my textiles—bright, colorful Kente cloth and a few mud-cloth pieces—to add warmth and texture. Candles cast a soft glow in the rooms and sweetened the air with rose, vanilla, and jasmine.

I took a seat on the couch and propped my feet on the coffee table, with Amos perched somewhat stiffly on my lap. I thought I'd better tell him a little bit about myself.

"I'm your new mom, Amanda Bell Brown. I'm named after my paternal great-grandmother and favorite diva in the whole wide world. Most people call me Amanda, and some even call me Dr. Brown, but you can call me Bell. That's reserved for the people who love me best."

Amos didn't say anything. I figured sugar gliders weren't very talkative. No problem. I'd fill the silence between us.

"I got you because I need someone to love. I hate to sound like one of those thirty-five-year-old career women who realize too late that they forgot to get pregnant. It wasn't really like that. I had a lot of hurts, but I don't want to talk about that. The point is"—I stroked his short fur, which made him recoil—"it seems the only prospect I have for marriage is my pastor, Rocky. That would be too weird; you'll see what I mean if you ever meet him. And then there's Jazz . . ."

Just saying his name gave me chills. How fine was he? Too fine. Fine like God didn't make him out of the dust of the earth that the rest of us mere mortals were made of. Jazz was made of something sparkly and inspiring. He intoxicated me. No, he made me feel, as Aretha Franklin sang, like a natural woman. But it could never work. He had issues. He kept using the word "unavailable." Not that he had a woman, mind you. Just an ex and a belief that he couldn't remarry. And God bless him, he had too much integrity to lead a woman on. Unfortunately for me, I didn't want anyone but him. And he'd never want me. Not really.

Even Amos didn't seem to be into me. I thought for a moment that, instead of Amos, I should have gotten a rocking chair and a pair of Birkenstocks and resigned myself to a depressed, childless spinsterhood. I told Amos, "I stopped seeing Jazz one month, two days, and three hours ago. I miss him. Now Christmas is coming."

I looked around my place, void of any yuletide cheer. *Well, Bell, that was smart, thinking of Christmas.* All I needed was to get some poisoned eggnog and put myself out of my misery. I rubbed the top of Amos's head. "I guess it's just you and me."

Either that head rub didn't please Amos, or he didn't like Christmas. He made a hissing sound like he was exhaling smoke from Hades.

The saleswoman hadn't said anything about evil hissing, and I hadn't read the manual.

Then he added to the hissing a raised paw—a gesture that did not look loving at all. I didn't have to be an astute observer of body language to see that I had myself a little problem.

I was on the couch, so I didn't have the luxury of backing away slowly. I hoped if I cooed and touched him affectionately, he'd relax and see that I was a "good touch" person. But when I gave his silken gray fur, with an adorable black stripe right down his back, just a tiny stroke, the rotten little stinker jumped on my sleeve and tried to kill me.

Our bonding session turned straightaway into *When Sugar Gliders Attack*.

The saleslady hadn't mentioned anything about aggression.

Amos scratched, bit, and clawed my pajamas like a veritable Tasmanian devil. I screamed. My pathetic manless life flashed before my eyes. I could just see my mother at my funeral, talking smack about me because I'd purchased, of all things, a *sugar glider*. "I always knew that child didn't have good sense," she'd lament.

Someone pounded on the door.

I leaped from the couch, still screeching, Amos still clinging and assaulting. While the vicious creature shredded my jammies and skin, I managed to unbolt my locks—a dead bolt and a spare, thanks to Jazz—and snatched my door open. I didn't bother to ask, "Who is it?"

There stood none other than the man my heart beat for, Lieutenant Jazz Brown, homicide detective. He had his pistol drawn, ready to protect my honor. I noticed, after swiftly taking in his general gorgeousness, four fresh, angry slashes on his face.

In an instant he took in my situational challenge, grabbed the arm that was being attacked, and started pumping it like he was trying to milk me.

I screamed louder.

"Stop all that noise!"

"What? Are you going to arrest me for disturbing the peace?" I yanked my arm away from him as hard as I could, which had the effect of hurling poor Amos across the living room. He landed with a thud on the couch, right in the middle of the cushions.

I hurried over to the couch with Jazz on my heels. My arm ached and throbbed from the battery it had taken.

Amos was as still as a stone.

"Oh, no," I wailed. "I think I killed him."

"Good." Jazz put his gun back in his shoulder holster. He walked to my door and locked it. "You shouldn't open the door like that, Bell," he barked. "I could have been anybody."

"It's *not* good if I killed him. I'm supposed to love, nurture, and protect him." I touched one of many tender spots on my arm. My motherly instincts hadn't kicked in all the way. I glared at Amos. "The little beast."

"Are you okay?" Jazz took my arm in his hands. He shot a look at Amos and shook his head. "I can't believe you chose this thing for a pet." He gently pulled back the wreckage that was my sleeve.

I ignored his comment and took in his perfect beauty, his sculpted and slender body. He was wearing one of his trademark suits—the brown one—and the effect of the color, contrasted with his creamy skin tone, made him look as good as a Hershey's Hug. He wore no overcoat, which was odd for a cold December night, but so was the fact that he was wearing his suit so late into the night. I didn't ponder it too much. Except for the ugly scratches and pinched expression, his white-chocolate face was as fine as ever. Yum. *Lord, have mercy on my Jazz-starved soul.*

I felt awful for poor Amos. What kind of mother was I, ogling Jazz while my baby could be lying there dead? I wondered if Jazz would arrest me for cruelty to animals. Looking at his relieved expression, I figured not. Still . . . I glanced at my fallen furry friend. "Jazz! He's so still."

"I'd be still, too, if you threw me across the room," Jazz said. "We need to take care of your arm, Bell."

But my parental guilt was growing like mold on a loaf of bread in summer. I started wringing my hands, like my mother did whenever I cut my hair. "Amos is hurt the worst. What kind of mom would I be if I tended to my wounds without making sure Amos is taken care of?"

"Bell, you're not his mom, and he's probably dead. Now, let's get some antibiotic ointment on you before you get an infection."

I had images of Amos on life support. *Beep, beep, beep.* "Maybe it's not too late. *Do* something, Jazzy. He could be getting brain damage."

Jazz looked at me like he *didn't* actually get paid to protect and serve. "What am I supposed to do?"

"Do CPR on him or something." Honestly, I was becoming more histrionic by the moment.

He laughed right in my face. "Now you're trippin'."

My maternal hysterics compelled me to yank on the sleeve of his suit jacket. "He's unconscious. You have to help him."

"I'm a homicide detective, not a vet. I can, however, shoot him in the head."

"Please, please, puh-leeeze, Jazz."

"You're crazy."

When begging failed, I progressed to physical assault. I started hitting him with limp-wristed girl slaps all over his chest while shouting in a staccato rhythm with the blows, "How. Can. You. Be. So. Cruel?"

Jazz tried to stop my flurry of blows to his torso. "Bell, stop it."

I didn't stop.

"Woman, I said . . ."

I kept it up.

"*Okay*," he bellowed, with a few added expletives. "What is up with all the violent women tonight?"

So it was a woman who'd scratched him? Interesting.

Jazz shot a very dirty look in my direction and dropped to his knees. He reached out his hand and gingerly shook Amos.

"You're supposed to ask him if he's okay first."

He gave me another look that said, *Shut up.* He turned Amos over, and when Amos didn't move—or hiss—Jazz steeled himself for the task at hand. "I hate you, Bell. And if you ever tell anybody . . ."

"*Brain damage, Jazz!*"

He groaned and put his mouth to Amos's, then puffed as if Amos were a big inhaler. It looked so utterly ridiculous that I started laughing. I couldn't help it. Besides, I reasoned that laughter was good for calming my frayed nerves.

Jazz looked up at me and hissed himself, something like "You think this is funny?"

"I'm sorry."

"You ain't right, Bell."

Before Jazz could get in another puff, or even a fur-covered chest compression, Amos sprang up. Jazz grabbed him with both hands, arms extended, holding Amos as far away from himself as humanly possible. "Where am I supposed to put this thing?"

I grabbed Amos's cardboard box off the coffee table and held it out. Jazz deposited him inside it, frowning, as if Amos were a piece of that aforementioned moldy bread and needed to be done away with. I delicately placed my precious cargo back on the table. "Amos and I thank you, Officer."

Jazz wagged his finger at me. "You owe me."

I winked at him. "What do you have in mind, big boy?" I got one of his toothpaste-model-like smiles for that one.

"What's that your great-grandmother used to say?"

I sighed. "She'd say, 'Don't start no stuff, and it won't be none.'"

"Take her advice, for your own good."

"I can handle you. I can't handle Amos, but you . . . Hey, what are you doing here, anyway?"

"Saving you. *Again.*"

I looked at his war wounds. "Jazz, what happened to your face? Did you get a sugar glider, too?"

"A *what?*"

"A sugar glider. You know, the furry little thing you just gave the kiss of life to."

"I don't need a wild animal in my life." He swiped at his pursed lips. "Give me a wipe or a washcloth or something."

"Don't get cranky with me. It's not my fault you don't like pets."

"I do like pets. *Pets*, Bell. Kittens. Puppies. Rabbits. You might even be able to sell me on a hamster or gerbil, but that thing . . . What the heck is it, anyway?"

I looked at him as if he were the most ignorant, uncouth man alive—the same way the saleswoman at the pet store had looked at me. "He's an Australian marsupial."

"Bell! People don't buy marsupials for pets."

I was getting sick of his attitude. "They don't yell at me, either, and if you don't stop it, I'm going to hurt you."

"Like you did before with all that pimp slapping?"

"I was under duress. Plus, I had to get you to act."

We were at a standoff. We stood there, shooting lasers from our eyes at each other. Those scratches on his face looked recent. When he finally looked away, I knew I'd won this battle. Having attained victory, I went back to more important matters. "What happened to your face?"

Suddenly, he wouldn't meet my eyes. "Tough night."

I snickered. "Yeah, me too."

He moved closer and tenderly lifted my arm again. It felt like little jolts of love shocking me. He surveyed the damage. I tried not to let him see me swoon.

"Let's get you cleaned up," he said. "You got any antibiotic ointment? And industrial-strength mouthwash?"

"In the bathroom."

"Come on." Jazz led me to my tiny bathroom as if we were in *his* apartment. Men. Always marking their territory. I glanced around. His presence here always made me feel like redecorating.

"Still think my apartment is shabby chic meets Africa?" I asked.

"It's nice."

"Thanks."

Not good. One of the things I loved most about being with Jazz was our verbal volleying. I couldn't believe he hadn't said anything clever or teasing while we'd walked to the bathroom. Of course, when we got in there and I handed him the Listerine, he got busy rinsing his mouth about three hundred times. Honestly, the man used up the entire bottle. He shrugged when he finished and gave me a sheepish grin. "I'll buy you another one, but c'mon. I had to do what I had to do." I wondered what else he felt like he had to do tonight.

I didn't have to wonder for long. He grabbed me by the waist, pulling me to him. I looked into his eyes. But what I saw there this time—unadulterated hunger—scared me. "Jazzy?"

He reached up and touched my hair. It had grown about an inch, and now my teeny-weeny Afro wasn't so teeny. I had braided it in microbraids, then unbraided it. It gave my hair a soft, crinkled look.

Jazz tangled both his hands in it and rubbed his cheek against it. *Ouch*, I thought for him. I had a vision of his blood mingling with my hair. *Ew!* Not a good image, but when he moved his face, the image went away. He started massaging my scalp. I get all soft and gooey when a fine man plays with my hair. "Your hair is growing," he said.

"My hair is growing?" I asked dreamily, as if I'd suffered from female pattern baldness and hair growth was a surprise.

"And you smell like peaches."

I snuggled a little closer. "I smell like peaches?" The peach-scented shampoo and body mist had also been a gift from Carly.

The head massage felt wonderful. And then, God help me, I moaned: "*Ummm.*"

"'Ummm' is right." By now he'd started rubbing circles on my back. "I missed you, Bell."

"You missed me?"

He laughed. "You're repeating everything I say, except you make it a question."

"I'm repeating . . ." So what? He was right, but I didn't care. Hadn't I told him I didn't want to see him again? Why did I ever tell him that?

Wait. I knew why I'd said that. I could never have a real life with him. *Shoot.* I couldn't let him just dance into my apartment like he was Gregory Hines and start molesting my hair. "Hold on, Jazz," I said, trying to push him away.

He nestled his face into my neck. "I am holding on."

"We need to deal with our scratches."

He let me go, and I got over to my medicine cabinet like I was on fire. I kept my first aid supplies behind the bathroom mirror. I didn't have a whole lot, but I needed to step away from that man. Goodness me, his touch had activated some warm and fuzzy feelings in me. In fact, I felt so fuzzy I could hardly pay attention to what I saw in front of me. I started furiously rooting around for the Neosporin and missing it, though I knew it was there. I thought taking a tough, efficient stance—like Nurse Ratched from *One Flew Over the Cuckoo's Nest*—was in order for both our sakes. "Now," I said, practically snapping my heels together like a Nazi soldier, "let's have a look at those scratches."

He moved over to where I stood. Too close. He reached around me into the cabinet, grazing my arm with his. My body's nerve endings went *Shazam!* I hate it when that happens. He knew he'd affected me, too. He gave me a slow, sexy grin but quickly got back to the task at hand. "Let's take care of you first," he said. "You might have rabies."

Rabies? "Thanks for the insight." My sarcasm couldn't mask a bit of irrational fear that he may be right even though I got him at a pet shop. *No wonder he rinsed so much.*

He gestured to my towel rack, where bath and face towels hung. "Are these clean?"

I nodded, imagining myself foaming at the mouth and Jazz having to shoot me, as if we'd gotten plunged into *Their Eyes Were Watching God.* Not romantic.

He turned on the faucet, washed his hands with my antibacterial hand soap, then wet a face towel and gently washed my arm. I winced. His eyes, full of sadness, regarded me. "I'm sorry I hurt you."

"It's okay. I'm just a big baby sometimes."

"No, Bell. I'm not talking about when I touched your arm. I'm sorry I hurt you when I, you know, when I said I was unavailable and all that."

"Jazzy . . ."

He took the ointment and administered more of his treatments to my battered arm. My pajamas were now officially ratty. Carly was going to stand on the roof and pound on her chest like King Kong when she saw them. I shook my head to clear the image and to clear Jazz's words from my heart: *I'm sorry I hurt you.*

When he was done, I washed my hands and went to work on his face. The mystery woman sure had gotten a hunk of his DNA.

I applied the ointment. It was his turn to wince. He grabbed my wrist. It startled me.

"Sorry. Did that h—" He pulled me to him, crushing me with his embrace. "I want you," he whispered in my ear.

Uh-oh. I wasn't ready for this.

In a pinch, intellectualizing is an effective diversion. "Uh," I said into his chest, "by 'want me,' do you mean you'd like to hire me as a consultant again? Or do you mean you'd like to be my man?" I tried to wriggle away, to no avail. "You could also mean you'd like to rip my bodice like we were the cover models on the romance novel on my night table. So . . . I really need clarification here."

But he grabbed my face and smothered any other questions I may have had with a definite pre-bodice-ripping kiss.

God, this ain't right. Amos chewed me up, and now Jazz is trying to take off my chastity belt—and I don't want him to stop.

I tried to buck up. *Okay. I'm Bell Brown. I'm tough. I am a strong black woman. Surely I can endure one kiss without it becoming an R-rated movie.*

But we were already at PG-13!

Okay, God; it's me again, I'm kissing him back like I'm going to rip his bodice. Apparently, I don't have any self-discipline. What's this going to cost me?

Jazz had hurt me. Maybe he hadn't meant to, but he had. We could do this, but in the end he was going to give me the sad story about him not believing in remarriage. I didn't believe in letting myself be used. I didn't care how battle-weary he was tonight.

I pushed him away again. "Stop it, Jazz. You're all over me

like T. D. Jakes on sinners. What's gotten into you tonight? Every other time we've kissed, it's been me who came on to you. Now you're . . . Well, it's like you're not yourself." I folded my arms. "Why are you even here?"

His voice had the same passion as his kiss. "I need to tell you something very important."

"What?"

Again he wouldn't look at me. "Bell, I did something wrong tonight."

"Jazz, what's going on?"

He ran his hand roughly through his brown curls. "Can we make it work? You and me? What I mean is, do you feel like you're capable of doing something you never thought you'd do— something that would compromise what you believe in—if it meant we could be together?"

What was I supposed to say? I wanted to be with him, badly, but how could I ask him to compromise what he believed in? That's not what love does. Not the First Corinthians kind. "Jazz, if we could have made it work, I think we would have. We were at an impasse that wasn't fair to either of us."

"So are you telling me that there's no hope at all for us? Please don't tell me that, Bell. That's the last thing I want to hear tonight."

I didn't know what to say, so I just stood there with my mouth agape, trying to figure out if Rod Serling was going to walk into my kitchen and begin his *Twilight Zone* monologue. I waited for Jazz to confess whatever it was that was deviling him. For a long time, neither of us moved. Finally, he broke the silence. "I was with Kate."

"Excuse me?"

His jaw tightened, and his eyes seemed to plead with me for understanding. "I've been with Kate tonight."

Without warning, my heart dropped to my bathroom floor. I backed against the toilet, which made my knees buckle. I ended up plopped down on the toilet seat. Thank goodness I kept the lid down. I'd have hated to fall into an open toilet bowl at a time like this.

So the bum had come to see me after he'd been with his *ex-wife*. And what did he mean by "been with" her? I couldn't believe his nerve. "You were with . . ." My strange repeat-after-Jazz speech impediment had begun to irritate me—but so had he. I jumped up—how threatening can you look on a toilet?—and marched into the living room and to my front door with him trailing behind me. I unlocked all those stupid locks he insisted I have and pulled open my door. "Get out of my apartment."

He placed his hand over mine. "Wait."

"Are you touching me? We've got a no-touching policy, or have you forgotten? We've also got a no-seeing-each-other policy, if I recall. So leave. Now."

He didn't move his hand. "I was with her because of you."

I snatched my hand away and slammed the door shut. I didn't know what was up with him, but that was the last straw. "You've got about two seconds to explain, or I'm going to send you back to her with scratches *I* gave you."

"Can we just sit down? I can explain everything."

"I don't want your explanation. If you want to be with Kate, do that, but don't come over here kissing on me when you're done."

Jazz gave me such an earnest, almost desperate look that I felt a little scared for him. "Please, Bell. I'm sorry. I can't seem to get through this night without saying and doing all the wrong stuff. I need a little help here. Will you just talk to me for a minute?"

I stood there, staring at him. I loved him, and it was obvious that he was in trouble. If the tables were turned, he'd help me. "Do you want some coffee?"

His exhale was so dramatic that it looked like he'd been holding his breath. He smiled at me, chuckled a bit, and raised an eyebrow. "Got anything stronger?"

"I'll put a cinnamon stick in it," I quipped. "I can't have alcohol in the house. I'm a pet owner now."

He smiled at that. "You'd better check on him."

I headed over to the coffee table and peered down at Amos. He was peacefully scratching at the cardboard walls of his box. I let him be and went into the kitchen. Jazz didn't follow me.

In five minutes I had the coffee brewed. I hollered from the kitchen, "How do you want your coffee?"

"Black, strong, and kinda sweet—like I want my woman."

Since he'd tried to lighten the mood, I followed suit. "I guess I'm not the woman you want, then, unless you want a little cream in this. You said I was the color of peanut butter."

"With aspirations to be an ebony queen."

"I am a queen—the Skippy Queen."

He laughed. "Last time you were Jif."

I walked back into the living room carrying a bamboo tray bearing a fresh rose and my two favorite handmade coffee mugs full of steaming Starbucks Holiday Blend. Jazz would recognize the artist who'd crafted the mugs. "Speaking of choosy moms . . ." I said, offering the tray.

As soon as he saw the mugs, he smiled. "My mom made those."

"I never saw an Addie Lee piece I didn't love."

That is, except for the Marriage Wish necklace she'd made for Kate. Actually, I loved that piece, too, but in a nasty way that brought to mind commandment number ten, *Thou shalt not covet.* Not to mention number eight, *Thou shalt not steal.*

I handed him the red ocher mug with the yellow spirals and mud-cloth pattern at the bottom. I took the indigo one with the silver stars, my favorite. She'd crafted the indigo and luminous silver glaze in a way that made the colors otherworldly beautiful. It took my breath away almost as much as Jazz did. I was so preoccupied by him that when I handed him the mug, it slipped from my hand. The moment it touched the floor, it shattered. My hand flew to my heart. "Oh no! It was my favorite." I wanted to cry.

Jazz jumped from his seat. "I'm sorry, Bell. This is my fault. You must be a nervous wreck with me acting so crazy."

"That was a rare one, too." I stomped my foot. "*Man.*"

He reached for my hand and clasped it in his, sending a wave of warmth through me. "I've got one of those," he said. "You can have mine."

"Are you touching me?"

He chuckled and withdrew his hand. "Don't want to break any more rules." He started picking up the big pieces of the mug. "I'll clean up this mess. Why don't you have a seat and chill for a minute?" He went into the kitchen for supplies to clean up my mess.

I plopped down, feeling dog-tired. Somehow the night had spiraled out of control almost as soon as I'd gotten home. "I've gotta get Amos's cage put together," I called to him.

He reappeared with a plastic grocery bag and a dish towel. He dropped the pieces into the bag and sopped up the coffee.

"Careful," I teased. "We don't need any more bloodshed tonight."

"Amen to that," he said. While he wiped up the last of the Starbucks, he threw this little gem out there: "I didn't sleep with her." He paused as if waiting for my reaction. But what was I supposed to say to that? It wasn't my business. Much.

"Will you go somewhere with me?" he said. "There's something I want to show you. And I still haven't told you what I came here to say."

Before I could answer, my cell phone rang in the bedroom. I sighed and thanked God for being saved by the bell, though I wished I could have been saved by *Bell.* I made it to my bedroom and picked up the phone off the night table. "This is Amanda," I said, using my standard phone greeting for friend or client.

"Bunny?" It was Carly. Her voice sounded like something was wrong.

It didn't take much to make me panic when it came to my mother or sister. "Carly, what is it? Is it Ma? Did something—"

"Everybody is fine. Bell, is Jazz with you?"

Honestly. Did she have man radar when it came to me? "Nothing is going on." We were still PG-13, for goodness' sake.

Her voice got very strange. "Is he in the room with you? Can he hear me? Don't say my name again."

"I'm in my *bedroom.*" I chose my words carefully, to appease her. "The answer is absolutely not, and won't be, so don't worry. Bye-ee!"

"*Wait*," she said. "Listen to me, Bell. You've got to get out of there."

Had everyone gone insane tonight? "What are you talking about?" I made sure I didn't say her name.

"Are you dressed?"

"Of course I am. I said nothing was going on." Well, I *was* dressed, albeit in shredded pajamas. They offered full coverage, even if they were from Victoria's Secret.

"Bunny, please, just get out of there. Don't let him follow you. And write down this address. I want you to meet me there."

"What is going on?"

"Just take this address down. And don't let him see it."

Great, I have to play cloak-and-dagger now. Can this get any weirder?

She rattled off the address.

"Okay. I've got it. What is this place?"

"It's Jazz's loft downtown," she said, her voice hushed. "I just got called to a crime scene there. His ex-wife, Kate . . . Bell, she's been murdered."

chapter
two

KATE'S BEEN MURDERED.

I heard Carly say it, but it sounded as if she'd spoken some archaic form of English that I only vaguely recognized.

"What?" I said.

My body understood. My heart pounded so hard it made my pulse thump in my ears. I tried to unite body and mind to make sense of what I'd heard, but my mind refused to cooperate. *Murdered...*

"Bell... are you there?"

"Yes, I'm..." My voice sounded strange and hollow, even to me.

Carly said something. I couldn't focus. I felt like the ground was shifting beneath me. I needed to root myself on to something solid and immovable, but everything seemed shaky.

Jesus, Jesus, Jesus.

"Talk to me, Bell."

"I'm coming."

"Come *now*. Try to keep him there if you can, and don't let him know you know anything."

I *didn't* know anything. I tried to focus on the facts—the few I had. *Who?* Kate. *What?* Dead. *When?* It had to be sometime between face scratching and Jazz showing up at my door with his gun drawn.

His gun drawn . . .

Had he shot her? The beginnings of a headache throbbed at my temples, commanding my attention and forcing my eyes shut.

Where? Jazz's loft. *Why?*

His voice pounded in my head. *Do you feel like you're capable of doing something you never thought you'd do . . . if it meant we could be together?*

Impossible. I couldn't believe he'd kill her for us to be together any more than I could make a bowl of alphabet soup into the great American novel.

Carly's instructions, *Get out of there,* bit into me with the frigid precision of a Michigan winter. "Okay," I whispered into my cell phone.

"Bell!"

"Okay." I folded it closed, cutting off the call.

I sank down onto the bed, wondering how I'd get out of there *and* keep him in my place.

"Bell?"

Jazz stood at my bedroom door, his lean body suddenly menacing. He'd pressed his shoulder against the doorjamb. He gave me a quizzical look. "Is everything okay?"

That man could read me like a John Grisham paperback— not that I wasn't obvious at the moment. I scanned his face. His expression looked more genuine than sinister. I squeezed my eyes shut. *Sure, everything is great, except for the dead woman in your loft.*

"What's wrong, Bell?"

"I have to go out."

"Now?"

When I didn't say anything, he moved to take charge. "I'll take you."

"*No!*" I tried to calm my voice. "I just have to . . . make a quick run."

"But I need to talk to you."

"I'll be back, Jazz." What choice did I have? It was my apartment. "Uh . . . just hang out. Will you put Amos's cage together for me?"

He did not look enthusiastic.

"I need to get some tampons."

He stared at me like I'd said I needed a leopard-skin body stocking. "Is it that time of month? Do you have to leave right *now?*"

What kind of man . . . ? A mere mention of a feminine hygiene product should have sent one of his species scuttling to the other side of the room. Since the dreaded "girl stuff" card hadn't worked, I'd have to go hysterical, which I was on the verge of anyway. "It's *not* that time of month," I screeched. "But I am a thirty-five-year-old woman *with endometriosis.*"

Now make it about him.

"Do you know anything about endometriosis?"

He opened his mouth but didn't answer, just stood at the door looking dumbstruck.

"That's what I thought!"

And then the big finish, with my eyes narrowed to slits and my voice a deep rumble. Very Joan Crawford. "You cannot underestimate my need for supplies." I stomped my foot, hard. "*Ever!*" I hoped I sounded like Joan when she said, "No. More. *Wire hangers!*" in the movie *Mommie Dearest.*

I rushed into the living room to snatch my black wool duster out of the closet. I pulled it on over my partially mangled pajamas. I grabbed the first pair of shoes I could get my hands on—ornate gold, jewel-encrusted, high-heeled pumps that went with absolutely nothing I owned but were really cute and only twenty-five dollars. I slid my bare feet into them, Carly's voice saying *Get out of there* driving me into a full-blown hissy fit.

With caution, he broached the question: "Is that what you're wearing?"

"Is this what I'm wearing?" Again my voice crested with more drama than I'd intended. "Are you my mother now? She's the only person who would ask me that. And my secretary, Maggie." I thought about it. "And Carly." The mere thought of those three, and the possibility of Jazz being a murderer, bolstered my hysteria. My hands shook.

He took a big risk in stepping a little closer to me. "It's just that . . ."

"It's just that *what?*"

"You look . . ." I could see him searching for the right word, treading carefully. "Upset, Bell."

"Of course I'm upset! I need tampons, and you're opposing me!"

He put his hands up as if he all of a sudden felt like praising the Lord. "Okay. I'll put the cage together, and you go handle your business. I'll walk you to your car."

"No! You don't have time to go strolling around like you're God's troubadour. I need that cage put together. Don't you see he's badly in need of a home? What kind of mom do you think I am, leaving poor Amos in a cardboard box after all he's been through tonight?"

And speaking of Amos . . .

"Uh. I'm taking him with me." I whisked over to the coffee table and swooped up Amos's box. I couldn't leave him with a man who might be a dangerous felon.

"Bell, are you sure—"

"Do. Not. Get in my *way*." My eyebrows nearly touched the ceiling.

He took a step away from me. "Fine. I'm out of your way."

I exhaled. The air I forced out of my lungs almost hurt coming out. I was sure Jazz could see me trembling. My heart began an Irish clog dance. I tripped twice going over to the door in my fabulous shoes, while Amos flopped around in the box. I finally grabbed the doorknob in hopes of steadying myself, but Jazz's arms caught my waist and pulled me up and against him. He turned me to face him, stroking my hair. "Maybe you should change shoes. You know how you and high heels are."

Our eyes locked. A knot twisted in my throat. "Jazzy?" Tears sprang to my eyes.

His eyes filled with concern. "What is it, baby?"

I whispered, "Baby, what did you do wrong?"

He didn't avoid my eyes this time. He smiled a bit. Brushed

a stray tear off my cheek and gave me a squeeze. "We can talk about everything when you get back. Don't worry, okay?" He pulled away and narrowed one eye. Chuckled. "I'm a little scared of you right now."

I couldn't return his silly grin. "I'm scared, too."

He kissed my forehead, then my lips. "It's not that bad. What I did was more stupid than anything. I—I just wanted us to be together." He squeezed my shoulders. "Go get your—you know, stuff. I'll be here when you get back."

I nodded again and rushed out the door.

———————

I don't know how the Love Bug got me to the address I'd discreetly tucked into the breast pocket of my pajamas. It was all I could do to steer, my iPod blasting U2 to blunt my thinking. It briefly occurred to me that a sunshine yellow VW Beetle sure was a happy-looking car to drive to a crime scene in. I'd have to rethink my vehicle choice—or at least color—if I were to continue sleuthing.

I tried to focus on Bono's scratchy tenor wailing "All Because of You." I replayed it over and over as Interstate 94 flew past me. I may have made it to the heart of downtown with my body in one piece, but my mind resembled an unassembled jigsaw puzzle.

Gonna need a little help here, Lord.

I gazed up at the impressive redbrick building. Back in the early 1900s it was a pharmaceutical company's warehouse. The space had been converted into lofts years ago, and now the high-end property right on the Detroit River was home to the city's most prominent shakers and movers—very cosmopolitan. How Jazz could afford it, even on a lieutenant's salary, was beyond me. I got a little mad that he'd never brought me here.

The requisite crime-scene gawkers ambled about, even in the cold, and uniforms kept them at a distance. The CSIs had arrived, but they hadn't gone inside. I saw Carly's Escalade parked on the street. I spotted her standing outside in the cold. I picked up Amos's box, got out of the Love Bug, and rushed over to her, surprised by the relief I felt just seeing her.

"Bunny." She gathered me into a hug. "I have never been so happy to see—" *Screeeeeech,* went the brakes on her affection. She thrust me away from her, holding me by the shoulders. "Are you in *pajamas?*" The word "pajamas" soared eight octaves higher, rivaling Minnie Riperton's famous refrain from "Loving You."

"You said leave *now.*"

"You told me you were dressed."

"As opposed to being naked."

"And what is up with those shoes?"

"You don't like them? I got them on sale at Ma's boutique. She let me have them wholesale for twenty-five bucks."

"Bell, we're at a crime scene."

"Last time I wore stilettos and a red silk halter dress."

"You have a point." She thought for a moment. "Actually, I've got a sexy little bustier and gold shorts that would—"

I did not want to hear about gold shorts on a forty-year-old woman, even one as striking as Carly. "Can we just get down to business?"

"Okay, but I will get back to you on the pajamas and shoes."

I had no doubt that she would. She jerked her head toward Amos's temporary home. "Is something moving in there?"

I tried to ignore her.

"Bell?"

Continued to ignore her.

"Bell!"

I gingerly opened the box. I didn't even look, but I heard the familiar hiss, followed by Carly's scream. "What in the *world*?" She tried to knock him out of my hand.

I snatched him away. "What are you doing? He's my baby!"

Carly stared at me openmouthed, like I was more shocking than Jazz possibly murdering his wife. "What *is* that thing?"

"A sugar glider."

She shook her head. "I don't understand you, Bell."

"I can tell you all about myself later, but I'm sure you asked me here for a reason."

"I *had* a plan, and then you show up dressed like Hugh Hefner, with a squirrel in tow."

"Sugar glider."

I'd challenged her with my unorthodox apparel and furry companion, but try dissuading Carly Brown when she has a plan. She snapped back into efficiency. "You're going to have to go along with what I say, no matter how you're dressed." She glared at me, looking frighteningly like our mother. "And put that thing away."

"I can't leave my baby in the car."

"Why didn't you leave him at home?"

"With someone who might be dangerous?" I clutched Amos's box to my chest.

"That *thing* looks dangerous, Bell."

And speaking of dangerous . . . "Carly, what happened here?"

Her brow furrowed. "What do you think? It looks like he snapped or something. I was scared to death that he could be with you, which he was. I thought you said you stopped seeing him."

"I did. Look, we'll talk about my social life later. What happened?"

"Did he act unusual tonight?"

I nodded.

Her hand flew to her mouth as if to stop whatever would come out. She practically threw herself on me and snatched Amos and me into a suffocating embrace. I let her hold us until Souldier, Jazz's colleague and best friend, interrupted our sisterly hug by rubbing my shoulder. I eased out of Carly's arms.

The handsome, dreadlocked CSI supervisor looked shaken; his cocoa brown skin actually looked pale. "Sorry we had to get you"—he regarded my pajamas—"out of bed."

"I wasn't in bed with Jazz."

His gaze darted to the ground and assured me I'd given him too much information. "Uh . . . nice shoes."

That worked for me. I wouldn't have to regale him with more unnecessary disclosures about my nonexistent sex life. Besides, it's always good to have a man's opinion about shoes. "Thanks."

He scratched the top of his head. "Did Jazz say anything to you—"

About murdering Kate? Nope!

"Nothing specific, Souldier. He just said . . ."

I did something wrong.

A bolt of fear shot through me. I clamped my mouth shut. After a moment I could offer: "He said . . . something about being with Kate." My gut twisted. "Have you gone inside yet?"

"Nobody can do anything until the medical examiner takes a look. Carly and I just got here. We took our time, waiting for you."

Carly took my hand. "Come on. You're going in with me. When we get inside, walk with your hands behind your back, and don't touch a thing." She took a deep breath, steeling herself for a task that had become much more personal than a routine death investigation. "Bell, don't throw up or in any way compromise the scene. This isn't like last time. The lead detective hasn't invited you in." She gave me another disgusted look. "Pajamas! And those *shoes*." She sighed. "Pray that we get away with this."

I said a silent prayer indeed.

I followed Carly to the building's glass double doors, guarded by a bored-looking uniformed officer.

"Dr. Brown," the uniform said to Carly. "She can't—"

"She's with me."

The officer took one look at my attire. "But—"

"But what, Officer? We need to get inside."

He nodded and let Carly and me brush past him.

We walked into a narrow corridor that led to the stairs. My hands stayed behind my back—awkward, since I held a box full of sugar glider. The corridor had a stale smell. I favored it, however, to the blessedly absent odor of the not-so-freshly deceased that had permeated the air at the previous crime scene I'd been to.

I climbed the black metal stairs on shaky legs, dreading what

I'd find in that fabulous loft, with every precarious step I took. When we arrived upstairs, I could see the door to Jazz's loft already open. I noted that it hadn't been forced open. A few uniforms huddled by the door.

Carly nudged me. "Stay behind me."

I followed her lead. Carly walked right up to the men and lifted her chin, and with a single look, they parted like the Red Sea. What a goddess.

But enough about her.

Take in everything, Bell.

I studied the room. Timber ceilings and cathedral windows with a spectacular view. Wide, open space, exposed brick walls graced with his mother's paintings. Shining wood floors you could eat off of. A gourmet kitchen with stainless-steel appliances. A forgotten takeout package from Luckey Chinese sat on the countertop. The bag was still stapled shut with the bill attached. I've eaten many Chinese takeout meals with Jazz. Judging from the size of the bag, he'd ordered for one tonight.

His cold food was just about the warmest thing in the room. The place had the sterile air of a property that hadn't been lived in yet. He had very little furniture. A big-screen projection television held court in the nearly empty living area. A black leather couch—that looked like an IKEA special—sat at comfortable viewing distance. Beneath it was an area rug as funky and colorful as the ties he wore.

Jazz apparently had mastered minimalism in his approach to home decorating. I knew exactly what he needed to make the place homey: me. Of course, the lack of a corpse would do wonders as well.

Carly stopped at two wet spots pooled just inside the door. Broken pieces of pottery caught my eye. *Aw, man!*

It must not have been a good night for Addie Lee's Starry Night mugs. So much for getting Jazz's. I briefly—and selfishly—wondered if he had two of them.

They're rare, clown girl! Besides, this is no time to ponder adding to my Addie Lee art collection.

Carly crouched down to examine the wet spots. Sniffed. Wrinkled her nose. "One is urine." A broken red fingernail lay beside it. She stood up again. "The other has no odor. It's probably water." Carefully, she walked out of the living area, toward a full-size bed perched in a corner by one of windows. *His* bed.

I followed her, hands and Amos behind me. Jazz's bed had a cast-iron headboard wrought into several hundred candleholders that he'd filled with white candles. Okay, maybe it wasn't that many, but they looked so beautiful, lit up as if in a sanctuary. A lovely patchwork quilt, made of a rich jewel-toned shimmery fabric, lay folded at the foot of the bed—no doubt another gift from Jazz's mother for me to covet. God have mercy on me, the things I could picture doing in that bed, if it weren't for the dead woman sprawled in the center of the mattress, looking frail and pitiful beneath the white satin sheet, which covered her partially clad body from the waist down.

I followed Carly over to the bed, my steps heavy, as if I had worn steel-toed work boots instead of my gold sparkly shoes. The former Mrs. Brown was not quite resting in peace, her body an odd pale blue except for her bloodred face. My heart plunged to my shoes.

Carly snapped a vinyl glove on her hand and pulled the sheet back, exposing the body. Kate had been posed in a most unflattering, sexually suggestive way.

A primal scream sounded in my head. My legs threatened to fold beneath me, and I stumbled into Carly. She turned swiftly and caught me, forcing me upright. Her half nod, a brisk downward thrust of her chin, gave me a little courage.

I muttered to her, "Excuse me, Dr. Brown." I tried to regain some semblance of composure and took a deep breath before I looked again.

Kate wore only a man's white button-down shirt. What must have been her clothing—a little black dress that I could have fit into when I was five—frilly black panties, a demi-bra, a garter, and thigh-high panty hose lay neatly folded on the floor by the bed, her black stilettos upright beside them.

Death pallor aside, Kate Townsend had to be one of the prettiest women I'd ever seen. When Jazz and I first met, he told me that I reminded him of a story about a monk and an actress. He was the monk, Nonnus, and I was his Pelagia, the woman who inspired him at first sight. Or so he said. After seeing Kate, I had my doubts. She had the kind of beauty that could awaken a man; I didn't. She and Jazz must have made a lovely pair.

I hate to admit how much that disturbed me.

She had fair skin, like Jazz, but a bit more tawny, and the same exotic biracial good looks. She couldn't have been over thirty years old. Her brown hair had been coiffed to perfection in a sweeping updo. White rhinestones dotted her crimson nails—nails now broken, as evidenced by the one on the floor near the urine. Some had been torn off completely—defensive wounds.

She didn't go easy. Good for you, Kate.

She was wearing false eyelashes, which gave her a dramatic Audrey Hepburn in *Breakfast at Tiffany's* look. A stunner. She'd obviously made a big production of how she looked tonight, the poor doll. Now her striking hazel eyes looked dramatic because they were bulging in wide-eyed terror. Mouth open, tongue protruding over her bloodred lipstick, competing with the unnatural ruddiness of her face.

Carly bent over the body. She manipulated the woman's open mouth, then prodded and turned her head. "She's still warm—no rigor yet. I don't think she's been dead over a few hours, if it's been that long." Carly shook her head, a look of disgust shadowing her face. I wondered if she'd been thinking he'd come to me right after.

A wave of nausea washed over me.

She pointed to Kate's neck, circled with angry red abrasions and contusions. She spoke directly to me: "You can see the external damage to the structure of her neck. I have no doubt that it's worse internally." She pointed to a thumbprint-size impression on the side of Kate's larynx. "These impressions are from his fingers."

"Whose fingers, Dr. Brown?" I asked.

It was a breech on my part, one she didn't respond favorably to. She shot me a hard look. "Her murderer's."

"Assuming the person is a he."

She ignored me, speaking in terse ME-speak. "The wounds are consistent with hand strangulation."

Strangling someone to death is not like shooting them—bam, bam, you're dead. It takes about four minutes for a person to die from strangulation. Four *eternal* minutes. I couldn't imagine Jazz being that angry or cruel.

Carly asked me, like the curious innocent she wasn't, "What kind of killer would do this, Doctor?"

Not my Jazz. I didn't respond.

She turned her attention back to the body. "The bruises indicate a *lot*"—the word emphasized for my sake—"of unnecessary force." She pointed to Kate's eyes. "She's got the telltale petechial hemorrhaging consistent with strangulation."

An image of Jazz's hands flashed before me. I blinked it away. *Just breathe, Bell. Think.*

I tried to act like a pro—as if the man I loved weren't the one who could have done this. "Carly, the urine on the floor by the door? Is that from the victim?"

"The crime lab will be able to tell us later, but it's common for a victim's bladder to void during this kind of violent act."

"Could she have been murdered over by the door, then moved to the bed?"

"She shows signs of lividity, although it's not fixed, which means she's probably been in this position for the short time she's been dead. Whether she died in this bed or not, I can't say."

A burly, balding, brown-haired man entered the apartment, ambled over to us, and stood by my side. His pasty white skin provided a sharp contrast to his curly dark hair. The poor soul needed vitamins or some sun. He had all the appeal and energy of a crumpled paper bag. He rocked back on his heels and regarded me curiously. Then he nodded and thrust out his hand, attached to an arm that looked like a pale ham hock. "Detective Bobby Maguire," he said, sounding as bored and irritated as a teenager. "And you are?" His bushy eyebrows curved up like twin question marks.

I shifted Amos's box to my left hand and offered my right. He shook it harder than was necessary.

Carly spoke up. "This is Dr. . . . uh, Dr. Amanda . . ."

"I'm a forensic psychologist," I said, as if that would give me permission to be there.

Carly chimed in, "She's worked another case with me. I wanted her to see this."

He shot an incredulous look at me, pajama girl. "What's your name again?"

"Dr. Amanda . . ." Saying Brown, when that was both Carly and Jazz's last name, seemed a bit like overkill. No pun intended.

"Dr. Amanda what?"

I gave him a tight, professional smile. "Dr. Amanda is fine, Detective."

He returned it with his own fake grin. "I didn't realize the medical examiner's office sent out forensic psychologists on death investigations."

Carly, still busying herself with the body, spoke with arresting authority: "I said she's with *me*." She grinned at him to charm the sting away. "I didn't say she was from our office."

He shrugged. "I see. Interesting outfit for a death investigator."

"Hey!" I said. I had absolutely nothing to put behind that. While my mind whirred, searching for data to fill in the blanks, my favorite sleuth came to mind with a lightbulb-over-the-head *bing*. "Have you ever watched *Columbo* on television, Detective Maguire?"

Maguire had to be at least fifty, just the right age to remember the popular show well. He nodded.

"He had his own special uniform." I raised my arms with a

flourish, drawing attention to both Amos's box and my clothing. "Pajamas and sparkly shoes are my version of Columbo's trench coat."

I put my hands on my hips, firmly gripping the handle on Amos's box while the poor thing flopped around inside. "Maybe this is what makes me comfortable so I can give my brilliant assessments. Maybe it helps me to ask important questions that will help you catch the nutjob who did this. Questions like: Why is she in the bed instead of over there by the door, where the urine is?"

I got a blistering stare from him, but after a moment his gaze softened in what must have been recognition. "Are you two related? You look like you could be sisters."

"Sir," I said, my hands still on my hips, but resisting the urge to rock my neck sistah-girl fashion. I moved closer to him in what I hoped he'd find an intimidating half step. "Are you suggesting that all black women look alike?"

Detective Bobby Maguire showed no sign of being put off by my question. He pointed a stubby finger at Amos's temporary dwelling. "What's in the box you've got there?"

I thought it best not to do the whole sugar-glider routine. "Detective Maguire, I'm sure you want me out of your way so you can work. If you'll excuse me, I really have to concentrate."

He smirked. "Don't let me interrupt, Dr. Amanda. I'm just the lead detective here."

I turned back to Carly. "Why would she be in the bed if she was killed near the door?"

Carly looked away, but Maguire didn't. "You don't know for certain she got killed near the door," the detective answered.

"Right." I looked back at him. "She just peed on the floor because she wasn't wearing her Depends."

"You don't know if it's her urine, and even if she did get killed by the door, it's not so hard to believe he could have moved her."

Bobby Maguire annoyed me. "Why would he put her in his bed?" I asked.

"Maybe he was sending some sort of message."

"What kind of message? It wasn't *her* he wanted in his bed."

"How do you know that? Do you know Lieutenant Brown?"

I panicked and raised my voice. "I know him."

"Do you?" Maguire asked. The question reeked with innuendo.

"She was his ex," I said, wanting to kick myself for making it crystal clear that not only did I know Jazz, I knew him well. But I couldn't seem to stop myself. "'Ex' means it's over."

"Not always."

"Why pose her like that?"

The detective sighed. "Maybe he wanted her to look sexy."

He knew good and well the message had nothing to do with Kate Townsend being sexy.

"Do you find anything about that pose sexy, Detective?"

Carly nudged me, clearly peeved. "I think you made your point, Be—Doctor."

"That pose," I said, ignoring my sister's prodding, "is humiliating. It's a message, all right, and not the kind made by a person in the heat of a crime of passion."

Maguire didn't bother to mask his diminishing patience with me. "What do you mean, Dr. Amanda?"

I walked back over to the door with him following. Carly stayed by the bed. I said, "Let's say, *hypothetically,* Jazz did strangle Kate. How would things have progressed?"

Maguire said nothing.

"We'll assume Kate came here for . . . *something.*" And I assumed it wasn't to be strangled to death. As a matter of fact, I knew what she had come for. The thought made my breath try to heave out of my lungs again, while my knees decided to get to know each other better. She had wanted what I wanted: Jazz. And in a way that was so personal, so intimate. It stripped my very soul to think that she had once had what I wanted.

It took every bit of professionalism, biofeedback training, minor acting skill from one high school play, and a quick, silent prayer for mercy to hold my body in check. I couldn't let Maguire and Carly see me fall apart. And maybe I needed to hold myself together for Kate.

Who was I kidding? I needed to be strong and see this through for Bell. What in the world had I gotten myself involved with? Or rather, whom?

Heaven help me!

"They argued. He wanted her to leave, which brought them here by the door. Maybe she didn't want to leave. It got physical," I went on.

Maguire chimed in, "Maybe she's the one who wanted to leave, and he tried to stop her with the little choke hold cops know all about." He shrugged.

I didn't like his take and kept rolling with my own not exactly stellar spin. "Maybe in the struggle, he grabbed her by the neck and started choking her." I held my hands out, shaking them as if strangling someone, but I could hardly stand it. I couldn't picture Jazz doing it. Not *my* Jazz. "The action took place right here." I took a deep breath. "She was dying. Her bladder emptied involuntarily."

I stopped. Shut my eyes against the image assaulting my mind. I saw Jazz's hands—the same hands that had delicately caressed my face this very night. Hands that had outlined my lips after I kissed him.

"No," I said aloud without intending to. He couldn't have. The thought of him doing the kind of violence evident at this scene drained me of energy. "Kate slumped to the floor." I became less aware of everything and everyone around me, except Maguire studying me as if he suspected me as the prime suspect. But the scene compelled me.

Dear God, what happened here?

My pulse drummed in my head, and my knees began to tremble. "She was dead," I said.

Bobby scratched his head, looking more bored than confused. "He'd drag her over to the bed."

"Are there drag marks on her heels?"

Carly cradled one of Kate's heels in her hand. "No."

"Then he picked her up and took her to the bed," Maguire said.

I was buffeted by an image—tender and golden—of Jazz sweeping me off my feet and into his arms on the night I met him. I could see him picking her up, just as he'd done to me.

"Why put her in his bed? There's no good reason for it," I said.

Maguire quipped, "So she can rest in peace." The two uniforms who had previously guarded the door snickered.

"Something else doesn't make sense," I added.

"What's that, girl Columbo in shiny shoes?"

"Why would he cover her from the waist down with the sheet if he posed her like that? I mean, I've known of murderers who have closed their victims' eyes or turned their heads. It's an effort to relieve the guilt. They don't want the victim's stare to accuse them. But that pose . . . it begs for attention."

"Maybe he posed her 'cause he's a slime bag—make that a *murdering* slime bag, Dr. Amanda. Your theories are interesting and all, but you're a shrink, not a homicide detective. It looks pretty clear-cut to me. Maybe they gave each other a little sumthin'-sumthin' now and then. It ain't unusual between exes. Things got crazy. He killed her, panicked, and left."

I looked at him with what I hoped were a whole basketful of cocker-spaniel puppy eyes. To no avail. "Detective Maguire, I just want to help you figure this out."

"You don't work for me. And I don't need you."

"Why would a veteran homicide detective leave a body right in his bed? He'd have more than enough knowledge of how to hide his crime."

"Like I said, he panicked."

"Or someone else killed her and wanted it to look like Lieutenant Brown did it. Maybe your perp was the person who called the police."

"Not possible."

"Why not?"

"Kate Townsend called."

I tried to wrap my brain around that. Dead women don't call 911. Maguire didn't offer any sympathy for my obvious confusion, so I had to ask, "How could the victim call?"

"I don't know. Maybe he beat her up first, left, then came back to finish her off before we got here. Maybe he was still here when she called."

"How long did it take your uniforms to get here?"

"Apparently, it took *too* long. Look, lady—"

"Doctor."

"Doctor." He frowned. "I don't know about your success rate as a profiler, but I've been a homicide detective for fifteen years. To me, it looks like the lieutenant snapped and murdered his ex. Now, if Dr. Brown is done with the body, I'd like to get my crime scene processed."

Carly grabbed my arm. "Thanks for your insight, Dr. Amanda." She focused her attention on Maguire. "Do you have any more questions for me, Bobby?"

"Nah. I'll see ya down at the morgue."

Carly yanked me away and marched me out of the loft. When we were outside and some distance from the detectives and CSIs now starting their work, she loosened her grip on my arm and let me have it. "That was a bit much, Bell."

"It doesn't look right, Carly."

"No, it *doesn't* look right, because there's a dead woman in there. You made some good points, but that doesn't mean Jazz didn't do it."

"He wouldn't have left her that way."

She rolled her eyes. "Are you kidding me? You don't know *what* he would have done."

"Jazz is a gentleman. He opens the door for me. Walks me to my car. He puts his hand on my back to guide me. Carly, he stands up when I come to the table. Every single time."

"You're still in love with him, Bell."

"Think about it, sis. Every scene leaves clues, both physical and behavioral. Bobby Maguire, you . . . You both read physical clues."

She put her hands on her hips and glared at me.

"Okay, you don't just read physical clues, but you have to admit, you'd be more inclined to lean on what the physical evidence says. Right?"

Carly sighed. "And that's a good thing. Physical clues aren't subjective."

"I read behavioral clues. The crime scene is pointing to a killer who is *not* a gentleman."

She touched my arm. "Honey, they haven't even finished processing the scene."

"But Car, I've seen enough to tell me it's unlikely that the Jazz I know did this. You saw how it was in there. The scene is organized. That's not a crime-of-passion scene."

"Bell, I'm a pathologist, not a behavioral scientist. I'm not sure what you're talking about. I saw broken glass, evidence of a struggle, and a dead woman. How organized is that?"

My gut told me I was on to something. At least I hoped that was what it was saying, as opposed to *You're about to puke.* "Her clothes were neatly folded. If they were about to get into, as

Detective Maguire said, a little sumthin'-sumthin', do you think they'd stop the action so she could put her clothes in a neat pile?"

"I wouldn't know her bedside manner. Besides, they used to be married. It's not impossible that she'd have done that."

"Maybe he left and she took off her clothes while he was gone. Like she'd try to seduce him again when he got back."

I gazed back at the bed. All those candles glowing like the hope of love. Had he lit them knowing she was coming? Had he lied to me? For a moment I felt like I couldn't breathe. Even the passing thought felt like a vise grip squeezing my lungs. It did worse to my heart. I shut my eyes and tried to remember I was a professional. I tried.

Carly shook her head. "It still looks bad."

"There's a broken mug near the door and urine on the floor, but she's in bed. It's weirdly organized. I admit, it may not all make sense yet, but it's enough to make me doubt that Jazz, if he'd killed her, would have done it this way."

"So you *are* saying he could have done it."

"No. I'm saying—"

"Bell, I asked you here because I wanted you to see this for yourself. Once I get her back to the morgue, I have to report what I see."

"What do you mean, Carly?"

"I don't know if I'll find anything that will clear him. His prints and DNA might be all over her. He could have done this."

"Carly—"

"I called the police on him."

I stared at her in disbelief. "You told them he was in my place?"

"What else was I supposed to do?"

"You could have let me talk to him first."

"I don't trust a man with a dead ex-wife in his bed being at my sister's apartment." She paused, looking deeply into my eyes, pleading, speaking as a woman who had seen too many dead bodies. "How well do you really know him?"

The heart is deceitful above all things, and desperately wicked: who can know it?

I closed my eyes. The Scripture had descended on me like the Holy Spirit in the form of a dove. *How well* do *I know him?*

chapter
three

I MADE MY WAY back home after stopping for over three hours—pajamas, Amos, and all—at the twenty-four-hour Starbucks at Arborland Mall. My head was still reeling from what I had observed at the crime scene, despite feeding my nervous energy with extravagant amounts of Toffee Nut lattes and espresso fudge brownies.

I'd put a few brownie crumbs inside Amos's box, and when my first latte cooled down, I'd given him a few sips of that in the lid. He now seemed a little high-strung, too, throwing himself against the cardboard walls. Whether it was from the caffeine I'd shared with him, or my frayed nerves rubbing off, I wasn't sure.

Jazz's presence was as palpable as if he'd been sitting beside me. Thinking of him, probably already on his way to jail, I made the effort to stop at the 7-Eleven near my place to get a box of tampons before I went home. I'd made such a fuss about them; it was the least I could do.

After I'd gotten to my apartment building and parked my car, I scanned the lot for the blue police-issue Crown Victoria that Jazz drove. I hadn't noticed it in my haste on the way out. Now I spotted the Crown Vic at the curb just beyond the front entrance of the building. I thought it odd that the police hadn't impounded it yet.

The poor Crown Vic. It looked so forlorn underneath the streetlight. I remembered when he'd parked it there once before, on the Friday night he'd waited hours for me to come home. That night we'd kissed in the triangle of light, and I'd still had some hope that we could be together. I recalled Jazz's words to me earlier this evening, as sharp and unexpected as a knife wound to the heart. *I just wanted us to be together . . . Do you feel like you're capable of doing something you never thought you'd do . . . ?*

My honest answer: Of course I've felt that way, but that doesn't mean I'd do something wrong. Or something *beyond* wrong.

I stepped out of my car, grabbed Amos and my iPod, and locked the door behind me, ever aware of Jazz's insistence that I keep my doors locked at all times. I sighed and shook my head.

Now what am I supposed to do?

A nagging question kept tugging at my consciousness: *How well do I know him?*

The weight of the sadness that settled on me made me feel colder than I should have, even in the brisk December air. I shivered inside my coat, clutching Amos's box and wanting nothing more than to hurry into my apartment, grab my Bible and my grandmother's quilt, and get alone with God.

I dragged myself up the three flights of stairs, hanging my head and cursing each step like Jesus did the unfruitful fig tree. By the time I'd made it to the last step, Amos's box was nearly grazing the ground. I hobbled on the high-heeled golden monstrosities I'd grown to hate.

My shoes didn't like me, either. I tripped on the last step. Poor Amos slammed into one of the cardboard walls of his box. In a flash, I anticipated the two of us splattered on the hard ground, but a pair of hands caught me—not before I crashed my head into the chest that went with those familiar hands.

"Ow," I said as Jazz righted me. I touched my forehead where it felt like the imprint of one of his shirt buttons had formed. He still hadn't gotten a coat.

"You'll break my ribs yet," he said with what I hoped was mock seriousness. I peered up to see him shake his head at me. "You're banned from wearing high heels, young lady—unless we're in private, of course." He gave me a wicked grin that belied the sobriety of the night's events.

My heart Riverdanced again. "What are you doing here?"

He tried to pry Amos from my maternal grip. I resisted.

"I was here when you left, remember? That whole 'put the baby's cage together' thing. Give me the box."

"No. I thought you'd be—"

He couldn't wrench Amos from my hand. "You thought I'd be in jail?"

My mouth went dry. "Actually, yes. I did." I couldn't tell whether my heart was beating so fast because he made me feel like a lovesick girl or because I was afraid of him.

"Let's just say I got a heads-up. No thanks to you." The set of his jaw and the terse edge to his voice let me know he wasn't pleased with me. We kept the sugar-glider tug-of-war going until it exasperated Jazz and he let go. "What? Do you think I'll hurt him, too?"

"Too?"

"I didn't mean 'too.' I meant—Bell, you know what I meant."

"No, Jazz, I don't know what you meant. When did you come back?"

"I just got here. I was debating whether or not I should wait for you. I wasn't even sure you'd come back tonight. Considering . . ."

An arctic blast of air, seemingly out of nowhere, sliced into us. Jazz rubbed his arms up and down the brown wool suit jacket—fabric that offered little protection against the harsh wind. "Are you going to let me in, or do you think I've been murdering women all night?" The brooding anger became evident in his sullen, menacing expression.

I shuddered. "That's not funny."

"It wasn't meant to be."

We stood there for a moment, neither of us saying a word. I wished I could see inside his head, not like a psychologist but like a prophet. I needed a godly kind of certainty to assuage the onslaught of images from the crime scene. I watched him. If I thought I had nervous energy, Jazz's glowering agitation begged release—and soon. I didn't want to be around when he found it. He scared me. I blurted out, "I didn't call the police on you."

"It doesn't take much to figure out what happened, Bell. Your sister called, told you to get out of the apartment, and *she* called the police. You should have told me what was going on."

My hands clutched Amos's box. It felt like my heart was beating in time to the jagged rhythm of the infamous shower scene in *Psycho. Steady, girl, this is just Jazzy.* I tried to keep my voice even. "It occurred to me that perhaps you already knew." I echoed Carly's question to me: "What was I supposed to do?"

"How 'bout trust me?"

"You showed up at my door out of nowhere with those scratches on your face. You're the one who said you did something wrong, and a half hour later, I get a call that your wife—"

"My ex-wife."

"Ex? She was half-naked."

"She had clothes on when I left. Let's talk about this inside."

My heart had become a drum machine, and someone had turned up the speed. "What makes you think you're going inside?"

"Bell, I have never hurt you, not even when you hit *me*."

I looked into his deep brown entreating eyes. They didn't seem harsh. Still . . . "Why should I let you in?"

"Because you know me. I just want to talk to you."

"Maybe I don't know you at all."

"You don't believe that."

I opened my coat, put Amos inside, hugged one arm to myself against the cold that had little to do with the weather. My heart was about to fly right out of my chest. Gooseflesh rippled up and down my arms. My knees shook in the silky pajamas. "How do you know what I believe? I haven't seen you since the middle of November."

"You broke up with *me*."

"How could I break up with you if I was never your girlfriend in the first place?"

"We had something special, and you know it, regardless of what we called it." He rubbed his arms again. "I don't want to talk out here. I'm freezing, and so are you. If you don't want to let me in, I'll leave, but I'll tell you this: Kate was alive and kicking—literally—when I left."

I leaned against my door, stalling for time, thinking about how much I'd enjoy an angelic visitation right now. "Why is it so important that you talk to me?"

"I want you to hear what happened from me. I may not get the chance to talk to you again."

I wanted to ask why he didn't think he'd get to talk to me again, but it occurred to me that none of the answers I imagined he would say were good. He could say he planned to run away or turn himself in and risk going to prison for the rest of his life.

He didn't look like a murderer. He looked like the guy I'd fallen in love with. The one with Daddy Jack Brown's toothy smile and Addie Lee's artistic streak. Fatigue framed his eyes. His scratches must still hurt—mine did. Maybe he hadn't eaten. He certainly couldn't go home. His loft was now an active crime scene.

I had a WWJD moment. What *would* Jesus do? Not in a rubber-bracelet, weird, Christian-subculture, Jesus-junk-wearing way, but in a breathing, incarnational, God-with-us way. Jesus had ascended to heaven; I'd have to be His presence here on earth. What was *I*, the placeholder for Jesus, going to do?

I reached inside my coat pocket and pulled out my keys. Jesus told us to visit those in prison, but should I hang out with someone who hadn't quite made it there yet? Someone who could be dangerous? My instincts told me to let him in, give him a cup of coffee and something to eat, but what if . . .

I looked into Jazz's eyes.

Am I right? Lord, is that what You'd do?

Jesus was God, and He was a man—a strong, able-bodied carpenter. He could take Jazz. I considered my own frame, straining toward five-two, slightly overweight, and wearing heels—no match for a six-foot-tall cop in excellent physical condition.

Could I trust my fractured instincts? Would it be kind or suicidal to let him in?

God, don't let me do something crazy.

Just then Jazz took my hand in his. He bowed his head and began to pray the Ninety-first Psalm: "He who dwells in the secret place of the Most High shall abide under the shadow of the Almighty. I will say of the Lord, 'He is my refuge and my fortress; My God, in Him I will trust.'"

I squeezed his hand, closed my eyes, and interrupted him with my own paraphrased psalm from *The Message:* "That's right—he rescues you from hidden traps, shields you from deadly hazards. His huge outstretched arms protect you—under them you're perfectly safe; his arms fend off all harm."

Jazz closed the space between us and rested his chin on the top of my head. I heard him take a deep breath. He wrapped his arms around me. "I would never hurt you, baby."

God, don't let my feelings . . .

I went back to the psalm, praying with all my might: "Yes, because God's your refuge, the High God your very own home, Evil can't get close to you, harm can't get through the door."

Jazz placed his index finger on my lips. He repeated the words "Harm can't get through the door." He gathered me into his arms. "You even pray in the words of *The Message.*"

"How do you know it's *The Message?*"

"Your enthusiasm for it persuaded me to buy a copy. The first thing I read was the Ninety-first Psalm."

I smiled at him. "You pray in the New King James Version."

"What can I say? I'm a modern kind of guy. Let's go inside, baby, please."

Had the Scripture spoken? *"Harm can't get through the door"*? Or did it count if you foolishly swung open the door and invited it in?

I love this man. I don't know what to do.

In a still-small voice whispering inside, I heard the shepherd of my soul say, *Let him in.*

I should have comforted *him,* but Jazz settled Amos in his cage and went into the kitchen to make *me* a cup of tea. He came out with the same tray I'd used earlier. My other favorite Addie Lee mug, the one he had used earlier, held a steaming brew of Lemon Zinger sweetened with Splenda that I'd requested. Not that I really wanted another drink of anything, but Jazz wanted to do something for me. "Jazz, how many mugs like the one I broke earlier do you have?"

"Just one. She made about forty for the gift shop at the Detroit Institute of Arts when they had some of her work exhibited a few years back. They're almost impossible to get now."

"Can I still have yours?"

"Of course. I want you to have it."

He didn't know it was broken? Or was he that good of a liar?

He set the tray on the coffee table and handed the mug to me. "Are you still cold?"

"Yes."

"We should get you warmed up."

"What do you have in mind?" That just flew out of my mouth—nervous humor defending me against the thought that Jazz, my Jazz, could be dangerous.

He grinned. "You don't want me to answer that." His fidgeting told me that he had his own case of nerves to contend with. He sat down next to me. Turned his knees and body toward me. "Can I get a blanket or something for you?"

I nodded.

Jazz gave my knee a little squeeze and went into my bedroom.

I called out to him, "Get the quilt that's folded on the chair."

Forget comfort food. I'd always found comfort in my great-grandmother's arms, which I felt in the soft, worn fabric of the cloth of my family's history. Ma Brown had pieced together a vibrant Star of Bethlehem, or North Star, out of odd bits of fabric from dresses, slacks, baby clothes, and beloved shirts. Each piece told a story. The star design itself, centered, in antique white fabric, had been a veritable map to help and freedom. The star points spread outward in bursts of color and texture, shooting from a center as multicolored as our family. It would be worth good money if I ever parted with it. Of course, it would have to be wrenched from my dead, bony fingers, I loved it so.

I waited for Jazz to bring it to me.

And waited.

"Jazz, what's taking you so long?" Gooseflesh crept up my arms. *Is there something in my room he could hurt me with?*

I scanned the living room for something I could defend myself with if I needed to.

Jesus, did I make a mistake in letting him in?

"What are you doing in there? Making a new quilt for me?" Panic rose with my heart rate.

"I'm coming," he said.

I didn't have the patience to wait. I shot to my bedroom door as if a cannon had propelled me. Jazz lay sprawled out in my bed.

He sprang up when he saw me. "Sorry," he said, his cheeks pinking.

"What are you doing?"

"I just wanted to lie down for a minute." He stood, grabbed the quilt off the chair, and gently wrapped it around my shoulders, as if I were made of glass and he was about to pack me in a box.

Hmm . . . pack me in a box? Somebody get me out of this Alfred Hitchcock movie!

"Are you *that* tired?" I asked, shaking the morbid me-in-a-box thought from my head.

He chuckled. "You don't want to know."

I didn't respond. I was preoccupied with trying to figure out if I should offer him the hospitality of my bed for the night. Not with me in it, of course. The shrill scream in my conscience suggested I should not.

He gave me a quizzical glance. "You *do* want to know?"

He had gone back to my original question about him being tired. I thanked God he hadn't read my mind. "Yes, please."

"I'm way too keyed up to be tired. I laid on your bed . . ."

"Please don't say 'hoping you would join me.'"

He laughed and shook his head as if sharing a bed with me would be as absurd as him joining the Universal Soul Circus. "Uh. Actually, I hadn't quite gone there, but . . ." A sly smile crept across his face.

"Don't start no stuff, Jazz."

"It won't be none, baby, okay? I just remembered the time I picked your lock and came in here to watch the game. Your bed smelled like the vanilla and amber stuff you wear."

"Anahita's body butter."

"I missed your scent."

"Jazzy—"

"I just want to be honest with you tonight. I don't know what the morning is going to bring."

I didn't know what to say. What *would* tomorrow bring? For that matter, what would the night bring if the two of us stood in my bedroom feeling nostalgic, not to mention vulnerable. "Let's go back into the living room and finish talking," I said.

"You're not nervous about being in a bedroom together, are you?"

"I'd rather talk in the *living room*."

He licked his lips and grinned, probably another nervous gesture, but I found it deliciously sexy. "Do you think I'd try to seduce you at a time like this?"

I can tell this is going to be a challenge.

"I think that both of us are highly emotional. Shall we go now?"

He moved toward me, his hand touching the small of my

back to guide me to the couch. He leaned in and whispered in my ear, "I just missed you. That's all." Between his tender touch, his warm breath at my ear, and the hug Ma Brown's quilt was giving me, I could have curled in to him and had a blissful nap.

He took a deep breath when we made it to the couch, and as I eased into the cushions, he offered, "Things got out of hand tonight."

I guess they did, if he ended up killing a woman. A chill crept up my spine. "Tell me everything that happened." I tried to sound as if I weren't shocked and that whatever he said would be heard without judgment.

"I called Kate a few days ago and asked her if we could meet at a restaurant."

No more thoughts of blissful sleep. Jazz plopped down beside me on the sofa. I tried to act like I didn't care that he wanted to take his *wife* to dinner and hadn't thought to take me in a month. "Why?"

"To be honest, I couldn't stop thinking about you and Rocky."

"Me and Rocky?"

"I had all kinds of visions of your nuptials, and there I was in love purgatory." He propped my feet on my coffee table and massaged them. Yum.

"That's silly. Rocky and I are nothing more than friends," I said, enjoying the attention he was giving my tootsies.

"*Good* friends. You know Rocky would marry you in a heartbeat if you gave him the chance."

"But I didn't. That's why we're only friends."

"Bell, I started praying."

Usually, I like it when people pray, but . . . "And then you called your *wife*?"

"She's not . . . She *was* my ex-wife."

I felt badly about what I'd implied in my jealousy; the poor young woman was on a slab in the morgue. "I'm sorry. Please go on."

"It got harder and harder to believe it was so wrong for you and me to be together. I respected you, Bell, as much as I could. I only tried to kiss you once—and got busted by my mom—not that I didn't thoroughly enjoy the kisses you gave me." He smiled shyly. "I tried to treat you like a sister in Christ, but God knows my feelings for you were far from sisterly. I didn't want to sin. I was scared."

"Scared of God?"

"Scared of the train wreck that could happen if we didn't do things right. Blame my mother. All that Church of God in Christ holiness teaching."

"Can you fast-forward to the murder?"

"I didn't murder anyone." *Blam!* He erected a wall between us that was almost palpable.

I paused, chastising myself for the foolish accusation that had flown out of my mouth. I'd have to do some business with God about my impatience. I hoped I could mount the wall and get him talking again. "I'm sorry, Jazz. Why did you want to meet with Kate?"

He didn't say anything. Now he avoided my eyes. A minute passed. I thought a bit of disclosure would help my cause. "I'm nervous. You have to admit it looks bad."

He nodded but didn't offer anything. We both sat back. I

thought perhaps the conversation was over. My mind returned to the crime scene. I thought of the evidence I'd seen. I couldn't shake the thought that nothing that I knew of him, other than the scratches on his face, pointed to him being a murderer.

"I want to believe you," I said.

He looked at me. I prayed that it was hope I saw light his eyes. He exhaled, and words tumbled out of his mouth. "Bell, I know it's stupid now, but I wanted to make sure she was okay. I'd made up my mind."

"About what?"

"About moving on. I was done being tied to her." He folded his arms across his chest.

"Tell me more about that." Ack! Therapist-speak. I couldn't control it sometimes.

"She knew my convictions. She knew I'd always feel bound to her, and she used it against me." He looked into my eyes. His begged for understanding.

I nodded to let him know I was still with him.

"When we first divorced, she'd come to me when she was mad at Christine, her partner, and we'd end up—" He put his head down, waited a beat, and gazed back up at me. Whether to determine if I'd be disappointed or what, I didn't know. "We'd end up in bed. I know it was wrong, but she could be very seductive."

It hurt me, an irrational response. He hadn't even known me at the time. I knew I shouldn't be taking it personally. As a therapist, I'd known scores of divorced couples who'd done the same— some even after one or both of them had remarried. Still, it made my heart sink to think he'd done it, too.

He slowly unfolded his arms, literally opening up to me. "It was during the months right after the divorce. It wasn't a good time for me, and it hasn't happened in three years, no thanks to Kate."

I nodded, afraid of what my heart would let fly out of my mouth if I spoke.

"Even after I stopped being with her intimately, she would come to me a few times a year and tell me she wanted to get back together. She said she was confused about her sexuality. Sometimes I think she only got together with Chris because I didn't give her enough attention. I felt guilty about that, like I forced my wife to become a lesbian, but Bell, I didn't want her back." His left leg shook. I assumed he was letting out some of the thick tension trapped in his body. "She wasn't the love of my life. I didn't even like her most of the time."

"Why did you marry her in the first place?"

"I told you, it was complicated. I'm ashamed to say she was supposed to be just a one-night stand." At this he turned his head away. "I'm not proud of how I tried to use her." He searched my eyes again, like he wanted my forgiveness. "I asked God to forgive me a long time ago, and I've suffered consequences you know nothing about, and I hope I never have to tell you. I'm not the man I was four years ago. I fooled around with her, and things happened that I didn't anticipate."

"What do you mean, Jazz? This is all vague to me. I thought you were going to be honest tonight—that whole thing about not knowing what tomorrow will bring."

"I am being honest. I married her because under the circumstances, I felt like it was the right thing to do."

I set down the mug of tea. "What were the circumstances? Are you saying you married her because you had sex with her?"

He shook his head and slouched into the couch, looking boyish and sullen. "It was time to slow my roll. I wasn't an angel, and my lifestyle finally caught up with me."

"Just because you thought it was time for you to settle down still doesn't explain why you married *her*. You could have had your pick of women."

"I'm afraid that's a misperception. I can't have my pick."

"Sure you can. You're gorgeous."

"Then why'd you let me go?"

I didn't answer. I didn't want to get into how letting him go was one of the hardest things I'd ever done. "Let's get back to why you married Kate."

"What difference does it make? It was only a month before she started cheating. With my female partner! And Christine wasn't the only one."

I thought of the crime scene screaming to me that a man she'd been involved with had killed her. "Could the other person she was seeing have been a man?"

"Why do you ask?"

"Could it have been a man?"

"I don't know. All I know is that she went back and forth between men and women, but she lived with Christine for most of the years since I put her out, so I figured she was mostly a lesbian." He stared at his hands. "Kate was hard to figure out. By our second month of marriage we were pretty much finished, and by the third, I was giving a lawyer a good portion of my income." Despite expressing his desire to move on, he clearly still felt guilty. I hoped it was guilt about his failed marriage, as opposed to another kind of guilt.

I knew Jazz well enough to know he wasn't going to tell me tonight why he had married Kate. There could be only a few options. I didn't want to think of any of them.

I took a sip of my not so hot tea and set the mug back on the tray. I repeated, "Let's fast-forward. You wanted to tell her you were moving on. What, exactly, did you mean by that?"

"I was coming back for you, Bell. I was obsessed with the thought that you would marry Rocky."

"I told you, nothing is going on between me and Rocky."

"He wants you."

"What makes you think so?"

"I'm a man. I've seen how he looks at you. He told me to my face that he was still in love with you. To my *face*!"

"That doesn't mean he and I are anything more than friends." I stared into his eyes. "So, you invited her to your house?"

"I offered to take her to dinner. I wanted to meet her at a public place."

"How did she end up in your loft?"

"She just showed up. We were supposed to meet tomorrow evening."

"She showed up, and then what?"

His posture changed. He rounded his shoulders as if he carried a heavy load.

Of guilt?

"I told her I wished her well and that I was going to . . ."

I leaned back into the cushions, slightly away from him. "You were going to what?"

"I told her some things about you, and she went ballistic."

Man, what do I have to do to coax information out of you?

"What did you tell her about me? Can you be a little more specific?"

He shook his head. "Always the therapist, huh?"

Why not? When I was Dr. Amanda Brown, I wasn't vulnerable Bell. But even if my defenses weren't up like the price of Italian shoes at my mother's boutique, I still burned to know his intentions. "What about me?"

"Is that a bit of narcissism I detect?"

"Will you stop it? I want to know what happened."

"I told her that I love you."

My heart soared to the heavens, then plunged back to earth, beating wildly. I couldn't decide if I was more excited or frightened, but for the moment I thought I'd better leave that comment alone. "What happened next, Jazz?"

"I just said I love you."

"I heard you."

Jazz's body armor went back up. Arms across his chest. Long legs stretched out and predictably crossed at the ankles. He leaned toward the armrest of my sofa, effectively distancing himself from me. For a few moments neither of us spoke.

I knew two things: I'd have to break through his defenses, and he'd resist me if I did so as a psychologist. I'd totally have to use my feminine wiles. I had only one or two, and they were full of dust, but I'd use them to keep him talking.

I moved my legs over so that my knees touched his thigh. He tried not to respond, but the tiny beginnings of a smile at the corners of his mouth betrayed him. I upped the ante and rested my palm on his knee.

God help us both.

His gaze flicked over me. "Kate tried the old seduction ritual." He removed my hand to let me know he was on to me.

I could feel my "Kate" jealousy rising inside me, but I couldn't stop it. "She got to you?"

"Just because she's good at it doesn't mean I wanted her. *You* get to me, Bell, without even trying, but when you do try, like you just did when you touched my knee . . ."

My stomach did a somersault. I grabbed my mug and took a heaping gulp of tea, then practically broke the mug slamming it too hard onto the tray. More attitude slipped out of my mouth: "Is that when she lit the candles and did a little striptease for you?"

Jazz shook his head, probably annoyed with me. "She tried a little verbal persuasion. When I didn't go for it, she started cursing and screaming. She lunged at me and got my face."

I didn't want to hear any more, but I couldn't bring myself to stop him.

He clenched and unclenched his fist at the memory. "It stunned me, 'cause she got a whole lotta Jazz underneath her fingernails. She came after me again. As a reflex, I grabbed her." He fidgeted, shaking one ankle, but he looked right at me and kept talking. Whatever lurked below the surface in him was about to shake itself free. "She kept trying to fight me, and I got more and more ticked off."

I expected an explosion, but his nervous energy stalled like the eye of a storm. A solemn look shadowed his face.

Here it comes.

"I pushed her away from me—hard—and she fell on the ground."

I held my breath and scanned his hands. No scratches. I thought about Kate's defensive wounds. She wouldn't have done that kind of damage to her fingernails by just scratching his face. She had clawed at whoever killed her. *Why doesn't he have scratches on his hands?*

Jazz gritted his teeth. "I have never hurt a woman in my life, but . . ."

He's going to say he choked her. I was wrong. I got him all wrong, and he's about to confess.

My blood turned to ice water. "But what?"

Again he stared at his hands—hands with no scratches. He clenched his fists. His face turned stony.

My voice turned to a whisper. "What did you do wrong?"

I closed my eyes and waited for what felt like judgment to fall.

chapter
four

SHOVED HER. Hard." He looked away. "I pushed her," he said quietly, his voice full of shame.

I stared at him. "What else?"

His head jerked up, eyes wide. "That was it. I know it was wrong. I have no excuse. I should have just walked away."

"All you did was push her down?" I demanded to know, cuttin' my eyes and rockin' my head.

He stiffened, knowing he would have to stand down. Brothas hate it when you go unadulterated sistah girl on them. "Isn't that bad enough?" He twisted his mouth into a frown. "Give me a break. You know I don't lose it like that, not even with violent women. Like you."

I ignored that last dig. Had to. Or we'd get all messed up, going in the wrong direction. "Jazz, if all you did was push her—" My mind swirled with bits and pieces that didn't make sense.

"I felt like doing more than that. While she was on the floor, that hellcat started kicking me with her stilettos. I grabbed my keys, stepped over her, and left. I felt stupid for letting her in. Then I felt bad. I wanted—no, needed—to see you. So I came straight here."

He hadn't even grabbed his coat. *But to escape the wildcat or in fear of getting caught?* "Why did you leave her alone at *your* place?"

"What was I supposed to do? Drag her out by her heels? Call my colleagues at the station on her and be ridiculed for weeks? I knew I never should have let her in, but when things escalated, I figured if I left, she'd cool off and go, even if she did a little property damage first."

"What else happened?"

Jazz sighed. "That's all that happened while I was there. Now she's dead." He sagged deeper, if that were possible, into my couch. "All because I wanted to be free of her."

"You were already free of her."

"No, Bell. I was divorced, not free. She was like an albatross around my neck." He looked at the floor. "And the fact that I'd married her ate away at me. My parents had a great marriage. My grandparents. All my brothers and sisters have great marriages. There was this part of me that felt obligated to work things out, but the other part of me hated Kate. Hated that I ever set eyes on her." He looked at me, his eyes pleading for understanding. "Kate always kept some kind of drama going on. I actually felt sorry for Christine for being her lover. I don't know how she could stand to look at Kate most of the time."

"Jazz—"

He jumped to his feet. "Just let me finish. Kate ruined my life. I couldn't so much as date because I thought I'd be doing something wrong. I spent three and a half years being lonely. Mad. Feeling like it was all over for me, and then you came along and kissed me, and after that, *baby*—"

"Don't, Jazz."

"Don't what? Don't want a life? Don't want to cut that dead-weight off of me?"

"'Deadweight' is probably a poor choice of words right now."

He glared at me.

I stood to face him. "I'm sorry to tell you this, Jazz, but you sound motivated."

"I *am* motivated. I want more."

"Motivated as in you have a *motive*—motive for murder."

He gaped at me. "Haven't you heard anything I said?"

"I heard it all, Jazz. I'm telling you what it sounds like."

He spoke slowly, calmly. "I felt so guilty, I couldn't bring my-self to *date* after my divorce. Do you think I'd *kill* her?"

I didn't answer. I'd known people to do worse.

He repeated, raising his voice this time, "I asked you if you think I killed her?" I thought Jazz might blow like Mount St. Hel-ens at any moment, and I didn't know what he'd do. I'd never seen him out of control. Not even right before he got shot in the line of duty. His eyes narrowed, and the veins in his tem-ples bulged. His head seemed to morph into a red ball of rage. I backed away from him.

"I don't *murder* people." His voice exploded, shattering my insides. "*I* put murderers *away!*"

I shrank away from his voice, tears springing to my eyes. Part of me needed to console him. My whole heart rent in two.

With one hand, he covered his eyes. He brushed away his tears with the other. The barrier of this heinous crime stood be-tween us. He stood only feet away, but it may as well have been a million miles. His shoulders shook with grief.

Oh, God, I loved this man.

"Jazzy?"

When I spoke his name, he sobbed, big heaving wails. I thought the sound would kill me. My heart couldn't take any more. He dropped to his knees and held his head. He choked out the words: "I didn't kill her."

I couldn't help myself. I went to him. I gathered him in my trembling arms. My hands stroked and rubbed his arms, back, head.

"I don't understand," he said, weeping.

I rocked him for a long time. Held him. Shushed him. Wiped his moist eyes with my cheek. Kissed each eyelid.

Bad idea.

We were okay until the eyelid kissing. He responded to my motherly gesture by giving me a soft, brief kiss on the lips. And then another. And another.

I closed my eyes, realizing I needed his tenderness as much as he needed mine. I willed myself to forget about murder. It reminded me of words that I'd heard in an old Billie Holiday song. Her haunting voice sang about knowing she was a fool, but she loved her man so. I was the woman in that blues song, and in his arms, I just didn't care.

The intensity of our kisses grew. The bodice-threatening smooch we'd shared earlier seemed chaste by comparison. While I was glad to see we'd gotten a momentary respite from our anguish, my great-grandmother, if she could see us from heaven, would have said we'd jumped out of the frying pan straight into the fire. Clichéd, yes, but mystical black women are entitled to use clichés. Besides, we'd moved from a hot place to a hotter place, and honestly, I wished she could leave the celestial realm for a moment to hose us down.

My good sense slowly began to return. Did I *really* want to be like Lady Day?

"Uh . . . Jazz?" I grabbed his hands, which were trying to make their way past my Victoria's Secret pajamas to the parts of me that were meant to *stay* secret, at least until vows were exchanged. "Didn't you say something earlier about not wanting to sin?"

His voice sounded husky with desire. "We're not sinning yet. You just moved my hands away."

"We're close enough. You don't really want to be intimate under these circumstances, now, do you?"

In answer, he covered my mouth with his. I wrenched myself away, showing impressive restraint for a woman filled with lust. "I think we're acting out in reaction to the stress we're experiencing tonight." I did realize that, while astute, my observations were not the same as saying "Please stop doing that."

"How can you make out with me *and* psychoanalyze me?" He showered my neck with kisses, not bothering to wait for an answer. His hands got busy again. Mine blocked his efforts. I still hadn't asked him to cease and desist.

"This won't make us happy, Jazz. The same challenges will be there tomorrow."

"It'll make parts of us happy. Parts of me are happy already."

Jazz Brown, the man I loved, was about to rip my bodice for real. When we'd shared our first impulsive kiss, I had told him I wanted to be in love, even if only for a minute. Shoot, that had happened in September. Now most people had their Christmas trees up! Didn't I deserve another minute of love—a few of them?

I tried to return myself to a place of rationality by analyzing the situation from a professional viewpoint. It was obvious that Jazz, unable to cope with the shock of his ex being murdered, was coping by using classic avoidance techniques—attempting to affirm life by making love.

Or was he fleeing his own guilt by pretending he hadn't been capable of performing such a heinous act? Was he just trying to distract me from the truth?

My Jazz couldn't have done it, could he? Hadn't the evidence pointed to a killer very different from Jazz? I told myself he couldn't have done such a horrible thing. The hands caressing my back and tangling in my hair could not have strangled a woman to death this very night.

Or could they?

On the other hand, I wanted to do what was right—for God, and for Jazz and me.

Needless to say, I was conflicted on more than one level. I silently prayed. God told us in His Word to flee fornication. It sure wasn't easy when you were practically starved for intimacy. Especially when the man of your dreams wanted it, too.

God, help me, I don't want to do something you don't want me to do. Help us get out of this mess.

Then I heard it. *Yip, yip, yip.* "What is that?"

He lifted his head and listened, and then an expression of annoyance showed on his face. "Ignore it," he said quickly, pressing his lips to mine.

When I gave his hand a hard smack, he stopped smooching

and groping to plead with me like a sixteen-year-old. "C'mon, baby, please."

As much as I liked having Jazz beg for my affections like a rhythm-and-blues singer, the noise had captivated my attention. Finally, it dawned on me what I had heard. "That's Amos. It's a sign."

"No, it isn't," he lied, his expression giving him away.

"Jazz, you know Amos is over there barking like a rat dog." The saleslady hadn't said anything about barking, either, and I still hadn't gotten around to cracking open that owner's manual. I laughed. *Don't tell me God doesn't have a sense of humor.*

Jazz eased away from me. "Amos is full of surprises, isn't he?"

"It's the barking of God," I said.

"Don't violate my brain with that thought."

"God once spoke through an ass. He can bark through a sugar glider." I laughed again, but Jazz did not find this divine intervention funny.

As inexplicably as it had started, Amos's yipping stopped.

I pulled myself up from the floor, trying to suppress another round of giggles. "Are you okay, Jazz?"

"I can't believe what just happened."

"We were out of control."

"That *did not* just happen."

"One day you'll look back on all this and laugh." I thought about it and cracked up again. "I'm laughing already."

"I don't think I will, Amanda."

"You're not calling me Bell. You don't love me anymore?"

"Not at the moment."

"You'll thank Amos for this one day."

"No, I won't."

He raked his hand through his hair and blew air from his cheeks. A blush crept up his neck.

I extended my arm to him. "C'mon, get up."

He took my hand and picked himself up off the floor. "I'm embarrassed," he said.

"Don't be. Thank God for Amos."

"Yeah, right. The prophet Amos! Did I mention that I hate Amos?" I rubbed his shoulder. He backed away. "We'd better go back to our no-touching policy. I'm not quite settled down yet."

"Truth be told, neither am I."

His shoulders sagged and he cursed, ignoring my no-swearing-in-Amos's-presence policy. "I'm sorry, Bell. I wasn't supposed to sin with you."

"I'm Bell again?"

"You've always been Bell. You were Bell at first sight."

"Jazz, we just made a mistake. We could have gotten in a lot more trouble than we did."

He sighed and walked over to my door. I followed him.

He turned to look at me with startlingly mournful eyes. "I can't afford any more mistakes."

"And what is that supposed to mean?" My reactions splintered. The psychologist in me wanted to analyze. Was it a confession of sorts? The other me, the shocked, scared woman, ached for more of his comfort, no matter how illogical it was. I thought it best to cling to whatever logic I had left. I tried to ignore the me who needed his love more than the truth. "When do you think they'll arrest you?"

"When they find me. *If* they find me."

"Jazz, you have to turn yourself in."

"No, I don't. I didn't kill anyone."

"If you run, they'll think you did it."

"They already think I did it."

"Will you at least consider turning yourself in? Please?"

He glared at me like I was asking him to go to jail for me personally.

"It's the right thing to do," I said.

He sighed. Shrugged. "Maybe. Probably." He sighed again. "I don't know. I don't want to go to jail."

I unlawfully touched his arm. "Let's talk some more. We could have more tea."

He responded by running his finger up my arm. "That's not what I want to have. You're tempting me."

"Coffee? With biscotti?" I offered, even though I was grossly overcaffeinated, hyped up on sugar, and flushed from almost having my bodice ripped. It would probably be three days before I could sleep.

Jazz smiled, a slow, seductive dazzler. "You're not listening to your great-grandmother. Don't start no stuff, and it won't be none."

Ma Brown would be so proud of him.

"It won't be none," I said, lying to myself.

"It will be if I stay. I promise you that, beautiful." He clapped both hands on my shoulders.

Maybe my MIA good sense had fled to him, but good sense meant nothing to me now. "Don't leave yet." Even as I said it, I wondered, *Why would any sane woman want a potential killer in her house?* I guess that was precisely it. I wasn't sane. I was wrapped up in the Jazz spell.

He searched my eyes. "Why are you doing this to me, baby?"

"Doing *what?* Nothing really happened. I just want to talk." Not true, but I couldn't bring myself to admit, even to myself, how good his desire for me felt.

"You know exactly what you're doing, and a lot happened. At least, it did for me."

So he knew I wanted him—needed him like I need air and water. Still, we'd stopped ourselves once. We could again. I still had so many questions to ask. *Just a few more moments with him, Lord.* Everything inside of me screamed no. I ignored everything. "Jazz, I want to see you again. I mean . . . I'd like for us to talk about this."

"I know exactly what you want. We're adults." His hands circled my waist, and he groaned before releasing me. "Under the circumstances—all of them—it's probably best if we stay away from each other."

"Please" slipped out of my mouth. I still ached for his touch.

He ran his hand across his smooth chin, and my fingers followed until he took my hand in his again. "You sure make it hard for a brotha to say good night."

A nervous laugh escaped my mouth. "I don't really want anything to happen . . ." A flat-out lie and I knew it. *God help me.* "But I'm feeling . . . so . . ."

"I feel it, too."

My ability to intellectualize abandoned me, leaving a gelatinous mass of feelings in its place. "Jazz, I feel a million different—"

"I know."

"I'm so scared. What's going to happen to you?"

"If they catch me, I'm going to go to jail, and I'll probably stay there until they find out who killed her. Only, they think I killed her, so they won't be real motivated to find someone else."

"Jazzy . . ." I had no idea what to say. It all seemed too enormous to figure out. The world was like ground zero, debris covering every surface around us, and my place was a sanctuary. "Stay with me," I pleaded. I wasn't even sure why.

He placed his mouth on mine. He hesitated and finally gave me a long, lingering kiss. "I want to stay. I want to hold on to you until whatever is going to happen to me happens. I want them to drag me away from you. That's why I should go, baby."

"Jazz . . ."

"Bell, you aren't yourself tonight, either. People only get so many sugar-glider barks before they do what's natural. You'd regret it, and I don't want you to have any regrets when I make love to you."

I nodded. God knows I didn't want to run out of sugar-glider barks. I had a lifetime of regrets. I didn't want to add another.

Jazz let me go. "I don't know what's going on, but Kate is dead, and the killer was bold enough to off her in my loft. Something could happen to you because of me."

I touched his lips with my finger. "But I just got you back."

He took my hand in his and kissed my fingertips. "I should have let you go when you told me you didn't want to see me again. I couldn't even protect a woman in my own loft—which is like a fort! What could I offer you now?" He placed my hand by his heart and kissed me on the forehead. "I wanted tonight to be the beginning of something beautiful for us. Now it looks like Kate wins again. Even in death, she wins."

"How could she win? She was murdered."

"And the police want me for it. That's how she wins."

"Jazz, a lot has happened, and you're right—neither one of us is thinking clearly. But you have to know the only person who is winning is the person who killed her."

He shoved his hands into his jacket pockets. "I shouldn't have come here. But honest to God, Bell, when I came here earlier, it was about you and me. Kate was alive when I left her." He sighed. "I'm so sorry. Good-bye, Bell."

"I'll see you later, Jazz. Right?"

"I don't think—" He squeezed his eyes shut. "I can't go to jail. I can't do that, baby." He opened his eyes again, and they were moist.

"Don't do anything crazy. Just turn yourself in."

"Make sure you lock all three locks. Be extra careful. Don't trust anybody."

Including you?

I closed the door behind him, dutifully bolted all the locks, and rested my back against the door, willing myself not to cry. I tried not to think about the fact that my body still burned for him—guilty or innocent—even standing alone in the empty space he'd left behind.

I cried anyway.

chapter
five

WHEN THE MAN YOU LOVE is suspected of murder, it's a grand excuse to beg off work. I called the Washtenaw County Jail and told my boss, Dr. Eric Fox, that I had a crisis of a personal nature. Next, I made a visit to my dear sister at the morgue rather than partaking of the more comfortable option of wallowing in self-pity for several hours.

When I arrived at the morgue, I had to go through the maze of security. Honestly, you wouldn't think the dead needed so much protection. I'd gone through the morgue's security checks once before, the day after I first met Jazz. It was like going through airport security bearing a ticking parcel. Finally, I made it to the double doors that led to the autopsy room. I took a deep breath and tried to prepare myself. Didn't Carly have a desk somewhere in the building? Was she always crouched over the dearly departed? I hoped this time she'd be on her way out of the autopsy room to fill out paperwork.

Nice try, but no prize.

I opened the double doors to the room where all the action happened. The place made me queasy. All those metal tables.

All those sinks and hoses. All those jars and saws and crowbars and . . . My head started to swim. Before the room began spinning, I focused my attention on my sister in the middle of the room wearing hot-pink scrubs, a lab coat, a surgical mask, and vinyl gloves. She held an eyeball in her hand.

Things suddenly got very fuzzy.

I don't know if the surprise on her face meant she hadn't expected to see me or she hadn't expected to see me about to give up my breakfast and/or pass out on the floor.

"*Woooooooo*" sort of slipped out of my mouth, followed by bobbing and weaving, even though my feet hadn't moved since I'd opened the door.

She came over to me, still holding that eyeball. "Snookums, what are you doing here?"

So it was "snookums" now. At any moment my sisterly moniker could change. She tried to hold me up with her elbows. "Carly, don't touch me with *the eye hand*!"

"Then stand up straight."

Couldn't do it.

My sister could be a ruthless dictator, like our mother. She directed, "Take a deep breath. You're wobbling, just like one of those Weebles you used to play with when you were a kid."

I knew she meant that I wasn't steady on my feet. But Weebles didn't have feet. They were egg-shaped dolls I used to take great pleasure in destabilizing. I couldn't help but think she was also alluding to my less than perfect figure. My defenses went up like the price of movie tickets. "Well, Weebles wobble but they don't fall down," I countered.

I'm sure Carly found that statement ridiculous. She responded the way she typically did when I acted dumb. "Whatever." Then she added cruelly, "Suck it up."

I sucked, but not quite up.

"*Do it.* I can't hold you like this. If you haven't noticed, one of my hands is full."

With that in mind—vividly—I did suck it up. Besides, she was too much like our mother for me to defy her in this kind of situation. I straightened my shoulders and hightailed it over to the nearest chair. Carly and her sidekick The Eye went back over to the metal autopsy table. She plopped the eye into a container of liquid.

"I hate this place, Car. Why couldn't you be a pediatrician or something?"

"Do I ask you why you couldn't be anything other than a psychologist?"

Actually, she had on several occasions. "Did you finish doing the autopsy on Jazz's ex-wife?"

She had her back to me, engaged in clanking around strange-looking tools and doing what looked to me like busywork. At last the reality dawned on me. She was purposefully ignoring me. She didn't want me there.

"Carly?"

She stopped clanging for a moment, not turning to face me yet, but kept arranging tools, more quietly. "I haven't started it yet. She's not the only dead woman in Wayne County, you know. Contrary to what you and Maguire think, I've got other cases. He's been pressing me all morning about it. I've had no sleep, no coffee, my mood is foul, and you shouldn't be here." She went back to banging things around.

"You weren't this hostile the last time I came here."

She stopped and turned to face me. Her face softened. "I'm not hostile now, honey. And last time you were here, your boyfriend's wife wasn't in a drawer wearing a toe tag instead of the Jimmy Choos she left at the crime scene."

"She's his *ex*-wife. Those were Jimmy Choos?"

Carly looked at me the way I'd looked at that eye. "I'd be much more comfortable if you had said he's your *ex-boyfriend*."

"Maybe he didn't do it, Carly."

"And you base this on?"

"He wouldn't have posed her."

Carly rolled her eyes. "That doesn't prove anything to me. The imprint of his hands extends all the way around her neck."

"How do you know it's the imprint of *his* hands? Did you find his fingerprints on her?"

"We weren't able to lift any prints off her neck, but that doesn't prove he didn't strangle her. And whose DNA do you think we'll find underneath her fingernails?"

I scooted up to the edge of my chair. "That will only prove she scratched him."

Carly threw her hands up. "Man!" When she could look at me again, the disgust in her eyes made me turn my gaze away from her. "Bell, how can you be this naive? I haven't known you to be so weak in a long time."

"Weak?" Did she want a catfight right in the middle of the morgue?

Her expression hardened. "You're acting like you've gone stupid—the way some *weak* women do after they sleep with a man and suddenly become blind to his faults." She cocked her head to the side and stared at me. The gesture punctuated her questions: "Did you taste that forbidden fruit last night, sis? Is that why you're temporarily insane?"

She wanted a catfight, all right. I wouldn't give her the satisfaction. "I am not weak, and Jazz didn't bed me." *Thank you very much, Amos.* But that whole "weak" thing grew on me like a tumor. Okay, I *would* give her the satisfaction. I sharpened my cat claws for an attack. "Even if he *had* bedded me, it would be *my* business, just like you sleeping with your fiancé is *your* business."

Meow! Rrrrr.

She recoiled subtly enough that if I hadn't known her so well, I'd have missed it. "Will you look at yourself, Bell? You want him so badly you can't even see what's right in front of you. Jazz is the prime suspect in a woman's brutal murder. Maybe you should have slept with him. Perhaps you would have found out he's just a man like any other, and you could take off those blinders you're sporting like Prada sunglasses."

That one was the perfect blend of smart, vicious, and fashion-conscious. She's truly our mother's child. But I still had my own stash. "Why do you want to see him as good for this so badly? Are you salty with him? Maybe because he wanted me instead of you?"

A referee appeared in my head—striped shirt, black pants, whistle. "*Foul!*" he yelled, calling me out of the game.

The idea had been just a tiny speck in my consciousness the moment Jazz noticed me in my red dress—the dress Carly had purchased for me to look amazing in. Men always noticed Carly first. After that, I didn't exist. But the night I met Jazz, I felt a heady sense of power—he'd been interested in *me*.

Carly threw her head back and laughed. "Oh, sweetie, your insecurity is showing like a cheap slip."

I couldn't think of anything after my mind processed the visuals for "cheap slip." We stood there glaring at each other, the silence as palpable as a thick fog. An endless minute passed. I looked away first. "I didn't mean that," I said.

"Oh, yes, you did, sis. But that's okay. I don't have to be a psychologist to know about this *stuff* we've had between us since you were a teenager. We should have had this little talk years ago."

"That wasn't a talk. It was a fight."

"Bell—"

I gave her the "stop" gesture with my hand. Carly and I were very close, but in a few notable ways, there was too much silence between us. I didn't want to discuss this. I never wanted to discuss this. So I opted to do what I did best. I avoided it. "I'm in way over my head, Carly. I need to find out what happened to Kate."

She knew my avoidance techniques and showed mercy by not pressing me any further about the matter of our "stuff." "I'm trying to help you, snookums. Step back and let the evidence speak. What if you're wrong about him? Do you think I want to see you here on a slab? I don't feel *any* allegiance to Jazz Brown, no matter how fine he is."

"But what if the evidence *is* speaking, Carly? What if it's saying it could be someone else? There's more to evidence than fingerprints and DNA."

She sighed. "I can't get through to you." She shook her head. "Maybe you should go."

For a moment I thought I should. Last night had proved to me that I was way too close to Jazz to be objective. But what I had seen at the crime scene gnawed at me. I couldn't give up so easily. "Can I see her?"

"You saw her at the crime scene."

"So what would it hurt for me to take another peek?"

Carly put a hand on her hip. Those purple gloves looked so good with the fuchsia scrubs. "What would it hurt? Try, first of all, my professional integrity. I did enough damage bringing you to the scene. Maguire is still questioning me about you. Second, Maguire could be in the building, and I don't want him to see you. This is *his* investigation, not yours. You shouldn't be poking around here asking for trouble. And third, you get all goofy in the presence of the dead."

"If Maguire has already been here and knows you haven't started the autopsy yet, he probably won't be back too soon. And I promise I'll be composed. Look, I'm fine." I nodded as vigorously as a bobblehead doll. "I even kept my cool when you had an eye, with those tubular thingies hanging off of it, right in your hand!" I shuddered to think of The Eye.

She pointed a gloved finger at me. "See? You're loopy already, just thinking about an eyeball. How am I supposed to show you the woman your man killed?"

"He's not my man." Not completely. "And maybe he didn't kill her. Please? One look, Carly, and I promise I'll never ask you to do anything like this again."

"I'm not buying in to your fulfilling some Columbo fantasy, Bell."

"I'm not sleuthing. Really." I was going to burn in hell for the lies I kept telling myself. And Jazz. And now Carly. *Lord, have mercy on my soul.*

But Carly knew me well. "I don't believe you."

"I just want to see what you see. Let me have a peek." Okay, seeing what Carly saw was way secondary to seeing what *I* wanted to see. More hot coals on the fire for me. *God help me.*

She crossed the room again and came back over to me. She pursed her lips and looked away. Finally, she sighed and returned her gaze to me. "One look, missy. And don't you ask me for another thing after that."

I got up from the metal chair and hugged her. "I don't know how to thank you."

She squeezed me back, avoiding touching me with her gloves, which she peeled off after she released me. "Thank me by seeing that he could be guilty." She tossed the gloves into a nearby trash can.

Before she led me out of the autopsy room and over to where Kate lay in repose, I grabbed her arm. "I'm sorry about what I said about you and Tim."

"You don't have to be sorry. I do sleep with my fiancé."

"My attitude smacked of self-righteousness. I have no right to judge you, especially as raggedy as I am. And just to set the record straight, Jazz and I got a little hot and heavy. It could easily have happened last night."

Carly's wise eyes looked into mine. "Last night?"

I nodded.

"All those times you were with him before and you raved about what a gentleman he was—you mean to tell me the two of you never *almost* let it happen until *last night*, after his wife was murdered in his loft? Don't you find that a bit odd? Not to mention convenient for him?"

I did, and the knowledge of it was killing me on the inside. "I don't want to go a few more rounds, Carly. Can we just drop this for now?"

She paused. "Whatever." Another heavy sigh. "Look. I'm sorry to be so witchy, but I'm worried to death about you, not to mention you kinda hurt my feelings."

Not a typical Carly admission. I had indeed fouled out. "I'm really sorry. I didn't mean to hurt you."

She crossed her arms and sighed, her stance telling its own story. She looked me squarely in the eyes again. "I know you think I'm the carefree little sex kitten, but I talk to God about more than you realize."

"I know you talk to God, Carly. Say a few words to Him about me today, will you?"

"I do every day, bunny, but I will especially today."

chapter
six

CARLY LED ME THROUGH another set of double doors and down a long corridor to a reception area. It actually seemed like a nice space, with the homiest-looking institutional furniture available. The jail had a similar ensemble. We went into a space beyond the reception area—plain beige walls, nondescript seating area, no personality.

A video monitor set up near the ceiling made it possible to identify a body by viewing an image on the screen. This particular innovation meant one didn't actually have to go into the freezer and get up close and personal with the dead. Carly must have thought she'd caught a break with this technology. She'd already reminded me of how I behaved in the presence of the departed. She motioned with her head to the monitor. "Stand here and watch the screen. I'll go inside, set things up for you, and you can take a peek from here."

"Can't I go inside? I'll be good." I smiled at her, giving her my most hopeful and innocent cherubic face.

Her shoulders sagged. "Tell me you'll be content to see her this way."

"You said you haven't done the autopsy yet, right?"

That question elicited an exaggerated eye roll. "I need some coffee."

"Let me go in the freezer with you. I promise when we're done, I'll buy you some Starbucks. Venti. And an almond biscotti. I will personally deliver it to you. STAT."

Carly, clearly unmoved by coffee bribes, put a hand on her hip. "You can't handle stuff like that."

"What? I go to Starbucks almost every day."

"I mean dealing with the deceased."

"Carly, look at me. I'm good to go."

She gave me that blistering frown she and our mother torment me with when I insist on wearing my hair "natural." "And you're wanting to do this why?" She knew why but had to ask, just like Ma would.

"Her body is as much of a crime scene as the loft was. I just want to see if there's anything I may have missed."

"You think we missed something?"

"No. I'm just saying . . ."

Make it about her.

"You were the one who invited me to the scene." If I thought this would garner any guilt, I was sadly mistaken.

"I asked you there so you'd ditch murder boy."

"Please, Car?"

"I don't like this. *I* shouldn't even be on this case. The only reason I am is because the chief is in Barbados, and he insisted that I do it because of the police connection."

"A quick look. That's all I want, and I promise I'm outta here after that."

She didn't have to worry. I wasn't known for tarrying at the morgue.

She punched in an electronic security code, and one hydraulic door sighed open. I followed her in, noting any physiological changes in myself that could swiftly render me in a horizontal position. All clear, rubber legs notwithstanding, I took in the cold—literally—room. It didn't strike me as being quite as scary as the autopsy room, with those metal tables and things that gave me posttraumatic stress syndrome just to think about—things like those horrible scales that you know weigh all kinds of disengaged organs.

Mind you, even though this area didn't spook me as badly as the autopsy room, nothing about it invited me to come and sit for a spell. The room was impersonal and clinical, with too much steel and horrid fluorescent lights. Metal drawers housing the dearly departed lined one long wall.

I tried not to think about what those drawers held. In my mind, some kind soul had chocked them full of designer shoes and handbags. Lots and lots of Manolo Blahniks and Hermès Birkin bags.

My little mind game didn't work. Goose bumps beaded my arms as the truth of my woeful environment invaded my conscious mind. I tried to hold fast to the false image just the same, to keep what fledgling bit of composure I could manage. I also hoped my efforts would keep Carly from throwing me out.

Carly headed over to the drawers and placed her hand on the handle of one. "Ready?"

"Yes."

I must not have convinced her.

"Ready?" she repeated.

"Yes."

She crooked a perfectly arched eyebrow at me. "Bell, are you *ready?*"

"Carly, are you going to keep asking me that? Like Jesus asked Peter, 'Do you love me?'"

In those ten seconds, she'd undermined my already nonexistent confidence, but she moved to yank the drawer open anyway, ready or not.

"*Wait,*" I shrieked.

Carly rolled her eyes again and sighed so hard I wondered if she was doing a yogic cleansing breath. "What now, Bell?"

"Uh—what have you done to her so far?"

She paused, her hand still resting on the handle of the drawer. "Do you know how we process bodies once we get them here?"

I shook my head.

She removed her hand from the handle and placed it back on her hip. "The first thing we did after we got a positive ID was take a bunch of pictures of her with the shirt on. After that, Souldier came in and got trace evidence. That's standard procedure."

I nodded again, just to let her know I was still with her.

"The next thing we did was get her clothes off. Take more pictures, gather more trace evidence, and when we get clearance from the police, we can wash her body and start the autopsy. The worst you'll see is what you saw at the crime scene, minus her clothes."

"I can handle that."

"There's one more thing."

"Yeah?"

"This is a sisterly warning, not a medical-examiner one."

"Okay, what?"

"That woman has perfect breasts."

Oh no. *Perfect?* Carly was not one to throw the word "perfect" around lightly. "Thanks for the warning. Open the drawer."

Carly slid the drawer open with a flourish to reveal the completely naked *goddess.* "Katherine Anne Townsend, the former Mrs. Jazz Brown."

"Oh no!"

Carly touched my arm. "You okay?"

"They *are* perfect! *She's* perfect. Dear Lord! I will never feel good about myself again. *Ever.*"

Carly laughed. "Of course you will. Just get an enhancement, like I did."

My eyes widened in horror. "You got *enhanced?*"

She looked around as if someone could hear us and would be scandalized. "Remember when I took six weeks off last year?" She pushed up her own perfect pair. "I got these babies."

And here I'd thought a good underwire bra was her secret.

She continued to hold her ample bosom. "I'm going to be the *finest* thing in the nursing home with these. In fact, when I'm dead and gone, they'll still be looking good." She released herself with a satisfied grin.

And speaking of dead and gone . . .

I gratefully turned my attention back to Kate Townsend, avoiding the area below her battered neck. Thoughts about my small, saggy disappointments dissipated as I took in Kate's horribly flushed face.

Her body is a crime scene. What do you see?

"You didn't find any prints on her, correct?"

"Correct," Carly said. I could hear the disappointment in her voice. She badly wanted some solid evidence.

"How 'bout trace?"

"We found fibers: a single brown hair that looks like Jazz's. Not much else that's not excruciatingly ordinary."

"Has your lab done a comparison with the hair?"

"Not yet, we'll get to it."

I tried to peer past Kate's impeccable double D's. "Is there anything unusual on her body?"

"You mean besides her broken neck?"

"Yes, Carly."

"She's got old scars all over her arms and thighs."

"What kind of scars?"

"Take a look. That's your area of expertise. Not mine."

Carly pulled out the drawer some more, revealing the tops of Kate's forearms. Rows of neat scars crisscrossed down both her arms and stopped midway between her inner elbow and wrist. They could easily be taken for cat or bramble scratches. Too perfect, though. A skilled wielder of a knife or a razor blade made these scars—scars she could hide with a long-sleeved shirt. My heart sank. Poor Kate.

I remembered that Jazz had said he'd grabbed her. I saw no evidence on her arms or shoulders that he had. He must not have grabbed her too hard, even if he had pushed her. Why had she fallen so easily? *She had on heels. She was still dressed when he pushed her.*

I didn't ask to see her thighs. I was sure I'd be traumatized. Not by the scars but by what I imagined were her perfect model's thighs. She hadn't been uncovered far enough for me to see them at the scene. Not that I wanted to then, either. "How old would you say the scars are?"

"Some aren't too old. Maybe a month."

"Anything else notable?"

"Her wrists. Looks like she botched a suicide attempt once upon a time."

I examined her wrists, careful not to touch her with my ungloved hand. Jagged, unsure white lines scarred the skin above her hands. It's harder than people realize to actually kill yourself by slitting your wrists. You have to go deep enough to get an artery, and arteries don't want to go easy. They'll try to spasm shut. It's possible to kill yourself that way, but it'll take a few hours to bleed to death. You'd have to be pretty committed. Apparently, Kate was not.

"Anything else?" I asked.

"No."

I gave Carly a just-between-us-sisters look. "Nothing?"

Carly abruptly shut the drawer. "She hadn't had sex, nor was she sexually assaulted, if that's what you mean, but Jazz still isn't looking like a choirboy to me."

"You've made that clear." I had made it through that ordeal. I felt exhausted and a little sick to my stomach. "I'd better go get your Starbucks."

"Don't bother, kitten. You must have taken off work. Just go somewhere and chill. Think things through."

She kissed me on the cheek, and I pulled her into a hug. "We'll get through this, right, Carly? I mean, we'll be all right. You and me?"

"You're my sister. Nothing is going to change that."

I gave her a squeeze and released her.

"Now, go," she said, "before Maguire sees you here."

"He's going to catch up with me eventually. The question is where."

"Let him do his job, Bell."

"I will."

That didn't mean I wouldn't do mine. If I could just figure out exactly what that was. But it had to be something; I was in this for a reason.

chapter
seven

GOT BACK HOME just before noon, and all I wanted were my
fuzzy pajamas—the awful, amazingly comfortable ones with
the permanent stains and the missing button, held closed by a
safety pin. Carly had made me throw them away.

With almost psychic ability, she and our mother can discern
when I have bad lingerie. I had secretly stashed away a pair of
peach flannel ones, with an appalling floral design, that I paid
seven dollars for at Kmart. I'd spilled grape soda on them during
one of my self-pity sessions that included a couple of two-liter
Faygos and bounteous pretzels. The grape soda left a stain, curiously shaped like a butterfly. It was a sign, I'm sure, something to
do with the cocoon of despair giving way to . . . Okay, maybe it
wasn't a sign, but I loved those fuzzy jammies anyway, almost as
much as I loved the blue ones I still mourned.

The sight of my "peaches" warmed me. They could probably
knock my sister unconscious in an instant, as if they possessed
some strange superpower to take down the highly fashionable.
Me, in the sleepwear of justice! Death to all oppressive fashioni-
stas! *Pajama Girl!*

I'd just—carefully—fed Amos a special yogurt/raisin treat

and put on a pot of Starbuck's Holiday Blend when I heard a knock at my door. I hadn't even had time to check the messages on my answering machine. I didn't get many visitors and held out the pathetic hope that Jazz would be standing there, looking handsome and needy, begging for my help. I fluffed my crinkly hair and opened my door for my dude in distress.

I got the distress part right but had the wrong dude in mind. Rocky stood in my doorway, looking crazed from worry. He'd gotten another "unique" hairstyle. Impressive clumps of his hair, grown out about four inches now, had been backcombed and teased into some semblance of dreadlocks. He looked very Anne Lamott—whom he'd been reading voraciously—only he was younger and was a really cute guy. An army-fatigue bandana held back his wild hair. Silver rings and Milagros charms adorned several blond locks that had strayed from the confines of the bandana. Khakis, a bright green Virgin of Guadalupe T-shirt, an army coat, and moon boots completed his wacky ensemble. He completely charmed me. I smiled at him. "Hello, Napoleon Dynamite."

"Babe!" he said, frowning, oblivious to my warm reception. It didn't matter what I did or said, I couldn't make this man stop calling me babe.

"Rocky, we don't date anymore. Stop calling me babe." Of course, he'd called me LaFawnduh for weeks after we saw *Napoleon Dynamite*. I supposed I should count myself blessed to be "babe" again.

"Where have you been? I saw Jazz on the news this morning. They suspect he murdered his wife."

"Ex-wife," I said. "And they didn't say they suspected him.

They said she was found dead in his home and they suspected foul play. *General* foul play, not specific."

"Uh, babe? Excuse me, but that doesn't make it better for me. So you knew this already?"

"I was at the crime scene last night," I said sheepishly. "Carly wouldn't let something like that pass without immediately letting me know what's going on."

"Duh," he said, sounding very Rockyish—and a snarky Rocky at that. "She probably didn't want him to, like, kill you." He still stood at my door. The way the conversation had gone, I didn't necessarily feel compelled to ask him in, and Rocky was gentleman enough to stand there until I did.

He tapped a moon boot. "How come you didn't answer your phones this morning? *Either* of them?"

The "either of them" part served as a not so thinly veiled criticism of what my friends and family believed were my fatal phone habits. I didn't have the energy to argue once again about why I frequently failed to answer my home phone or to carry or charge my cell phone. My answers never proved satisfactory anyway. I relented and rolled out the welcome mat, so to speak.

"Come in, Rock," I said. "I've been gone all morning. I just got home. I was going to check my answering machine." I had a good old-fashioned one, complete with a cassette tape. It never cut me off, only asked me if I'd like to rerecord my message.

Rocky shuffled inside my apartment, scowling at me. "You didn't call me as soon as you found out what happened? Every day you inch me out more and more. And I'm not the only one."

"What? Is there a small-group meeting about my social life?"

"No," he said. "It's a *large* group." He smiled to soften the blow. Before a sassy retort could form in my brain, he spotted Amos. My instincts kicked in andI thought I'd have to rescue him, but that man's eyes lit up, and he grinned like a five-year-old with a new puppy.

I stared at him. "You know what that thing . . ."

I didn't have to ask. Rocky nearly bounced over to the cage and started clucking at Amos. What's worse, Amos clucked back. The saleslady hadn't said anything about clucking. The scene unfolding between Rocky and my "baby" stunned me so profoundly, I forgot to shut the door to my apartment. I trailed behind Rocky. "Be careful. That thing is dangerous."

But Rocky already had his hand in the cage. Amos went right into his palm. No shrieking, biting, or attempted murder. Rocky laughed. "You've got a *sugar glider,* babe?" My very cool-looking, tattooed, emergent-church pastor squealed with pure pleasure. Of course Rocky would know what a sugar glider was. Nobody else in my life would but Rocky. It just made sense. No doubt about it, if I were ever to relent and marry him, we'd certainly have a lot of fun together. Rocky could make anybody happy.

Okay, not me, but most people.

Suddenly, I wanted him to lacerate me with comments about my boyfriend choice. Instead, he completely ignored me in favor of the cluck/love fest. I was jealous of a pastor and a marsupial. "Could you please put him back in his cage, Rocky? I don't want him to get used to strangers."

Rocky shot me a hurt look, his puppy eyes big and watery. Amos's eyes, also staring at me, looked sad, too. "Babe, I'm not a stranger."

Shoot.

The genuine pain I heard in his voice made it clear I'd get whatever holy tongue lashing he had in mind, just for being jealous and insecure, not to mention a lousy friend.

Rocky placed Amos back in his cage, and Rocky's puppy peepers, so reminiscent of Amos's, fixed on me. "Just because you treat me and everybody in your life like we're strangers doesn't mean we are. I happen to be your friend—your good friend—and I love you. I'd be more than a friend if you'd let me."

"Rocky, please don't. Not the blond boy-toy bit."

He replied with his standard "But we'd be holy and stuff."

My Rocky. He wasn't a stranger, but how was I supposed to admit how much I hated that my sugar glider liked him better than me? Not to mention the discussion about my being a hermit, which I'd promised I'd change. His impromptu proposition didn't help matters, either. I was ready to offer him yet another lame apology when my spidey senses kicked in and my gaze went to the door.

Detective Bobby Maguire filled my open door frame, looking rough and ready—that was my great-grandmother Ma Brown's way of saying he looked like he'd slept in his clothes.

"Well, well, well," he quipped, "if it ain't girl Columbo in pajamas. And she has company. Am I interrupting you? I see you got on your workin' clothes." He leered at me, no doubt putting me and Rocky in a compromising position in his greasy little head.

"Welcome, Maguire," I said. "My company was just leaving."

Rocky looked at me. "I was?" No way I'd let him hear Maguire drill me. I didn't care how compelling his eyes were.

"You sure are," I said. With that, I hustled Rocky right out the door and allowed Maguire inside.

His overcoat, an olive green disaster, looked worse than Columbo's, and underneath, he wore my favorite television personality's awful brown suit. An equally atrocious leather-look briefcase hung on his shoulder. I wondered if he compensated for his lack of fashion sense by doing stellar police work. Honestly, he was the antithesis of Jazz. Nothing stylish or fine about him.

He looked at me as if I annoyed him just by being at home. That didn't stop me from being a gracious hostess. "Would you like to have a seat, Detective?"

"I certainly would, Dr. Amanda."

I pointed to the sofa. "Make yourself at home. I'll be back in just a minute."

I grabbed my bathrobe from my bedroom, put it on, and tied the belt, thinking that one day I should stop entertaining in sleepwear. Maguire hadn't moved from where he stood.

"Don't be shy." I swept my arm out like a game-show hostess. "Welcome to my humble abode."

He glanced around, no doubt sizing up my personality based on my décor. Fortunately, I'd gotten rid of ridiculous items, such as the three-foot-long decorative bean pod I'd once wielded as a weapon when I thought Jazz was an intruder. I hoped Maguire liked my Rachel Ashwell's shabby-chic-with-an-African-flair hookup.

"Nice place."

The good cop instead of the Good Housekeeping Seal. At least, I hoped he was a good cop.

"May I take your coat?" I said. *To the Dumpster.*

"Thank you." He had good manners—when he wanted to use them. He slid out of his coat and handed it to me.

"Have a seat." I smiled at him.

Seal or no, he eased himself onto my couch slowly, as if it were a bed of nails instead of a cute velvet classic. His suit didn't look particularly clean, and it smelled of stale cigarettes and booze. I sat in a chair across from him. He set the pleather briefcase on his lap.

I paused to analyze him. I didn't need a psychology degree to see that Maguire regarded me as if I'd talked too much in his class and he had come to rap my knuckles with a ruler.

"Imagine my surprise at seeing *you* here, Dr. Amanda, when my assignment was to interview the last person my prime suspect was with last night. What an amazing coincidence."

I expected that kind of sarcasm from Maguire. I gave him another smile and no bait to reel me in with.

"Exactly what is your relationship to Jazz Brown?"

I could tell Maguire wanted to assimilate my brain like the Borg on *Star Trek*. In an open homicide investigation, resistance would be futile. I'd have to play it smart, though. "Jazz and I are colleagues. We worked together on a case a few months ago."

He crooked an eyebrow. "What case was that?"

"The Jonathan Vogel and Damon Crawford murders."

He nodded slowly again. I could see the pistons in his brain firing. "I worked on that case. So, how come I never saw you at the station or nothin'?"

"*Detective* Maguire, I didn't realize *Lieutenant* Brown needed to report every detail of his investigation to you."

He nodded, no doubt planning how to throttle me. "You're not gonna be a nice gal, are ya?"

I gave him my wide-eyed innocent look. "Who me? I'm a lamb. I'd be happy to help you with your investigation. Pro bono."

And speaking of reporting details of an investigation, I heard a knock at my door. Great. Another slumber party. I silently prayed it wasn't Jazz. The news hadn't reported that he'd been captured yet.

"Excuse me," I said, beaming a fake smile at Maguire. "Who could this be, *Detective Maguire?*" I yelled the last part just in case it was Jazz.

It wasn't Jazz, but the man was nearly as breathtaking. I stood there, confused, trying to figure out who the good-looking, mysterious white guy with the dark hair and darker eyes was. He wore a very nice gray pin-striped suit—Armani, I was sure of it—beneath a black camel-hair coat. His distressed leather gloves looked both hip and expensive. Good-looking stood about six feet tall, 190 pounds or so. He looked a little older than me, with a hint of gray at his temples. He had an air of new money about him, an utterly tasteless tie hanging on his neck, the one bit of excess in an otherwise flawless and restrained presentation. My mother would have liked him, but she'd have grilled him about the tie.

No, she'd have grilled *me* about it.

The tundra had more warmth than his stare. He may have been at my door, but he looked annoyed to find me home. I got an initial "uh" out of my mouth, but I refused to let his displeasure at finding me home stop me from getting down to business. "May I help you?"

His eyes seemed to thaw, albeit slowly. "Amanda Brown?"

Not *Dr.* Amanda Brown, which almost everyone in a professional capacity called me. I wondered if he was playing at pulling rank somehow. He thrust out his hand for me to shake. "I'm Officer Archi—"

Maguire yelled from the sofa, "That's just Archie. He's IAD."

Archie nearly broke several of my hand bones while shooting lasers from his eyes at Detective Maguire.

Archie had been dispatched from the Internal Affairs Department—a cop's cop. His icy demeanor indicated the bad cop had arrived. I suddenly felt naked in my pajamas and bathrobe.

I asked him in, told him to have a seat, and excused myself. A guy like Archie demanded real clothing. I dressed, made a pot of Earl Grey tea—not using my remaining Addie Lee mug—and sat down with the men. Maguire claimed the sofa, while Archie and I sat in chairs. We formed a weird triangle.

Maguire started. "You mentioned you worked on the Vogel-Crawford case pro bono. Are you sure Brown didn't offer a little sumthin'-sumthin' to take care of you?"

The big rat. Now *he* was bad cop.

"The definition of pro bono, Detective, is that I worked for no pay. *None.* Not that I think you should concern yourself with my compensation. You may want to keep in mind, however, that the perpetrator in that case was *apprehended.* I'm hoping you'll actually do such exemplary work on *this* case."

Maguire glared at me, then gave me a fake smile remarkably reminiscent of the ones I'd showered him with. "I don't think you should concern yourself with my work, Dr. Amanda—"

"I don't suppose you have an alibi for Lieutenant Brown?"

Archie interrupted, boring those cool brown eyes into mine. I tried to study his body language. His stolid bearing gave few cues to the inner man, his facial expressions as unmovable as Sean Connery as 007.

"He came here at approximately nine-thirty last night."

"Are you sure?" He cocked his head slightly in a gesture he probably thought begged my trust. Good cop.

"I'm reasonably sure. I'd been at the pet store until they closed at nine. It's five minutes from my house. I came in, showered, and got ready for bed, and Jazz arrived right after that."

Maguire didn't hesitate. "He came to tuck you into bed?"

I ignored his implication.

Archie dismissed Maguire's rudeness with a wave of his hand. "Carly, *your sister*," Archie said, to let me know he was on to me, "estimated that Ms. Townsend was killed around nine P.M."

"Perhaps I do have an alibi for him, then. It would have taken him a minimum of forty-five minutes to get here, *if* he was blazing down the freeway."

Archie slowly nodded.

Maguire quipped, "Maybe he came right after he killed her."

I turned to Maguire. "What time did you get the call from her?"

He ignored me.

Archie filled the silence with "How well do you know Jazz, Dr. Brown?"

Oh, I'm "Doctor" now?

"I know him well enough to doubt that he did it, Archie." I gave him my most open posture and sincere look. "I mean that."

He regarded me closely. I wished I knew what he was thinking. "Is Jazz your boyfriend?" he asked.

"I wouldn't say that."

Maguire's yank on the stalled zipper of his ancient briefcase managed to steal my attention away from Archie. When he finally got the thing open, he pulled out a picture frame wrapped in an unmarked plastic evidence bag. He handed the diptych—two frames connected—to me.

I took it, and my heart cartwheeled. I addressed both men: "It's me." In my red silk halter dress—the dress I'd worn only once, on the night I met Jazz. I wasn't smiling. The second one was of Jazz holding me. Very closely. Someone had taped a clear label at the bottom of the frame that held the picture of Jazz and me: "Mr. and Mrs. Brown." I'd never seen the photo before. "Was this in his house?"

"It was in his desk at the station."

I handed the picture back to Maguire. He tucked it back in the briefcase and fought the zipper closed again.

"Those pictures had to have been taken at the Vogel crime scene. He was just praying with me."

"Interesting way to pray," Archie said with a smirk. He added, "Were you with *your sister* that night, too?"

"Yes. She had no intention of taking me to a crime scene. It was my birthday, and we were celebrating. She'd hoped she wouldn't get a call while we were out."

Maguire's gruff voice clashed with Archie's velvet one. "Brown don't usually have all kindsa people hangin' around his scene. How did you get inside?"

"I had on a really cute dress."

Archie said, unsmiling, "I'd say that's a very sexy dress you had on."

I hadn't said "sexy."

Archie went on, "Seriously, how'd you get in?"

"Is this an interrogation?"

Archie gave me a crooked grin. "It's nothing like that, Dr. Brown. I'm just asking a few routine questions."

"I really am a forensic psychologist. I got inside the scene of the crime because Jazz invited me to take a look."

"Are you a profiler?"

"It would be unethical if I said profiling is an area of expertise for me, but I do work with criminals every day." I added, like an idiot, just because he was cute, "And I watch *Body of Evidence: From the Case Files of Dayle Hinman* on television all the time. She's a profiler. That's gotta count—like extra credit or something." My face burned as soon as that came out of my mouth. Honestly, I'm a train wreck when I talk to good-looking men—at least at first.

Both he and Maguire looked unimpressed.

Maguire leaned toward me. "Let's be straight with each other, Dr. Amanda, huh? Both of us want something. You want your boyfriend cleared. I want my killer apprehended."

"He's not my boyfriend, Maguire."

"Maybe we can help each other."

Detective Bozo didn't seem to get that I worked with cops every day, and I knew the good-cop routine when I saw it. "I'd really like for us to help *Jazz*, Detective Maguire."

He put the horrible briefcase on the floor. Leaned toward my chair. "Are you his lover?"

"Absolutely not," I answered too quickly.

My response must have piqued Archie's attention. "Do you want to be?" he asked.

"I don't see how any answer to that question could be pertinent to your investigation, Officer."

"Carly is worried about you."

Score one for the IAD guy. He smiled. I planned my sister's death.

"I don't blame her, Amanda," he added.

So now I'm just Amanda again? Oh, he was smooth. But he'd underestimated me. I could play buddy-buddy, too, with both of them. Maguire first. I eased back in my chair. Stretched my spine out to lengthen my posture to my full height—minuscule though it was. "What time did Kate call the police, *Bobby*?"

"We're talking minutes, *Mandy*. It had to be minutes before she died."

"Don't call me Mandy. How many minutes?"

"She called at nine-oh-nine, Amanda."

"He'd have to take a rocket to get to my house by nine-thirty."

Archie, his demeanor as cold as marble, said, "Maybe you got your time wrong."

"Maybe you got your prime suspect wrong. What did she say when she called?"

"She said he'd beaten her. Again."

My eye twitched. Archie noticed, I was certain. A hint of a smile curved the corners of his mouth upward a tiny bit. Score another one for IAD. I tucked that painful piece of information inside.

This time Maguire studied me for a long time. He knew Archie had unnerved me. He jumped all over my vulnerable state. "How could anybody other than Jazz get to her so fast? What do you make of that, Dayle Hinman wannabe?"

"Wouldn't that be *your* job to make something of it, or are you a homicide detective wannabe?"

Maguire threw his head back and laughed with gusto. "I can see why Jazzy is in love with you. You're a card."

A wild card. He had no idea. "What makes you think Jazz is in love with me?"

"He protected you like a man in love."

"You've spoken to him?"

"He turned himself in last night." He and Archie seemed to watch for my reaction. I tried my best to give them a poker face.

"Did he confess?" I asked.

"What do you think?" Maguire asked.

"I think you need to look for more suspects. When is his arraignment?"

Maguire shrugged. "This afternoon, maybe."

"That's fast," I said. "Do you think he'll bond out?"

Archie answered, "I hope not. For your sake."

"You don't think the man Maguire said protected me would harm me, do you, Archie?"

"Maguire said he protected you. I didn't. If you ask me, he protected himself."

As much as I wanted to know the specifics, I didn't ask. I shot Maguire a look. "What did you mean when you said he protected me?"

Again Maguire leered at me. "I meant just what I said, Mandy. I know you were with him last night, but that information didn't come from him."

Carly!

"It would have been in his best interest to use you as an alibi. He refused to mention you. Sounds like love to me, Mandy."

"It doesn't sound like that to Archie. And don't call me Mandy, Maguire."

Archie fired another question at me: "What did Jazz say when he got here?"

Another change in direction. These two were trying to work me like the Minnesota Multiphasic Personality Inventory, a personality evaluation tool we used at the jail. Were they kidding? I administered the test three times a week. They'd have to work a little harder to break me down.

"Jazz said, 'Hold still.'"

"'Hold still'?"

"A vicious animal was attacking me."

"Is that where you got those scratches on your hands?"

"Yes. And speaking of scratches, Jazz didn't have any on *his* hands. He would have if he'd choked her to death."

"I found the scratches on your boyfriend's face interesting."

"He's not my boyfriend."

"Did he act unusual?"

"How long do you think those candles were burning, Archie?"

He look flustered. "What?"

"The candles? On that fabulous bed. See, I'm a woman. A woman you insist is into Jazz, and I don't mean the music. One of the first things I noticed when I walked into that place, which I'd never been inside before, was the bed. Those candles. They weren't burned down very far. Like they hadn't been lit long. Don't you think that's odd?" I leaned forward in my chair toward Archie. "Kate was alive when Jazz left his loft. I'll bet she lit those candles when Jazz left. If she called you at nine after, she was breathing when he was on the road. I'm his alibi. Jeff Gordon couldn't get here that fast."

Archie pulled his cool back together just that fast. "Did he seem agitated?"

Still leaning forward in my chair, I gave him my most earnest expression—the one I used when I was trying to get my mother to give me something from her boutique at the wholesale price. "She was strangled. Hand-strangled. That's a very personal way to kill someone. The murderer had to get his hands dirty, so to speak, and most likely scratched."

Archie pelted me with questions: "Did he seem contrite? Irritated? Strange in any way?"

"If you and Maguire think he's my boyfriend, why would he need to put her in his bed, especially if he suspected she'd called the police and they were on the way? How did they get in the house without a warrant, anyway? No way you could have gotten a warrant for a mere domestic-dispute call, even if the alleged perp was a cop."

Archie's Adam's apple bobbed. Ha! I'd unnerved him. Or he was thirsty. Man, he was hard to read.

Maguire answered this time. "The door was open when our uniforms got there."

On Mr. Lock All Three Locks's loft? "Open as in unlocked, or open as in wide open?"

He sighed, running a hand through his greasy, thinning hair. "Wide open."

I shook my head. "C'mon, Maguire! You can't tell me you believe a seasoned homicide detective—a lieutenant in the city of Detroit—would leave his door wide open, with a dead woman in his bed, visible from said door."

"People do funny things when they're hyped up."

"That's not funny, Detective. That's insane."

"So is brutally murdering a woman," Archie said.

"You're right. Which leads me back to my first point. Maybe Jazz didn't do it. If my timing is correct, he wasn't even home to do it."

Maguire yawned. Stretched. Burped. He finally got around to asking, "Did you look at the clock even once the whole time he was with you?"

"No, but—"

"You could have been off on the time."

True. I had been stressed. I easily could have taken a longer shower than I'd realized, but I didn't think so. "I'd bet, on everything I've ever known about people, that he wouldn't have put her in his bed like that."

Maguire raised those question-mark eyebrows. "Because that's where you belong?"

"You're the one who said you think he loves me."

"And you're the one who said he ain't sleeping with you. Men do things. Things they don't want their pretty, churchgoing girlfriends to know about."

"Maybe they do, but there are things he wouldn't have done."

Archie stood. Our time was up. "I wouldn't call that irrefutable evidence, Amanda."

I stood, too. As sincerely as I could, I said to Archie, "I'm not going to deny what you already know. Jazz and I care about each other, but we didn't work out." I needed an ally. I hadn't impressed these two, and frankly, either of them would do. I went for Archie first. "You're a cop's cop. You know how hard it is to have a good, stable relationship with a cop."

And then Maguire. "This isn't about me at all, Maguire. I'll tell you why I'm not convinced Jazz is the man for this. He didn't love or hate her enough to invest that much in her. He wouldn't have thrown his life away for Kate. He didn't have the passion to commit this crime of passion."

Maguire gathered his awful briefcase into his arms and stood with us. "You're gonna hear from the lawyers soon."

Great. Lawyers, too. "From the DA's office?"

"You'll probably hear from both defense and prosecution." He glanced at Archie. "Internal Affairs is gonna want another crack at ya, too."

Archie gave him an annoyed look; I guessed he didn't like Maguire speaking for him. He stepped closer to me. "I *will* be in contact." He'd turned into bad cop again. *He must be good in an interrogation room.*

Bobby Maguire, however, looked back at me with absolute honesty in his blue eyes. "I've seen people do worse than your boyfriend did—for less." He fumbled with his briefcase and finally thrust out his hand for me to shake, which I did. "Step away from this, girl Columbo," he said with a frown. "This ain't television."

"I'll keep that in mind, Bobby."

He nodded. "Please do, Amanda."

chapter
eight

I TOLD MYSELF TO BE a good girl and stay out of this, like Maguire had said. He was right. Carly was right. If I'd taken the time to consult Miss Mary Mack's doctor, nurse, and lady with the alligator purse, I'm sure they'd have said the same thing. And they'd have been right. I had to face the facts. I was in love with Jazz Brown, and I couldn't look at this case with any objectivity.

But three hours after Maguire and Archie had left, I sat in the Love Bug, parked two houses down from the Palmer Park home of my pretend in-laws. I watched the paparazzi hovering around Jack and Addie's home like buzzards. I deliberated whether I should go inside the artsy Tudor—a place I loved even more than my mentor Dr. Mason May's office. I wanted to go inside. I wanted to see Dad Jack and Mom Addie. But I didn't want drama from the press any more than they did.

I can't go in. I should go back home, gorge myself on abundant quantities of chocolate, and go to sleep—for about three weeks.

I probably would have sat there ruminating for the next two days, but Jazz came outside, sealing my fate. Frankly, upon seeing him, I was inclined to not only go to him but to marry him, move in, and give him many sons.

The press attacked him with questions before he even reached the sidewalk. I could hear the shouting from my car.

Where on earth is he going, knowing they're out here?

He had to be having a really bad day, but the jeans that fit oh so right, and the caramel-colored turtleneck sweater—cashmere?—made me want to open my arms and say, "Come to Mama!"

And speaking of "Come to Mama," he was walking toward the Love Bug. The press trailed behind him like rats following the Pied Piper. All I could think was: *My mother is going to kill me if she sees me on television looking like this.* I'd put on a black knit itty-bitty T-shirt complete with a tiny front pocket. This sexy little number came from Carly. I wore it with a pair of hip-loving jeans stuffed into black suede cowboy boots I never wore because they made me feel wild and carefree, and most days I couldn't handle that kind of freedom. A new black Stetson, with untamed black-and-white feathers across the brim, topped off the ensemble. I also wore my big silver hoops that shouted "diva." Over everything, I wore a slimming leather jacket with a hint of western flava—to go with the hat and to finish out the look. Since I'd arrived in that get-up, you would have thought I'd have known Jazz would be there.

A flash of insight upset my precarious internal balance. I hadn't gotten all tarted up hoping he'd be around, had I?

I hated looking within. I avoided it as much as possible, because most of the time, I saw something unsavory that destroyed my wholesome self-image.

Jazz reached the Love Bug, and I rolled down the window to fuss at him. "You should have a coat on. You'll catch your death of pneumonia."

He looked at me incredulously. "Get out of the car, don't say anything, and come with me."

I didn't have the heart to give him a hard time.

The throng before me reminded me of being in downtown Manhattan at lunchtime. People were everywhere, sucking me in to them. Jazz pulled me through the crowd, fielding the intrusive questions with his cold, hard gaze, but they kept pounding him. "Lieutenant Brown, who is she? Is she your girlfriend?"

He finally maneuvered me into the house, locked the door, and gave me the same glare I'd gotten from Archie earlier. I shuddered. I'd had enough evil-eyed cops for one day. "Don't look at me like that."

"What are you doing here, Bell?"

I wagged my finger at him. "You know, I won't recommend they keep you on the welcome committee."

His eyes began to warm. "I'd probably welcome you *very* warmly if I'd asked you to come. I seem to remember telling you we shouldn't see each other right now."

"Oh, it's okay for you to stop by unannounced after I told you to stay away, but I come here and it's—"

"I can't believe you're bringing that up now."

"You hate it when I'm right, don't you? Where's your coat?"

"In my loft, with everything else I own."

He helped me out of my coat. Always a gentleman. Well, most of the time. His eyes scanned my body as closely as an MRI, and he plainly liked what he saw.

I liked that he liked it.

After he hung my leather jacket in the closet, his hand moved predictably to the small of my back, and the sparks preceding the fireworks started. I turned, and our eyes locked. A blush crept across his cheeks.

"You feel it, too, don't you, Jazz?"

"Shut up. What are you trying to do to me, anyway? Coming here looking all fine." He shook his head. "Let's go into the living room."

I smiled.

"You're going to drive me crazy, woman."

"That's okay. I'm a psychologist. I can help you with that."

In the living room, Jack and Addie swept me into hugs. Jack clapped my back. "Hey, baby. Thanks for coming."

He made me feel needed in their time of crisis. "Of course I'd be here, Dad," I said, shooting Jazz a smug look.

"I hope you're praying," Addie said.

"I sure am, Mom."

As usual, they looked fabulous. Like his gorgeous son, Jack had on a pair of jeans. Honestly. I seldom saw old-timers with Jack's easy grace. Today he wore expensive Girbaud jeans with a circa-1980s multicolored sweater, which made him look like a white Bill Cosby as Heathcliff Huxtable. His Claire Huxtable had on one of the caftans she lounged around the house in, this one winter white with a meandering design stitched in gold thread. A matching head wrap covered her honey-blond Afro. The gold bling on her wrists and neck made me salivate.

My folks.

Just being in their home made my heart sigh. It was beginning to look a lot like Christmas at the Browns'. Seasonal touches mingled with the always present bohemian beauty. Angels and Santa Clauses—both black and white—stood a foot high on the hand-painted ceramic floor. The Mexican-inspired colored walls, and the African and Southern folk art that graced them, had been accented with boughs of holly and endless lengths of evergreen. Addie's paintings, bold and evocative, had been scattered throughout. A humongous rubber tree, with branches stretched out like an invitation for a hug, stood looking stately in one of Addie's ceramic pots on the floor. Those rubber-tree arms inspired me.

I reached out to hug Mr. Unavailable, despite his resistance. I circled his waist and snuggled against him. He melted in my arms and whispered in my ear, "Wicked little minx. You know I can't resist you."

I whispered back, "Maybe it's not you who can't resist someone."

Jack interrupted our little lovefest. "I'm glad you're here, Bell. We can put our heads together and try to talk this thing through."

I got excited. Jazz had told me that he, his dad, and his mom would often brainstorm about cases, the way he and I had when we'd returned to the crime scene two days after Jonathan Vogel and Damon Crawford were murdered. I had so many questions, which Jazz and his father—two veteran cops—could help me work through, even though they couldn't have had a bigger conflict of interest.

Jack led us to the kitchen table. Crab cakes were frying. Heaven help me! How I loved that kitchen. More of the brightly colored tiles graced the floor and countertops. The furniture—warm woods with simple Quaker lines—complemented the jewel-toned window and a bright, multicolored batik table covering.

Addie rubbed my back before I sat down at the table. "Want some crab cakes and corn on the cob, baby?"

"Umm-hmm."

She went over to the sink and got busy readying a plate for me, in between turning crab cakes sizzling in the cast-iron skillet.

Jazz smirked. "You think you can save some room for a cup of coffee? I'll put it in one of Mom's mugs."

"Only if that's to go," I said with a wink.

Jazz smiled. "Ma, Bell's trying to heist your pottery."

"Don't listen to Mr. Snitch, Mom," I said, laughing. "He offered up one of those mugs like a prize. I think he's trying to win favors from me."

She hooted. "Well, honey, take the mug and give 'em those favors."

"Jazz! Your mother is as naughty as your dad."

"You ain't seen naughty yet," Jazz said, winking. "These two . . ."

Jazz's mother placed a hand on her chest and assumed an expression of such haunting piety that she could have been a statue in a Catholic church. "Jazz Christopher Brown!"

Jazz *Christopher*?

She laughed. "You know I'm deeply holy. You mustn't say things that will mislead our dear sister Bell."

Jack sidled up behind her. "You're something that starts with an *H*, all right, but it ain't 'holy,' baby." He smacked her butt, and got a pot holder upside the head. She giggled, and he pulled her into a snuggle. They nuzzled each other's neck and sighed contently.

Jazz came over and pulled up a chair by me. "Sickening, aren't they?"

"I think they're sweet."

He swung an arm behind my chair and leaned in to whisper, "They give a brotha all kinds of ideas about growing old with somebody. You know what I mean?"

I nodded. "Too bad we're not seeing each other."

Jazz frowned.

"So move your arm," I said. He'd get no slack from me.

He complied, looking salty at my rebuke.

Jack sat down with us, scooting his chair close to the table so he could lean his elbows on it. "Let's get started." He looked at me. "This is old hat for us, baby. Why don't you kick us off today?"

"I wouldn't know where to begin, Dad."

"Start with your most burning question."

Did your son kill Kate? Because if he did, I'm going to have to take back that whole thing about marrying him and giving him many sons.

"Okay, Dad. My burning question is, who'd benefit from Kate's death?"

He leaned in and narrowed an eye. "Is that really your burning question, baby?"

"Uh."

"I think your question might be, is Jazz a murdering nutjob? Go ahead and ask it."

I didn't say anything.

He put his hand over mine. "Ask it, baby."

"Is Jazz a murdering nutjob?" I shrugged and tried to laugh it off.

Jack gave my hand a squeeze. "You're asking the wrong person. Why don't you ask Jazzy?"

I turned to Jazz. He kicked out his legs and crossed them. His arms followed suit. We stared at each other. Neither of us said a word.

He kept his gaze steady on me but spoke to his father. "We had this conversation."

"But she didn't ask you, did she?"

Jazz didn't respond, just kept looking at me with those delicious brown eyes. "Don't put her on the spot, Dad."

"She came here on her own. That says something."

Jazz smoothed his hands over his pants. "I don't think anything I say right now would matter."

I looked away, hoping their discussion would get me off the hook.

Addie brought a steaming plate of corn, fried okra, and crab cakes to the table. She paused before she set it in front of me. "I'm not a police officer or a psychologist, sweetie. I'm just a woman. But if the man I love was accused of something as ugly as this, no matter what I believed, I'd have to ask him."

Jazz sputtered, "Ma! Who said Bell is in love with me?" His defensive posture dissipated as he bolted upright.

She glowered at him. "Don't be stupid, boy. Of course she's in love with you." Her glare made a grown man—a big, tough cop—wither. Shoot, she made me wither, too. Ma Brown would say Addie Lee was readin' my mail.

She put the plate of food in front of me. Nothing like a heaping plate of soul food to make a girl forget her troubles. Jazz apparently knew this. But before I could pick up my fork—

"Just ask me," he yelled. "Maybe we can get on with trying to figure this thing out."

I looked at him. Still mute. Crab cakes had splintered my focus.

He got louder. "Ask me, for crying out loud."

I got a little loud myself. "Didn't I ask you at my apartment?"

"No, you didn't. Not once."

"Well, doesn't that tell you something?"

"Look, if you don't want to participate, why don't you just leave?"

"You can't put me out. This isn't your house."

Jazz looked to his parents.

"It isn't your house," Addie said calmly, pulling up a chair. "Besides, I like her."

Jack chimed in, "Me, too. Keep fighting. You're probably close to a breakthrough. I think it was your turn, Bell. Nice and loud, now."

"Gladly!" I shot lasers out of my eyes at Jazz. "As I said, *Lieutenant Brown*, the fact that I didn't ask should tell you something."

"Yeah, *Dr. Brown*. It tells me you're too scared to ask."

That was it. I jumped up from my seat. "I'm not scared of you. Maybe I just don't happen to believe you're guilty."

He stood, too, and darn it if he wasn't a whole head taller than me. "Then it shouldn't be a problem for you to ask, should it?"

I stood on the chair, stealing a peek at Addie to see if that was okay. She nodded to spur on the taller me. "Fine. I'll ask, if that will satisfy you." But I remained silent.

"Today, Bell."

"Fine! Are you a . . ." I stopped. Wasn't "Are you a murdering nutjob?" *Jack's* question?

We glared at each other, me still standing on the chair. What was *my* burning question? Certainly "How well do I know you?" was near the top. But the burning, won't-let-me-rest question that I had to know? I had to ask it in my own words. A simple question, really, yet so hard for me to ask.

Jazz spoke softly. "Come on, Bell. Ask me so we can get past this part."

Suddenly, sadness nearly toppled me over. I didn't want to put up a brave front anymore. I gazed at my hands and then at Jazz. He looked even sadder than I felt. I said, "Do I really know you? It's only been a little over three months since I laid eyes on you for the first time. And one of those months you were gone from my life."

"We can spend a lifetime getting to know each other. I gave you all I could of me in those months." He held his hands out in a helpless gesture. "I gave you all I got."

Jack came to his son's defense. "He really did, Bell. Listen, I asked Addie to marry me after we'd known each other a month. What do your instincts tell you about him?"

My attention went to the loving couple. Addie nudged him. "Let them finish, Jack."

I turned back to Jazz, climbed off the chair, and sat down. He sat, too. "Did you beat her?" I asked.

Jazz looked surprised. "You got questioned already?"

"What do you think?"

"Maguire?"

"And Archie. IAD."

Jazz slammed his hand on the table and muttered an expletive. "That's just great. Bobby *and* Archie tag-teaming you. Both of them hate me." He paused. "Did they tell you I beat her, or did they say they'd gotten calls that she said I'd beaten her? There's a difference."

Archie hadn't said Jazz had beaten Kate. He'd said that was what *she* said. The difference cheered me. "But you told me yourself she made you mad enough to want to hurt her."

"That doesn't mean I beat her—or killed her. Bell, *you* make me mad enough to want to hurt you."

"How do I know I can trust you?"

"I saw you put a gun to a man's head—a man you were mad enough to kill. How do I know I can trust *you?*"

My mind went right back to my apartment, that awful day in September when I'd confronted Gabriel, the man who'd nearly beaten me to death—the man I'd thought might have raped me while I was unconscious. I had wanted to kill him. Everything within me had screamed for me to pull the trigger. Jazz's voice had talked me away from the edge of that precipice. Would I have shot Gabriel? Even *I* didn't know. I gathered all my courage and whispered, "Did you kill Kate, Jazz?"

"It was my fault."

If I hadn't been seated, I'd have dropped to the ground as if he'd killed *me*. I wobbled like a Weeble again, quite a feat sitting in a chair. "*What?*"

He touched my knee. "What I mean is I didn't strangle her to death, but I left her alone and vulnerable. I didn't protect her. As far as I'm concerned, she's dead because of me. I killed her."

Jack marched over to his son and smacked him across the back of the head. "You big idiot. This isn't the time to play nobleman. Haven't I taught you anything about women? Bell wants you to assure her that you aren't responsible for a heinous crime. You're supposed to tell her you didn't kill Kate, and that's all. Now try that again. Starting with the question it took us four days to drag out of Bell."

The tension drained right out of me when Jack Brown gave me one of those Jazz look-alike smiles. "Sorry," Jack said. "He rolled off the couch when he was a baby. Ain't been right since. We work with him. Let him try that one more time."

I tried to suppress my laughter. I looked Jazz right in his eyes, my confidence blooming like a flowering tree. "Did you kill Kate, Jazz?"

"No. I did not. But I should have protected—"

Jack groaned. "Please tell me you didn't say all that when they interrogated you! Addie, I told you that boy ain't got good sense. Could you tell him to just say no?"

Addie gave Jazz a real head-rockin', don't-give-me-no-smack sistah-girl look. "C'mon, now, baby boy. I didn't raise no fool. Just like the Reagan administration told you when you were a teenager. Just say *no*."

He smiled for his mama. "No." He slanted his smile Bellward. "No, Bell. I did not kill Kate." His eyes searched mine, and I didn't think I'd ever seen more honest eyes in my life.

I *wanted* to believe him.

"But I should have been—"

His parents said in unison, "Shut up!"

Addie got up from her seat, went over to Jazz, and rubbed his shoulders from behind. She placed a motherly kiss on his cheek. "You didn't strangle her, and you aren't going to jail for whoever did. I know you feel like you're responsible, but you left her so she would be safe. What happened after that is not your fault. Now let me grab a plate for you, baby." He got another smooch. Why didn't my mother kiss me like that?

chapter
nine

AFTER WE'D STUFFED ourselves on crab cakes, Jack ushered us into the living room, practically forcing Jazz and me onto the love seat, while he and Addie stretched out on the sofa. Actually, it was Addie who stretched out, lazily resting her head in Jack's lap and her feet on the armrest. Jack propped his feet on the coffee table. "Okay, kiddos," he announced. "It's time to brainstorm. Here are the rules, Bell. Everybody has to give input. No theory is too crazy, and no question"—he shot me a look—"now that we've got the important stuff out of the way, is out of line."

"Got it," I said.

"And don't freak if we say something that sounds inappropriate. Cops use humor and other weird stuff to deal with the intensity of the issues in front of us."

"Health-care professionals do the same," I said. "Coroners, too. People in high-stress jobs tend to make light of things in a way outsiders could see as cruel."

"Good," Jack said. "Glad you understand."

"Where do we start?" I asked, leaning forward, eager to let

my brain begin what it loved to do: solve puzzles of the human mind.

"We start with dissecting the crime scene. Since you were the only person here who got a gander at it, you need to tell us what you saw."

We all knew I shouldn't be talking about this with them, but as far as I was concerned, all was fair in love and war, and this was both. I took a deep breath and mentally transported myself back to the scene. I wanted them to see everything just as I'd seen it. "I got there and noticed there was no sign of forced entry. In fact, Maguire told me later that Jazz's door was wide open when the police arrived."

That raised eyebrows on all the other Browns in the room.

"Right by the door, there were two puddles. One was most likely water. Next to it, one of Mom's pottery mugs—your Starry Night one, Jazz—was broken. The other puddle was urine. I think Kate was strangled right by the door."

"My mug was broken?" Jazz asked me.

"Yes."

"So you were just checkin' me out when you asked for it the second time?"

"What do you expect?" I said. I smiled, hoping that would ease the sting of my distrusting him. To judge from his somber expression, it didn't.

"Go on," Jack said.

"The way Jazz has the loft set up, I could see the bed from the doorway. All those candles were lit. Which reminds me: Jazz, how often do you light those candles?"

"That's the thing. I haven't lit them since . . . uh . . . in fact, I'd gotten new ones because the old ones reminded me of . . ."

He didn't finish his thought, thank God!

"When did you buy the new ones?" I asked.

"A week ago."

"Why?"

"I felt hopeful."

"About what?"

"Not about Kate!" was his terse reply.

Jack cleared his throat. I turned my attention to him. "What?"

"You may not want to continue that line of questioning," Jack said.

"I thought you said nothing was off limits."

Jack Brown's face transformed as he did a spot-on Jack Nicholson imitation. "You can't handle the truth."

Addie chimed in with a chuckle. "Baby, why don't you go back to the crime scene and away from that bed. Take it from us, Jazz's hopes are not something you want to talk about at this moment. There will be plenty of time for that when this mess is cleared up. We promise you."

"But the candles. I had a thought about—"

"Forget the candles," Jazz said.

"Fine. Kate was in the bed with the candles I can't mention, leaning against the wrought-iron headboard. She'd been covered with a sheet. Her clothes were in a neat pile by the bed. She had on a tailored white man's shirt—the kind that Jazz wears when he's not wearing sexy cashmere turtlenecks with his jeans."

I winked at him. He tried unsuccessfully to suppress a smile. I'd made that little comment to break the tension in my neck and shoulders that remembering the crime scene was causing. "Her face was beet red, and her eyes and tongue . . ."

"You don't have to describe that, baby," Jack assured me. "We know what a strangled vic looks like." Addie rewarded his kindness with a hand squeeze.

I sat up straighter. No matter how I shifted my position on the comfy sofa, nothing would make what I'd say next comfortable. "Here's the thing, everybody. She was posed."

Jazz's brow furrowed. He frowned. "What do you mean, she was posed?"

"I mean someone placed her body in a sexually suggestive position postmortem."

Jazz looked horrified, as I'd suspected he would. "Posed!" he said. "Who the—"

Addie asked, "Was there any evidence of a struggle besides at the door?"

"No. His place was neat as a monk's cell; he hadn't even opened the Chinese takeout." *He couldn't have known she was coming if he had dinner for one. If he never took off his suit. If the candles were for . . .*

"I had just gotten home and set it on the countertop. I had enough time to get my coat in the closet. The woman was practically lying in wait"—he forced an exhale from his lungs—"for her own death. Poor Kate." Jazz appeared deeply disturbed by what I'd said about Kate being posed.

We all sat quietly for a few moments. Jazz got up from the love seat. "I need a beer. Anybody else want anything?"

"I'll take a Corona, son," Jack said. Addie didn't ask for anything.

"You can refill my coffee," I said. "My mug is on the kitchen table."

Jazz went into the kitchen. I suspected he needed to excuse himself because no matter how much he may have disliked Kate, he certainly didn't want her dead. I looked after him, wishing I could help.

"He'll be okay," Jack said, "as soon as we get this figured out." He took a deep breath and started in on me again. "Is there anything else we need to know, baby?"

"Maguire told me that it was Kate who'd called the police. She told them Jazz had beat her up." I waited for a reaction. Neither he nor Addie looked like they thought this was unusual. Either they were used to Jazz beating up women, or they knew she was lying. "The police responded to the call, saw his door open, went in, and found her dead."

"Freaky," Jack said.

Addie nodded.

"Okay, Bell," Jack said. "What is your *second* burning question after, Did Jazz do this?"

"I want to know who would benefit from Kate's death."

"Good girl. Spoken like a true detective."

Jazz ambled back into the room, two Coronas in one hand and a steaming cup of joe in the other. He set my mug on the coffee table in front of me, then handed his dad a Corona before plopping back down on the love seat beside me. He took a long swig.

"Jazz, give her a kiss," Jack said.

Jazz nearly choked. He looked confused. "A kiss?" He set his beer down on the floor.

"Yeah. You changed the rules to this process at the jazz festival, remember?"

"Dad, what are you talking about?"

As soon as Jack mentioned the jazz festival, I knew.

Dad expounded like he was trying to explain something to a small child. "Jazzy, when your mother and I walked up on you and Bell at the festival in September, you were about to kiss her."

Jazz's expression changed from confusion to disbelief. He could see it now, too.

"Your mother said, 'Jazz Brown, what do you think you're doing?' And you said you and Bell were working on a case. Do you remember that, son?"

"Dad—"

"Do you remember?"

Jazz nodded.

"So you must have changed the rules, and now we have to kiss to work through a case. Frankly, I like the new rules. Now, kiss your girlfriend. She's been giving us some good stuff to work with."

"We agreed not to see each other anymore."

"I didn't agree to that," I said.

"Of course you didn't, sweetie," Addie said. "That's why you're here." She cast a disdainful eye at Jazz, as if he were a complete buffoon. "Now, give Bell a kiss."

Jazz looked flustered. "Bell, do you want me to kiss you?"

"Not now," I said.

"See," he said smugly to his parents.

I reached into my purse and pulled out a tin of wintergreen Altoids I kept for breath-freshening emergencies. I opened the container and shook a heaping amount into my palm. "But as soon as I finish these . . ." I popped several minty orbs into my mouth.

Jack and Addie cracked up.

Jazz blushed furiously.

While the three of us waited for my mints to dissolve, Jack went on. "Let's look at the police's first suspect: Jazz. Why would they think you'd want her dead?"

Jazz sighed. "Because she was in my place and in my bed. They want an open-and-shut case, and I can't say I blame them."

Jack agreed with a nod. "Besides the fact that nobody wants to work hard, why *you* for this, son?"

"Maguire's tack, at least in the interview, was that I was still seeing her, and we'd had a lovers' quarrel."

Addie snorted. "Wrong! And even if you were still seeing her, why kill her?"

"You got that right," said Jack. "You two had a nasty divorce. If you wanted to kill her, you'd have done it when it counted."

Jazz added, "She was still living with Christine. Maguire implied he thought I was jealous."

"Yeah, but she's been with Chris for almost four years. A little late for that. Plus, everybody knows you've got a love jones for Bell."

"Everybody?" I said, Altoids nearly slipping out of my mouth.

Jack waved away my concern. "Pretty much. Cops talk."

Addie joined in. "And speaking of cop gossip, it's common knowledge that Miss Kate loved some other boys—and girls—in blue."

"And it didn't matter if they were married or otherwise unavailable," Jazz said. "Which brings me to my question: Who would want her gone? I'd look first at the people she's closest to."

"Spouse or significant other," Addie said.

"Christine?" I asked.

"Exactly," Jack said to me. "That reminds me. You said she was wearing Jazz's shirt, and her own clothes were in a pile by the bed. Let's dissect that, but first Jazz has to kiss you. Go ahead, Jazzy. Make me proud."

Jazz cocked his head to the side. A bit of pink spread across his cheeks and ears. "Dad! She doesn't want . . ." His face had to be red-hot.

"Kiss her."

His eyes pleaded with me. "Will you tell them you don't want me to kiss you?"

I loved that Jack and Addie were determined to play matchmaker. The least I could do was participate. I crunched the last of the mints and swallowed them. "Bring it on, Jazzy."

His parents practically roared with laughter. Addie sat upright for the show.

Jazz nodded slowly, undoubtedly plotting to bring me down. "I'm gonna make you pay for this, Bell."

"Bring it, don't sing it, okay?"

He laughed. "A'ight. Come here, heifer."

I cracked up. "Oh, I'm 'heifer' now? You'd better kiss me

good, 'cause don't nobody call me 'heifer' but my mama." *And my sister. And my secretary.*

Before I could lick my lips, that man had me hemmed up against the love seat with some sugar so sweet I thought I'd go into a diabetic coma. He released me with a satisfied grin. "Did I bring it?"

I couldn't answer because he'd stunned me into silence. Jack tried to revive me with "Now, about Kate . . ."

Oh yeah. We're on a case. I cleared my throat and continued, "Jazz told me last night that she'd tried to seduce him and got mad when he didn't take her up on her offer. According to him, she was dressed—"

"She *was* dressed." Jazz scowled at me. "She had on her little black getup."

I ignored him. "As I was saying, *if* she was dressed when Jazz left, she had to have taken off her clothes with the intent to try to seduce him again when he returned." Now I turned to Jazz. "What time did she get to your place?"

"Maybe eight-fifteen."

I started calculating in my mind. If she arrived at eight-fifteen, and by eight-thirty or -forty they were at it and he stormed out, she could have sat there stewing until nine and then decided to switch gears and seduce him again. Light the candles. *How long does it take to light all those candles?* He didn't come back because he was en route to see me, which meant she'd been there alone for some time. So she was angry. She was in his shirt. The candles were burning.

I said none of this aloud because of the candle connection.

Addie took the Corona from Jack's hand and had a sip. "Maybe she got to thinking he'd reject her again. You know what they say about a woman scorned." She handed her hubby his beer.

I let Addie know I had the same suspicions. "I can see that—Kate fuming, feeling rejected after she'd gone to such an effort. She had on false eyelashes, for heaven's sake!"

Addie went on, "So she got mad and called the police with the story that he'd beaten her up. It wouldn't have been the first time she'd done that."

Jazz agreed. "That was definitely Kate's MO. The uniforms would have taken their time getting to my place. They knew Kate. They wouldn't have wanted to deal with her."

"So you think they purposely made her wait?" I asked

Jazz answered, "They'd have dispatched somebody right away. It would cover their butts if anybody ever had to investigate what happened. But would they have gotten there ASAP? That depends on the uniforms who got the call. The rookies would want to please the good lieutenant and get there quickly."

Jack added, "But not so much the uniforms who resent you because they think your pretty face—which bears a striking resemblance to your dad's—got you further than good, solid police work did." He turned his gaze to me. "Not everybody on the force likes Lieutenant Pretty Boy."

"Dad," Jazz warned.

Addie asked, "What if the killer got two for the price of one?"

"What do you mean, baby?" Jack put his arm across the back of the couch.

"I mean, what if the killer had a bone to pick with both Kate and Jazzy?"

Jack nodded enthusiastically. "Oh yeah, baby. Come to Daddy."

Mom went to "Daddy," lifting her torso to kiss him as if Jazz and I weren't even in the room. I nudged Jazz. "I want to be like them when I grow up."

"Who says you have to wait till then?"

Oh yeah. This was going to be an interesting night.

When the sweethearts finished nuzzling, I brought up Christine again. "Wouldn't Chris be the first one on the list of people who had a bone to pick with both Kate and Jazz?"

Jack stroked Addie's arm. "I know I'd be ticked off if my woman was half-naked in her ex's apartment."

"How would Christine know Kate was with you, Jazz?" I asked.

He raked his hand through his hair. "Kate wasn't known for her discretion. She was crazy enough to tell Chris."

"That doesn't sound right," I told him.

"We're not talking about right. We're talking about Kate," Jazz responded.

"What was she like, Jazz?" I asked

He sighed. Slumped back into the love seat. "Pretty. Model-pretty but nuts."

With perfect double D's, my mind tortured me. Before I could calculate how long it would take to afford my own surgery, Jazz went on, "She could be very flirty. Fun, even. She knew how to make you feel like you were the most important person in the world. For a minute. Then she'd turn on you."

"What do you mean?"

I watched him carefully. His eyes shifted left, and his head tilted slightly up. He was remembering. Eyes shifting right indicated lying. "She'd, like . . ." He shook his head as if he were seeing something unpleasant and trying to shake it out of his mind. "She'd consume you. She was so intense. Her need for you would just . . . obliterate you."

My mind whirred. "Was she insecure?"

"Unbelievably so. She was a *very* good-looking woman and knew how to work what she had, but by the end of your first date, you'd have figured she thought she was a troll."

Does he have to keep mentioning how good-looking she was?

"Was she self-destructive?"

Jazz didn't need to think about that one. "Not just self-destructive. She was destructive *period*. She knew how to make an enemy, and she was her biggest."

"Did you know she was a cutter?"

His eyes cast downward. "It was pretty hard to miss, even in the short time we were together. I didn't know how to help her, Bell. Honest to God I didn't."

In my quest for information, I'd almost forgotten about Mom and Dad.

"Bell, what did you mean she was a cutter?" Addie asked, her brows drawn together in genuine concern.

I let Jazz answer. "She cut herself with razor blades, Mom."

"On purpose?"

"On purpose."

Addie looked at me. "Bell?"

"I'm afraid it's not uncommon, Mom. It's a way to escape internal pain by shifting the focus to physical pain. It's a symptom of a very hurting person."

Addie pressed a hand to her heart. "I didn't like her very much, but Lord, I hate to think the poor child was that bad off."

Jazz put his head in his hands. "She was so messed up. I feel bad for her. For all the times I had wished she was out of my life, I wouldn't have wished what she suffered on a dog. I should have just let her rage at me the other night. She'd have calmed down and gone home."

"She attacked you, Jazzy. You don't know what she would have done," I said. Poor Jazz. He looked like he bore the weight of the entire world on his broad shoulders—and the weight was beginning to crush his spirit. "Which brings me to this question," I said. "Maguire said Kate called the police at nine minutes after nine. Could she have called someone besides the police, too? Someone she may have believed would comfort her? Even if it was unknowingly at her own peril?"

Jack, Addie, and Jazz said in unison, "Christine."

"Is Christine strong enough to strangle Kate to death?"

"Chris could rumble with the big boys," Jack said.

"Strong woman?"

Jazz smirked. "Yeah. A real soldier, and she and Kate had been known to play Rock 'Em Sock 'Em Robots."

I chuckled at Jazz's reference to another popular seventies toy. Me with my Weebles, and him with his battling robots. I thought for a moment. "Would Christine want to frame you?"

Jack answered, "She would if she didn't want to go down for Kate's murder."

Jazz shook his head. "I don't think she would have tried to frame me. She felt bad about her affair with Kate. Not bad enough to end it, but she tried in the best way she knew how to let me know she was sorry. Chris didn't really have beef with me."

"The way the killer posed her really bugs me," I said, thinking out loud.

Jazz shuddered. "I don't even want to try to picture it. What's your take on it?"

I loved it when he got into my work. "My take is that somebody wanted to punish her. I like a man for this," I said. "I'd like to have a peek at Kate's little black book—the book that you all say is filled with cops' names." I asked Dad, "Do you think they'll pull phone records?"

"Absolutely. What all did Kate have with her?"

I thought about the scene. "I recall seeing her dress, undies, panty hose, and shoes, but no purse. That seems strange. A girl without a purse."

Jazz said, "Kate never went anywhere without her purse. It was where she kept her makeup. She wouldn't be caught dead without her makeup."

"She wasn't caught dead without it." I could have kicked myself like Jackie Chan for my jealousy. I took a deep breath. "Maybe whoever killed her took her purse."

"Good cop thinking, baby," Jack said, a mischievous twinkle in his eyes. "Jazzy. I think you're going to have to marry this girl."

Addie grinned like a wedding planner on the make. "I'm a licensed missionary. I can marry you two right now."

Jazz dropped to his knees and picked up my hand. "Will you marry me, Bell? 'Cause your crime-solving expertise . . ."

I gave him a stern look. "There's the small matter of a dowry."

"I have a sizable Addie Lee artwork inheritance."

"Sold!" I said, loud and proud.

"I now pronounce you man and wife," Addie said. "Jazz, you may salute your bride."

Jazz stood and gave me a brisk military salute. With precision, he turned and reseated himself. Instantly, he was back in the groove. "We still need to consider who else, besides Christine, Kate could have contacted."

Addie leaned forward. "Let's say she had another girlfriend, or even a boyfriend. She didn't seem terribly particular about gender. So let's say she was bored with Christine, got rejected by Jazz—"

"Kate couldn't stand rejection," Jazz said. "It was like her kryptonite."

Jack added, "Maybe she called her other lover for comfort while she waited for the police."

"Maybe her other lover *was* a police officer," Addie said.

"I don't think a uniform called to the scene would have killed her, but in light of Jazz's investigation—"

"Dad!" Jazz seemed angry with his father.

"What?" I said, confused, looking from Jack to Jazz.

Jack caught himself. "Never mind, baby. Moving right along."

Jazz's mouth became a hard line. "Game over."

"Game over?" I asked. "Why? What investigation is Jazz involved in?"

The three of them looked at me like I'd caught them wearing white shoes after Labor Day.

"Forget about it, Bell," Jazz said.

"What happened to the 'no question is off limits' clause? This is the second time I've gotten shut down."

"That question is."

I went kitten on him, stroking his leg with my shoe. "Aw, baby. Tell me. I'm your wife."

"Ha!" he said. "If you were my wife, I'd have you under control, and I wouldn't have to worry about you trying to play Columbo."

Under control?

I blasted him. "First of all, you sexist ape, if I were your wife, you couldn't control me in any way, form, or fashion. Second, *Lieutenant Brown*, Columbo is a brilliant, deceptively disarming detective who always catches his killer."

"Woman, Columbo is a television character who never got beat up like *you* did the last time you tried to play detective. And did you just call me an ape?"

"No. I called you a *sexist* ape. You called me a heifer. We're even, Old MacDonald. E-I-E-I-O."

We glared at each other until Jack broke the tension. "Their first fight as a married couple. Ain't that the cutest thing? Why don't y'all kiss and make up."

I stood. I hadn't slept well since Sunday night, and now it was Tuesday afternoon. All the drama abruptly settled on me, and all the coffee in the world couldn't keep at bay the exhaustion now weighing me down. "Like Jazz said, game over. I'm going home." I stretched, yawned, and walked over to the sofa to kiss my pretend mother- and father-in-law good-bye. I felt brave. "I love you," I said to them both. "I'll see you soon." I hugged Jack first, then Addie.

Before Addie let me go, she whispered, "Don't be mad at him. He's just trying to protect you."

I gave her a squeeze to acknowledge that I had heard her, but I didn't make any promises.

Predictably, Jazz stood up. "I'll see you out. Maybe." He put his arm around my shoulders, and I grudgingly let him lead me to the foyer. I made my resistance evident. "Stop it, wife, or I'll pull the 'submit to your husband' card on you."

"I don't have to submit to you. I'm not really your wife. If I were, you wouldn't be holding out on me."

He reached into the closet, pulled out my leather jacket, and helped me into it. "I'm not holding out on you, Bell."

"You are."

"Did it even cross your mind that I do real police work—not the Columbo kind? I'm talkin' the kind that can get even seasoned officers killed."

"I know you're a cop, Jazz."

"Then you should know I can't discuss with you everything I do. For your own safety."

"You told your mom and dad. How unsafe could it be?"

"Dad is a retired cop, and Mom's been a cop's wife most of her life."

"Your mom just married us. I'm a cop's wife, too."

"Nice try, Bell. Can you just drop it? For me?"

I gave him a salty look.

"C'mon, baby. You gotta see things are rough on a brotha over here."

I hated it when he was right, especially when it interfered with what I wanted.

He rested his arms on my shoulders. "Bell," he said calmly, "stop being difficult."

"I'm not being difficult. I just want to help, and I feel like you're not telling me something important."

"You did help. You brainstormed and came up with some good stuff."

I sighed and lowered my head.

He stepped closer and rubbed the back of my neck. Pulled me into a hug, touching his forehead to mine. "I failed Kate." His voice grew husky. "But I'll be lost if anything happened to you. And I mean that literally."

Well, when he put it that way . . . "Okay, Jazz."

He held me away from him and gave me a long, searching look. "Really?"

"Yes," I said, pouting.

"Don't look so pitiful. You're supposed to like this whole 'protect the woman you love' thing."

A smile I didn't intend to give him slipped out. "I do like it. Especially the love part. Say that again."

"That would be redundant. Now be a good girl and stay clear of me until I get this mess straightened out."

I looked at him, uncertain.

"We can do this, Bell. You didn't seem to have a problem with not seeing me this past month."

"But we just got married." I put my hands on his hips and pulled him close.

"Don't start no stuff, *Miss* Brown."

"That's *Mrs.* Brown."

"Stop teasing me, minx."

"Don't call me minx."

"Move those hands, Dr. Brown."

I obeyed. Reluctantly.

He gave me a deliciously naughty grin. "Now, let's go to bed."

"Excuse me?"

"I can tell you need more sleep. I picked your pocket when I pulled your coat out of the closet. I've got your car keys. You are frighteningly easy to victimize."

"I don't believe you!" I fished around in my jacket pocket. No keys.

Jazz reached into the front pocket of his jeans and then dangled the keys to my Love Bug in front of me. "You're not going anywhere until you get some sleep, *wife*."

So that was what he meant when he'd said *maybe* he'd see me out. I hit him. "I'm not your wife, you big primate. Give me my keys."

"I'll show you to the guest bedroom. And be glad we've got religion over here. Otherwise I might be tempted to do my husbandly duties, *Mrs.* Brown."

Honestly!

Later, I was glad he made me stay. Once my head hit the pillow in that cozy guest room, with the red-clay-colored walls and the red Moroccan and Turkish tapestries piled on the bed, I slept more peacefully than the dead, holding in my arms a hand-sewn rag doll Addie had made.

Give me a break. I could have filled my arms with someone else.

A little after 11 P.M., I crawled out of bed. I padded into the

living room and saw no sign of Mom and Dad. Jazz snoozed on
the sofa, still sitting up, with a remote control in his hand, the
colored lights from the television flickering across his face. Dear
Lord, how fine was he? He took my breath away. *How did I ever
turn your head?*

I eased myself onto the sofa beside him, my desire to leave
dissipating as I studied his magnificent frame. He looked more
tired than usual tonight. More vulnerable.

The eleven o'clock news blared on, Jazz being the top story,
but only Jazz. *I guess the mystery woman in the little yellow Beetle
isn't newsworthy. Thank you, Jesus.* I put my hand lightly on Jazz's
knee. "I'm so sorry for your trouble, baby."

I didn't know if he'd awakened when I sat down, or if my
gentle touch had stirred him, but he curved his arm around me.
"What was that song you told me your great-grandmother used
to sing to you about trouble?"

"'I'm So Glad (Trouble Don't Last Always).' She favored Sam
Cooke and the Soul Stirrers singing it."

"Trust her."

I nestled close to him and closed my eyes, Ma Brown's image invading my consciousness. Her spirit seemed to lean inside
of mine, as heavy with hope and sorrow as the blues. Or a Negro
spiritual. I heard her singing in my soul:

> *Well you know, I'm so glad*
> *I know that trouble don't last always*
> *I know that trouble don't last always*
> *I know that trouble don't last always*

Oh my Lord, I wonder, what shall I do
Oh my Lord, I wonder what shall I do.

A heavy sigh escaped my lips. *My Lord. What shall I do, in-deed?*

chapter
ten

A PPARENTLY, it's virtually impossible to get information out of homicide detectives when they don't really want to give you any.

Wednesday morning Jazz showed me no love when I tried to pry Christine's last name, rank, and serial number out of him. Neither did Jack, despite my attempt to turn on a considerable amount of charm. Even Addie took their side—the traitor! Whatever happened to sistah-to-sistah solidarity?

I thought I might have more luck with Detective Bobby Maguire; after all, he hadn't totally shut me down at my apartment. So I headed down to his "house"—the Detroit police department.

Honestly, I watch way too much television. The Detroit police department looked like every old-school police station you'd ever see on the tube—from *Barney Miller* to *NYPD Blue*—it had too little space, even less inspiration, and a bunch of crabby occupants. I came upon Maguire's hulking figure, in that same terrible brown suit, hunched behind a desk that seemed like the Grinch's heart: three sizes too small. He noticed me and motioned with his head for me to come over.

"What?" he barked, probably unintentionally. "No pajamas? No sparkly shoes?"

I'd caught Maguire in his ever present foul mood. He looked like he'd be willing to give up about as much information as I'd get from a stone gargoyle.

"Have a seat," he said, sighing deeply. He rustled around in a brown paper sack for some kind of food, which, judging by the impressive grease stain it created, would ensure his untimely death. Adding to that the fact that hunger just about guaranteed extra grumpiness, and I had a veritable recipe for him to not be willing to cooperate with me.

"Whaddya want, Dr. Amanda?" he asked without any fanfare. From his sack, he pulled a hideous mound that vaguely resembled a sandwich. An unrecognizable meat product hung precariously off the bun, which appeared to be made of high-density foam—*old* high-density foam. He examined it. Sighed. Rolled his eyes and took a bite.

I watched with the morbid fascination of a looky-loo at a twelve-car pile-up, bodies strewn across the freeway. *Dear God, he's chewing it! He's gonna swallow. Oh . . .* I looked away.

"I just wanted to talk to you," I said between grimaces.

"Whaddya wanna talk about, girl Columbo?" he said, forcing me to look back at him and the sandwich of doom.

"I just wanted to ask you one more thing."

"Just one more thing. Like your television idol, right? Didn't I tell you to step away from this?"

"That was a command? I thought you'd merely made a helpful suggestion."

He took another bite of the abominable sandwich, ignoring

me for a bit while he chewed, until finally: "What's your question?"

I had to force myself to focus, making a mental note to buy him a decent meal—soon. "It's about Christine. I understand she and Kate had been known to fight."

"And where did that understanding come from?"

"So they fought?"

"Most couples fight."

"Like Rock 'Em Sock 'Em Robots? Most couples don't punch each other's heads off."

He chuckled at my mention of the toy. "Don't you think I've talked to Chris?"

"Did you pull phone records? Kate's cell? Jazz's phone? Christine's?"

"Lemme do my job without you checking up on me."

"What did Christine say?"

"That's police business." He somehow managed to say that around a disgusting mouthful.

"Does she have an alibi for the night of the murder?"

"Does Jazz have one?"

"Yes. Me. Is she a suspect?"

"Is Jazz a suspect? To *you*, girl Columbo? Because he's the primary suspect to *me*. Did you talk to him yet? Did you ask your boyfriend if he killed his wife?"

"Ex-wife. And as a matter of fact, I did ask him. He said no, just so we're clear. Didn't he tell *you* he didn't do it, Bobby? Anyway, I know Christine doesn't work for the Detroit police anymore. Does she work for the Royal Oak police department?"

Maguire reclined in his cheap vinyl office chair, which didn't have a recline feature. The chair groaned in protest like only a pleather chair could. Honestly, did the man hug trees and not eat his animal friends? Did he have a moral objection to *real* leather?

He put the awful sandwich back in the sack. I almost made the sign of the cross out of gratefulness. I looked into his eyes. "You're not going to tell me anything about her, are you?"

"You don't work for me, girl Columbo. You need to step away, like I said. You also need to think about choosing your boyfriends more carefully."

"What's her last name, Maguire? That's all I want to know."

"You said you only had one question, but you've asked four or five."

"You didn't answer any of them."

He stretched again, and the chair screamed for mercy. "Come back in your pajamas and magic shiny shoes, and maybe we'll talk pro to pro, but right now you need to go home unless you wanna have a little chat with IAD."

"I'll find out, Bobby. How many detectives named Christine can there be in Southeast Michigan?"

"Who said she's still a cop?"

"I just want a last name."

"You got a last name: Brown. Now go home."

I stood and thrust out my hand for Maguire to shake. I think it surprised him, but he took mine in his and shook it. He didn't stand up, but a half smirk twisted across his lips. "I'm on it, Amanda."

"I hope so, Bobby."

"Let me do my job, and you go back to talking to the nut-cases at the Washtenaw County Jail."

"Okay." I turned to walk away.

"Oh, Amanda?"

I turned around, hoping he'd had a change of heart and, for the price of a smile, would tell me everything I wanted to know about the case. I grinned at him.

"Call your mother."

Shoot! I didn't check my messages. Of course Ma called. The last thing I needed was Sasha Brown stalking me. As soon as she caught me—and she would—I'd get the talk. On steroids.

———————

I truly hoped Maguire was on it, as he'd said. This case had to be a nightmare—not just for the people involved but also for the department.

Speaking of the department, no sooner had I turned away from Maguire than I bumped right into Officer Archie IAD. "Excuse me," I said.

His hands cradled my elbows. His brown eyes, not warm and delicious like Jazz's, studied mine. "Remember me?" he said. "From Internal Affairs?" He held me as if he and I were having an internal affair.

I took a good look at him. He wasn't as striking as Jazz, but he could certainly hold his own. Again I marveled at the Detroit police's good-looking crew. They didn't make them like that in Washtenaw County. I nodded to acknowledge him and stiffened like a board, hoping he'd catch my body language and let me go. "It's nice to see you again, Officer."

His eyes flickered down past my unbuttoned coat to my conservative clothing, stopping at my unimpressive breasts. Appreciation shone in his eyes. Apparently, his version of sexy clothing was anything worn by a woman. I tried to wriggle away, which he allowed. "Do you have a moment? I've been looking for you," he said. "Did you get my messages?"

"I'm sorry, I didn't. My cell phone battery died."

"You certainly can be elusive."

"I've been with friends," I said. Honestly! Did everyone check on me?

He caught my alarmed expression and gave me a smile that didn't reach his eyes. "I'm sure you'll find you're going to be quite popular in the next few weeks."

"I don't doubt that I will be."

He touched the small of my back to lead me to a desk he must have pilfered from some poor, unsuspecting detective. I felt none of Jazz's warmth in his gesture. He sat down behind the desk. "Why don't you have a seat, Amanda," he said. He didn't pull out my chair for me.

I seated myself in the metal folding chair by the desk. "I'm sure you have a lot of questions for me, Archie," I said, "but I already told you and Detective Maguire all I have to offer."

"Why don't you tell me all that you *know*?"

Smart man.

"I know Lieutenant Brown got to my apartment at around nine-thirty P.M. How could he have killed a woman who was alive when he was on I-94, on his way to my apartment?"

"You have no way to prove you were aware of the exact time he arrived."

For the first time in a long time, I hated that I rarely watched anything other than TiVoed shows I could view at my leisure. Nothing rooted me in time that night, other than leaving the pet store. "It took me nearly an hour to get to Jazz's loft. I know it wasn't that long after nine that he got to my place."

He smiled at me. "Those certainly weren't business hours, were they, Amanda?"

"I guess it depends on what his business with me was."

Another fake smile. "You're a very good-looking woman, but I wouldn't take you for his type."

I swallowed hard, and he noticed. I had on a plain navy blue suit. White high-collared blouse. He must have known that with my frumpy clothes, *I* wouldn't take me for Jazz's type, either. I pursed my lips. I didn't care for how he and Bobby Maguire had conducted this investigation. Both were too focused on the wrong angles, and neither seemed to want to fight for his colleague. I ignored the comment about my type. "It's possible that Jazz didn't do it. How could he have gotten to my apartment so soon if he'd killed her after she made that phone call?"

"You realize that your boss, Dr. Fox, doesn't appreciate your involvement with Jazz Brown."

I didn't appreciate Archie discussing me with my boss.

Archie continued, "He didn't approve of your work on the Vogel-Crawford case, which ended up with you being hurt badly." I heard no hint of compassion in his voice. "He doesn't want you involved in this case, either, which we both know is much more personal. Isn't it?"

I could see Archie's brilliance. He knew how to get a girl's attention, but I needed him to know I was no wimp, despite my poor choices at times.

"What I do on my own time is my business, Officer."

"Dr. Fox feels differently. According to him, you ended up having to take three weeks off work because of your injuries. He also believes your credentials do not qualify you for the work you've done with our department. He doesn't believe you have any business being involved with any of our cases."

"I didn't work for the Detroit police department. I worked for Lieutenant Brown, privately, as an expert on cults and toxic churches, which *is* my area of expertise. That has nothing to do with my job at the county jail."

"You don't want to *embarrass* your *boss* by dealing with a dangerous man, do you? Lieutenant Brown is all over the news."

"This is a conversation I'll take up with Dr. Fox."

"I'm sure you would if he could find you. You didn't go to work yesterday."

"I'm entitled to a day off."

"I'm sure you are, Dr. Brown. Were you with Jazz?"

"I said I was with friends."

"The DA is looking for you. You'll probably be called as a key witness in the prosecution's case. You shouldn't be talking to Lieutenant Brown."

"I haven't heard from the DA as of yet. I can talk to whomever I want. Now, if you'll excuse me, I really have to be going."

I stood. He didn't oppose me.

"We'll talk again, Amanda," he said. "I'm not the enemy."

"According to the laws of this fine country we live in, a man is innocent until proven guilty. It would do you and Maguire well to keep that in mind."

"You are not a police officer, Amanda, nor, I assume, are you an expert on the laws of this country. It would do *you* well to keep that in mind."

If I felt hopeful at all, it was only because I was sure of this: Jazz's family believed he was innocent, and regardless of what was happening, he still had enough of his swagger to convince me that he felt confident the real killer was going to be found. I knew somehow that even if Archie IAD and Bobby Maguire dropped the ball, Jack Brown, and even Jazz, would see to it that someone picked it up. I also knew that despite the carnage of their failed marriage, Jazz believed Kate deserved justice. And Jazz did justice beautifully.

These thoughts whirled around in my head as I walked away from Archie's makeshift desk. I stopped in a small corridor and sat in a plastic chair, trying to think everything through. Why hadn't Archie pressed me for more information? What was he up to? And had that been a hint from Maguire about Christine not being a cop? Or had it been a rabbit hole for me to fall into?

I dug a notepad and pen out of my purse. I always recommended that clients in my private practice keep a pen and pad handy to write down dreams, questions, fleeting impressions, even full journal entries. I'd gotten out of the habit myself but had at last taken the initiative to toss those tools into my main purse—an excellent Birkin knockoff I had hustled off my mother.

I jotted down Christine's name with a big question mark beside it. I'd already tried to find her through directory assistance. No luck.

I was saying a silent prayer for help when I noticed a tall twentysomething black woman with endless legs in black leather pants headed toward the exit. Those pants were topped by a classic white wraparound shirt. Perfectly executed cornrows crowned her head and flowed to her shoulders. Her bold silver-and-leather cord necklace and enormous silver hoops—much bigger than mine—made me break the commandment about not coveting. She carried a Coach Hamptons leather business tote, in mint condition, that would cost me half a month's rent. If she lived in Detroit, it might have cost all of hers. I looked past all the things to covet and realized: she looked oddly familiar. Then very familiar. I realized to my delight that she was one of my youth-group babies from way back in the day. "Kalaya?"

My little missy had grown up right nicely. Ms. Class with Sass stopped in her tracks. "Miss Bell?"

"Kalaya!" I jumped to my feet. I loved that kid. I hadn't seen her in years. She was one I'd taken a special interest in. She was bright, funny, and talented. "I can't believe it's you! Look at you, pumpkin."

Honestly, it looked like she was blushing under all that brown skin. "Yeah. You remember me with the bad posture and even worse skin. And look! I grew into my head. Finally."

"I always thought you were beautiful. You're even more so now. Your eyes are stunning."

"If you like cow eyes."

I gathered her into a hug, and she flopped around like nobody hugged her anymore. When I released her, she looked uncomfortable. She avoided looking at me with what she'd described as her cow eyes.

"So what are you doing with yourself now?" I asked.

She took a deep breath. Shrugged. "I did the college thing: journalism. Now I'm doing the career thing: journalism. It's dope, but I work too hard. No man. No life. I have a student loan I'll be paying until I'm fifty, wireless Internet, and a cat named Patron Saint of All Things Literary."

"Must be a challenge to call him in for dinner. But who am I to talk? You don't want to know about my pet. What church do you go to now?"

Her body language said none. "Bell, I know what you want."

Her avoidance of my question gave me the answer. But she was right. I wanted to know why a sweet kid like Kalaya, who had loved the Lord so much, had given Him up. Though a righteous man falls seven times, he rises again. I wanted her to be safe in the arms of Jesus. His blood would cover her fall, no matter what it was. I could testify to that.

But that wasn't all I wanted. After that I wanted her height and her purse. I'd go with the jewelry next.

"I want you to make your way back to Jesus. How 'bout that!" I said.

She smirked. "Maybe. Someday." She put a hand on her hip. "You don't waste any time do you?" She cocked her head. "But neither do I." She leaned toward me. "Like I said, I know what you want."

"Do tell."

She stepped closer. "I heard your conversation with Maguire. I can put you in contact with Christine."

Okay. She did know what I wanted. Kalaya wasn't a little kid anymore. She was a tough negotiator.

"Shall we take a walk, Kalaya?"

She raised her eyebrows as if to say "What are you waiting for?" But what came out was "Yes."

I stuffed my notepad and pen back in my Birkin knockoff. Kalaya pulled a business card from her fabulous tote. She stuck it in front of me. "I'm a crime reporter for the *City Beat*. Ever hear of it?"

I took her card. Kalaya Naylor. How could I be so obtuse? How many Kalaya Naylors could there be? She was an ace reporter. And here I was thinking I'd just coincidentally stumbled upon my lost sheep.

"Who doesn't read the *Beat*?" I said. The *City Beat*, a funky Detroit tabloid, had wide distribution in the suburbs. You could find a copy, even in Ann Arbor, at any good bookstore or newspaper stand. It boasted the best news coverage of all the local rags put together. I'd read many of Kalaya's riveting articles, most of which specialized in corrupt politicians. I would have recognized her name ages ago if I had been prayerfully paying attention. "I'm a fan. I should have known that was you."

"It was a long time ago. Let's keep moving." She looked over her shoulder.

We navigated our way through the maze of desks. Officers glared at us saltily. Whispers swept behind us.

Kalaya spoke softly. "You may not have made the paper yet, but you're famous. You're the sistah who's got all that *Jazz*."

"You don't have your facts straight. I'm currently unattached, and Jazz and I have never officially been a couple."

"Word is he's diggin' you like a grave." She leaned in to me with a conspiratorial whisper. "The scuttlebutt has it that you and he were an item until you dissed him."

"You don't think I'm going to discuss my personal life with a reporter, do you?"

She waved away my concern. "Don't think of me as a reporter. Think of me as an old friend." Then, with a wicked grin, "So, Jazz has issues, huh?"

It was my turn to incline toward her and whisper, "He does *now*."

A delighted whoop exploded from her mouth. "I always liked you, Bell Brown. Of course you must have known that, seeing the way I followed you around like a puppy."

Her eyes betrayed the longing in her soul. I knew what was behind that look. I'd lived with it far too long, until people like Mason and Rocky and a few others refused to let loneliness swallow me whole. Kalaya missed being loved.

I stopped. I touched her wrist but let her go so she wouldn't freak out on me. "Who else is in your life besides the Patron Saint of All Things Literary? A girl needs more than a cat with a long name."

"I have a boyfriend. I see him once or twice a week." Her eyes shifted away. She frowned. *She's not happy with the boyfriend.* I didn't even think she realized it.

She drummed her fingers on her thigh. I read her body language like the Psalms in *The Message*. Not long into a conversation, most people forget they're talking to a psychologist. Guards go down and they unwittingly give me all kinds of information.

"I know Christine," Kalaya said, shifting to her current comfort zone—business. "I've got all her information, including her phone number and where she lives. I'll take you there myself if need be."

"I've got a feeling there's a big 'but' involved."

"A 'but' as big as my mother's, and my mama's got a big ol' butt."

I chuckled at her analogy. My own mother did not have a big butt, but I wished she did, if only for a day. It would be sweet revenge for all the poor wide-loaded women she viciously slandered. Including me. "What do you want, Kalaya?"

"I need a girl Columbo," Kalaya said.

"I'm sorry. I can't help you."

Kalaya's gaze bored into me. "Isn't that who you told Maguire you wanted to be?"

I'd been had.

"Look, I've got some information that might be important. I want to write a story that'll have everybody from here to Ohio talking." She lowered her voice. Didn't even lean in toward me. She was a master at this. "Just hear me out. Kate Townsend was murdered. Lieutenant Jazz Brown was fingered for it. That's all I know."

I glanced around the station. I was standing in a roomful of Detroit's finest and not so finest. I could very well be in the same room as Kate's killer. Who could hear us? We were in plain sight. Was it wise to let people see me with a reporter? And what about Kalaya? Had God sent her to help me? Or me to help her? Or both?

"We'd better get out of here," I said. I walked swiftly, and though Kalaya had the long, gorgeous gams, she struggled to keep up. Adrenaline shot me out of the station house like a rocket. Finally, we reached the corridor and continued down the hall, our heels clicking in time.

Kalaya chattered behind me. "Maguire said they're going to issue a statement tomorrow afternoon, but I think you know something that won't be in that statement. Give me some Dr. Carly Brown insider information. Help a sistah out."

"If you heard most of my conversation with Maguire, you know I'm scrambling for information myself."

"I find that hard to believe."

I looked at her. Young, ambitious, quirky, even, with her own spin on classic style. Not a conventional beauty but striking. Kalaya knew how to work with what she had. At the *Beat*, she'd proved herself to be a writer to watch. I didn't have any idea what measures she took to get her fantastic stories, and I didn't know if I wanted to find out. Jazz had enough trouble in his life without me talking to the press, especially when I didn't know a thing. Not really. "I'd be reluctant to help you at all, especially if it meant hurting someone I lo— someone I know."

Kalaya regarded me with a thoughtful gaze. Kindness reflected in her eyes. "You've still got a love jones for him, don't you?"

I didn't say anything.

"Would it help if I told you I don't think Lieutenant Brown had anything to do with this?"

"It may."

"I don't think he killed her. And I've got very compelling reasons." She drummed her fingers on her thighs again, telling me without telling me that she wasn't sure I'd help her. "I need a little more information."

I still didn't know if I could trust her. *Okay, Lord, what am I supposed to do?*

Feed my sheep.

Can you be a little more specific, Lord?

Kalaya fished in her purse again and pulled out another card. She shook it as if small flames threatened to engulf it and she had to diffuse the fire. "Christine Webber. She does private security now for a company called First Watch. And I'll bet she could use a very kind psychologist right now. She may reveal all sorts of things in that discussion." She held the card out until I took it.

She'd put in my hand exactly what I'd come for. The card looked legit. I said a silent "thank you" to Jesus and took it from her. Now what would she require me to give?

She grinned victoriously. "Can I buy you breakfast?"

Feed my sheep.

I nodded. *I guess I'll be buying the breakfast.* I hoped in agreeing to go, I hadn't agreed to sell a piece of my soul or, worse, Jazz's. But I only wanted to help him. Talking with Christine could yield some useful information.

What are you doing, Bell?

"We'll have to make it fast," I said. "I have work to do. And I'm buying." Not just because God had said so, either. I needed to feel like I'd have some power in this relationship, whatever it was.

And, God, show me what this is.

Kalaya led me to a coffee bar and café called Motown's Java Jive. With the exception of the framed and mounted Motown 45s and classic autographed photos of artists such as Stevie Wonder, the

Jackson Five, and the Supremes, it looked like any other coffee bar that served overpriced food.

I hadn't eaten since the crab cakes at Jazz's parents' house, but in the last three days, I'd had enough java to hold me until Jesus offered me a cup in His kingdom. However, Kalaya's clipped tone and air of quiet desperation for fuel hinted at her growing a Medusa head if the barista didn't get her a fix soon.

We got our orders—Kalaya recommended an amazing-sounding sweet-potato-and-pecan-pancake confection—and we sat down at one of those ridiculously tiny tables common in coffee joints. Kalaya had a cup the size of a stockpot full of steaming brew and the pancakes. I opted for a modest-sized cup of cinnamon tea to go with my pancakes. As good as those sweet-potato pancakes looked—with candied pecan syrup spilling over the edges—the lingering image of Maguire's sandwich haunted me, killing my appetite. The few bites I managed were magnificent, but not enough to stave off the imprinted image.

I still wanted to know what Kalaya wanted, and I didn't know altogether if I could trust her, but I had certainly felt the Holy Spirit leading me to feed her, and feed her, body and spirit, I would.

Now caffeinated, Kalaya became charming and chatty again. The Motown theme of the coffeehouse provided fodder for her to tell me all kinds of ancient gossip about the artists, most likely gleaned from the owners, who treated her like she had stock in the place. Once the chatty flow ebbed, she relaxed against the hard metal chair, sated and ready to get down to business. "I met with Kate twice last week," she said.

"What for?"

"She contacted me about a month ago. Said she read my work and loved it. She wanted me to do an exposé on"—she paused—"how can I put this delicately? Some of her friends."

"I assume you mean her many lovers?"

"Exactly. So you know she was kinda stank?"

"I don't know if that's the word I'd use, but yes, I'd heard she could live fast and loose—playing both sides of the gender game."

"What do you think that was about?"

"I'm still working on that," I said. "But I suspect she had some vulnerabilities from her early childhood. She needed power to compensate for her powerless childhood. If she could gain sexual power over both women and men, she could lessen her chances of being a victim."

Kalaya looked like she was trying to decide whether to reveal her next card. "What if her lovers were all powerful people?"

"Politicians? Cops?"

"Yeah."

"She may have viewed them in an ambivalent way: as powerful people who could both reassure her of her own power and be her protectors. The problem would be if she sexualized her need for power and security until they became unhealthy obsessions."

"Why, if she viewed them as protectors, did she seem so eager to hurt them?"

"Like I said, I'm still working on what I think about Kate's personality. Even if I did come up with some theory, it wouldn't be gospel. People are complicated." The Scripture slipped to my consciousness again.

The heart is deceitful above all things . . .

Kalaya took a sip from her enormous coffee cup. "She wanted me to do a kiss-and-tell story about her extracurricular activities."

"Why you? Don't you write more about corrupt politicians?"

"Maybe there's a politician out there who shared her bed and wanted that to be very discreet."

That hadn't even come up in the brainstorming game at Jazz's parents' house. "You're saying a lot of maybes. I take it she didn't tell you any specifics."

"She told me details. Crazy, salacious details—just enough information to make it easy to guess she was talking about well-known people—but not enough to know exactly who they were." Kalaya sighed and fiddled with one of her cornrows.

"Did you try to get any names out of her?"

"I wouldn't have been doing my job if I didn't. She wouldn't give anybody up yet."

"She say why?"

"No, but I have a theory. She had a diary with all the info in it. I think she wanted money for it, but she hadn't hit me up for any yet."

"What do you think she was waiting for?"

"I'm not sure. She may have been talking to someone else—a rival paper."

"Maybe she was protecting someone."

"Why would she do that if she wanted me to do an exposé?"

"For the same reason she'd meet with you and then not give you anything you could really work with. She could have been conflicted, and from everything I'm learning about Kate Townsend, 'conflicted' isn't a stretch. Did anyone know she'd been talking to you?"

"I have no idea. The thing is, a lot of people in the city know me—people I don't know. A tip-off could have come from anywhere."

I shook my head and took a sip of my tea. The cinnamon smell acted as an aromatherapy agent, chasing my low-grade depression to the shadows. "She also could have kept the diary for leverage. To protect herself. And then there's the revenge, hence the exposé."

"That could certainly pose a threat to her. How did she die?"

"What makes you think I know that?"

"Dr. Carly Brown is your sister. You can't tell me she wouldn't give you a heads-up. C'mon. I've got a sister. I *am* a sister."

I chuckled. "Maybe Carly doesn't cut and tell."

"What would a little detail hurt?"

"The police don't release all the details because some could be instrumental in an interrogation later. They could give insight into the case that only the killer could have."

Kalaya rolled her eyes. "Yeah, yeah, yeah, sistah. Throw me a bone here."

I sat back in my seat and crossed my arms, putting on my emotional armor. She had been generous with me. I could give her a little something without compromising the case. Couldn't I? "I can tell you this, and only off the record: her manner of death was personal."

"Personal like what?"

"You shoot somebody, and you don't get your hands dirty. You stab somebody, and that's personal. Do you know what I'm saying, Kalaya?"

"Are you saying she was stabbed to death?"

"Absolutely not. I'm not going to say anything more specific about how she was killed except that it was personal. You'd do well not to print that she was stabbed."

She nodded. "Why do you want to talk to Christine?"

"I want to check her out."

"Are you trying to find out if she's the kind of woman who could, say, stab a sistah to death?"

"You're a bright woman, Kalaya."

"I only met her once. I think you're barking up the wrong tree, but do your thing, girl."

"I will, thanks to you. Why aren't you talking to her yourself?"

"Everybody thinks I'll make them the front-page story." Kalaya tilted toward me. "Find out if she still has the diary."

"What if the police already have it?"

"Then find out if they do."

"I'll do that. It's the least I can do for what you've given me."

She dug in her Hamptons business tote again and removed car keys. Once again I considered snatching the bag and running. It had snowed, however, and I decided I'd probably slip on the wet concrete outside and give myself a concussion.

"Call me," she said.

I nodded.

"We want the same thing," she said.

I wanted to find a killer. I didn't know if she wanted that or to break a story that would make her career.

Soon enough, her motives would be clear. Thinking about it, I got a tiny Holy Spirit nudge. I also realized something sobering. Soon enough, so would mine.

chapter
eleven

I HAD TO GO IN.

It was, after all, *my* office. I paid the rent there. Clients came and paid good money to talk to me. *I am an adult! I can buy a bottle of wine without getting carded. Shoot. I'm more than an adult. I'm thirty-five years old. In some people's minds, I'm middle-aged. If you ask me on a bad day, I'm pushing old age.*

Still, I didn't want to go into my overpriced little office on State Street. I approached the door tentatively. Surely they were lying in wait—the purple-wearing, red-hatted ninja twins. One of them, a former blonde and now a stylishly white-haired curmudgeon, was my secretary, Maggie Harold. Her vicious best friend, Sasha, was my mother.

I didn't mind Maggie so much. The petite fireball at least belonged in my office. I kept her on because her exemplary skills in typing, filing, answering phones, handling clients, and well, handling me, offset her generally ill-tempered deportment. Most days, when I walked in the door, she'd give me a full wardrobe-and-hair evaluation—usually negative—but after the first cup of coffee, she'd have me settled in to her well-oiled machine.

I worked with mentally ill people. While most were your

garden-variety mild neurotics, or even healthy people in need of a little guidance, I did have a few truly sick clients. I needed Maggie's pit-bull office-management style as sure as I needed the *DSM-IV*.

However, I did *not* need my mother at the office. I could just see her. She'd surely be at *my* desk, in *my* big, yummy purple Italian-leather chair I'd just purchased as one of many belated birthday gifts to myself. I called it the throne.

Ma would pounce on me like a tiger. After all, I hadn't called her for two days, when I knew she'd be worried sick. *Lord, have mercy!*

I turned the door latch. Unlocked. Maggie, at least, was in there. I said a prayer for mercy and forgiveness, took a deep breath, and went in.

I didn't see them until they were on me—suddenly attacking on both flanks. Maggie gathered an impressive portion of the crew collar on my itty-bitty black sweater into her fist. My ear wilted in my mother's kung fu grip. I don't know how that woman got such perfect aim. She hadn't taken ahold of my lobe like that since I was in the ninth grade and she found out I'd let Elvin Curtis French-kiss me behind our dogwood tree in the backyard.

"Maaaaaaa!" I howled.

She talked in a staccato rhythm. "Amanda. Bell. Brown. What. Do. You. Think. You. Are." And, with a harder tug, "*Doing?*" Her last word came out with the force and authority of the Last Trump.

At least Maggie released me, though she wiped her hands together as if she'd soiled herself by touching my sweater. Maggie posed little threat in the presence of Sasha, who I believed had been military-trained to destroy me.

"I'm trying to start my workday, Ma."

"What is that you're wearing?"

"Huh?"

"What are you wearing, you little narrow-tailed yellow heifer?"

Uh-oh. Only the worst infractions made my mother refer to me as a bovine. While the name was common in my teenage years, I didn't get "heifer" much now. I quickly moved to the psychologist part of my brain and analyzed what she'd said. First: "little narrow-tailed"? To her, a little narrow tail was a diminutive rear end, the kind belonging to a child. She believed I had acted childishly. And she'd pulled the color card. A "yellow heifer" was so much worse than a plain old heifer. Name-calling notwith-standing, a sobering reality hit me harder than her ear twisting. *I've scared my mother to death.*

I thought addressing what she'd said about my skin color would be the least troublesome subject to broach and possibly delay "the talk," on steroids—at least until I could get to my desk. "Mama, I think I'm more the color of a square of Brach's caramel, not a true yellow, really. Someone told me I'm a nice shade of peanut butter."

"I don't care what color you are. What do you have on?"

She really *didn't* care what color I was. Nor did she care—much—that I'd come to work in less than business-casual attire. She knew my jeans, cowboy boots, and practically sprayed-on sweater meant a fine man was on my radar. "Did you spend the night with a *murderer*?"

Not a good question. She wanted to know if I'd spent the night with Jazz, who was supposed to be innocent until proven guilty in a court of law. If I said no, I had not spent the night with a murderer, she'd say I was lying to her. On the other hand, if I said yes, she'd kill me. Really, she'd take my life, just as she'd given it to me. Not for having a sleepover with a person she believed killed someone, but because she'd be convinced we had shared a bed, and God knew we hadn't.

"Answer me," she shrieked. "Did you sleep with a *sociopath*?"

Bad question again. If dozing in an upright position in close proximity to another sleeping person is "sleeping with" him, then I was guilty as charged. However, if she wanted to know whether Jazz and I knew each other in the biblical sense, well, absolutely not. Not to mention Jazz was not a sociopath. Still, her hand crawled like a tarantula up my earlobe to the cartilage at the tip, which really hurts when someone—even if she's sixty-seven years old—grabs it.

"Mommy . . ." I whimpered.

"*Answer me!*" she roared.

"But you asked me two different questions. First you asked if I'd spent the night with a murderer, and then you asked if I'd slept with a sociopath. Which one do you want me to answer?"

"Both!"

I hoped to high heaven none of my clients were milling about in the reception area. "Maggie? My clients—"

"Nobody is here," she said, utterly lacking in compassion. "I canceled all your clients for today and Friday."

"You canceled my clients? Why?"

"Because your mother and I are going to kick your butt,

Amanda Bell. You will need time to recover, heifer." She said this as matter-of-factly as she would say "You have a noon lunch appointment."

I stared at her, unbelieving. Maggie had on a pair of lavender wool slacks and a matching sweater. She'd pulled her hair into an elegant chignon. Delicate amethyst and diamond earrings hung in her lobes, which my mother hadn't assaulted like she did one of mine. Hearing this sweet-looking, elegant woman calling me names and threatening to kick my butt, and knowing she'd ambushed my business, was just wrong.

My mother, resplendent in a fuchsia knit dress with fabulous drape, continued her torture. "I want to know where you've been and why you've come to work looking like a video hoochie."

"Wait just a minute, Ma!"

"Don't interrupt me. Were you with him?"

I didn't care how she phrased it. I didn't want to answer her question. She progressed to what my great-grandmother would call "smacking me upside the head."

"Ouch! Ma, don't hit me! I just went to talk to his parents. He happened to be there. I hadn't had any sleep, and he insisted that I stay in the guest room. His parents were home the whole time. That's it."

She glared at me. So did Maggie.

"Can I get to my office now?" I asked.

My mother didn't respond, and I took that moment to zoom past her at breakneck speed to my office. I'd hoped to escape any additional assaults and sit quietly at my desk, healing. She wouldn't beat down a sistah who was sitting innocently at her desk, would she?

Ma followed. I sat in my purple chair, eyeing her warily. She lowered herself onto my couch. Yes, I have a couch. It works for me. Clients seem to enjoy it as they recount their joys and pains, but I've also been known to have a nap there now and then.

Ma regarded me for a moment before establishing some normalcy between us. She began, as Maggie would, with a clothing evaluation. Part two. Without fail, she'd start with . . .

"I've never cared for you in black."

"Thanks, Ma."

"The boots look cheap."

"They are cheap, Ma. The real ones are a hundred dollars more than your mortgage. These are Blahnik-*inspired*."

She threw her head back with a snort. "Without the style and excellent craftsmanship."

We sat quietly for a while, and I knew from her troubled expression that her concern had gone beyond my shoe budget. She crossed her legs, still amazing after sixty, and looked away from me. "I didn't know what had happened to you, so I called the police." Her voice broke, as did my heart when I heard it.

"Mama, I wouldn't do anything to purposely hurt you. I got caught up in all of this and just wasn't thinking straight. I should have called you."

"You're going to kill me. I need my nitroglycerin." She fanned herself for emphasis. "You shouldn't make an old lady exert herself that way."

First of all, I had not asked my mother to attack me. Second of all, my mother's heart was healthier than mine. She did aerobics at a chichi gym in downtown Detroit frequented by local celebrities, was twenty-five pounds lighter than I, was a perfect

size four, and had me convinced that she was an immortal. But all
I managed to eke out was "You don't take nitro, Ma."

"Well, I'll need to now." She swept her mid-shoulder-length
salt-and-pepper hair behind her shoulder in a nervous gesture.
And speaking of hair: "You look like Don King," she said.

"Ma, I had a cowboy hat on."

"Which should have prevented your hair from sticking up
like you've been electrocuted. Can't you get a perm, Bell?"

More silence between us.

"How is Addie holding up?"

"She's doing fine, considering." I shifted in my chair and
inclined toward my mother, hoping to gain her empathy. "She
and Jack don't believe Jazz had anything to do with Kate's murder."

"Of course they don't. He's their son."

"But Mama, Jack is a retired cop with a praiseworthy record.
Don't you think he would choose justice over Jazz?"

"If you were in trouble, I'd take you on the lam, and we'd live
out our days in Brazil getting sun." She thought for a moment.
"You'd have to wear a big straw hat and sunscreen, though. If you
get too much sun, you'll start to look older than you already do."

Thanks . . .

"Jack wouldn't take Jazz on the . . ." I didn't want to resort to
dialogue from old movies on the Turner Classic Movies network,
like her, but I couldn't think of anything better. "He wouldn't take
him on the lam."

"You don't know that. You're not a parent."

Just a friendly reminder of my barrenness.

I couldn't argue with her. Nothing I had to say would make

her feel better anyway. I sulked, my desk a barrier between us that felt as big as the Grand Canyon, until she made a brave effort to cross it. "I don't like to interfere with your personal life, but I want you to stop seeing him."

No, she didn't like to interfere with my personal life. She *loved* to interfere with my personal life. Still, I had never seen my strong, beautiful mother afraid, and I'd seen her almost every-thing. She had appeared unfazed even when she and my father divorced after she had been out of the workforce for twenty years. Breast cancer? She'd beaten it like eggs for an omelet—and we never once saw her cry or feel sorry for herself. I got up from my purple throne and went to her. She scooted over on the couch to accommodate me.

Suddenly, my head felt too big for my shoulders. Fatigue and tension weighed on my neck. My ear still hurt. "He doesn't want to see me, Ma. He doesn't think it's safe. You don't have to worry about me being with Jazz."

She looked surprised. "Really?"

I nodded.

She harrumphed. "I almost respect him for that."

I lay my head on her shoulder. "I slept for thirteen hours, and I still feel tired."

She wrapped her arms around me. "When you were just a little thing, I used to sing you 'All the Pretty Little Horses.' Do you remember that?"

I smiled. "I remember. And you'd rock me. You used to do that until I was way too old for it."

Ma laughed. "Yes, you were nine years old the last time I sang it to you. You'd been outside playing and came inside and announced I didn't need to sing to you anymore." She rubbed my arm. "You said, 'I'm mature now.'"

I chuckled. "No way I said that."

"That's exactly what you said. It tickled me at the time, but later, when you ran back outside to play Barbies with your *mature* little girlfriends, I cried."

"Really, Ma?"

"You were my baby. Nobody wants to lose her baby. Do you understand what I'm telling you, ladybug?"

"Yes, Mama." She hadn't called me "ladybug" since I "matured." I nestled closer to her, and she squeezed me. We sat like that for a long time, Maggie not once interrupting us. When the quiet—pregnant with questions she wanted to ask and answers I'd hesitate to give—threatened to engulf us, she began to hum and finally sing:

> *Hush-a-bye don't you cry*
> *Go to sleep-y little baby*
> *When you wake, you shall have*
> *All the pretty little horses.*

If she thought I was being immature, it didn't bother me at all.

chapter
twelve

UNFORTUNATELY, warm and fuzzy moments with my mother did not last. Shortly after her lullaby, she resumed tormenting me on the topics about which mothers torment daughters who have disappointed them. After spending a month with her in the half hour that followed, I prayed for respite. God answered my prayer just before noon, when Ma opted to go to lunch with Maggie. The dish they'd devour would be me, for sure. I didn't mind. I decided to redeem some of the time I'd lost by paying Christine Webber a surprise visit.

I arrived in Royal Oak, hoping she'd be home, not knowing if I was burning very expensive gas in vain. Kalaya had let me know that Kate's funeral would be at eleven o'clock the following morning. I hoped to catch Christine at home with a network of friends and family who could help her through this tragedy.

Christine and Kate's house was a small, neat A-frame on a quiet street close enough to walk to downtown—primo real estate at a premium price. SUVs filled the driveway and spilled into the street. I got out of the Love Bug and made my way to the porch. The lace curtains that dressed the open windows made it easy to see the bustle of activity inside. A multigenerational group of people—mostly women—milled about, holding drinks and plates of food. I knocked on the door, saying a quick prayer for help that started with something like *Lord, I know Jazz wouldn't like this, but* . . . and waited to see if help would come.

A short, thin white woman of about fifty, with spiky white hair and Tammy Faye Bakker mascara, opened the door. She had on a white faux-fur miniskirt that truly would have made my mother need nitroglycerin tablets, especially having seen it on a woman this age. A red long-sleeved cashmere T-shirt with a skull on the front and black-and-white stripes on the arms topped the skirt. Outrageous electric-blue platform-heel boots, circa '73, completed the ensemble. I smiled at the woman and gave her a few thousand dance-to-your-own-drummer points.

"Are you here for Chrissy?" she said warmly.

Thank God for fur-skirt lady. "I'm with the Washtenaw County Jail," I said, as if that had any relevance whatsoever to the case. "I just have a few questions for her."

Fur-skirt lady's face fell. Apparently, Chris had been questioned, and her friend didn't look like she appreciated the implications that came with that. She probably also wondered what in the world Washtenaw County had to do with the case.

I briefly touched her elbow. "I'm not a police officer. I'm a forensic psychologist. I'm just doing a brief psychological autopsy. I only want to know what Kate's last days were like. I'd really like to help the police find who killed Christine's partner."

This seemed to appease her a bit. She moved to the side, allowed me to enter, and pointed through the crowd. "She's over there by the futon."

"Thank you." I realized my social graces were lacking. "I'm sorry. I'm Amanda."

"Tori," she said.

"Do you think you could discreetly let her know I need to speak with her?"

"Sure."

Fur skirt meandered her way through the mourners, and I followed her to where Christine sat in the center of a sofa, flanked by two women and a man draped lazily on the sofa's arm.

All I could think was *Wow*. Christine was stunning. She had the regal presence of Maya Angelou. Snatches of a Maya poem, *Phenomenal Woman*, came to mind: *Pretty women wonder where my secret lies. / I'm not cute or built to suit a model's fashion size.*

No, I wouldn't call her cute, but she had the formidable presence of a queen. Long jet-black dreadlocks flowed down her neck. She was dressed like Addie Lee, in an amazing silk caftan with an African-inspired print. Bone bracelets crept up her arms. Unlike Addie, she had muscle tone—I could see that even through the caftan. Her arms resembled a boxer's. Jazz must not have been kidding when he'd said she could rumble. *Float like a butterfly, sting like a bee*. And with the size of her hands, that would be some sting. She had a definite edge about her, ghetto toughness, like she'd seen too many bad things in life and had grown a hard shell around her soft center. I'd seen this in other women cops—though not all—and in women who'd lived on the streets for a long time.

Tori whispered something in Christine's ear, and Christine looked up at me. She sized me up in that way I'd seen only cops do. She stood and gestured with her head toward a hallway. I went with her, all eyes in the room following us for about two seconds before their attention went back to the people in the room who were far more interesting than me.

She opened a bedroom door; coats were piled high on the bed. The room was decidedly feminine, with Laura Ashley florals, tastefully done. A soft shade of lavender colored the walls, matching the lavender-and-lilac flower print on the bedspread. Chris pushed the coats to the side and made a place for me to sit. "Sorry I don't have any place else to take you. As you can see, the house is full." Her voice sounded both melodic and authoritative, a smoky, Jazz singer's alto. She could have been an old-school African-American actress like Cicely Tyson. I wondered how a woman like this ended up being a cop; what tragedy—if any—had driven her to the job? She eyed me warily. "I didn't expect this many people. Kate's family took over all the funeral arrangements, and I'm"—she sighed deeply—"just here with my sistahs, trying to make my way through this . . ." Whatever else she would have said, she swallowed. She regarded me with the cool detachment of a person who needed to keep her hurt at a minimum. "Tori said you're from the Washtenaw County Jail. What do you have to do with Kate's murder?"

"I'm doing her psychological autopsy."

"Why is that? Wayne County hasn't sent anyone here for that. Why would Washtenaw?"

"I'm on my own, Ms. Webber."

"Call me Chris."

"Okay, Chris. I'm looking into Kate's death privately. I happened to be on the scene at her death investigation."

"Why is that?" Chris kept her expression even. "She wasn't

found in Washtenaw County. You're a little far from home, aren't you?"

"The DI on call asked me to attend. I'd worked with her on another case."

She stared at me but didn't question me on it.

I tried to sound like I actually had a reason to interview her. "Someone brutally murdered your partner. I want to know who would do that to her, and I'm committed to trying to find him."

"Or her?"

Interesting. A guilty person would take every imaginable opportunity to draw attention to someone—anyone—else. As a former homicide detective, she'd know that. What was she doing? "I'm not a police officer, Chris. It's not my job to interrogate you."

"I'm not sure why you're here at all. I'm hoping you'll tell me."

I cleared my throat, a nervous gesture I should have been conscious enough to avoid letting her see. "I'm a behaviorist. I look at people. Watch what they do. I find patterns in behavior. I believe my work can help me discover who's responsible for her death."

A tight smile spread across her lips. "I do the same thing." She paused. "I'm not implying that I'm still a homicide detective, but I still take care of people."

Interesting choice of words: *I still take care of people.*

"If you'd be kind enough to answer some questions, I'd like to get a clear picture of who Kate was, how she spent her days, and who she spent them with."

Chris cocked her head and sized me up again. "Why are you investigating on your own?"

"The woman you love is dead. She needs all the help she can get."

"What's in this for you?"

"I saw her, Chris. No one deserves to die that way."

She shook her head slowly, closed her eyes, then turned her head and gazed to the right. Her expression collapsed to a flat, disengaged affect. Christine had gone to some terrible inner place.

Wait. Her eyes had shifted right. In memory. Had she seen the crime-scene photos? Would Bobby Maguire have told her what Kate looked like? About the pose? Or was she just imagining Kate as she looked now, at the funeral home? Either image would be horrible enough, but I'd seen something in the way she'd shaken her head.

Chris asked a question. I'd been so deep in my own thoughts that I didn't hear her. "Excuse me?" I said.

"I said what's your name?"

"I'm Dr. Amanda . . ."

God, can I just borrow my mother's maiden name for a minute? It's really not convenient to be a Brown right now.

Of course, Chris in no way possessed the unflappable mien of Bobby Maguire. She wouldn't let me get away with just Dr. Amanda.

"Your last name, please." She commanded it. She must have been fierce in homicide.

"Brown. I'm Dr. Amanda Brown."

"Brown?"

I nodded.

She grunted. Shook her head in disgust. "Amanda Brown,

also known as Bell. I should have seen it. You look just like her."

I didn't want to ask, but how could I not? "Who are *you* speaking of?" I asked, not so much feigning innocence but giving her the opportunity to tell me whom she thought I looked like. At least that's what I hoped she would do.

Chris's regal posture stiffened considerably. Tension seemed to gather in her shoulders and arms. She clenched her sting-like-a-bee fists. "You're here for Jazz." A statement, not a question.

"I'm here for Kate."

She didn't raise her voice, but she inclined toward me with a venom-dipped whisper. "I know exactly who you are. You look just like your sister, Carly Brown. You're Jazz's woman, and you're not here for my Katie. You're at the wrong house, girlfriend. I suggest you leave now, or things may get ugly."

Did everybody know about Jazz and me? And when did I become his woman? Not to mention she just said I need to leave and could start reciting Mohammed Ali quotes any minute—and not about floating butterflies!

"This isn't what you think, Chris. Yes, I want to help Jazz, but I don't think he did it."

"Why would you? You're his woman."

"There are others who don't think he did it, either."

I watched her reaction. One carefully sculpted brow subtly lifted. My theory had surprised her. "Keep talking," she said. She unfurled her stingers.

"Kalaya Naylor met with me this morning. Do you know who she is?"

"She's that reporter for the *Beat*. Kate met with her a few a times."

"I'd gone to see Bobby Maguire, and Ms. Naylor wanted information. She approached me. She told me about Kate's story. Did you know what she was trying to do?"

Chris sighed, pushed the mound of coats to the side, and lay against them. "Kate always had some crazy hustle going on. She drove me absolutely nuts with her schemes. I knew about it and told her she needed to drop it. She could upset a lot of people with that mess. She could make a lot of enemies."

"Do you think she told anyone else she planned on getting Kalaya to do an exposé?"

"No. As indiscreet as Katie was, she wanted the story to be a surprise. She didn't advertise it to the people she planned to call out."

"And you're sure of this."

Chris nodded. "Reasonably." She paused and fiddled with one of her dreadlocks.

"I have two thoughts about this story she wanted to do. One: maybe whoever hurt her didn't want his wife or significant other to know what he'd done, even if he wasn't a person who could sell newspapers. Two: Kalaya and I suspect she'd snagged someone who wasn't a cop. Maybe a politician. Someone who'd want to keep a low profile to keep from hurting his career."

"What makes you so sure it was a man?"

That question again? "Look, I'm not saying that I'm an expert profiler, but I am seeing patterns emerge."

Her eyes widened almost imperceptibly, but I noticed. Was that a flicker of fear I saw? "What patterns?"

"She had something done to her that a woman wouldn't do." I watched her carefully for any sign of reaction.

An unmistakable flash of recognition showed in her eyes. "And what was that, Dr. Brown?"

Dr. Brown? The first time she's used a name for me. She's letting me know I've touched a nerve while acknowledging my expertise. Very interesting.

My mind whirred like a hard drive trying to process what was happening here. I went back to the scene. In my mind, I saw Carly pulling back the sheet on Kate's body, a sheet that had no business being there if she'd been purposely posed. What murderer covers a body?

One that's ashamed. One trying to hide his crime. Or . . . someone who feels empathy. Someone who loves her?

"Where were you on the night Kate was murdered?"

Chris stood. "You'd better go," she said, obviously seething.

I stood. "Did you see her at the scene?"

"No." *Delayed timing. Stiff posture. No facial affect. She's lying.* "I was at my mama's house."

Now she'd mentioned an alibi, a bad one—who wouldn't name her mother as an alibi?

I'd lost ground with her, and I couldn't afford that. There was no way I'd build rapport now. I went for the gusto and let her know she was off the hook for now. "I believe the person responsible knew her intimately and yet had a profound dislike, even hatred, of her. Perhaps hated himself for being with her."

"That sounds like me most days."

More confessions. "Did Kate have some kind of diary, Chris?"

"You need to leave. I have a funeral tomorrow."

"I understand."

"Do you? Because I don't. I don't understand why I'm putting a beautiful, vibrant, thirty-year-old woman who had her whole life ahead of her in the ground tomorrow."

"Are you getting grief counseling?"

"That's for her *real* family. All I get are the whispers. I don't even get to sit with her family at the front of the church."

"Talk to someone about your feelings, Chris. It'll help you."

"I just might do that. I might even need to talk to a professional. Do you understand what I'm saying, Dr. Brown?"

An invitation?

"May I speak with you after the funeral?"

"Perhaps," she said. "I'll see how I feel."

A
S SOON as I got home that afternoon, I kicked off my cowboy boots, slipped out of my coat, and went to Amos's cage. My poor neglected sugar glider.

I opened the door to his cage, guarded yet optimistic. He must have missed human contact since I'd seen him last on Tuesday. This time he didn't hiss like the spawn of Satan merely because I'd come within three feet of him. I stuck my hand in the cage, praying, *God, please don't let Amos try to kill me,* and breathed a sigh of relief when the animal didn't rip into my wrists.

He came willingly into my hand, and I spoke to him in the low, soothing tones I used when an inmate at the jail was about to have an unfortunate psychotic episode that would not be beneficial to my person. Amos seemed pacified by my efforts, and I made the mistake of rubbing just behind his ear.

He hated it.

"*Haaaaaach*" emanated from his mouth, and it sounded so profoundly creepy that I could have sworn I'd seen a menacing green mist pour out with it. "Jesus," I whispered, "there's something wrong with Amos. I think he's possessed."

I didn't think Amos appreciated my diagnosis. That thing went after the mound of my thumb with gusto.

"What*ever*!" I yelled like a teenage girl. I'd had just about enough of Amos's incursions into my tender flesh. I set him on the end table where his cage rested, not even bothering to put him safely back inside. "You're on your own, you little beast. And I hope a vicious mouse gets you."

Amos hates me. And I'm stuck here with him. Can my life get any more depressing?

I shouldn't have wondered. As soon as I did, the telephone rang. I picked up the phone and heard the voice of Dr. McLogan, a friend of Mason May and the fertility specialist I'd seen about my endometriosis. The kindly silver-haired Irishman had seen me for the last few years, and I considered him almost as much of a friend as Mason did.

"Bell, my dear."

"Hi, Dr. McLogan."

"I'd like to see you as soon as possible. Can you come into my office in the morning?"

I worked at the jail on Thursdays, but my caseload happened to be light right now, and I didn't have any testing scheduled. I supposed the county could get along without me one more day. I still had a glut of personal days I hadn't taken. "Sure, what time would you like me to be there?"

"How about ten o'clock?"

"I'll see you then." A pause, more pregnant than I wanted it to be, followed. "Dr. McLogan?" I asked fearfully.

"It's not the best news, dear one."

Uh-oh. He'd gone from "my dear" to "dear one," and there was a difference. "Is it really bad news?"

"It could be. Bring your friend with you." He meant Rocky. I'd taken him with me the last time, and we'd actually discussed him being a donor for me.

"Okay," I said. The doctor rang off, and I found myself standing in the living room, listening to the buzz of the dial tone in my ear.

It's over. I'm never going to have a baby.

The throbbing pain in my hand snapped me out of my trance. When the tears streamed down my face, I told myself it was because my hand hurt.

After I'd tended to my war wounds—physical and emotional— I called Kalaya Naylor and asked her to meet me at my place. She would be a welcome diversion. I didn't have time to clean up my apartment much, but was hoping the easy grace Kalaya had exhibited in conversation would extend to her skipping the white-glove test when she entered my humble abode.

When she arrived, she walked into my place with a smirk. It didn't look like my mother's smirk; it actually seemed affirmative. She took off her coat without me asking her for it, and she put it in my closet herself. She'd exchanged her earlier outfit for sweats, K-Swiss sneaks, and a Sarah Lawrence sweatshirt.

As her eyes swept the room, I couldn't help wondering if she was evaluating me. That should have made me uncomfortable, but from Kalaya, it was about as disagreeable as a little sister looking into a big sister's purse just to see what mysteries it held.

She closed my closet door, and "I love your apartment" nearly burst out of her. "It's dope."

"Shabby chic meets Africa, I've heard."

"But heavy on the chic."

"My mother would say heavy on the shabby."

"That's a mother for you."

I beckoned her into the living room, and she looked around as if she'd never seen flea-market furniture before. In my defense, I said, "I get a little crazy at open markets."

She shook her head. "But you change everything. You make it hip. This is all so DIY." I was glad she was into the do-it-yourself movement, too. Maybe I'd find in her a partner to haunt the thrift stores and flea markets with in the spring.

Kalaya fingered an armoire I'd found around Halloween. I'd painted it a color that the paint manufacturer called Ashes of Roses, and I'd added accents with gold leafing. The color and the piece's whimsical beauty had made me think of the miniseries *The Thorn Birds*—which I hadn't seen in years—and had inspired me to buy the series on DVD. One lonely night when I'd ached for Jazz, I'd plopped down on my bed and watched it. When I'd finished, I'd made a little prayer corner by putting a few things I loved on top of the armoire. Candles, the prayer beads Jazz had given me, a little picture of him I'd taken with my cell phone's camera, and a picture of Ma Brown were all arranged artfully and prayerfully. I'd go to my little sacred space and light a candle, then pray for Jazz and me, thinking of the priest and Meggie and marveling at how simply loving the wrong person can cause so much pain.

"What's the shrine about?" Kalaya said.

I didn't detect any sarcasm in her voice. "It's not really a shrine, just a place I set aside to remember some things in prayer."

"Do you pray that you two will work things out?"

"I won't answer on the grounds that I might incriminate myself."

She chuckled. "What's up with the sweet-looking old lady?"

"She's there to give me strength."

"Who is she?"

"My great-grandmother and namesake. The first Amanda Bell Brown."

"Maternal or paternal?"

"Paternal, but my mother adored her, and she adored my mother."

"Is she Native American? Look at those cheekbones."

"Her father was part Cherokee and part Irish Scot. Her mother was a slave. A real mixed bag, she."

"Ah, miscegenation."

"Ah, indeed."

We headed over to my sofa and sat side by side. I propped my feet up on the coffee table. She looked at me sheepishly. "Go ahead," I said.

She stretched those long legs out and crossed them on the table. "Girl, you are truly my friend. So, whatcha got?"

"Off the record."

"Come on, Bell."

"Off the record, Kalaya. I shouldn't have even been at the

scene of the crime. Telling you anything could compromise the investigation. In fact, you knew Kate. You'd been with her in the last weeks of her life. You could be a suspect yourself."

Her mouth dropped. She sputtered, trying to find words that wouldn't come out.

I cracked up. "Jazz did that to me once. I had the same reaction."

She gave me a playful shove. "You nearly gave me a heart attack, fool."

"Ah-ah-ah. In Matthew 5:22, Jesus said, 'Whosoever shall say, Thou fool, shall be in danger of hell fire.'"

"Girl, I've been in danger of hell fire for a long time, and it has nothing to do with me calling you a fool."

"Jesus can take care of that, you know. Why don't you go back to Him?"

"Because I've strayed way too far. Hey, can you just tell me what you've got and proselytize me later?"

"You promise to hear my 'go back to Jesus' pitch?"

"Is it a good one? Or are you going to give me some of those J.T.C. tracts that used to terrify me when I was a kid?"

I laughed, remembering the little black-and-white cartoon tracts that Chick Publications had put out for years. "Do they still make those tracts? I may do both."

"Yes! And any time I see one, I get the willies."

"I promise my Jesus pitch won't give you the willies. I'm all about being relational these days. That's how we do it at the Rock House. I'll love you back to Jesus in practical ways."

"I'm gonna hold you to that." She swept back her long cornrows. "Now, tell me what you've got and then give me some snacks. What kind of relational witness are you, anyway?"

I still couldn't decide how much I could trust her, but I needed her. She was my only real ally in trying to find information. Even the Browns weren't being helpful. "Let me feed you." Just like Jesus told me to.

"The kind who's trying to lose twenty-five pounds." I got up and headed into the kitchen. "I have Christine at the crime scene."

Kalaya shot up off the couch like fireworks. She zoomed into the kitchen. "For *real*?"

"For real." I opened my snack cabinet and found a box of Nabisco 100 Calorie Packs Cheese Nips. I held them out to her.

She groaned. "Those are so lame."

"Not to big girls."

"You're not big."

"The only other snacks I have are Oreo Thin Crisps."

"Like these things?"

"Yes."

"We're so not friends anymore."

I put the box back in my cabinet, leaned against the counter, and thought a minute. "I can grill you a chicken breast."

"We're friends again."

"You're awfully high-maintenance, Kalaya."

"Is that why nobody hangs out with me?"

I went to the fridge to pull out the chicken breast I'd thawed for dinner. Fortunately, I'd planned on having stir fry the next night and had an extra one. I grabbed the chicken, a bowl, and the spices for a marinade. I mixed the whole thing with a little olive oil and lemon juice and let it sit on the countertop.

"Nobody hangs out with you, probably because they think you'll write about them in your scathing political pieces."

"That was a rhetorical question."

"Sorry. I couldn't resist."

"I'm overrated, you know."

"Glad to hear it. What do you want to drink?"

"You got margarita fixin's? Lots of tequila?"

"Nope. I've got bottled water, Crystal Light, and Diet Pepsi. I used to have wine, but I got rid of it for Amos." I padded into the living room.

"Amos? You got a new boyfriend?"

"Not quite."

"I'm intrigued. Tell me about this Amos."

"Anybody ever tell you you'd make a good therapist? Three-fourths of my job is asking some variation of 'tell me about that.'"

"Mine, too. Maybe you should be a journalist. I'll take a Pepsi."

"Pepsi it is."

"Don't try to distract me with career choices. I haven't forgotten about Christine. Or this Amos."

"I know you haven't."

"So which do you want to tell me about first?"

"Amos, since he's standing right behind you."

Kalaya turned, looking confused, until her eyes went to the floor. Then she let out a scream that could pierce your eardrums. "What is that thing?" She pointed wildly at him.

He hissed, which made her scream again and run out of the kitchen.

Amos scurried out of the room behind her. The poor thing. People kept having bad reactions to him. I'd be unfriendly, too, under those circumstances.

I calmly called out to the living room, "It's a sugar glider." I didn't mention his homicidal tendencies. I returned to my chicken marinade as if a screaming reporter tearing out of my kitchen was normal. "I'm surprised you don't know that. You're a journalist. You're supposed to have all kinds of arcane knowledge."

"I have a fact checker," she yelled. "He knows everything. *Shazam!* Did you see its crazy, beady eyes?"

I laughed. "Shazam" must have been her toned-down version of an expletive.

I washed my hands in the kitchen sink. "He doesn't have beady eyes. His eyes remind me of my pastor Rocky's, and Rock has the kindest eyes in the world."

"Remind me not to meet your pastor."

I walked back into the dining area. Kalaya stood flush against a wall as if Amos were the size of a mountain lion instead of a Beanie Baby. The poor woman was shaking like one of my clients on Haldol. I said, "Have a seat. You look like you can stand that Pepsi right about now."

"I don't want a Pepsi. I need that margarita I talked about. A strong one. A pitcher, in fact."

"You'll be okay in a minute. I'm a psychologist. I can help you process this experience."

"I need more help than you can offer. I may need to hear that 'go back to Jesus' pitch sooner than I realized. That thing scared me to death." She fanned herself. "And speaking of death . . ."

Always the reporter. "Have a seat, Kalaya."

She peeled herself off my wall and dropped cautiously into a dinette chair. "What's this about Christine being at the crime scene?"

"She saw something. She won't admit it, but I can tell."

"How?"

"She lied. I talk to liars all day at the jail. Bad ones. That's probably why they're in jail. If I could gain her trust, I think I could weasel a confession out of her."

"You think she did it?"

"Anything is possible. I think she did something, for sure. It's what I saw at the scene. A big clue says someone who loved Kate was at that scene."

"You're my new best friend, Bell."

"You're just saying that to get at my chicken."

"The chicken I don't smell cooking?"

"It's marinating."

"So why would Christine be there?"

"Maybe Kate called her and told her Jazz beat her up. She said she was at her mother's. I wonder how close that is to Jazz's loft."

"I can find out." Kalaya drummed her fingers on the table. "Do you know Kate's ETD?"

"Carly estimated Kate had been dead a few hours or less. We went inside for Carly to pronounce her at eleven-thirty P.M. Maguire said she'd called the police at nine-oh-nine. Kalaya, Jazz came here that night. He showed up no later than nine-thirty."

"Wait. Who called the police in that short amount of time?"

"Kate Townsend did, if you can believe that."

"Holy Moses!" She took furious notes. "You're sure about the time Jazz got to you?"

"Pretty sure. I purchased Amos from Exotic Petz that night. I was there until right before the store closed at nine. It's five minutes from my house, and as soon as I got home, I took a shower and put on my pajamas. Jazz came right after that."

"Did he call you before he came? There would be phone records."

"Unfortunately, he just showed up."

"Did you look at a clock?"

"No, but—"

"So you really have no proof of what time he arrived? No stand-up-in-court proof?"

"Well . . ."

I didn't have to finish my statement. She'd stopped listening. I could practically see her mind working. Her fingers tapped on the table. "Did Maguire pull phone records for Kate and Jazz?"

"He's not telling me anything."

"Maybe Kate called Christine and she went to Jazz's place mad because her woman was at her ex's loft. She easily could have killed her. She's an intimidating woman. Don't let those fly African clothes fool you. Did you see her hands?"

"I saw them and her fists. But I don't think she strangled Kate. Just because Chris is a daunting figure and a liar doesn't mean she killed her partner, even if they used to fight."

Kalaya shrugged dramatically. "Then again, what do I know? I don't kill people."

"At least not physically."

"Ha, ha, ha. I don't kill people with my words, either. I happen to be an ethical journalist. Mostly. If I weren't, I'd be scooping every paper in the metro area right now. What are the stats for domestic violence in same-sex relationships?"

"What, am I your fact-checker now?"

"Come on, Bell."

"It's just as prevalent as in hetero relationships, only the gay victims receive fewer protective services."

"Do you think Chris abused Kate?"

"Here's the thing. Of the two, Chris was obviously physically stronger, but that doesn't tell me about anything except their body types. I've been gathering information, and from the picture I'm putting together of Kate, she could very well have been the dominant partner—especially emotionally—and the dominant partner is the abuser across the board."

"Kate abusing Christine? I don't see it."

"Think about it. Kate was a serial cheater and, to judge from the psychological profile I'm gathering, probably a pathological liar."

Kalaya nodded. "Yeah. I did find out that she'd filed several reports that Jazz beat her up—none of which could be verified."

"She was also a cutter. She slashed her arms with razor blades. What do all these behaviors have in common?"

"You mean besides being nutty?"

"I wouldn't say 'nutty' is quite a clinical term. Try again."

She sighed. "I don't know. They could be a cry for help, but they could also be manipulative."

"Exactly. She was unstable, couldn't keep a job, was unpredictable, hated rejection. I think Kate had a personality disorder."

"Like what?"

"I think she was borderline."

"What's that? I don't have my fact-checker available." She winked at me.

"Borderline personality disorder is a severe psychiatric condition that presents as extreme emotional instability."

Kalaya gave me a deadpan stare. "I'm not a doctor, I just play one on TV. You wanna break that down for me?"

"I'm saying, this is what borderline personality disorder looks like: A person would have all those characteristics I just described in Kate, and more. She'd be an interpersonal-relationship nightmare."

"No wonder Jazz swore off dating. That is, until—"

"Shut up, Kalaya."

"I'm just sayin'—"

"Stop saying. Now, I'm only speculating, but if Kate was borderline, she'd have had the potential to make a lot of enemies."

"That's obvious. The question is, which enemy killed her?"

"Chris wouldn't give up information about the diary."

"Darn it."

"Are you toning down your language for me?"

"Yes, I am."

"I think the Holy Spirit is after you."

"Leave it be, Bell."

"You know I'm not going to do that if you're ripe for the harvest."

"If I'm ripe, I'll take a shower. How are we going to find out who she was seeing right before she died?"

"Whoever it is—and I think it's a man—he had to leave some

kind of trail. He couldn't very well take her home with him if she was a secret. They had to have their little rendezvous somewhere, and probably not the house she shares with Christine."

"True."

"There has to be a trail. Somebody knows who he is. I think Christine is going to talk to me again, maybe after the funeral tomorrow. I think she wants to unburden herself to a nice psychologist."

"Oh, yea-ah! Coolness!" Kalaya put up her hand to give me a high five, which I heartily returned.

"So, how is Jazz?" she asked.

"What makes you think I've been with him?"

"Who said I thought you've been with him? You're telling on yourself."

"Busted. He's fine."

"I know he's *fine*, but how is he doing?"

"I couldn't tell. I was too busy looking at how fine he is."

She giggled. "You're silly."

"Seriously, he's doing okay. How'd you know I'd talked to him?"

"I got a friend who works for Channel Seven. I saw the footage of you at the house. I told her you weren't significant."

"You did that for me?"

"Who knows? I may need a favor someday."

"A real altruist, eh?"

"I'm working on it," she said. She grinned and rubbed her tummy. "And next time dinner is on me."

"Don't worry about it. I've got a feeling we'll be sharing a lot more meals."

"Do you mind?"

"It will be my pleasure."

I was going to trust God that sheep weren't vicious animals.

Sometimes a girl just has to have a pampering day. After I extracted Kalaya from my couch—my goodness! That girl needed friends—I hustled over to African Essence and let the sistah braiders work their magic on my hair. I got Kalaya-style cornrows that boldly cascaded down my back. I may have looked like an over-the-hill Alicia Keys, but I could do worse.

Next stop, my friend and former prayer partner Lisa Kane's downtown pampering paradise, the Lady Day Spa. She fluffed, primped, and primed me as often as I let her, which was not nearly as often as she would have wanted. And she let me know it, complaining every time I saw her.

I'd talked Lisa into staying open after hours to give me the works. She took one look at me, and her blue eyes registered surprise. Then the petite dark-haired cutie, draped in a white lab coat and scrubs, grinned. "Wow!" she said in her faint Kentucky-by-way-of-Maryland drawl. "This is a different look for you."

"A new friend inspired me. I think it's kinda sexy."

She raised an eyebrow. "Sexy! Uh-oh. Come on in here, Mandy Bell. You're gonna get the works, all right. And we might just have ourselves a little Bible study, too."

"What? Did I say something wrong? Come on. I just want to be cute today." Nobody else in the world had permission to call me Mandy Bell. But it sounded great when Lisa said it.

"You didn't say 'cute.' You said 'sexy,' and what's worse, you do look sexy. What's going on, girlie?"

"Lisa! You're a sexy woman. You make women feel beautiful every day. It's what you do. I'm just here so you can do what you do for me."

"Mandy Bell. You know I don't have any problem with women looking sexy, but I've known you for ten years and have never seen you try to look sexy. Have you changed your style or what?"

I blushed. I didn't dare tell her I'd changed my style since the night Jazz showed up at my door with scratches on his face and a dead wife in his bed.

"Well?" Lisa persisted. "Where are your boring blue suits and too much black?"

"In the closet. I can't wear them to a spa day, can I?"

Lisa sighed. Although it looked like she'd given up, I knew she'd bring the topic up again later.

I distracted myself by taking in the sounds and the sights of the place. The walls had soothing, soft greens and blues painted in waves and swirls, like the ocean. Scattered about was soft sand-colored furniture that you could imagine adorning a summer house in the islands. CDs pumped out nature sounds, chanting, or jazz, especially Lady Day. It smelled like heaven in there. I went right to the dressing room in back, peeled off my clothing, and put on the fluffy white robe Lisa had waiting for me. In the massage room, I disrobed and climbed on the massage table, tight as a drum, smelling Nag Champa incense.

Lisa opened several bottles of essential oils and her special signature-blend massage oil. "I want to begin with an aromatherapy massage. You need calming, healing oils right now, the emphasis being on 'calming.'"

Lisa got started trying to work the kinks out of my shoulder. "Relax, Bell."

"I am relaxed."

She worked in silence for five minutes or so. "You're seeing him, aren't you?"

"Who?"

"Jazz. Of television fame this week."

"When did you start watching the news?"

"When Rocky told the whole church to pray for the two of you. And what do you think you're doing, young lady?"

Lisa and I are the same age, but somehow, she's older. "I'm being a friend. They're in short supply for him right now."

"You, a friend? Friends are always in short supply for you."

That stung. I got quiet.

She stopped working and stroked my hair. "I didn't say that to be a meanie. But you've gotta admit, you haven't made much of an effort to spend time with those of us who love you. And now this guy is in trouble, and you show up talking about being sexy. How could I not be concerned?"

"I know I won't win any awards for being a friend in deed, but I'm working on it. Jazz needs me. More than you. More than Rocky. I just want to help him."

"You're in love with him."

"People say that like it's a crime. What's wrong with loving somebody?"

"What if he's a murderer?"

"I don't think he is."

She stared at me until I wilted. "Okay. I'm not one hundred percent sure, but there are some things—"

She smacked my back, hard, then continued to knead my muscles. I could tell she was trying to be objective, even though she hadn't been since I'd walked through the door. "You can't do anything for him all knotted up, you know." We didn't speak for a few more moments, while Lisa kneaded my shoulder muscles. She broke the silence. "Are you praying *The Divine Hours* with us?"

"No, but does saying 'Oh my God' count as prayer?"

"Yes, but you could add to that, you know. When was the last time you came to church?"

"Uh. Two weeks?"

"Try again. We've been doing *The Divine Hours* since the end of October."

The Divine Hours was a modern prayer book based on the Book of Common Prayer. Compiled by Phyllis Tickle, it had changed Rocky's life, so he'd gifted the Rock House with it by implementing a churchwide practice of the spiritual discipline of fixed prayer four times a day. I'd been at church when Rocky had announced we'd begin. But I hadn't returned since then? "Has it been that long?"

She karate-chopped my neck. "I've never seen you this tense. You can't be his savior, Bell."

"Whose?"

"His."

I huffed. "What? You suddenly can't say 'Jazz' now? You said it a few minutes ago. You're playing it on your CD player."

"And you're snooping, aren't you?"

"Sleuthing."

"Same thing. Being a friend is one thing. Sleuthing, which *sounds* much safer than it is, is another. Let the police handle it. You know what happened to you last time."

No one in my life would let me forget. "Someone has to help him. Even the police think he did it. I'm not so sure."

"And how do you know?"

"I don't. Not for certain. But I just don't think he's guilty."

"That isn't good enough. You're making *me* tense."

"You don't have to worry about me, Lisa."

"Let me be the judge of that." She worked in silence for a few minutes. "Is there something else going on with you physically?"

"Why do you ask?"

"You're literally fighting your own body. What's up?"

I didn't say anything.

"What is it, Mandy Bell? Spill it." She brushed back a lock of dark-chocolate-colored hair and stopped to refresh her hands with a fragrant lemongrass oil.

"Since the murder, when I've been with Jazz—"

"You're not having sex with him, are you?"

"No, I don't mean I've *been* with him. I mean . . . it's like we're gasoline and fire."

"You mean you're fighting with him?" Her hands went back to work on my neck.

"No, we're not fighting. Well, yes, we are, but I always fight with Jazz. What I mean is we're an inferno. It's like suddenly, we can't keep our hands off each other. It's not like before."

"That worries me. It sounds like the law of diminishing

returns is at work. You need more and more stimulation to achieve the same . . . I don't know, high or something. It's like an addiction in a way."

"You think I'm getting addicted to touching him?"

"I'm saying you seem to need more."

"That doesn't sound good."

"It would be fine if you were engaged and planning to be wed soon, but you're not. As I work on you, I get a sense that you're at war with your body. All this stuff is going on. You're bearing a lot of burdens right now. Heavy ones. You're like . . . a donkey!"

Okay, that whole donkey image did not please me.

She went on, "You said your prayer life isn't what it should be, and you aren't the best at attending church right now. What kind of support and accountability do you have to help you deal with all this stress, not to mention the temptation of having a very good-looking, very needy man in your life?" She paused in her lecture, kneading me harder. "And now you want to look sexy for him."

"Who says it's for him?"

"If it were for you, why choose *now* to get sexy? Girlie, how long do you think your purity is going to last with a man like that? And I'm going to go out on a limb here, but my guess is that he's not quite himself right now. How can you expect him to have the strength to be godly at a time like this?"

"He's not strong, though he's trying. And I'm trying, too. I'm resisting him, Lisa, as much as I can."

"What are you going to do?"

"He wants me to stay away from him until this mess is straightened out."

"Smart man. But are you?"

"What do you mean? Of course I'm going to do what he says."

"I know you, my friend. You're not going to stay away."

"I am, Lisa."

"You're in over your head."

"I know."

"Can you go away? Go to the cabin and chill by the lake. You won't have clients during the holidays. Just go up there with your Bible and a couple of books. In fact, leave the books."

"I can't leave."

"Not if you think you're going to save someone, you can't."

"I'm not trying to save him."

"Exactly what are you trying to do?"

"I don't know. I just want to help him. He's my friend."

"He's more than that, and you know it."

I let out a deep, cleansing breath. "I dunno, girl. I keep reaching into my bag of tricks to find something to help me figure this out, and I keep coming up empty. I can't intellectualize this. I'm a bundle of feelings right now."

"In a body that's desperately trying to contain all those feelings. You're going to blow a gasket if you don't find release."

I laughed. "That didn't sound very clinical."

"I'm not a psych major anymore. I can be my sassy Southern self. Are you sure you're not going to be hanging around him?"

"Yes. He told me to stay away. I think he means it."

"Don't be too sure about that. Can I tell you something as a sister in Christ?" She made feathery movements up and down my spine.

"Uh-oh," I said. "'Sister in Christ'? You're about to slam me, aren't you?"

"No. Now, can I tell you?"

"Go ahead."

She stopped working, stepped around to face me, and fixed those blue eyes on mine. "Things are happening. Awful things. If you two aren't careful, you're going to do what's natural and find consolation in each other. You could easily end up in bed together, because both of you are vulnerable. Then what are you going to do?"

Slam!

I took a deep breath. I didn't have an answer for her.

chapter
fourteen

I FELL INTO A FITFUL STATE of unrest after making all the phone calls possible to concerned friends and family. I talked on the phone until one in the morning, glad for the distraction, but in the quiet of the night, I couldn't stop thinking about my conversation with Lisa.

You could easily end up in bed together, because both of you are vulnerable. Then what are you going to do?

I thought sleep would be a welcome reprieve from my inner chaos. At last I dozed. However, under an hour later, I heard a loud pounding at my door. I scrambled to rouse myself and stumbled into the living room.

I glanced at Amos's cage. I feed him, keep his cage clean, but does he protect *me*? Nary a sound. Obviously, his repertoire did not include barking to actually ward off people about to break my door down in the middle of the night. I gave him a dirty look. I hadn't made it past the couch when I heard a key go into the lock.

Is that Ma? Or Carly? And with the ordinary magic of opening a door with a key, presto! My door opened. "Jazz!"

"Not so loud. You'll wake your neighbors."

"And you don't think anybody heard all that pounding?"

"I pounded thoughtfully."

"When did you get a key to my apartment?"

"When I purchased the locks."

"I didn't say you could have a key."

"I buy the locks, I get a key."

"No wonder the guy only gave me one set. I just thought he was cheap! How could he give you my keys?"

"Can I help it that people assume things because we have the same last name?"

"Why are you here?"

He didn't say anything, and I took a good look at him. I'd never seen Jazz disheveled. Even though he had on a cashmere turtleneck and jeans, he looked about as polished as Maguire. He hadn't slept well. His face was rough with stubble. He'd definitely had more than one beer.

"You shouldn't drink and drive."

"I didn't. I drank in your parking lot. A lot. No pun intended." He smiled at me. "You can take my keys if you want to."

"Jazz, you shouldn't be here, especially in this condition."

He looked me up and down. "You're looking way too fine tonight."

Dear Lord, so was he.

I realized I was quite underdressed. Impulsively, I looked down at what I had on. No ratty pajamas tonight. In an effort to sustain the feel-good that my new hairstyle and Lisa's diligent body work had wrought in me, I'd put on a slinky silver gown with a slit that I'd have to do business with God about.

Jazz's eyes told me he liked the look, and my body told me I liked Jazz liking it.

Need a little help here, Lord.

I gathered the fabric together in a makeshift chastity belt—most unsuccessfully.

"A little late for that, baby."

I dropped the skirt of my gown. "I'd better put something on."

"Yeah, you'd better."

I hightailed it to my room like I was on fire, and I was! Unfortunately, he followed me. He stopped at the door. "You know, no matter what you put on, I'm not going to forget that gown."

I sure hoped he wouldn't. And I wouldn't forget the smoldering look he gave me.

God! You really gotta help me out here!

"What are you going to do to stop me from running my fingers through those braids?"

That ain't helping, God.

"Running," I said, thinking maybe God had heard me after all, "now, that's a plan. I'll run as fast as I can."

"Sounds good. I get to chase you. I'll catch you, too."

I couldn't help myself. I still wanted to play naughty with him. "What if I escape?"

He gave me a slow, sexy grin. "You won't want to before I'm through with you."

"Can you excuse me, please?" I wondered how I was going to resist him when he'd been drinking and his defenses were down. I didn't need help to get my defenses down when it came to him.

My body felt fine-tuned to respond to him whenever he so much as came into my line of vision.

When he didn't move, I went back to frantically searching for my robe.

"It's in the living room, Bell."

"What?"

"Your useless covering. It's on your couch."

"My robe is not useless. It's . . ." I tried to get out the bedroom door. Honestly, I really did want to do the right thing, but he blocked me with his very hot body.

"Is this silk?" He rubbed the small of my back.

I closed my eyes in ecstasy. "Um-hmm."

"Lovely."

"I'm glad you like it."

"Not the gown. You're lovely."

"Jazz, we're going to go in the living room, and you are going to sit on the couch. I'm going to grab my robe. There's a Bible on the end table. You are going to sit there and read it like a good boy."

"The Bible?"

"Yes."

"Okay. I'll start in Genesis, where God said a little something about it not being good for a man to be alone."

"Okay, don't read the Bible."

"All that being fruitful and multiplying."

"I said don't read it."

"I could read the Song of Songs . . ." He inclined his long body close to mine. "'I have taken off my robe. How can I put it on again?'" He pinched my robeless waist. "Did you read the Song of Songs tonight, too?"

"That's not in there."

"Yes, it is, my beautiful Shulamite. She also said, 'My beloved put his hand by the latch of the door, and my heart yearned for him. I arose to open for my beloved.'" He grunted. "I've got my hand by your door latch. Maybe I can get you to open for me."

"You've got your hand by my door latch, all right, but I ain't opening nothin'! Now will you move so I can get my robe? Please."

His hands went around my waist. "How fair and pleasant you are, O love with your delights. This stature of yours like a palm tree—'"

"See, you're wrong. I'm short. I'm more like a shrub."

"'And your breasts like—'"

I screamed, "Jazz, if you say one word about my breasts—"

"Could you cut it out? I'm trying to quote Scripture here."

"How do you know all of that? Who memorizes the Song of Solomon?"

"I did. Last month, when I was trying to figure out how to win you back from emergent boy. Now, back to those twin fawns."

"I don't have fawns. They're more like . . . Chihuahuas."

Oh, Lord. How much is that enhancement going to cost me? Maybe Carly will help.

"'Let now your breasts be like clusters of the vine, the fragrance of your breath like apples, and the roof of your mouth . . . '"

I swooned.

"I'll tell you in a minute," he said with a wicked grin. He

gathered me into a kiss that left me as liquid as a puddle on the floor.

"Baby," I whispered. I hadn't meant to call him that, but there seemed to be two Bells, and one of them was in the mood for love. Okay, both were, but one of them was at least a little rational. She took over. "Will you wait just a minute on the couch for me?"

"You'll hurry."

"Um-hmm."

Man, I did not want him to step away from me.

He squeezed me and kissed my neck. "Don't make me wait too long."

I smiled in answer, trying desperately not to rip his clothes off his body.

He finally got away from my bedroom door. I closed it, pushed the bed in front of it—more to protect him from me than the other way around—grabbed my cell phone, and ran into the closet. I punched Kalaya's number as quickly as possible. She answered sleepily.

"I need help," I said.

"*Bell?* Is that you? Where are you?"

"I'm in my closet."

I could hear her struggle to wake herself. "Wha—? Your closet? Are you safe?"

"No."

"What's going on?"

"Jazz is here."

"Did he hurt you? Should I call the police?"

"No. He's quoting Scripture."

"What?"

"He's quoting the Bible by heart."

"I'm sorry. I don't see the problem."

"It's the Song of Solomon."

I waited for the realization to hit her.

"Oh. You *are* in trouble. What do you want me to do?"

"Come over here. I want to do it with him!"

"Now, I've heard of kinky, but—"

"Stop talking crazy, Kalaya. I need you to get me out of this."

"I can't come over. I've got company."

"Then I need you to pray!"

"Why didn't you call one of your Christian friends? I'm a backslider. God is mad at me."

"I can't call my Christian friends. They know Rocky, and they'd tell."

"Who is Rocky?"

"My pastor and ex-boyfriend."

"You dated your pastor? Ewwwwww."

"He's cute. And wonderful. Listen, Kalaya, everybody would be mad at me if they knew I let Jazz in and that I'm very, very interested in getting to know him better tonight. You're the only one who doesn't think he's guilty. So pray! For me! Not him. You can pray for him later."

"I told you, I'm not even alone tonight. I need prayer about that myself. God is mad at me."

"God loves you. He's not mad at you. And He needs you to accept Jesus as your personal savior right now, so you can help me."

"Is that your pitch? I was expecting some really profound theological treatise full of deep psychological insight—that whole 'The Lord is married to the backslider' thing—and all you come up with is 'Accept Jesus so I won't sleep with my boyfriend'?"

"Fine! You want a pitch? How 'bout this one: God loves you and has a wonderful plan for your life. That one got a *lot* of mileage. Now, repent so we can pray."

"I was planning on easing into it after several thoughtful discussions with you."

"Kalaya, the Holy Spirit is obviously working on you. Maybe that's why He brought us together. Praise God! But if you don't ask Jesus into your heart right now, I'm going to come over there tomorrow with some Jack Chick tracts."

"You wouldn't."

"I would. I'm talking the old-school, really scary ones. I'm coming with 'This Was Your Life,' Kalaya. You remember that one, don't you? The one with the big movie screen playing every evil thing you've ever thought or done?"

"That's the one that traumatized me."

"It traumatized *everybody*. That was Chick's point, to literally scare the hell out of us. Or scare us out of hell. Now do it."

"All right, you spiritual bully. But you lead the prayer."

I led her in the sinner's prayer, the kind on the back of those tracts. By the end I could hear her sniffling. I felt terrible.

"Kal, I'm sorry. I'm so selfish. I didn't mean to scare you."

"It's okay. I'm crying because . . ."

"Because what?"

"Because I just asked Jesus into my heart, and it feels good."

"Glad I can help. Now can you pray for *me*?"

"Um. Okay." She whooped. "Wow. This feels so dope. I'm a Christian again."

"Kalaya, this is about *me*!"

"You're going to have to work on that selfish spirit."

"Be a Christian for a week before you judge me, okay?"

"Okay. Let's pray."

She prayed a prayer, and honestly, it wasn't bad for a person starting over. Carla had taught her well back in the day. I felt stronger already. By the time she'd finished and we'd talked another twenty minutes, I felt ready to brave what she'd called "all that Jazz."

Only I didn't hear anything out there. I hung up to go investigate.

"Jazz," I called.

Nothing.

I pushed the bed away from the door. I slowly opened the door and peeked out. I could see him on my couch, his head lolled over to the side. He'd fallen fast asleep. And he was snoring!

I fell to my knees. "Thank you, thank you, thank you," I mouthed to the Lord, thrusting my fist in the air. "Yes! See, Lisa, I have support. I have accountability."

I padded back over to my bed, still not in its rightful place, grateful for another sugar-glider bark, so to speak. But Jazz was right; we'd get only so many of those. He'd fallen asleep because of the late hour and the alcohol. But what would stop us next time from going further than either of us were ready for? "Lord, don't let there be a next time. Give us strength. And please help him through this awful crisis. Reveal Kate's killer and bring him to justice."

I again thought about what Lisa said about me ending up in bed with Jazz. There had to be a way to flee fornication if the Scriptures told us to do it. The Word said: no temptation has seized you except what is common to man. And God is faithful; He will not let you be tempted beyond what you can bear. But when you are tempted, He will also provide a way out so that you can stand up under it.

I hear you, Lord. You are faithful. Help me be faithful, too.

I crawled into my bed, alone, and put the covers over my head. I prayed for my way of escape.

chapter
fifteen

I DIDN'T GO back to sleep. I went to Meijer, a twenty-four-hour store that sold everything on earth. I got new towels, toothbrushes, soap, deodorant, razors, and men's socks. Then, after cajoling a poor employee who looked to be Jazz's size into helping me, I picked out a pair of khaki pants, a leather belt, boxer briefs, and a black silk-blend henley.

Upon arriving home, I showered, dressed, applied copious amounts of makeup, and by six o'clock in the morning, looked fabulous in tailor-made black wool slacks and a tight red mohair sweater Carly had given me for Christmas last year. My new braids swung around my shoulders and grazed the pearl-drop earrings dangling from my ears. Sasha would be proud.

At eight-thirty Jazz stretched his long legs, yawned, and did a double take upon discovering my captivating beauty. I'd sat in the chair across from him with Rilke's *Book of Hours* in my hand, hoping it would make me look deep and profound.

"Good morning," he said, unable to peel his eyes away from me.

"Oh, hi." I threw my words out there like he woke up on my couch every morning and I was tired of him.

"You look very . . ."

I raised an eyebrow that Lisa had expertly groomed last night.

"You're very beautiful, Bell."

Mission accomplished.

"Would you like some breakfast, Jazz?"

"Only if you can stand me for another second."

"I can stand you."

"I'm not sure I can stand myself." He put his head in his hands, took a deep breath, then looked at me again. "About last night. I was way out of line. I'm sorry."

"Things happen. We got through it."

"I don't feel like I know who I am anymore."

I looked at him. I had no idea what he meant. I wanted to play psychologist, but he'd only call me on it. I'd have to rely on prayer, and I wasn't known for being a prayer warrior.

Jazz sighed, a forlorn expression shadowing his face. "May I use your bathroom, please?"

"Sure."

I'd frantically cleaned it. He'd better use it.

He went into the bathroom and came out moments later with the khakis in his hands. "Uh, are these for me?"

"Um-hmm." I kept pretending to read.

"Bell?"

"Yes, Jazz?"

"Why are you doing all of this?"

"You need a friend."

"Is that what you are? Just a friend?"

"Does it matter? I'm here for you."

"I want you to believe I'm innocent."

I didn't say anything.

"You're not sure, are you?"

"I'm not sure about anything. I'm not even sure about what's going on inside of me. I'm a regular doubting Thomas these days."

"But I'm no Christ. I don't have nail prints or a sinless life to show you. And I'm fresh out of miracles."

"Then why don't you just be Jazz—a man—and we'll keep looking to the Christ who has the nail prints and a continuous supply of miracles."

"I hate that you're not sure I didn't do it."

"I said I'm here for you. Take it or leave it."

He took it and left the subject alone. A sly smile crept across his lips. "Maybe I'm the one who shouldn't go anywhere. You know I like it here. All this place needs is my big-screen television . . ."

"Jazz?"

"And some man stuff. It's already starting to get that manly smell."

"No, it's starting to get that smelly smell because you stink. Please go take a shower."

He did a dead-on Ricky Ricardo imitation: "*Lucy*, I'm hooooooooome."

I hurled a throw pillow at him, laughed, and said, "Don't get beside yourself, Jazzy. Ricky and Lucy were *married*."

"Now, there's a thought," he said. He went to the bathroom and closed the door behind him.

I didn't dare ponder what he'd said.

When I heard the shower door close, I shot into the kitchen

and removed his breakfast from the take-out containers from the Breakfast Nook—eggs Benedict, strawberries, and orange juice—and transferred them onto my own plates.

Who said I was domestic?

He came out of the bathroom ten minutes later, looking better than a T-bone steak after a week of Lean Cuisines. He had on the clothes I'd set out for him. I'd set the dinette table for us and was pretending to wash the skillet I hadn't used.

"I'm impressed. I didn't take you for a morning person. It's not even nine o'clock, and you've gotten me right and made this wonderful breakfast." He winked at me. "Or, at least, you put it on the plates."

"Hey, I went to the restaurant and got it, too."

His arms circled my waist. "You're sweet." He kissed me on the cheek, then turned me to face him. "I could get used to this." He pulled me closer and planted a soft, lingering kiss on my mouth.

The room got very warm. I pulled away. "Okay, that's enough."

He chuckled. "Enough? I just got started." He massaged my neck.

I took hold of his wrists. "Please stop."

"I just want—"

"I know what you want."

"Do you?"

"I'm pretty clear on it. You're the one who quoted the Song of Solomon."

"Is that a sin?"

"You tried to seduce me."

"I quoted biblical poetry to you. I told you how pretty you looked."

"You did a lot more than that."

"And a lot less than what I wanted to."

I pulled my hands away from his.

His jaw tightened. "What? Now we can't hold hands?"

"You don't seem to realize that I'm affected by things like that."

"Now I'm offending you?"

"You're teasing me."

"I'm touching you."

I took a step away from him. He made no effort to close the space between us. "Jazzy, can't we just be honest? Isn't that what you asked for the night Kate died? Let's be honest about what's going on between us."

He laughed. "Honest? Okay, let's start with you. You're sending me all kinds of signals that you're loving the attention I'm giving you. Maybe you're the one who's being a tease."

"I'm not being a tease."

"Look at you. You've never dressed like this around me before. You want me to notice every curve of your body, and I have."

"I didn't even know I'd see you last night," I said, trying to divert him from his shamefully true statement.

"That doesn't mean your look isn't for me. You may not have known I'd be here last night, but you knew when I fell asleep on your couch that I'd be here this morning. I've never seen you wear so much makeup."

"Maybe I want to look pretty."

"The makeup you wear most of the time is pretty. Red lipstick is sexy. You want me to desire you."

"I'm just trying to pamper myself," I defended with an out-and-out lie.

"I stand corrected."

He moved over to the table and sat down. "Do you mind if I eat?"

"Go ahead."

But he only picked at his food. He drank the orange juice in one big gulp. His clipped movements and his banging the utensils on the table told me he had a problem with the direction our conversation had taken.

"Why didn't you ever invite me to your place, Jazz?"

"Why would I have a single woman in my apartment?"

"I don't know what you mean."

"Yes, you do."

"Kate was there."

"I didn't invite Kate there. She just showed up." He stabbed at his eggs.

"Did you have other women over?"

"Not since I got married," he barked.

"Are you getting upset?"

"Why should I?"

"That doesn't answer my question."

"I'm not in the mood for your verbal Olympics, Bell." He picked up a fork and nearly threw it back down again.

"Why are you mad?"

"Because *you* can't be honest."

"I *am* being honest," I said, but I wasn't really certain what I was being besides confused.

"You act like you don't want me to desire you, but you have a problem because I didn't take you home, where it would have been very difficult for me to be a good boy. You also act like desire in and of itself is a sin. What have we done? Kissed?"

"Your hands seem to be busy lately."

"You're right, Bell. I'm sorry. I happen to want to touch you. I'm a man." He stood. "I shouldn't have come over here."

"And that's another thing. Why did you come, when you're the one who said we shouldn't see each other? You said it wasn't safe."

"I guess I think it's safe now."

"There are more ways than one to be unsafe."

"Have I violated you? Because the last time I checked, you were unsullied by me." He glared at me when I didn't answer. "Look. I'll leave."

"You don't have to leave."

"I don't have to leave? What do you want from me? Do you want me to stay, or do you want me to leave? Do you want me to think you're sexy? Or do you want me to think you're a nun? Just a hint, if you're going for nun, you might want to try again, 'cause what you have on is *sexy*."

"All right, Jazz! You want the truth? I want you to think I'm attractive."

"You already know I think you're attractive. You're raising the stakes, baby."

"What about you? You say we can't see each other, and then

you show up here. You say you don't want to sin, and then you can't keep your hands off me. Why did you come here?"

"Why do you think I'm here?"

"I'm in no mood for your verbal tricks, either."

"A'ight, Bell. I came here because they took my badge, my gun, and my car. Because my parents put up their house to bond me out of jail. Because time is passing, and the person who killed Kate is a ghost. You wanna know why I came here? Because you wear tight jeans, little sweaters, and red lipstick for me. It feels good to touch you. And you smell good. And here's a big revelation for you, Bell. Chasing you around your apartment is preferable to sitting at my parents' house, wondering whether I'll go to hell if I kill myself. I don't want to spend the rest of my life in prison for something I didn't do."

The words hung like missiles in the air. I didn't think he meant them. *He couldn't mean them, could he, God?* "It scares me when you talk like that."

He looked at me, his Godiva-chocolate eyes mocking. "Could Bell actually be admitting to me that she loves me? Was that all it took? One little-bitty admission that I'm thinking of offing myself?"

"You know that I'm required to address this." I waited for him to pounce on me, as nearly everyone does when they think I'm being a psychologist and not a friend. Frankly, right now I couldn't be more than clinical. If I were, I might blow it all by being truly honest. I hoped my body language didn't betray the depth of how his words affected me.

Jazz remained silent.

"Are you seriously considering harming yourself?" I said.

"I'm not going to kill myself, Bell," he yelled. He raked his hand through his brown curls. Lowered his voice. "At least not today." He sighed. "Really. It was just a thought."

"Jazz, you're under a great deal of stress—"

"You're not my shrink. Try being what I want you to be right now."

"And what is that?"

"You don't dress like that at work. Why do you have that on?"

"I asked what you want me to be right now."

"Maybe I want you to be the woman who dresses like that for me."

"Be careful, Jazz. I think you missed some honesty there."

"It takes a dishonest person to know one, doesn't it?"

"I'm being as honest as I can," I said. "Here's a little more for you: I have very strong feelings for you, physically and otherwise. But I don't want to commit sexual sin. I won't win any prizes for my devotional life, but I'm trying my best to hold on to all of the God I have. That's the best I can do right now."

"I don't want us to sin, either. I mean that, Bell. You wanna know why I'm here? I'm here because I need you. That's the best I can do. Don't make me leave today."

"I have things to do."

"I can stay here while you're gone."

I tried to interject a little humor. "You're not going to make yourself at home too much, are you, Ricky Ricardo?"

"Today is her funeral."

"I know."

"I need you today."

For a moment neither of us spoke. I looked at him and saw

that he'd managed to come up with a pair of puppy eyes that rivaled the king of puppy eyes himself, Rocky. Those eyes broke my heart.

"Finish your breakfast. You're going with me," I said.

"Change your clothes or we'll be staying in," Jazz said.

Now, that was honest.

"You've got yourself a deal, Mr. Brown."

chapter
sixteen

I CHANGED INTO a completely boring navy blue pantsuit and a white blouse. Something I'd wear not only to my private practice but to the jail. Jazz's comment? "Yeah. That'll work."

I had to practically force him to get inside the Love Bug. "I hate this car."

"It's *my* car. You don't have to get attached to it."

"Yeah, but I have to ride in it. It's yellow, Bell."

"You like the yellow walls in my apartment. You said they're soothing."

"But a Love Bug isn't soothing. I feel silly in this car."

"It's soothing to me. Just get in, Jazz."

He finally did—with an attitude.

I breathed a sigh of relief. One challenge handled. Unfortunately, the next would be how to tell Jazz that he and I, and *Rocky,* would be going to see my fertility doctor together. One big, happy family.

"Where are we going?"

"I have to stop at my church first."

"The Rock House?"

"That's my church."

"You're going to go see your *boyfriend*?"

"Stop calling him that. Everybody knows Rocky and I are no longer an item. I don't have a boyfriend."

He didn't correct me by saying *he* was my boyfriend. I plotted to take him to several high-profile places in the Love Bug as punishment.

After much complaining and pouting on Jazz's part, we got to the Rock House. Jazz shot out of my vehicle like it was about to explode. Honestly, it was a fully loaded new Beetle, not an old busted-up hippie car. Why he had such an adverse reaction to it boggled my mind.

He walked briskly to the front door of the building; I had to hustle to keep up with him. "Is he even here?" Jazz asked.

"He's the pastor. He does show up now and then."

"And who made him a pastor, anyway?"

"Try God. Might I add, he's great in this ministry."

Jazz grumbled, "That better be all he's great in."

"Your jealousy is ridiculous. And it's even worse than before. What is wrong with you?"

"What's wrong with me? Try being up for a murder rap. Surely that gives ol' puppy eyes the competitive edge for your affections."

I shook my head. "Ol' puppy eyes isn't pursuing me." He wasn't, really. I mean, maybe a comment here and there . . . "And green isn't your color, Jazz. Your jealousy was cute at first, but now it's annoying." I fished around in my purse for my keys.

"You've got a key to your church?"

"That's a privilege of being the pastor's girlfriend." I looked at him. He'd turned red-faced, and not because of the cold. "I just said that to mess with you."

"You ain't right, Bell."

"But you love me anyway."

"Whateva."

I put my key in the door, opened it, and could hear the music coming from the sanctuary. "Switchfoot. Rock's favorite."

Jazz rolled his eyes.

We walked down the corridor that led to the sanctuary, past a welcome center with brochures and free booklets and metal racks filled with bread from Food Gatherers for anybody to take.

As we reached the door, the last riffs of "Stars" wailed from Rocky's electric guitar. I smiled before I opened the door, knowing that this favorite song of Rocky's would have him jumping up and down. He'd be singing with all the skill and passion of Switchfoot's front man, Jon Foreman, whether he had an audience or not. But the moment he finished, without a pause, he went right into another song. A song I hadn't heard in a long time. I had a visceral reaction to it. I stopped cold.

Why is he playing that song?

Before I had time to check my reaction, I swung the door open, and there was Rocky, guitar in his hands, rockin' away. Elisa St. James—the sweet, pretty, green-eyed sistah who'd saved me from certain death in the last case I'd worked on with Jazz—sat in front of him, engrossed in his performance, which was apparently for her alone.

Well, not for her alone. Elisa was now seven months pregnant, and Rocky's head was bent, singing his heart out to Elisa's pregnant belly—or rather, its inhabitant. Rocky was serenading her with *my* favorite childhood comfort song, but the special rock-and-roll version he'd arranged for the baby we thought I'd have with him. He'd gifted me with it when he and I were in love and he'd asked me to be his wife and have his children. This was before he knew I wouldn't be able to have a tribe of little Rocks like he wanted. Before either of us knew that, ultimately, that would be the reason we'd break up.

> *Hush-a-bye don't you cry*
> *Go to sleep-y little baby*
> *When you wake, you shall have*
> *All the pretty little horses.*

I felt like someone had kicked me in the stomach. My breath caught in my chest.

Jazz's hand went to my back. "Are you all right?"

But I couldn't speak. I couldn't tear my eyes off Rocky and Elisa, she looking at him with absolute delight on her face, he looking at her as if seeing her for the first time, then turning his attention to sing to her babe within.

They're falling in love. He's singing her baby my *baby's song. The baby I never . . . the baby I'll never . . .* I swallowed hard. A tiny "Oh . . ." escaped my mouth.

"Bell?" Jazz whispered in my ear. He tried to pull me away from the door but didn't succeed before Rocky saw us. He finished the song with aplomb.

"Babe," he said, smiling. "I hope you don't mind. It's the only lullaby I know. I wanted to sing to Elisa's baby."

Elisa's head spun around to look at me. She looked like I'd

caught her kissing my boyfriend behind the bleachers during prom.

I couldn't say a word, just stood there with a smile pasted on my face. Mortified.

"You ready to go, babe?" Rocky asked, totally oblivious to my pain.

Elisa's face fell. I don't think she could have hidden her disappointment if she'd wanted to. "Are you and Bell going somewhere?"

"I'm going with her to see her"—he censored himself—"doctor." He looked Jazz over. "At least I thought I was."

Jazz didn't miss a beat. "Actually, Rocky, Bell came by to tell you that we don't need you. I'm taking her. You can stay here and keep doing what you're doing. You kids have fun."

Rocky looked confused. "Are you sure, babe?" His brown eyes said, "Didn't he just kill somebody?"

All I managed was a hoarse "Don't call me babe." Somehow, saying it to him that time filled me with a sadness that I thought would kill me.

Babe. Soon I wouldn't ever have to ask him not to call me that. He'd call Elisa his babe. He'd call the fatherless child—this one he would surely step in to raise—his babe, just as sure as he'd sung a lullaby to it. It all fit together. I could see God's plan working out. Elisa needed someone to love, and so did Rocky. I just wished it didn't leave me feeling so bereft of hope.

I closed my eyes. My legs trembled, and my eyes pooled with tears.

Rocky put down his guitar. "Are you okay? Are you sure you want to go with him?"

I nodded. "I'm sure, Rocky."

Rocky didn't looked convinced. "Why do you look so upset, babe?"

He could be so naive at times. Again, lamely, "Don't call me babe."

Jazz got busy. "We had a little *lover's* quarrel this morning." "Lover" was emphasized just to torment Rocky, who remained oblivious to Jazz's implication. "She's still salty with me." Jazz grabbed my hand and pulled me to him. Touched my cheek. Looked in my eyes with so much love. "I'm so sorry, Bell." He didn't mean our argument at all, bless him.

A tear fell down my face. He wiped it away. "Aw, baby. Look at you. It'll be all right." Jazz looked at me, then at Rocky. "I'd better get her out of here."

Rocky moved toward me, but Jazz stood between us, rolling his shoulders back, ready to rumble, no doubt. "I'll take care of her, Rocky. Why don't you just enjoy what you were doing with Elisa?"

Rocky grabbed my wrist, but it was Jazz he spoke to. He spoke softly, but his eyes were serious. He wasn't good at being a lion, but he tried. "I don't think I want her to go with you, man."

"I think you'd better let her go, *man*."

Rocky held fast to my wrist, even though I knew he saw Jazz as a threat. "Babe?"

I gently pulled my arm out of Rocky's grasp. "Jazz is right. You and Elisa looked like you were having fun. And Jazz is—"

"Innocent until proven guilty in a court of law," Jazz said. He whisked me out the door and down the corridor.

"Don't look back," he whispered. "Just act like you really want to go with me."

I didn't need to act. I *did* want to go with him. I wanted to go with him to wherever he wanted to take me. I didn't care at the moment what he'd been accused of.

I heard Rocky's voice calling behind us, "Babe, wait."

Jazz returned his call. "Rocky, don't call her babe."

He took my hand and led me to the sanctuary of my happy yellow car. He didn't even complain about getting in.

chapter
seventeen

POOR JAZZ. Not only did he have to endure entering the Love Bug but he had to drive it to Dr. McLogan's office, hand me Kleenex, and speak to me in soft, comforting tones. He didn't ask me any questions, just offered assurances that everything would be all right.

When we pulled in to the parking lot, I realized that I hadn't told Jazz much of anything, including where we were or why we were there. I touched his knee. "This is my fertility doctor. I'd originally asked Rocky to come with me, but . . . well, you know."

"I see," Jazz said tersely.

I paused. "I'm not sure you do see, Jazz. I just asked Rocky—"

"You don't owe me an explanation."

"I think you may have the wrong idea. If you think—"

"Look, I don't really care. I'm here because I showed up at your door, and now you're stuck with me."

"But, Jazz—"

"Can we please go inside, if that's what you need to do?"

I sighed. *Men.* Honestly! I wanted to give them up for a monastic life. Rocky gave Elisa my baby's song and thinks I'm dating a murderer. Now Jazz thinks I asked Rocky to go to the fertility clinic with me for God only knows, but I can just about guess, why.

Jazz escorted me to Dr. McLogan's suite on the fourth floor. The office had been decorated in a manner similar to other institutions where people go because something horrible is going on in their lives—jail, morgue, "I can't have a baby" clinic. Their attempt to create a soothing atmosphere fails miserably with awful paintings hung on walls, painted in terrible "healing" colors, and cheap furniture that tries to say "home" but never does.

I'd finally stopped crying, and we sat in the waiting room on a big floral sofa. Jazz sat at an unusual—for him—distance from me.

"Are you okay, Jazz?"

He made a gruff, inconclusive noise.

"You just seem a little . . . put off. I know I made quite a spectacle of myself at the church."

"At least *that* was honest."

"What's that supposed to mean?"

He glared at me. He opened his mouth to speak, but Dr. McLogan interrupted us. "My dear, it's good to see you."

I smiled at the kindly old leprechaun. His suit, always a tad long for his short frame, sagged on his thin shoulders. But his green eyes twinkled with fire and mischief. He tucked a wisp of too long, once red hair behind a big, round, mouselike ear and grinned at us.

"Thank you, Dr. McLogan, this is my—"

Jazz thrust out his hand. "I'm Jazz."

Dr. McLogan shook Jazz's hand, and I could tell Jazz gave

the poor man a crushing squeeze. "It's a pleasure to meet you." His gaze shifted to me. "Will Jazz be joining you?"

"I'm her man," Jazz answered for me.

I shot him an icy look, to which he replied, "Come on, baby. Biological clocks are tickin'."

Dr. McLogan looked at me, clearly amused. I rolled my eyes. "I guess Jazz is coming in with me."

On the way to Dr. McLogan's office, Jazz swung his arm around me like he owned me. He swaggered to the tenth power.

I plotted his destruction. "Why are you acting like this, alpha male?"

"Who's acting?"

I elbowed him in the ribs with a harsh whisper: "Cut it out."

He harrumphed at me. I hate being harrumphed at.

Before we'd even gotten through the door, Jazz bombarded the doctor with questions. "So can she have a baby or not?"

Dr. McLogan looked taken aback but answered graciously, "We're here to discuss that possibility." He motioned for us to have a seat, which we did in the two upholstered chairs across from his massive cherrywood desk.

Jazz started up immediately. "Why don't we cut to the chase. Yes or no?"

Dr. McLogan paused. He actually seemed tickled by Jazz's antics. "Well, Amanda knows it's possible, but it won't be simple."

"Why not?"

I decided to spare Dr. McLogan the rest of this inquisition. "I'm sorry, Dr. McLogan. Jazz clearly has a mood disorder that's flaring up. Not to mention horrid manners. Not to mention a bit of psychosis, as he thinks he's 'my man.'"

"Mason's told me about Jazz."

"You know Mason?" Jazz grinned. "My man." He swung an arm out to give Dr. McLogan five, which Dr. McLogan readily offered.

I frowned at the two of them bonding. "If you two are finished, continue with"—I gave Jazz a withering Addie-like stare so he would stay quiet—"what you were saying, Doctor."

Jazz shuddered. "You looked just like my mother when you did that."

"Dr. McLogan," I prompted the man again.

He shook his head at me. "Well, I'm afraid the medications you've been taking are not as effective as I'd hoped they would be."

We'd tried every available medication on the market to stimulate ovulation in my failing ovary—the ovary that endometriosis hadn't ruined. I'd paid an obscene amount for all the prescriptions my insurance didn't cover.

"So now what?" I asked.

He leaned forward, reached a hand across his desk, and placed it over mine. "Amanda, I asked you here because you've reached a critical point in your treatment."

"What are you saying? What kind of critical point?" My heart stumbled around in my chest, running into things.

"I'm afraid you're out of time, my dear. I told you a few months ago you shouldn't wait much longer."

"I'm out of time?"

"If you really want to try for a baby, you need to do it now. *Now*, dear one."

Jazz and I exchanged a look.

Dr. McLogan continued. "I'd like to give you a shot of HCG today to induce ovulation, and try the intrauterine insemination procedure in the next few days."

My heart felt like it had stopped. "In the next few days?"

"I warned you it would come to this. If you don't move forward now, the procedures will become more expensive and more invasive, which means more risky. They will also be far less likely to work, my dear. And I must say, at your age, it wouldn't be worth the risks." He sounded like my mother.

He leaned back in his seat. He had good leather seats that didn't squeak when he moved. "Would you consider the possibility of adopting?" he asked.

"Dr. McLogan, I'd really like to have a baby. I missed . . ."

I missed everything. I gave it all to Adam, the nutjob who I left God for years ago, and I lost it all.

When I didn't finish my sentence, Dr. McLogan spoke. "I asked you to bring someone with you because I'd like to talk about what kind of support you have for going forward with the artificial insemination using an anonymous donor. Who will support you in this?"

I sighed and jiggled my leg. "That's a good question. My sister, Carly, doesn't care one way or the other."

Jazz jumped in with a little revelation of his own. "She's been talking to Mason about this for months. He thinks she should reconsider becoming a single mother. He told her he believes parenting is too hard a task to go it alone if you don't have to. I agree."

"Thanks for your input, Jazz," I said, throwing him a dirty look.

He ignored my sarcasm. Now that Dr. McLogan was his boy,

Jazz got bold. "So she's really thinking of getting inseminated with an anonymous donor's, uh . . . donation?"

Dr. McLogan nodded as if that were the saddest news he'd ever heard. "We've discussed it."

Jazz to me: "You can't be serious, Bell. What if you get pregnant by a nutjob?"

"Jazz, do you have to be so obnoxious today? At this moment?"

"Do you have *anyone's* support for doing this?" Jazz asked me.

I didn't speak.

"You don't, do you?"

My defenses went up like strip malls in the suburbs. "I don't necessarily have to use an anonymous donor," I said. "I did have a friend who considered volunteering."

"What friend?"

"A friend, Jazz."

"Name him."

"I don't want to."

"You don't have that many friends—especially males." A look of horror swept across his face. "Don't tell me you asked your *boyfriend*."

I shot a look at Dr. McLogan, then back at Jazz. "I don't have a boyfriend."

Dr. McLogan chuckled. "I thought Jazz was your boyfriend, dear."

"I'm her *man*."

Dr. McLogan seemed amused. "I see."

Jazz's attitude grew worse by the second. "He *must* be your boyfriend. You asked him to father your child."

"Why are you so jealous of Rocky?"

"Maybe because you want to have his *baby*."

"I also wanted an anonymous donor's baby. He wouldn't be my boyfriend, either."

Jazz's shoulders curled in, and he sank in his seat like a sullen little brat. "You can't have a baby with Rocky."

"Who even said it's Rocky?"

"Who else would it be? Mason? Of course it's Rocky. Did you bring him here before?"

I didn't answer.

"I can't believe you. You never brought me here, and I told you twice that I'd help you."

"You did no such thing."

"I did. Once in your apartment—"

"The day I fainted? You were kidding."

"Says who? And I offered when you were in the hospital."

"You said that because I thought I could be pregnant by a nutjob."

"I said that because I wanted to help you have a baby." He went into a full snit. "I'm disappointed. You never once considered me, did you?"

Was he for real? Of course I had considered him. He was my dream man, but I wouldn't dare ask. If he'd said yes, I'd have wanted much more than his baby.

Dr. McLogan smiled. "Would you two like to be alone? Mason told me you were like this."

"No!" we said in unison.

Jazz jumped back on his soapbox. "*Rocky!* How can you consider *Rocky?* Have you ever looked at his head?"

"What's that got to do with anything?"

"Let's just say I can see why his parents named him Rocky. You wanna mark your kids with heads that look like the four inner terrestrial planets? Maybe you do. You, Rocky, and little Mercury, Jupiter, Venus, and—"

"It was just a thought," I said. "A fleeting one. And Venus is a very cute name for a girl."

Dr. McLogan stood. "I'll leave you two alone for a minute." He stepped quietly away from us.

No sooner than the door closed behind him did our bickering stop. Jazz folded his arms across his chest. His tight-set jaw and sad brown eyes told me that not only was he angry at me, I'd hurt him.

I tried to get back in his good graces. "It was right after I stopped seeing you, Jazzy. You'd said you were unavailable. I didn't think I had a future with you, and I desperately wanted a baby."

"You thought you had a future with *Rocky?*"

"I thought I'd always have a friend in Rocky."

"You didn't think you could be my friend?"

"No, Jazz."

"Why not?"

"Because my feelings for you go far deeper than they ever did with Rocky."

He looked at me, and I thought I saw a flicker of hope in his eyes.

"Jazz, I never meant to hurt you. It's just that . . . I'm afraid I'm fairly desperate when it comes to this. I want a child badly. More than anything else in the world."

Besides you.

He peered at me. "I want one badly, too. You have no idea how much."

I didn't say anything. I didn't know how to address that.

Jazz still looked dejected. "You were going to bring Rocky today, not me."

"Just for moral support. Dr. McLogan said to bring someone with me. I knew this would be bad news, but I had no idea he would say I needed to have a baby right now. You told me you didn't think it was safe for me to be around you. That's why I didn't think to ask you to come. And Rocky is . . . well, he's like a rock to me."

Jazz didn't respond.

I sighed. I didn't want to have to explain myself to Jazz. I didn't want to sit there consoling him while the reality that I would most likely be childless struck me with brute force. "I'm not going to have a baby with Rocky. I'm not going to have a baby at all." I choked on the last word. Saying the truth out loud brought a fresh wave of tears, but Jazz didn't come to my rescue.

Man, can't a girl get some sympathy around here? Did he hear what I said? I'm not going to have a baby. As in at all!

I thought I'd give Jazz a hint that it was time to comfort me now. "Jazzy . . ." I croaked.

He didn't say anything.

"*Jazzy!* I'm suffering here. Helloooo."

He looked over at me. "Yeah. Bell . . ."

I gave up and grabbed the Kleenex myself before I had an unfortunate accident involving snot. He didn't seem to notice that I'd progressed well into self-comfort. In fact, he seemed lost in his own thoughts. I touched his knee. "Jazz?"

"I married her because she got pregnant."

I sat back in my chair. I knew it. Why else would he have married Kate? "What happened? Did she lose the baby?"

"She aborted it two weeks later."

"Jazz, why?"

"I don't know. I discovered by accident that she'd had an abortion. She never told me why she did it. I got so angry that I wouldn't speak to her. I shut her out for a month."

"And then she had the affairs."

"And then I divorced her. We never had a marriage."

I didn't feel a need to reply.

"I wanted the baby. I would have tolerated her, honest to God, just to have the baby. I wanted a son. I have always wanted a son."

I scooted my chair close to his. "I'm so sorry, Jazz."

"Every time you told me about your little girl, I was right there with you. I knew all those feelings. I just didn't want to talk about my own baby drama. I still want a son—"

"You have plenty of time to—"

"—with you."

"Excuse me?"

"Tell Dr. McLogan we want to do it."

My heart pounded so fast I thought Jazz would be able to see the imprint of it coming out of my blouse. "Tell him we want to do *what?* 'Do it' has a street definition, too, you know."

He turned to face me and took both my hands in his. "We can do it all, baby."

I snatched my hands away. "How are we going to do it *all*? Jazz, you happen to be in a lot of trouble right now."

"I know what my circumstances are." He paused, his Godiva-chocolate eyes boring into mine, making my peanut-butter skin tingle. "How could I be worse than a total stranger?"

"Their donors are well screened."

"So am I. I come with references."

"References?"

"Jack and Addie. My brothers and sisters. Mason May."

"Mason?"

"I've been in counseling with Mason, too, twice a week since I met him."

"You have?" I could have fallen out of the chair. "Why?"

"I wanted to know if I could remarry. He didn't tell me what to do. He helped me to make the decision for myself. I chose yes. I chose you." He took my hand in his. "Choose yes for me now, Bell."

I felt like I had just been plunged into a parallel universe where the most gorgeous man on the planet wanted me to be his wife and his baby's mama. My mouth flew open. "Yes to what? What are you asking me?"

"I want us to have a baby. I want you to marry me."

"Are you kidding me?" Oh yeah. I was on Planet Shock right now. I was sure if my heart beat any faster, I'd fall dead where I sat.

"I'm serious." He squeezed my hand. "Don't you see? You can have what you want, and you don't have to do it alone. You can have your baby and, in the package, get a father for him, and grandparents, and uncles and aunts. And a husband. I can take care of you. I *want* to take care of you."

That beat the heck out of cuddling with my sugar glider! My head was like the tornado in *The Wizard of Oz*. Amid the wreckage in my brain appeared images of the people in my life who would be horrified if I married Jazz now. If I thought I had little support for artificial insemination, I'd have zero for marrying a man who could be a murderer. "How are you supposed to take care of me? Are you forgetting that you're suspended from your job? How am I supposed to marry you with all this going on?"

"I can't give you a baby without marrying you."

"I didn't ask you for a baby." But the idea compelled me like a lover calling me into a dark corner for some forbidden intimacy—an intimacy I wanted with everything in me.

Jazz looked at me with an intensity I had not seen before. "Don't have an anonymous donor's baby, and don't miss out on the opportunity because of what's going on with me. This is just a nightmare we're going to wake up from. Have *my* baby, Bell. Marry me for the security you'd get."

Rational Bell warred with the other Bell—the one with the sexy clothes and willing body. The one who shouted to my soul, "Yes! You love him. Marry him." And my soul heard her loud and clear. And the third Bell, the insecure one who knew no man this good could ever want her for long, couldn't trust that her deepest dreams could come true.

Rational Bell squeaked out, "What security? My whole point is that your life is horribly *insecure* right now."

The pitch of his voice rose. "I didn't do it."

"Jazz, you're starting to sound like Samuel L. Jackson in . . . every movie he's ever made."

"You really do think I killed her, don't you?"

I didn't answer him. I had gone over that crime scene a million times in my head. It didn't seem like he'd done it, but I also knew I didn't *want* to see Jazz as good for a murder.

Again those dark, delicious eyes enticed me. "Trust me."

"Jazz . . ."

I could have what I wanted. This was better than Willy Wonka's golden ticket. He was offering a ticket to one endless Jazz fest. And I wanted to go, but nobody else would appreciate my presence there. I could choose Jazz or everybody else.

He slumped back in his chair and turned his head away from me. His mouth flattened into a hard line. He didn't even glance in my direction when he said, "No one has to know we're doing this."

The idea intrigued me. *No one has to know?* "How will no one know if we have a child?"

"Until this mess blows over, and it will, we'll keep it a secret. After that . . . we figure out the details. When you conceive, you'll have the protection a marriage offers."

Rational Bell spoke out loud. "I don't need protection. I've been taking care of myself for a long time."

Insecure Bell wanted to say, *There's no security with a man like you. You'll leave the moment someone more beautiful comes along. And that won't take more than a minute.*

Jazz continued to plead his case. "What if the pregnancy is difficult and you can't work? You barely have enough for the procedure. Who would support you?"

Irrational Bell shouted in my head: *He's got a point. Marry the sexy beast!*

"Shut up," I said aloud.

"Excuse me?"

"I'm sorry, Jazz. Go on."

He gave me a quizzical look but continued. "What if you had a catastrophic illness? You know it can take years to get disability. My *wife* would have access to my health insurance, not my *baby's mama.* C'mon, Bell. You're a shrink. You know marriage protects you more than any other arrangement."

Irrational Bell belted out a rousing chorus of "The Wedding March," followed by a sultry rendition of Marvin Gaye's "Let's Get It On."

"Will you please stop?" I told my saucy alter ego.

"Bell, I don't want to stop. We can make this work. It could be business. Like a—what do you call it?—a marriage of . . . of . . ."

Mind-blowing SEX with the finest man ever, said Irrational Bell.

"Convenience," I filled in meekly.

It'd be convenient, all right, she said, doing the Snoopy dance—and black people, even black alter egos, don't do that! *I'll bet he's a* monster *in bed,* she shouted with glee.

And speaking of monsters, said Rational Bell, *what if he killed her? What if you're wrong? Or, just as bad, what if he didn't do it and is convicted anyway? You'll be a prison widow.*

But you won't be a prison widow today, Irrational Bell said. *He's out of jail on bond today. Take that brotha home and have your way with him.*

He doesn't really want you, Insecure Bell whispered from her corner. *Not really.*

For a moment I felt like I was having a psychotic break with reality. Jazz's proposal had triggered multiple personality disorder in me. I desperately tried to control Irrational Bell's enthusiasm.

Who are you kidding? I'm no alternate personality. I'm YOU!

Jazz must have taken my silence personally. "You got any other prospects? Other than *Rocky*? Or do you want him instead?"

"I wish you'd stop with the Rocky barbs. I could have married Rocky if that was what I'd wanted."

"Say yes, Bell."

Rational Bell got behind the wheel. I thought it best to let her drive. "You are in no position to take on a wife. What if—"

"I'm going back to work for the Detroit police department. I'll retire as captain one day. I'll have a son with you. I'm not going to go to prison."

"But what if you do?"

His demeanor changed. He went iceman. "I'm not."

"Jazz, it could—"

"God won't let me go to prison for this, because I didn't kill anyone. And you need to get with that reality."

"That's admirable faith—"

"I'm done with this conversation. If you want a baby, take the shot, we'll get married in the morning, and I'll get you pregnant. This really shouldn't be a hard decision. Not if you want a baby like you say you do. Or are you dishonest about that, too?" He stood abruptly. "I'll be in the waiting room. Tell him your decision."

I stood. "Will you wait a minute?"

"No. I won't. Your time is up, and according to you, so is mine."

"Look, I'm sorry. I just—"

"Choose: baby or no baby. Whateva. Or go with having a little Rock head, or Baby Nobody. It's your call. Don't expect me to sit around yammering about it."

He left the room, with me standing there, my mouth wide open.

Idiot, Irrational Bell said, then she left me alone, too.

chapter
eighteen

N OT ONE WORD. Not a single utterance all the way home. Jazz wouldn't respond to anything I said or toss me so much as a glance. He had enough people telling him he'd go to prison for the rest of his life. He didn't need me to join the chorus. He couldn't work. He didn't even have his Crown Victoria for comfort, like I had my Love Bug.

But he had to know what he'd asked had been unreasonable. He didn't think I'd be foolish enough to marry him under these horrible circumstances, did he? No matter how badly I wanted a baby—or him.

At last we reached my apartment. I parked in my space and tried to make him laugh by sounding like Lucy Ricardo doing an imitation of her husband: "Hunneee, we're hooo-oooome."

He glared at me.

"That was Lucy Ricardo pretending to be Ricky."

"Don't quit your day job."

"Oh my goodness! It *talks.*"

It stopped talking.

"I'm sorry, Jazz."

Nothing.

"You finally talked to me. Will you please say something more?"

Nada. He just got out of the car and came around to open the door for me. Always the gentleman.

I stepped out of the car, and he followed me toward the building. His attitude didn't prevent him from putting his hand on the small of my back to guide me up the stairs and to my door.

"Thanks, Jazz."

Nothing.

"I'll see you later."

Nothing.

"Fine. Don't say anything." I dug in my purse for my keys. I must have taken a little too long for Mr. Strong Silent Type. He took the liberty of taking out his own set and opening the door.

"You need to give me that set of keys," I said.

In answer, he waltzed into my apartment like Fred Astaire. I followed him, bewildered. He took off his coat and hung it in my closet.

"Excuse me? You want to hang out, but you won't talk to me?"

He helped me out of my coat. Placed it, too, in the closet.

"Stop doing gentlemanly things when you refuse to speak to me. Are you planning on hanging out here? Because I have things to do this afternoon."

"So go."

"Oh, you want to talk now?"

"No, but you refuse to leave me alone." He went into my kitchen and opened my refrigerator.

"What are you doing?"

"I'm looking for something to eat."

"Why?"

"Because I'm hungry."

"You can't just come in here like you own the place when you're barely speaking to me."

"I'll bet Rocky can. I'll bet Rocky can make himself at home."

"Rocky is speaking to me."

"He looked pretty busy with Elisa, if you ask me. And you can forget about having a baby with him. I think Rocky's got a baby now."

"You can be a real jerk sometimes, Jazz."

"So can you, Bell."

He foraged around my entire kitchen for something appealing. "Do you eat anything besides Lean Cuisine and hundred-calorie Nabisco snack stuff? It's a bunch of chick food in here. What are you doing? Trying to model now?"

"I happen to want to lose weight."

"For what?"

"Because I'm overweight."

He snorted. "You're trippin'." He made his way back to the refrigerator. Got frustrated and swore when he couldn't find anything suitable to eat.

"Don't cuss. Amos."

"Which reminds me. I didn't see him in his cage. Why isn't he?"

"He's part of the family now. He's free to roam at will."

"Excuse me? The rodent that tried to shred your arm is family?"

"Sure. He got nicer once I gave him his freedom. We actually have cuddle times now."

"At least someone does."

I stuck my tongue out at him.

"So you're going to let him wander around the house, with no access to his food and water, in an apartment that's not sugar-glider-proofed, just because you want him to be family."

"I'm letting you do it!"

"I can fend for myself. He can't."

I pointed to the corner of the room where I'd put a tiny water and food dispenser and gave Jazz an evil grin.

Jazz shook his head. "I still don't think it's safe."

I suddenly had a picture in my head. Animal protective services coming to take my baby and put him in foster care . . . *Don't think about* babies, *Bell.*

"I didn't think about him being unsafe."

Jazz sighed and shook his head, no doubt thinking how awful I was but taking pity on me. "Maybe not. I don't know."

"Really? You don't think I'm a terrible mother?"

"Not if I practically begged you to have my baby. However, I'm not impressed with you as a sugar-glider owner." He stood in the middle of the kitchen, miffed. "You don't have any food for a man." He went back to his futile search for "man food" in my refrigerator.

I thought about what he'd said. "I don't have a man."

That seemed to really get his ire up. "What am I, huh?" With one movement, he was right on me. I didn't think a quarter inch of space stood between us. He said in my ear in a hoarse whisper,

"Don't think I'm a man, baby? Do I need to show you how much of a man I am?"

I'd noticed his manliness, all right. We could have powered metropolitan Detroit with the masculine/feminine energy that crackled between us. And as far as his hunger went, he gave me a lusty look like I was on the menu.

I muttered lamely, "I thought you wanted to eat."

He stormed over to the fridge and slammed the door shut. "Yeah. I want to eat, all right. Only you don't have food fit for anyone with a Y chromosome. Probably on purpose. You don't really want a man, do you? That's why you didn't marry Rocky. And that's why you won't marry me. One good thing I can say about Kate. *She* wanted to marry me."

"She didn't want your baby, though, did she?"

His reaction was so subtle that anybody else would have missed it. For a moment neither of us spoke. He broke the silence. "I suppose I deserved that."

"Actually, you did not."

"Are you sure you won't marry me? We fight like a married couple."

"I think we should part ways before we shed blood."

He smiled. "Uh, I think I'm bleeding already."

"Did you miss it? I've been trailing blood since we left Dr. McLogan's office."

Jazz crossed his arms across his chest, body armor in place. I realized my body armor was already on. We stood there a few more moments, Jazz rocking back and forth on his heels, me tapping my foot on my tile floor until his stomach growled and we both laughed.

"I can leave, Bell. I just wanted to be with you today." He looked away from me. "The funeral . . . I really wanted to be with you."

"I've got take-out menus. You can order in."

We both dropped our armor. Went to each other at the same time and held on as if there were no murder, no doubts, nothing but love between us. We whispered our apologies and administered the gentlest of touches on hands, cheeks, hair, arms.

He took my hand and walked with me to my living room. We sat on the sofa together.

"I'm worn out, Bell. I don't have any more tricks. No more manipulations. I've sat all these weeks with Mason, trying to find some way to be with you. It's over now. I just love you. I want to spend my life with you. All the barriers standing in the way are gone for me."

"But not for me."

"Do you love me?"

"Of course I do."

"Do you want to have a baby? With me?"

"Yes."

"Then marry me. It can be our secret. No one else has to know."

"You did the secret-wedding thing. It was a disaster that your family and friends still razz you about. Do you want to try that again?"

"I don't, but I'm not the one who needs this to be a secret. I married Kate and kept it a secret because I got her pregnant. I didn't want to marry her. She embarrassed me. You're the one embarrassed here. Not me."

"You don't embarrass me, Jazz, and neither does the idea of marrying you. My problem is that marrying you right now will frighten my family out of their wits."

"Will it frighten your family—or you?"

He had a point. He waited for me to answer.

"I don't know, Jazz. This isn't easy. You're a cop. Put yourself in my position." It felt like a fifty-pound weight sat on my chest. "I want to say yes, but I need to think this through. I need to go out. I have some important things to do."

He sighed. "I'm going to order us some food. Come back to me, okay?"

"I will." I didn't think I could help myself. "Besides, this is my apartment."

He smiled at that, and he didn't smile much anymore.

chapter
nineteen

I ZOOMED STRAIGHT OVER to Christine's house in the Love Bug, and as before, a throng of women filled the place. The smell of patchouli and too many bodies scented the air. This time, fur skirt didn't meet me at the door; I was able to walk in and go right up to Chris. She wore a black outfit that reminded me of Jackie Kennedy's widow suit. She looked as elegant as before, even in her grief. "My condolences," I said.

She gave me a tiny smile, full of sadness. "Would you like to go somewhere and talk?"

"Sure."

Predictably, we went back to the same bedroom. Again, coats were piled high on the bed. This time a chair sat in the room. She offered it to me, pushed the coats out of the way, and reclined on the bed. She looked exhausted. "I put my best friend in the ground."

"I can't tell you how very sorry I am."

"I wish I could have gone with her. You know?"

I nodded.

"What will I do without my sweet Katie?"

I sat silent.

She pulled a silver parka over herself. "You wanted to talk to me. What can I do for you, Dr. Amanda Brown?"

I leaned forward in the chair. "Actually, I thought you may want to talk. I thought you could use a listening ear."

"There's not much to talk about now, is there?"

"Tell me about Katie."

She hugged herself under the parka. "Tell you about Katie . . ." Her voice turned wistful. "I'd never seen a woman that beautiful. She looked like a doll baby."

"So I've heard."

God, deliver me from being jealous of a dead woman.

Chris smiled, a faraway look in her eyes. "When I got paired with Jazz, everybody thought we'd get together. Partners have that chemistry sometimes."

"Had you come out at that time?"

"I didn't know I was a lesbian then. I mean, all my life, I've been attracted to women, but I had always dated men—the few who could handle me."

I nodded. She'd be hard to handle.

"The guys at the station teased me because they knew Jazz is a good-looking man, but he was a pro. He never approached me. I don't think I was his type."

Although I burned to ask what she thought his type was, I resisted. "All that speculation must have made for an unpleasant work experience."

"Not really. Cops have an odd sense of humor. They talk a lot of trash, but they don't mean anything by it. Jazz stayed focused. Did his job." She thought for a moment. "He was no angel. He had plenty of women, but he didn't take them seriously. He was a bit of a rascal."

I hated that she'd told me that. Rascals weren't near the top of my list of personal favorites.

"And then Kate came along. He didn't take her seriously, either, which made her go after him more. We all thought it was funny. Next thing you know, they were married."

"They must have had compelling reasons."

Christine paused a long time, her eyes staring and unfocused. "She was pregnant."

"He told me that was why he married her."

She looked right into my eyes. "No. I mean she was pregnant when she got killed. Two months along. We always had our cycles at the same time. I confronted her about it. She wouldn't tell me who the father was, but I think that was why she went back to him."

"To who?"

"Jazz."

I tried to keep my jaw off the floor. "Why would she go to *him*? You don't think Jazz got her pregnant again, do you?"

"Kate had her regrets when it came to Jazz. When she'd get mad at me, she'd talk about wanting a do-over with him. She'd actually try to get him back at least twice a year."

"She told you this?"

"When she was upset. But there was plenty she didn't tell me."

"He wouldn't sleep with her when she came back."

"Is that what he told you?" She laughed. "Of course that's what he told you."

I told myself that Jazz didn't lie to me, but it felt like she'd plunged a knife into my gut, then twisted it. I inwardly prayed a futile *Please God, don't let it be true* and blurted out a question that I knew would make me sound like a lovesick schoolgirl. I couldn't stop myself. "Did Kate tell you she was still seeing Jazz . . . that way?"

"Kate didn't have to tell me she was seeing somebody—a man. I've been with men. I know how we do. She was definitely still sleeping with him."

I wanted to cry. "But could it have been someone other than Jazz?"

"She carved his initial on her thigh."

"Excuse me?"

"She used to cut herself. She always left little messages on herself. She'd put a *B* on her left thigh, and the word 'bad' just above her bikini line. *B* stands for Brown, doesn't it?"

I kicked myself mentally. I should have looked at the rest of her body. Carly hadn't said anything specific about what she'd cut into her body. I tried to picture the crisscrossed marks on her arms. They'd been patterned, but not in a way that would have suggested a letter of the alphabet. Were there pictures? Surely Carly would have photographed that.

I didn't like the way Chris smirked at me. She had the upper hand, and I felt a need to upset the precarious balance between us. "*B* stands for more than Brown. Do you know what that 'bad' thing was all about?"

"I've upset you," she said.

I tried to shake it off. "I don't think he killed her. And I don't think he was seeing her."

Again that mocking smirk. "I'm sure you don't."

She was getting on my nerves. I decided to splurge. "I don't think you killed her, either, Chris."

She looked startled, but just briefly. Oh, she was a cool one. "You're absolutely right. I didn't."

"But you were there, weren't you?"

Her hard brown eyes stared me down, unblinking. Body language is a funny thing. Say a person lies. The defenses start at the top of the head, but the farther down you go, the more giveaways become apparent. Her eyes stared hyperdiligently at me, but her mouth lost it. Her bottom lip trembled, almost imperceptibly, but I caught it. "I don't know what you're talking about," she said.

"You covered her up, didn't you? No woman should be seen like that. You loved her. You wanted to give Kate her dignity back."

Our eyes locked.

Lord, let me get through to her, please.

"I said I don't know what you're talking about."

"You were there, Christine. You covered her. It didn't make sense to me, that her killer would pose her like that and then cover her up. Somebody else had to do that. It's a gesture of caring."

"I wasn't there."

"Cops aren't the only ones who can spot a liar. You wanted me to know you did that."

"You don't know me," she said, which let me knew I was right on.

"Yesterday you kept implying your guilt to me. Bobby Maguire didn't get it, did he? He came here and didn't *see* you at all, and you don't like that. You are too regal not to be seen. It was like that when you were with the Detroit police, too. You had to fight for people to take notice of you because you're a woman. Right, Christine?"

She gave me a feral grin but didn't speak.

"You resented all the Bobby Maguires you've worked with. You resented Lieutenant Pretty Boy, too. Everything came so easy to him, didn't it? Position. Women. *Kate*."

"What's your point, Brown?"

"Bobby Maguire didn't see what you did at that crime scene, and you wanted someone to see. You know that if he couldn't even see something that clear, it leaves her real killer out there."

Her hard stare fell first, and then, like dominoes falling, her shoulders slumped and her tough-babe exterior dissolved. Her eyes pooled with tears, and her voice became a whisper. "Who would do that to my Katie? What kind of person would hurt her like that?" Christine cried like a little girl.

I went to the bed, sat down, and held her, remembering those church mothers who had rocked me many a day after I'd left Adam and come home a battered, broken woman. In my mind's eye, I could see their Velveteen Rabbit–like Bibles, love-worn until the pages fell out, and the cheap leather covers softened and cracked around the edges. Romans 12:15, highlighted or underlined by ancient, shaky hands: "Rejoice with those who rejoice. Weep with those who weep."

I wanted to stay with Christine, be a friend to her in her time of need, but she had a houseful of people for that. I needed to get back to the business at hand. I released her. "Be honest with me, Chris. You don't think Jazz did that to her, really, do you?"

She shook her head. "I don't see it. Not the Jazz I worked with, but that doesn't mean he didn't do it. I've been surprised before."

"Are you going to tell Maguire you were at the scene?"

"Look. Katie and I had a fight a few months ago. I choked her. I hurt her badly. I didn't mean to, but I did. She took pictures to the local police."

"Were charges brought against you?"

"No. She didn't go until a few days afterward. She filed a report, but she said we'd fought and I'd hurt her. She hurt me, too. I have my own pictures."

"Does Maguire know that?"

"I don't think so, but I don't intend to volunteer that information. I didn't kill her. We fought, but she would start it. Every single time. She was rough. Rougher than she looked. Kate was a little crazy."

I shook my head. "You seem like a strong, powerful woman. Why did you put up with her?"

"Katie was a marvel. For the rest of my days I will never find another person as passionate as she was."

A picture of Jazz came to mind. I knew exactly what she meant.

Christine crossed her arms and slumped back against the coats, putting distance between us. I accepted her signals and moved back to the chair.

She glared at me. "I didn't kill her. If Maguire finds out I was there, he's going to think I'm good for it."

"I only want to find out what happened to her, just like you. Too much time is passing. If we don't find out who did this soon, you know the chance that we'll find him at all will diminish with each day that goes by."

She smoothed her long dreadlocks with one hand. "I know."

"Tell me about Kate's day-to-day life. What kind of people did she hang out with?"

"All our girlfriends are in this house. You can look around you to see who we spent our time with: fierce women. Beautiful, bold feminists. Then again, Kate tended to blend in with whoever she was around." She fingered a dread. "She still favored the sense of safety she felt around cops, but she had settled down—as much as she was capable of. There was only me and one man in the end."

I nodded. "Who do you think would hurt her like that?"

Chris shook her head slowly and swiped at nothing under her nose. "I can't think of anybody who would degrade her like that. Not a soul." She shrugged. "But how well do you really know anybody? I do things all the time and don't know why. I took my partner's woman, and my life hasn't been right since."

I do things all the time and don't know why . . .

She glanced at the door. Twice. Our little chat would be over soon.

"Did you follow her to Jazz's?"

"No. She called me. She was playing her games. She knew I was at my mama's house. Mom lives over on Mount Elliott. I could walk to Jazzy's loft from there. Kate wanted to make me jealous."

"What time was that?"

"About nine o'clock. At first I wasn't gonna go."

"What changed your mind?"

She chuckled. "I was jealous. I left about half an hour or so later."

I stored the jealous-lover part in my brain to process later. "How long did it take to get there?"

"About five minutes."

"What happened when you got there?"

"I walked up to the building, and the door was wide open. Jazz never left his door open. You know how he is."

Mr. Lock All Three Locks and never answer the door without asking the knocker to identify him- or herself. "So you went in?"

"Yes. She was in the bed, exposed and . . ." Christine cast her eyes down, and they filled with tears. "My Katie," she whispered.

"I'm sorry, Chris. I know this is hard for you. Did you see anyone?"

She wiped her eyes with her hands and sniffed. "Nobody. But I smelled something."

"What?"

"Lagerfeld."

"What?"

"I smelled Karl Lagerfeld cologne. Jazz doesn't wear cologne."

"You're sure?"

"I was his partner."

"I'm sorry, I know Jazz doesn't wear cologne. At least not usually. What I meant is, are you sure it was Lagerfeld?"

Christine nodded "My daddy wears it all the time. I know Lagerfeld. It's heady stuff."

I gave her my most sympathetic look. "Who could have done this to your partner?"

"I don't know, but I'd swear on Katie's grave it's a cop," she said.

"What makes you think so?"

"Cops were her thing."

I inadvertently went into therapist mode. "Will you tell me more about that?"

She stood. "You're the shrink. All I can tell you is she had a thing for cops and a thing for do-overs."

I took my cue and stood up. "Can we talk again?"

She nodded. "Give me your number. I'll call you if I think of something."

"Can I ask you just one more thing?" *Sheesh! There goes my Columbo bit.*

"Of course."

"What about the diary?"

"I don't know where it is. I've been looking for it since she . . ."

"If you think of anything—places she may have gone with whoever she was seeing—if you find a receipt or a scrap of paper with a phone number on it . . ."

"He could have done it. Jazz could have killed her." She went silent again. Seconds passed. "Sometimes Katie made *me* want to kill her, but I loved her. I will never love anyone like that again. I died with my Katie."

I looked at her—this statuesque, regal woman. I thought about the pain she must have suffered to love Kate. It reminded me again of *The Thorn Birds.* Kate was Christine's thorn tree—the one she had spent her life searching for—and when she'd found her, she'd pierced her heart on Kate's sharp thorns.

For a moment I felt afraid, and not for Christine. I realized Jazz may be my thorn tree. I was afraid of what lengths I'd go to be with him.

"I'll talk to you soon, Chris. Thank you." I gave her my hand and cringed as she squeezed it unusually hard.

"Sorry," she said. "I don't know my own strength sometimes."

I left the house, wondering if she'd inadvertently told me something else about herself and the case.

How well do we really know anybody? The question kept popping up. I rode back to Ann Arbor with the Scripture riding shotgun.

The heart is deceitful above all things, and desperately wicked. Who can know it?

I shrugged. "You've got me, Lord."

By the time I got home, Jazz was nowhere to be found. He'd left a note on my bed that read:

> *Love of my life,*
>
>   *I know you're scared. I'm scared, too. Let's remember the Scriptures say there is no fear in love; but perfect love casts out fear. You are perfect for me. Let me love you.*
>
>   *Will you meet me at 3 P.M. in Mason's office tomorrow? Please, Bell? He won't let us have our honeymoon in there like you wanted—I remembered! heh, heh—but we can get married around all those books. See. I can make you happy. Dr. McLogan and Mason's secretary*

*will witness. It won't be a secret. Bring someone else who
loves you, and even more people will know. Let yourself be
happy for a change. It's okay to have what you want.*

Jazz

There was one problem. Nobody else I loved would come.

chapter twenty

DIDN'T SLEEP. How could I? I had to make a life-changing, potentially life-obliterating, decision in just a few hours.

I'd given my heart before. And I knew what happened when you did. You opened yourself up for someone to destroy you. But I wanted Jazz so bad. I wanted a baby. I wanted Jazz's baby. But what if he destroyed me? I couldn't live through that again—especially from the man who had captured every part of me.

Jazz kept calling me, but I didn't answer the phone. I talked to Carly once. I told her that I'd gone to see Dr. McLogan and that he'd said I needed to get the procedure done *now*. I hinted that I was considering Jazz as a donor. Carly got so furious she almost had an aneurysm. I thought I'd have to call 911. I figured if I added the tiny bit of information that I might marry him the following day, I'd kill her dead. And Carly's reactions in general registered about two thousand degrees cooler than my mother's.

I didn't have many friends to concern myself with. For once that was a good thing. Rocky didn't even want me to *go* anywhere with Jazz, so I could presume he wouldn't be among the wedding guests. Lisa was worried about me as well. She'd be relieved that I'd decided to marry rather than burn, but she'd prefer he be cleared of all charges first.

Lord, have mercy!

Did I *have* any other friends? I could count Elisa, but I still smarted from the jealousy I'd felt as I'd watched Rocky singing to her baby *my* baby's song.

My baby. I could have my very own baby. A long shot, yes, but a shot! With Jazz. And I could *marry* Jazz!

Then why did I feel so sad?

I shoved that question into an internal closet and locked the door, turning my attention to the only other friend I could think of—God's little sheep He had asked me to feed: Kalaya.

I sat on the side of my bed. Picked up my cell phone. Wrestled with myself. I didn't know if I should drag her into this or not, but I didn't want to think it through alone. She may have been a baby Christian, but honestly, what kind of Christian was I? And yet my internal conflicts were too much to bear without a girlfriend.

I punched her number in. She answered right away, her voice bright and perky. Obviously, she'd had her vat of coffee.

"Kal?"

Through the anguish in my voice with that one word, she must have sensed the war going on in my head. "Bell, are you okay?"

"Yeah. Will you go shopping with me?"

"Sure, but . . . Did something happen?"

"I went to the doctor. I got some bad news. There's more, but right now I just need to shop. Are you sure you can spare a few hours?"

"I'll take two weeks off and shop in Paris with you, if that's what you need. I'll do that if that's *not* what you need. Are you sure you're okay?"

"I'm not really okay."

"Where are we shopping?"

"I don't know. Let's just say I know the softer side of Sears all too well. I need to break free. You may need to lead this little excursion."

"Do you need me to drive?"

"Probably. And I may need you to do something else for me this afternoon. Can you take the day off? I'll pay you for your time."

"Girl, you don't have to pay me. I'm down with whatever you need. Will you tell me what's up when I get you?"

"Always the reporter, huh, Kal?"

"Naw, girl, I'm a nosy friend. When should I come?"

"As soon as you can."

"I'm leaving right now."

I hung up the phone. I hadn't known if I could trust her that day in the police station. Now I thanked God for her. She was a proverbial ram—well, sheep in the bush whom God had sent to help me in a tough situation.

Even though she was a reporter, Kal didn't press me—no pun intended—for information. She let me sit quietly in her Toyota, lost in my thoughts.

I let her choose the mall, telling her only that we needed "girl stuff." We bypassed the local Briarwood Mall and drove farther, to Twelve Oaks, which looked for all the world like Briarwood to me. Okay, it did have a few more upscale stores. All right, a lot more. It boasted a Nordstrom, an Aéropostale, a Betsey Johnson, and other names I didn't know, but they smelled rich. They were places I couldn't afford.

I trudged through the parking lot, Kalaya darting worried glances at me intermittently. We walked around aimlessly for ten minutes, and when I finally stopped, she looked confused. "This is where you want to go?"

I shrugged. "I guess."

She looked at Victoria's Secret, her eyebrows raised. "Okay."

I ambled inside, feeling utterly depressed and confused. A saleslady in a black suit asked if we needed help. I needed help, all right. I told her I needed some time. That was an understatement. But I didn't have time.

I looked around, feeling like I was in some kind of teeny-weeny-bra-and-panties nightmare. They were all coming at me, thousands of them, all at once, set to a screeching horror-movie sound track, and none of them was my size. "Oh, Kalaya. I'm too fat for this."

"You so aren't too fat. What size do you wear?"

"Ten. But I'm short. I don't do size ten like you do."

"Cut it out. What exactly are you looking for today?"

"I'm looking for Victoria's secret. I thought the secret was that she got rich selling overpriced drawers to suckers like my sister, but apparently, she's on to something. And it ain't about money. That's what I'm looking for! Do you think they have books about that sort of thing here?"

"They don't sell books here. And I'm not sure that's the kind of book you should be reading."

I scanned the store and moaned. "You want to know what's wrong with me? I feel like I'm an awkward, geeky fifteen-year-old in Carly's underwear drawer. But I'm not fifteen, in Carly's shadow. I'm thirty-five. And the finest man I know—the finest man I've ever known—wants *me*! Not Carly! Me!

"I should be able to do this kind of shopping without an escort. I should be able to feel good about him desiring me. Right? I don't need to have anyone's permission to be loved, do I? Or to be sexy?"

Kalaya cleared her throat. "Bell, could you lower your voice? People are staring."

"Oh."

Still. My indignation hadn't burned out. I stormed over to a bin full of frilly wisps of fabric not much larger than shoelaces that were supposed to be underwear. I fingered through them, thinking that you-know-where would freeze over before Jazz would see one of them on me.

Kalaya trailed behind me. "What happened at the doctor's office?"

"He told me if I don't have a baby now, the chances are I never will. And then Jazz asked me to marry him. Right there in the office. He wants us to have a family together. Starting today. At three." I grabbed a red thong from the bin and got really disgusted. I held it up. "What is this? How is a full-figured woman supposed to be covered wearing dental floss?"

Kalaya didn't seem concerned about thongs. She squealed. "Really? He proposed?"

"Oh," I said, the weight of it all hitting me. "Jazz proposed. He asked me to marry him. I think I'm going to be sick." I started wobbling like a Weeble. I was sure Kalaya was too young to know what that was. I didn't bother to explain.

She took my arm. "Okay. Easy now. Do you want to sit down?"

I buried my head in the thongs. "I don't want to sit down. I want to pick out something that's going to devastate, thrill, and delight him."

Okay, I so didn't like my head buried in the thongs. I pulled myself upright. I wandered over to a display of Pink pajamas. They seemed tame, manageable, by my standards. I could breathe around the Pink stuff.

"I haven't shopped in Victoria's Secret without Carly dragging me in here since . . . Kalaya, I've never shopped in Victoria's Secret by myself! I feel lost in here. And you know what's funny? Yesterday I felt sexy. Today, when I can make being sexy legal, I don't know what to do. I don't know if I should get red, or white, or black—or anything, for heaven's sake. And this is just lingerie! God help me, what am I supposed to do about a wedding dress?"

I walked briskly to a display of angel wings only to flee them in despair. I definitely didn't belong around the angel wings.

I found a display of bras that looked bright and colorful. Something teenagers would wear. "Kal, I just said I don't remember how to devastate a man. The truth is, I have never in my life devastated a man. I have barely gotten men's attention. What in the world am I supposed to do with a man like Jazz Brown?"

I grabbed a Kool-Aid-orange bra, size 36DD. "Kate had

bosoms like this. That dead woman has the power to destroy my self-esteem!" I felt tears cloud my eyes. "She was five years younger than me. Gorgeous. I can't compete with that. And what about the wedding dress? Should I get a black one? Because lemme tell you . . ." I couldn't stop the tears now.

"Bell, you did not sleep with Jazz."

"No, I slept with a few *other* men. Maybe more than a few."

"That was years ago. You earned your virginity back."

"What if he did it, Kalaya?"

"What if who did what?"

"What if Jazz did that unthinkable thing everyone else thinks he did? What if he killed Kate and I got this all wrong?"

"You know you don't believe that."

"I'm so scared."

"I know you are. But you have to ask yourself what you're really scared of. Are you scared he's a murderer, or are you scared because committing your life to a man is terrifying?" She took my hand. "Look. Kate Townsend was up to no good, and whatever she was playing at, and whomever she was playing with, had nothing to do with Jazz. I asked Kate about Jazz. And she got miffed. She knew he was diggin' you. *She* brought you up. She said he was so-called in love."

"You didn't tell me that."

"I didn't think I needed to. I thought you knew he loves you."

"Will you be my maid of honor?"

"Of course I will. Now, let's get you some great lingerie. You'd better let me help you out. Unfortunately, I got mad skills in this."

"Will you help me pick out a dress, too? I'll buy you whatever dress you want."

"Are you kidding? I'd love to find you a dress. But I'll buy my own dress. And we'll get some shoes, and our hair and nails done. Girl, we gon' get fine for Mr. Brown today. And I'm treating you to the pampering and beauty treatments. And we'd better hurry. We don't have much time. You are going to be so dope. Don't you worry, Bell. I'll take care of you."

I let her do just that.

chapter
twenty-one

KALAYA AND I ARRIVED looking so dope, to use Kalaya's language, that I thought Jazz may not be able to drive once he partook of me.

The dress we'd chosen for my nuptials was a startlingly beautiful white satin cocktail-length formal. Soft fabric twists provided a bit of sass to the simple halter neckline. It was like the red dress that I'd met him in, but all grown up; softer, wiser, and ready to take a walk down the aisle—or across a few feet of office space—to meet him. Sasha would be proud. Of the dress, that is.

However, she'd take a belt to my backside if she knew what I was doing. Just the same, I wanted my mother there. I wanted what I'd imagined in my girlish dreams so many times before: her hands flying like doves around me as she fussed over satin, lace, and my long, flowing veil. The clucks from her and Maggie. Ma saying, "You should have worn a Wonderbra." And Maggie: "She needs a *miracle* bra" Then Carly: "Honey, you just need a *miracle*."

We stood in the bathroom, Kalaya primping and me pretending that I wasn't preoccupied with bigger concerns than makeup running if the threatening tears appeared.

Don't you cry, girl. You're going to be fat and sassy next Mother's Day, with a belly full of Jazz's baby.

I couldn't help it. A tear slid down my cheek, and it took my mascara with it on its trip down south.

Kalaya turned me to face her. "Oh, honey."

"I'm sorry. I miss my mother and sister. And Aunt Maggie."

She gathered me into a hug. "They'll celebrate later. At the baby shower."

"What if he really doesn't love me? What if he's just doing this to have a baby?"

"Bell, that man can have a baby with somebody else if he wants to. He wants you. *You*, honey." She stepped away from me long enough to grab a piece of tissue. Wiped my face with it. "Let's go in there so you can marry the man you love. The man who loves you. Okay?"

"Okay."

I followed her down the hall. At Mason's office, she knocked on the door. Another wave of panic hit me. "Nobody is here to give me away."

Kalaya opened her mouth, but no sound came out. She shook her head. That was something she couldn't do.

Dr. McLogan opened the door. He held a bouquet of Madonna lilies, roses, and baby's breath. "Jazz bought these for you," he said.

I reached for them, tentative, amazed. Roses, baby's breath, and lilies were the favorite flowers of Mary the Blessed Virgin. Jazz had chosen flowers that symbolized chastity, fidelity, miracles, mother and child.

Lord, have mercy.

What am I doing here?

Dr. McLogan saw my face. "Oh, you poor dear. What's the matter?" He stepped into the hall and closed the door behind him.

I fell apart. "Jazz picked flowers about Jesus' pure mama, and I'm so awful. And what if none of this works out? And my daddy isn't here. I'm supposed to walk in there on the strong arm of my daddy, and he's not here . . . And what if this doesn't work out? I'm so scared. I don't want to make another mistake. And . . ." I snuffled and tried to hold back the sobs.

"Oh, my dear one. I'll loan you these arms of mine. They aren't very strong, I'm afraid. But they're good arms. I've delivered many of God's little ones with them."

I must have wailed for a full five minutes while Dr. McLogan soothed and Kalaya rubbed my arms and back. Both of them huddled around me, hemming me in, reminding me of a verse I loved.

> *You hem me in—behind and before;*
> *you have laid your hand upon me.*

Did God still have me hemmed in? Or had I broken free, about to wreak havoc in my life once again? Should I stay or should I go?

My heart desperately wanted to stay. Desperately wanted to be loved and to give love—to Jazz. To pour everything I had, and everything I was, into him.

But pouring out opened the door for poison to come back in. It left my heart vulnerable.

After I pulled myself together, Kalaya hugged me long and hard. She pulled away. "You're doing the right thing, Bell. You are. Don't be afraid."

Dr. McLogan took my face in his hands just as my daddy would. "Mason and I are right here, dear girl. And we wouldn't do anything or allow anything that would hurt you. You know that. We'd do everything to protect you."

His hands, dry and powdery, continued to cup my cheeks. "You'll get to have a real wedding later, and everyone will be there, but right now it's best to do this quietly. Everything will be fine, dear one. Jazz is a good man. I wouldn't be here if I didn't believe that."

I nodded, wiped my face, and turned to Kalaya. "Is my make-up okay?"

"Girl, it looks like we wasted our time in that bathroom."

Dr. McLogan chuckled. "I'm not an expert at these things, but it looks like you've made a bit of a mess. You are a lovely bride just the same."

Kalaya nodded. "He's right."

"Okay."

"If it helps, he's as nervous as you are. But for different reasons."

"He is?"

"He loves you, dear one. Let's get in there. Your husband-to-be is anxious to see you."

I hooked my arm in Dr. McLogan's. He opened the office door, and everything disappeared—the beautiful leather furniture, the dark, brooding wood, the books, the African art, all of it gone. All but Jazz. His head was down, but as the door swung open, he looked up, and his face changed before my eyes. Suddenly, he had the face of a little boy filled with delight. For a moment I glimpsed in him the child I hoped I would kiss, comfort, and mother someday—my own son. "Dear God," I whispered.

I don't remember moving. I only know that one moment I was clutching Dr. McLogan, and the next I was facing the most beautiful man I'd ever seen, our hands clasped over the gap between us. And that fine, fine man began saying things to God about me. And he sounded like he meant them.

Mason asked him a question: "Wilt thou love her, comfort her, honor, and keep her in sickness and in health; and, forsaking all others, keep thee only unto her, so long as ye both shall live?"

I looked into Jazz's eyes—delicious brown eyes, soft and warm as Ma Brown's double-chocolate brownies. They were calling to me, calling me to trust. To love.

Jazz nodded a tiny, just-for-me nod. "I will," he answered.

Mason to me, in his "God's trombones" voice: "Wilt thou have this man to be thy wedded husband, to live together after God's ordinance in the holy estate of matrimony?"

Oh, yes. How does one stay anchored to the ground when a dream is coming true? And yet how does one fly when chained by fear and uncertainty? Truth was, this marriage had little to do with a baby and everything to do with the deepest desires of my heart.

"Wilt thou obey him and serve him . . ." Mason's voice disappeared into the sound like the adults on Charlie Brown cartoons talking. *Wonka wonk wonk wah wah.* Then his words startled me out of my consuming questions. *Obey and serve?*

"Amanda?" Mason said softly.

"I'm sorry. Could you clarify 'obey'?"

He tried to suppress a smile. "That means you'll do what he asks you to do, pumpkin."

Obey and serve? Ugly events from my past gave the words a sinister meaning. "Is that effective immediately?"

"Effective as soon as you say 'I will.'"

"Even before you pronounce us?"

Mason laughed. "I told you you'd have your hands full with this one, Jazz."

"So I see," my husband-to-be said. He didn't sound amused. He leaned toward me. "Just say 'I will.'"

"Are you going to make unreasonable demands?" I asked.

"I just promised to love and comfort you for as long as I live. Now stop torturing me and say you'll obey me."

"But—"

"Are you planning on opposing me in something important to you while we're standing here?"

"No."

"Then say 'I will' so we can go on."

I looked at him, then at Mason, who thought this was funny. Kalaya nudged me. "Say it," she hissed through a smile.

Peace slid over me from some other place. "Okay, I will."

Jazz rolled his eyes.

Mason instructed Jazz to give unto me a ring. It was short notice, so I expected something basic. But Jazz took my hand in his and pulled out a stunner. It was a one-of-a-kind breathtaking vintage Addie Lee Brown creation from the late sixties, when she'd made a brief but amazing foray into metalsmithing. She'd created a band of Madonna lilies and vines in white gold dotted with diamonds. There was only one like it in the world. The last I knew, it had been on loan to the Smithsonian Institution. I'd seen it there when I lived in Washington, D.C., and I had fallen in love with it. And Jazz was slipping it on my finger. Which meant he must have told his parents.

So much for our secret marriage.

I may have lost a large portion of our wedding ceremony staring at my ring.

Jazz yanked me back to it when he said something like "*Wonka wonk wonk wah wah* with my body I thee worship . . ."

Wait! With my body I thee WHAT?!

"Pardon me?"

Kalaya snorted.

"Tell her again, Jazz," Mason said patiently.

"I said, if you were *listening*, dear . . ." That "dear" had a definite edge to it. "With this ring I thee wed, with my body I thee worship, and with all my worldly goods I thee endow."

"What do you mean, 'with my body I thee worship'?"

"You couldn't focus on the 'with all my worldly goods I thee endow' part, could you, Bell? I offer you all my stuff—"

"With my body I thee *worship*? I've been daydreaming about my wedding vows since I was eight. I've never heard that. I would have remembered body worship."

Kalaya whispered in my ear, "It's what you've been dying for, girlfriend. Take it and run!"

I waved her off.

"Can we talk about this later?" Jazz asked.

"But you made a vow. You told God you were going to

worship me with your body. I want to know what you plan on doing."

"I'll *show* you when we get home. Can we get on with this?"

"Look, I think we need to ease into this slowly, and body worship doesn't sound like a slow process." I thought about that. "Well, maybe it does. But I . . . maybe I'm just not ready for all of this." I looked at Dr. McLogan. "I mean, all that obeying and serving is bad enough, but now . . ."

He smiled at me. "Just go with it, dear."

I turned to look at Mason.

"I think you'll enjoy whatever he has in mind, pumpkin."

I said to no one in particular, "I'm not sure I'm cut out for matrimony now that we're getting down to the business of obeying and serving and body worship."

"Are you nuts?" Kalaya asked. "You've got one of the finest men in Detroit who *adores* you and is willing to *worship* you with his body! Don't question it. Take it!"

"Thanks," Jazz muttered, still looking at me in astonishment.

"The vows are a little outdated, aren't they? Maybe we should bring them up to the current century."

Jazz sighed heavily. "Did I just vow to protect her?"

Mason answered, "You did, Jazzy."

"I said I'd love her, too, didn't I?"

"I'm afraid you did."

"And it's too late to take it back, isn't it?"

"You've made vows, son. Let's go on."

Jazz thrust his hand into his pocket and pulled out a plain gold band. He handed it to Mason, who handed it to me.

Mason took a deep breath and looked at me with raised eyebrows. "Ready, pumpkin? We really should move forward, or it will be too late to have your baby."

"Okay," I said. "What's next?"

"You say to him, 'With this ring I thee wed.'"

I took Jazz's hand. Slipped the inferior band on his ring finger. "With this ring I thee wed . . ."

A smile crept across his face.

"What?" I asked.

"There's more. You remember that 'with my body I thee worship' part, don't you?"

My eyebrows reached for the sky. "I'm supposed to say that, too?"

Jazz gave me a wicked grin. "Lay it on me, baby."

"I'm not saying that."

"Say it. You promised to obey me."

My mouth flew open. "That is so not fair."

He waited.

"It sounds a little blasphemous."

"Say it."

"You're going to want to do nasty things with me."

"I wouldn't use the word 'nasty.' The marriage bed is undefiled, baby."

"But I'm not Anglican. I'm a little uncomfortable with the whole concept of—"

Everyone present yelled, "Say it!"

"With my body I thee worship. Are you all happy now?"

"I sure am," Jazz said. "Now what about all those worldly goods?"

"And all my worldly goods I thee endow." I stuck my tongue out at him.

"Watch it. I may have plans for that tongue."

I looked to my godfather for help. "Mason!"

"You just promised to worship him with your body."

"Kalaya? Help me."

She wagged her head. "I'm on their side."

I couldn't win.

"Let us pray," Mason proclaimed. And in his "booming angel's" voice, my spiritual papa asked God's blessing upon us. He asked that we live faithfully together and that we love each other. Then he clasped our ringed hands together. I didn't feel electricity, just love—warm and binding—flowing between us.

Those whom God hath joined together let no man put asunder.

Then Mason said words that would change our lives forever. "Forasmuch as Jazz and Amanda have consented together in holy wedlock, and have witnessed the same before God and this company, and thereto have given and pledged their troth either to other, and have declared the same by giving and receiving of a ring, and by joining of hands; I pronounce that they be man and wife together. In the name of the Father, and of the Son, and of the Holy Ghost. Amen."

It was done. I was my beloved's, and he was mine. Before I could process it, he'd gathered me in his arms for his salute.

I almost protested. This felt so right and so wrong all in the same moment. But his face came near mine and captivated me. He wore cologne, something sweet, sexy, and manly. And when his lips touched mine, I opened my mouth to kiss him as fully and deeply as I could.

I surprised him, but he poured himself into me in his kiss. My heart pounded, and I could feel his own heartbeat thump through his suit. I put my arms around his neck.

Try to enjoy it, girl. He's going to figure out pretty soon you're no Kate, and it's all going to be over.

We kissed and kissed, all sweetness and passion, and for a moment I was happy. I was Mrs. Jazz Brown. I had the finest man I'd ever known, and I didn't even have to change my stationery.

How blessed was I?

For a moment.

chapter
twenty-two

FTER THE CEREMONY, Mason's secretary, Joan, had a little wedding cake and some refreshments for us. I managed to make it through the festivities, taking the required post-wedding photos. Somehow. In the photo with Kalaya, she held my hand and squeezed it reassuringly. She beamed a little too much at me and sometimes gave me knowing nudges. I frowned and nudged her back.

I was able to paste a smile over my fears. My mind didn't splinter off into the different Bells who had emerged in Dr. McLogan's office the day before, but all of their voices buzzed about my brain like mosquitoes at my ear.

I survived my "reception," the well wishes and blessings, and the kisses from the few people who supported me. And now I had to walk away with my husband. Thank God I hadn't arrived with him. That meant I didn't actually have to leave with him. He walked me to the Love Bug, holding my hand. It felt sweet, wonderful, and scary. I didn't want to be alone with him. What I wanted was for Kalaya to help me sort through the chaos in my head.

Jazz hesitated as if he suddenly felt shy around me. "I didn't sleep at all last night, you know. And even after your phone call today, saying a sort of yes, I didn't think you'd show up."

"I didn't know if I would, either," I said in a brief moment of total honesty.

"Are you sure you're okay with this?"

I wasn't sure. I was a little terrified. I didn't want to be a thorn bird dying for a love song. I wanted to be safe in my little world with a mother who would need nitroglycerin after I told her what I'd done and a sister who loved me despite our "stuff." I wanted friends who fussed because I didn't spend enough time with them, and to solve crimes I watched on TiVo or DVDs. Being a wife terrified me.

All I said to him was "I married you, didn't I?"

He gazed at me, a sober expression on his face. "Not quite the answer I was looking for. I love you, Bell."

And I love you, too—maybe too much.

"You're not going to go all mushy on me, are you?" I asked.

"We haven't gotten a chance to talk today, but I know you're unsure about this. I can see the 'come to me, go away' in every part of your body language. I'm going to honor that. I hesitate to say this because I don't want to push you before you're ready. But part of the reason we married *today* was because of the time line. We *are* trying to have a baby."

"Jazz, I know what we're trying to do."

"So why don't you just focus on that and not worry about anything else?" He leaned against the Love Bug. "Do you want to be together right now?"

"Jazz!"

"No, I don't mean like that. I mean, do you want to just be

around each other? We could have a nice dinner or go to a movie. We could talk. We could play Scrabble. We—"

"Scrabble? First of all, I would beat you horribly in Scrabble. Second, do you believe we'd end up playing board games with a license to worship each other's bodies?"

"Isn't that why we did this now?"

He did have a point.

"Look, Bell. I don't want you to be alone. This was a huge step you took today."

"Maybe *I* need to be alone right now."

I hated the words falling with ease from my traitor mouth. I wanted to be with him every moment, but I was scared to death he didn't really want to be with me. How could somebody like him truly love me? There had to be a catch. I knew I was missing something. But what? I had to protect my heart until I knew what that something was.

"When did you get so stoic? It used to be you who couldn't keep your hands off," he said.

"I couldn't help it. You're too fine for words."

We don't go together. You're the handsome prince, but I'm an ugly stepsister. And if I let go of my control now—

"You don't think I'm fine anymore?"

"Jazzy . . ."

He shrugged. Stepped back a bit from me. "How could you think I'm fine when I'm out of jail on bond? Nobody facing the possibility of life in prison is fine."

"Let's not go there."

"You don't even want me to tell my parents we're married?"

"But you did, didn't you? How else did you get that ring?"

"I didn't tell them. I got the ring weeks ago. I planned to ask you to marry me long before I did at Dr. McLogan's. That's why it was no surprise to Mason. The whole thing with the candles? I was planning on bringing you to my home. I hoped that would be *our* bed. My great-uncle made that bed. It's been in my family for generations. I thought you'd love it."

Now he tells me. "Oh, Jazz. Why didn't you tell me before all of this?" I felt like a deflated balloon. This whole thing had exhausted me. I needed to get him cleared. I needed to sort out my insanity. I wanted us to get on with our lives—together. But how?

"Let's do something tonight, Bell. Anything."

"I have some things to work on."

"Okay. I admit it. It's *me* who doesn't want to be alone right now."

"I have some things to attend to. They're really important, Jazz."

"What are you so busy with? We just got married. Let *me* be important!"

He had no idea. It *was* him I was busy with. And he'd be livid if he knew exactly all I'd be up to.

"It's just stuff," I said.

"Tell me. You're supposed to obey me."

"Shut up, Jazz. I have to go." I put my hand on the door handle of the Love Bug.

He grabbed my wrist. "Don't leave yet."

I pulled away from him. "Stop it. I'll see you later. I promise. I just have things I need to do."

"Why are you acting this way?"

Because Kate had perfect double D's. Because you're prettier than me. Because men like you would never even look at me, much less marry me. Because a freakin' thorn has pierced my heart, and I'm not sure about anything except that it feels like this once-in-a-lifetime love song is killing me. Because you didn't do it. Did you?

"I have to go."

I left him standing there and practically slammed the door to the Love Bug in his face.

Shut up, Jazz?

Stop it?

I'll see you later?

Could I have been any meaner to him? All the way home, I wondered why I'd acted like a jerk. Was it too much for him to ask to spend some time together? If it had been me clamoring for *his* attention, wild animals wouldn't have kept him from me. I could hear Mason's voice in my head: *Wilt thou love her, comfort her . . . ?* And Jazz's answer: *I will.*

So where was my comfort for him?

Okay, I didn't actually agree to comfort him. I said I'd obey and serve him.

Of course, the Holy Spirit didn't let me get away with that thought.

Are you serving him?

"Lord, give me a break, huh?"

You said you would love, honor, and keep him, in sickness and in health.

"I can't handle this, God. I need him to be free and clear of this murder rap, and then we'll be okay. I can play the happy housewife then. Okay?"

God went silent on me.

I went into my bathroom and stepped out of the satin gown. My breath caught.

I married him today.

The thought made my knees wobble, and I sat down at the edge of the bathtub, holding the dress to my heart. I shook my head, grazed my hand over my braids, and sighed.

Buck up, girl. Today is your wedding day.

No comfort there.

I stood to look in my bathroom mirror. My tired face, still a bit puffy from crying, stared back at me. "You're okay, aren't you? I mean, not a raving beauty, but not bad. So what if you don't have double D's."

I turned to the shower rod and spotted a hanger. Hung up my wedding dress carefully before going back to the mirror. I stared at my image a long time. "Mirror, mirror, on the wall, who's the fairest . . ."

He is.

Kate was.

Truer words had never been spoken. I didn't care how many vows we exchanged, Jazz belonged to the beautiful people, and I did not. He easily could have chosen a modeling or acting career instead of law enforcement. He could have had any woman he wanted. Even the Beyoncés of the world would line up for him. Mere mortals like me would always pale in the bright, shiny light of people like him.

The thought depressed me. I imagined the years passing by. In my mind's eye, I saw Jazz and me at a restaurant. He's sixty but has the rakish good looks of his father, only more so. Women still stare at him, giggling, trying to make eyes at him from across the room. Younger women. Beautiful women. Women whom he, even in his sixties, could get pregnant. While I, with my withered womb, look like a hag beside him.

There were scores of tiny lines at the corners of my eyes. I had frown lines deeper than I wanted them to be. New wrinkles showed up with regularity. My black braid extensions had a few twists of gray hair within them.

This was worse than being with Rocky, when I'd obsessed with "When he's forty, I'll be forty-seven. When he's fifty, I'll be . . ." But not once had I ever believed that Rocky loved me for anything other than just plain old me. Rocky didn't go out with fashion models. He'd rather have a woman he could worship God with. He wouldn't mind that I had Chihuahuas instead of fawns for breasts.

I closed my eyes. Opened them again to brave my reflection. "Mirror, mirror, on the wall, why would he want me at all?"

My conscience answered: *Because you're* there, *silly.*

I nodded. That explained it.

Jazz had guarded his heart for three years, and by surprise, I had knocked that wall down with a kiss when he'd least expected it. He'd told me even then that he was unavailable. When I'd told him to leave me alone, he had. He hadn't heroically come after me. He hadn't stalked me. Phoned me incessantly. He may never have come back to me, but Monday his pregnant ex came to his loft to talk. A woman he'd once gotten pregnant. Who knew what they'd discussed or what kind of impossible do-over they'd both longed for.

Now Kate was dead, Jazz could be on his way to prison, and I had married him in a last-ditch effort for both of us to have a child.

What was worse? I loved him. I turned on the water spigot and splashed water onto my face before I looked at myself. "Mirror, mirror, on the wall, who's the biggest fool of all?"

It was kind enough not to answer me.

———————

If I'd carried a day planner, my day would have been noted as follows: *Friday, December 20, marry the man of my dreams. Talk to Bobby Maguire about keeping him out of prison.*

I actually didn't want to talk about that, but keeping Jazz out of prison had been my goal as sure as my name is Amanda Bell Brown, now with a "Mrs." preceding it. That afternoon I trudged my way over to Detective Maguire's desk at the Detroit police department and found him leaning over a box of Krispy Kreme doughnuts, pondering his choices.

Honestly, the man's cholesterol had to ascend to the heavens. By distracting him, I thought I'd do a little intervention and buy him some time on the heart attack he was courting. "Hi, Bobby."

He didn't look at me at first. In fact, he flat-out ignored me.

"Chocolate-covered or glazed? How to choose? Heaven help you."

He sighed. Turned away from the box of temptations. "Girl Columbo. What brings you to my house today?"

"I thought I'd treat you to a healthy, guilt-free lunch."

"I don't feel guilty about my lunch."

"I'm sorry to hear it. You know why I'm here, Bobby."

He sighed again. "Doughnut, Amanda?"

"No, thank you, Bobby. Any more suspects?"

He went over to his fake-leather chair. Flopped down like he suffered from chronic fatigue. "I made an arrest, Amanda."

He didn't offer me a seat, but I took one anyway. "Yes, but when will you arrest the *right* person?"

"Have you talked to your mother about this?"

"Yes."

"So have I, and she thinks I have the right man."

"She's not a law enforcement officer. How about you actually do some *police work*. Investigate. Interview people. Interview more people. And then perhaps interview more people."

"Apparently, she and your sister have had difficulty reaching you this afternoon, even though you didn't have to work. All she wanted to do was tell you what Carly shouldn't have told her."

"And what's that?"

"We got his DNA results."

I braced myself. I knew what he'd say, but it would hit me like a Sherman tank just the same.

"Your boyfriend's skin is under his wife's fingernails."

It took my breath away. I collected myself and said, "I could have told you that. But what about the hair you found? Did you match the hair to his?"

"Your boyfriend has brown hair."

"You have brown hair, Maguire."

"It ain't my hair."

"Is it Jazz's hair?"

He leaned back in his chair, which made a very unpleasant noise under his weight. "We don't know."

"You don't know? Surely you'd be anxious to say the hair was a match?"

"We lost it."

"*What?*"

"We lost that piece of evidence."

"I cannot believe that, Bobby. How could you lose that kind of forensic evidence? Jazz Brown sure doesn't have it. It sounds like a setup to me."

"Keep your voice down."

"How am I supposed to stay calm with this kind of incompetence going on? A man's life is at stake."

"A man with brown hair and his DNA under his dead wife's fingernails."

"She's his *ex*-wife, Maguire."

"Nice ring, Amanda."

I touched my wedding band protectively. I had started not to wear it, but it was so beautiful . . .

"Didya get married recently, Amanda? Your mother didn't tell me that."

"What makes you think I got married?" I knew my body was betraying me. The tiny beads of sweat forming at the top of my lip. The tremor in my voice. A tiny twitch in my left eye. It screamed all the information Bobby Maguire wanted to know, and I couldn't help it.

"The wedding band on your finger."

Among other things I'm sure he wanted to add.

"Who says this is a wedding band? Lots of single women wear rings there. Maybe it's a promise ring."

"What'd he promise?"

"Maybe it's just a cute ring that I want to wear."

"Maybe you got married."

"Did you know she was pregnant?"

"Who, Amanda?"

"Kate Townsend."

"You mean the *former* Mrs. Brown."

"Did you know she was pregnant, Bobby?"

"The *former* Mrs. Brown *was* pregnant. My question would be, how'd you know that?"

"*Ms. Townsend* was pregnant."

"We told your sister not to give you any more information regarding the *former* Mrs. Brown."

"Ms. Townsend. I didn't find out she was pregnant from my sister."

"Who's your source?"

"Was it his baby?"

"Why don't you ask your husband?"

"Why don't you ask my mother if I'm married? Are you going to answer my question, Bobby?"

"Whether or not she was pregnant is police business and the *former* Mrs. Brown's personal *affair*, Amanda."

He went back to picking doughnuts out of the box.

I didn't know what happened. One moment I seemed to be okay. I knew I was stressed. I knew he was irritating me, but when he seemed to dismiss me for doughnuts . . . My hands seemed to act of their own accord. They shot out and slapped the box off the desk and onto the floor.

I found this strange woman who looked like me yelling, "Listen to me. I'm sick and tired of playing games with you. A woman was brutally murdered, and one of your own was accused." The room went quiet. Everyone stared at me. "You people are supposed to be there for him. He would die for you. For any one of you. And what is this? You let him down because he's good-looking?"

Bobby put on his body-language armor. He crossed his arms and wiped his hand across his mouth. "Take it easy, Amanda."

"Don't tell me to take it easy. I'm taking this hard. You're letting down somebody very important to me."

"Why don't you sit down, okay?"

"Why don't you get up and find out who did it." I turned all the way around slowly. "I know it was a cop. And I'm telling you, I'm not gonna rest until I find out *what* cop. Do you all hear me? A cop killed Kate Townsend."

Bobby Maguire grabbed my arm. "Sit down."

I snatched my arm away from him. "I'm serving all of you notice. I won't rest. Until—"

"*BROWN!*" a voice shouted behind me.

I turned. Archie IAD stared me down with fire in those ordinarily cold amber eyes. His chiseled features were distorted into a mask of rage.

Maguire stepped in front of me. "Amanda was leaving, Archie."

"She'd better be leaving. Fast. And let me tell you something,

Miss Brown. If I ever see you in this building again, you'd better be on your way to jail, or you will seriously regret it. Do you
understand me?"

I didn't say anything, which put him in a bigger rage.

"Do you?" he shouted.

Maguire sighed. "I'll make sure she understands. I'll talk to
her, Archie."

And on the way out of the building, he did just that.

chapter
twenty-three

L
ORD, I WISH *I didn't have to go home to an empty apartment
today* was my silent prayer of desperation as I wearily
climbed the stairs. In the hall leading to my door, I could
smell something rich and exotic cooking. *Mercy,* I thought. *I wish
I had some of that food.*

I should have wished for ten million dollars and a trip to
the islands while I was at it. As soon as I unlocked my door and
swung it open, a strong breeze from a Caribbean kitchen blasted
me in the face.

Jazz came out, still wearing his suit from the morning, sans
the jacket. His tie was gone, and the top three buttons of his shirt
were undone. They teased me to take a few more down and reveal what treasures lay below.

In his Ricky Ricardo voice, he bellowed, "*Lucy,* I'm hooo-
ooome."

I laughed. *What a charmer he is.*

The smells may have been island, but the look of my place
had a distinctively Christmas flair. As I scanned the room, my
eyes lit on one delight after another. He'd set up a Christmas tree
in the corner of the living room, near the table Amos's cage sat

on; the decorations, still in their boxes, were piled beside it. "You brought Christmas with you," I said.

Sweet and mellow Christmas sounds drifted from my CD player in the living room. A bottle of bubbly chilled in one of my saucepans on the coffee table. I laughed at the sight of it. Eggnog, sugar cookies, presents! He'd done it all.

"You silly man," I said, hanging my coat in the closet. "What are you doing here?"

"I had to come back to get my . . . you know."

I kicked out of my snow boots. "Your what? Your toothbrush?"

"Sure. Why not? Among other things. And since I knew I was coming, I brought some man food and a little holiday cheer with me."

"You really do think of everything."

"You have no idea. Yet," he said.

"I'm not going to touch that one."

"Aw. Where's your sense of adventure, my bride?"

I started to protest, but he'd hung Christmas lights all around, and everything looked twinkly and full of promise. "I'm in a really cranky mood," I said.

He stepped over to the coffee table. "We can't have that, my queen."

I groaned. "Don't start with the queen stuff."

He looked surprised. "You have a problem with being called my queen?"

"Next thing I know, you'll be giving me an African name and writing bad poetry about me being your Nubian sistah."

"Is that an Adam thing? I didn't mean to trigger a bad memory."

Lord, God! Help me. I got upset because he'd called me his queen. I felt a soft Holy Spirit nudge. *You're afraid he'll get to be king.*

Not right now, God, okay?

I sighed, looking at Jazz's embarrassed expression. My braids felt like they weighed a ton. "That one was my fault. I'm sorry, Jazz."

He laughed. "Calling you baby is fine with me." He reached for me. "Come here. Let Daddy take the edge off."

I went to him. Couldn't help myself. "Daddy?"

"I'm practicing. Have a seat."

I sat on the couch, lulled by the warmth in the room, the smells, the heat from his hand rubbing circles at the back of my neck. "How does that feel?"

It felt heavenly, but something in me wouldn't allow me to enjoy it. Maybe it was the conversation with Christine. Maybe the one with Maguire or Archie. I felt frustrated and more than a little angry. I stiffened and pulled away. "What are you cooking?"

He reluctantly released me. "I'm finished now. It's jerk chicken, peas, and rice."

I asked more harshly than I intended to, "How did you find time to do all this?"

His expression hardened a bit. "I don't have anything else to do these days."

Why didn't I just shoot him? A kinder option than death by hostility. "Sorry."

He stared at me. "Where've you been?"

I'd already led off with my "How did you find the time?" comment. Why not suck all the joy out of the room? "I said I had some things to attend to."

"You've been gone for hours. What things?"

"Jazz, I'm a little busy. That's all. What do you think, now that you're my husband, you can demand to know where I am all the time?"

"Actually, I can, and I'd have no problem telling you where I spend my time."

I didn't respond.

He tried to recover his good mood. "Are you hungry?" Then it tanked again. "Or did you have a moment of being not so busy and eat dinner?"

"I'm hungry, Jazz. And tired. Too tired to tango with you."

"I'm not here to tango. At least not this way. I thought doing these things for you would make you . . ."

"What?"

"Never mind."

We sat in silence for a moment. I didn't feel like we could kill the mood any more than we had. "Your DNA test results came in."

"I know. I talk to my lawyer every day."

"So you know it's your DNA under her fingernails."

"We both knew that, Bell. And I'm not talking about me and my lawyer."

"Did they test the baby's DNA?" I asked, as if that were an innocent question.

He sank back into the cushions. "What are you talking about?"

"Did they test Kate's unborn baby to see if it matched your DNA?"

"I don't really know. He didn't mention that to me."

"Did he mention your ex's pregnancy?"

"No."

"Did he know about it?"

"I pay him very good money to know as much as he can." We were quiet. Several minutes passed. "Why don't you ask me what you really want to know? Your—as my dad would say—burning question."

I decided not to dillydally around this time. I tried to plunge in, but all that came out was "Did you . . ." I tried. Honestly, I did, but suddenly, it felt like something was squeezing my chest.

"Try again, Bell. Your burning question."

"Did you see her while we were falling in love?"

"What do you mean, did I *see* her?"

"You know what I mean, Jazz."

"If you mean did I ever come across her, yes. I told you, a few times a year she came on to me. Ask your burning question."

The anger simmering inside went to full boil. Rage bubbled out of my mouth. "Did you sleep with her during those times?"

"That's your question? C'mon, baby, we went through this at my parents'. Ask me what you want to know."

"I want to know if you knocked her up." I couldn't believe I'd use such coarse language with him.

"No, I wasn't sleeping with her, and I didn't knock her up."

"When did you find out she was pregnant?"

"When she came over that night."

"So you two must have been nice and cozy. All that intimate personal conversation."

"I wouldn't say it was all that."

"A beautiful woman in a skimpy black dress telling you all her little secrets? She must have gotten some encouragement from you. Why else would she try to seduce you?"

"Kate never needed encouragement for that."

"Were you *really* good friends with her?" I practically spat the words at him.

"Not at all."

"Oh, but she told you her secrets sometimes."

That pretty woman with the perfect body and the face of an angel. That woman so unlike me.

He blew air from his cheeks.

"You didn't turn her away, did you?"

"No, but I didn't touch her."

"Why not?"

He shrugged. "I'm a decent guy."

"I heard you're a rascal."

He didn't respond.

"What would the two of you talk about?" My own posture went on the defensive. I crossed my arms over my chest.

"She did most of the talking. She either talked about wanting to be with a man again, or she talked about some madness between her and Christine."

"Madness like Christine choking her?"

"How did you know about that?"

I crossed my legs. "Did you know Christine hurt her badly enough that Kate took pictures?"

"I'm the one who took the pictures for her. She was in pretty bad shape, and I told her to go to the police. You could see bruises around her neck in the shape of Chris's hands. How did you know that?"

"So you were her protector?" *All I had to do was tell you to go, and you walked away from me without a fight.*

"It doesn't appear that I was, does it?"

"It appears that she knew she could go to you when she was in trouble." I wanted to ask him: *Did you still want her?* But I couldn't.

"A lot of people in trouble come to me. She needed help. I took pictures. That's it."

"What did you talk about with her on Monday?"

"Do I have to recount every conversation I've ever had with her?"

"No, just the one you had with her right before she died."

Did you still love her?

He shifted his position on the couch. Turned his body toward me. His knee touched my thigh. "What do you want to know besides whether or not I was still into her?"

I couldn't bring myself to ask. "Why did she tell you she was pregnant?"

"She felt nostalgic."

"Nostalgic?"

"She said it made her think about us."

"Did it make *you* think about the two of you?"

His eyes bored into me. "Yes. You may want to keep in mind that wasn't a pleasant memory for me."

"Whose baby was it?"

"I honestly don't know."

"Why didn't you mention her pregnancy when we were brainstorming at your parents' house?"

"There were a few things I didn't mention at the house."

"I noticed that."

He touched my hand and I took a deep breath. "What do you want to know, Bell?"

I want to know if you love me—if you really love me.

"What was the big secret that your family knew but you wouldn't tell me?"

He cradled my hand in both his. "That's not what you want to know."

"Tell me!"

"Okay. I was involved in an undercover investigation. Apparently, we had a dirty cop, and we thought he may be in homicide. I was working with IAD to try to find out who it was."

"With Archie?"

"How do you know Archie Dandridge?"

"I met him. Not a very charming man."

Jazz hmmphed. "Good ol' Archie, my childhood rival, doing what comes naturally." He shook his head. "No, I don't imagine you'd like him. He'd have a ball with you, though, just because you're mine." He grazed his hand through his hair.

"I'm not yours."

"I've got a license that says you are."

Neither of us spoke for a minute.

"You *have* been busy, Mrs. Brown. Obviously, you've had a little talk with Christine. You've spoken with Maguire. With Dandridge. Remarkable for a woman I asked to stay out of this."

"I'm in it. I'm married to the prime suspect! What could your undercover investigation have to do with Kate?"

"I asked you not to sleuth. I told you it could be dangerous."

"Do I look like I'm hurt?"

"You want the truth? Yes, you look hurt! There are more ways to be hurt than physical."

I faced him again. Took a deep breath. "What happened with the undercover investigation?"

"You're not going to acknowledge what I just said?"

"The investigation, Jazz."

"When Kate died like that, I initially thought someone had sent me a message. I didn't like that message."

"What kind of message?"

"That they knew I was on to them and they'd make my life hell. Killing Kate was a whole lot more cruel than killing me. I'd go to prison for the rest of my life for that. And who knows, maybe they had a little vendetta against Kate, too."

"And you couldn't tell me that?"

"I didn't know if they got Kate because it was Kate, or if they would have hurt anybody who happened to be in my life. It occurred to me that maybe they'd want to devastate a cop by hurting the woman everybody in Detroit called my girlfriend."

"So why are you here now?"

"Because IAD figured out who the dirty cop was. He had a solid alibi for the night Kate died."

"What was it?"

"A bullet in his head since Sunday. They found him Tuesday

morning in his apartment. He knew we were on his trail, confessed his crimes on a cassette tape, and took the easy way out.
And that's that. Anything else you want to know?"

"What kind of cologne are you wearing?"

"Lagerfeld."

"*Lagerfeld?* When did you start wearing that?"

"I don't wear it often. I thought today was special."

I felt like he'd knocked the wind out of me. But he hadn't
been wearing cologne when he came to me Monday night. Had
he? Wouldn't I remember that?

"Anything else?"

"Not at the moment."

"Bell. Souldier told me that they also found leather under
her fingernails. Whoever killed her had on leather gloves. Very
expensive brown calfskin leather. I don't have any leather gloves.
If I did, I'd probably go with black ones. And certainly not expensive calfskin ones."

That bit of news brought my emotions swinging back to the
calm side. "That's good."

"It's not the most compelling evidence in the world, but it's
something."

"Something beats nothing."

"They're going to see that it could have been someone other
than me."

I wasn't so sure. I eased my body deeper into the couch
cushions and propped my feet up on the coffee table. I considered drinking the entire bottle of champagne. I was about to
reach for it when Jazz ran his finger up my arm with electrifying
results.

"Mind if I ask you a few questions?" he asked.

"Yes."

"I told you everything you want to know. Be fair."

"Who said all is fair in love and war?"

"Is this love or war?"

I stood up. "I'd like dinner now." I tried to walk toward the kitchen, but he stood, too, and took my hand in his.

"Oh, no, you don't. I've got a burning question."

The way he looked at me, more than that was burning.

"What is it, Jazz?"

"What happened between the kiss you gave me this afternoon, when you became my wife, and now?"

"I don't know what happened," I lied.

He stood and put his arms around my waist. He looked into my eyes. "I think you need a little bit of that comfort I vowed to God today that I would give you."

"I hate this, Jazz. I hate thinking about all of Kate's tawdry little entanglements. I hate wondering if you're the man I think you are. And I hate wondering what's going to happen to you. Maguire thinks you're guilty, and that pompous Archie Dandridge—"

"I'm not one of Maguire's favorite people. He's in the camp that believes my face got me my position. Dandridge has hated me since the seventh grade."

"They're not even entertaining the idea that someone else could be responsible. That's terrifying to me."

"It is to me, too."

"Are you scared?"

"Of course I'm scared. I'm scared to death."

"What are we going to do?"

"*You* are going to stop sleuthing. And *we* are going to pray very hard that God will do what *He* does: take care of us. Do justice. All of that, baby. I see you got a copy of *The Divine Hours*. We're going to start using it. We pray the hours at my parish. It's not this version, but it's similar. We can make our life work. You, me, and God."

"It seems like we should do more than pray."

"We can do more than that."

I looked up into his kind eyes. I felt hopeful for the first time that day. "What else can we do?"

"Do you know what I came back here for? What was so important to me?"

"I'm guessing it wasn't your toothbrush."

"It wasn't."

"Did you leave your cell phone or wallet?"

"Nope."

"The clothes you had on Wednesday?"

"I came back for my wife."

"Jazz. I'm just an ordinary woman. I don't look like Kate—there is nothing about me that—"

He silenced me with his finger to my lips. "There's nothing ordinary about you. I love you, Bell."

He leaned down and placed a tender kiss on my lips. Just a tiny kiss. Sweet. Hunger and need for him consumed me. He took my hand in his and walked me to the bedroom door.

"Mrs. Brown?"

I didn't say a word.

"Let me show you that you are the only woman I've wanted since the moment I saw you in that red dress."

Even if he didn't truly love me, maybe this could be enough. Father, forgive me, for I know what I'm doing.

I squeezed my husband's hand and let him take me wherever he wanted to go.

chapter
twenty-four

I WATCHED HIM SLEEP, taking in the line of his jaw. His full, intoxicating lips, with a bit of a smile about them. The eyes shut tight beneath his strong masculine brows. The Irish nose, just like Jack's. The soft brown waves of his hair. His stunning beauty.

You are comely, my love.

I squeezed my eyes shut, only because they had filled with tears. I could not cry. Not in his arms. "Oh."

My bones had turned to liquid. His loving had made me a storm. I was wet skin, a tangle of languid limbs flush against him. I could almost feel my blood rushing like wind to find its way from my heart to my head, hands, fingers, feet, toes. I could hardly move, but the tempestuous waves crashing in my soul demanded release. Jazz's comforts were spent. I needed the Lover of my soul.

I'm so sorry, Jesus.

But all I heard in reply were those gales of grief within, threatening to crush me. Hot tears slid down my face.

"Please, God," I whispered, "I don't want him to wake up and see me crying."

We were perfect, every moment of our togetherness—like jazz—all soaring notes, brazen beats, and complicated melodies.

Spent, I knew I had given him everything I had. I had opened the door of my soul to this man, giving him the power to devastate me. The knowledge spawned fear, giving way to fight or flight.

I chose flight.

The strength to move away from him surged inside of me. I slid out of his embrace, pulling my great-grandmother's Star of Bethlehem quilt over my body. Jazz only stirred, still deep in slumber.

I tightened the quilt around me. There were stories in that quilt. Lessons. Strength and direction. Ma Brown had told me in the time of the Underground Railroad, if a runaway slave found a house with the quilt of the North Star flung around the roof, someone would be there to help them. A guide to take them safely forward.

"Where is my someone?" I cried into my fist, clutching the quilt. "I need help, right now. I don't know where to go from here."

And as in the eye of the storm, my soul went silent, and I heard God speak to me the words my great-grandmother had said to me until the day she died: *Call on Jesus.*

But I didn't call on the Lord. He seemed a little too far away. I wanted comfort I could hear in a voice sweet and familiar. A voice that would not let me down in a time of trouble. I wanted the man who'd prayed me through the worst days of trying to piece my life back together, even though at the time, he was little more than a goofy kid who loved the Lord.

I wanted to talk to my pastor.

I snatched my cell phone from my nightstand and punched in Rocky's number, padding quietly into the living room. It was late, but he'd take the call no matter what time it was. I stood in the corner of my living room, across from the naked Christmas tree in the other corner. I slid down to the floor, listened to his phone ring, and waited for the comfort of my friend. It occurred to me that maybe he wasn't home. I was just about to hang up—

"Hello?"

His voice sounded lively. He wasn't asleep at all.

"Rocky," I whispered.

"Babe?"

"Hi."

He could tell something was wrong. He spoke as softly as he would to a newborn. "Hi, babe. What are you doing?"

"I'm sitting in the corner."

"Why are you sitting in the corner?"

"Rock, do you think you could be with someone if you loved them but you knew they would never love you the same way?"

"I know I could. You know I could, too."

"I don't deserve you."

"That's not true. It has nothing to do with what anyone deserves. It's just love, babe."

I laughed, despite my pain. "I'm scared, Rocky."

"Scared of what?" I could hear the alarm rise in his voice. "Has someone hurt you?"

"I don't know." I dissolved into tears.

I could hear Rocky shushing and soothing me with his voice, as honey as his blond hair. "Babe, what happened to you?"

"It's what could happen. What must happen. I'm sure of it."

"What could happen?"

"I just need you to pray for me. Can you pray for me?"

"I will pray. Just tell me one thing."

"What is it, Rocky?"

"What did he do to you?"

Another wave of tears, sharp and cutting as a blade, assaulted me. Between sobs, I choked out the words: "I just want to be safe. And to be loved."

"You don't know how to be loved, babe. I've been trying to love you for seven years."

"I'm so sorry. I'm—"

"What did he do to you?"

"How do you know it was—"

"Who else would it be?"

"I wish I'd never met him."

"What do you mean?"

"I feel things with him. I do things—"

"Are you okay?"

"Yes. No. He didn't do anything. I can't explain it. I'm a little confused. I'm feeling so scared. Just pray for me, okay?"

"Okay. I will. Will you stay on the phone with me?"

"I can't, Rocky. My heart is broken."

I heard his voice catch as he said, "Mine, too."

"I'm so sorry."

"So am I."

I hung up the phone without even saying good-bye. I rocked myself in that corner, sobbing and wiping my nose on my favorite quilt.

Ten minutes later, I heard a soft knock at my door. It certainly wasn't Jazz. And my mother and Carly had keys.

Oh God, what have I done?

I dropped the quilt on the floor and pulled on my robe, rushing to the door before Jazz could hear. Rocky stood there. His cheeks and nose were pink, and his eyes red-rimmed and teary. "Babe." He pulled me into his arms.

"Rocky, you shouldn't have come."

"I needed to know you're okay."

"Please, you have to go now."

"I'll fight for you. I will."

"You're not a fighter, Rocky. You're a turn-the-other-cheek guy. You're the disciple who rests his head on the bosom of Jesus."

"I want to be with you. Let's try again."

"It's over between us. You have to go now."

"I know you love him, I know you want to be with him, but pick me. Guys like him, they have everything. He doesn't need you like I do."

"He doesn't have everything, Rocky. His life is a mess right now."

"He has you. He has everything I want."

I glanced at my bedroom door, worried that Jazz would hear us. "I'm not everything you want."

"I knew he'd take you away from me."

"Let me tell you something, Rocky. I can't be with a man like him. I'm in some kind of crazy dream. I'm not meant to be with an Adonis or a god. Guys like him don't pick me. They don't pick me."

"I pick you. I love you. Be with me."

I stepped out of his embrace. "Shhh. Listen to me. I saw you singing to Elisa, and there was something magical and beautiful there."

"That was dumb and insensitive of me. I shouldn't have done that. I'm a blockhead. I'm sorry."

"I saw something in the way you looked at her. In the way she looked at you. Something undeniable. Let yourself have it."

"I just made a mistake. I wanted to make her happy."

"You *can* make her happy, Rocky. Do it."

He shook his head. Stepped up to me and tried to gather me in his arms but hesitated. "I've loved you for a very long time. I'm always going to love you."

Oh, this hurt. Rocky really was my rock. He was always the love I could depend on. The love that didn't demand anything of me. The one I knew would never leave me for the perfect woman. To Rocky, I *was* the perfect woman.

I cradled his sweet face. "Let me tell you something, okay, babe?" I whispered. He loved it when I called him babe. "I'm a psychologist, and I know these things." I smiled at him, and he smiled back through his unshed tears. "You've believed I'm the only one for you for so long that it's automatic thinking now. It's not true, Rock. You just think it's true because you haven't really looked at it in so long. But think about our lives. We don't see each other that way anymore. We haven't dated for over a year, and you do great without me. I see how you look at Elisa—"

His voice dropped to match my whisper. "I'm sorry. She's so pretty. I don't mean—"

"You do mean it. And that's good. 'Cause she needs a good man like you to help her with that baby, and all the other green-eyed, towheaded babies you'll give her. She's twenty-three. She's got many babies in her. She has what you need, not me."

"I don't care about the babies. It's you I want."

"It's not."

"Just let me show you. Let me show you how much I want you."

The second man who'd said something like that to me tonight.

Rocky gathered me in his arms and kissed me so softly and tenderly that my heart broke in a thousand pieces. I didn't know how to stop him and tell him that I was ruined for any man, including my husband, who lay sleeping in my bed.

At least I thought he was sleeping—until I heard his voice cut into me like a machete.

"Did you ever get that déjà vu feeling? Like you've done this whole thing before?"

Rocky released me. He looked confused at seeing the half-naked man standing at my bedroom door. Then the reality of the situation dawned on him. "You slept with him" came out of his mouth. A statement, not a question.

I stood centered between the two most important men in my life, my husband and my pastor and friend. I felt like the woman in the Bible caught in the act of adultery, waiting for the first stone to come crashing into my head. Jesus chased her accusers away, but where was He now? The only thing I could think to say sounded hollow, even to me: "This is not what it looks like."

Jazz laughed. "It's not? It looks like you crawled out of bed with me to go lock lips with another man. Correct me if I'm mistaken."

"It's not what it looks like."

Rocky spoke. "Which one of us are you talking to?"

"Both of you."

Rocky's face had turned as stony as his name. He moved toward my door, turned back to me, and asked what he already knew. "Did you sleep with him?"

"What?" Jazz said. "Is that a sin?" He shot a look at me. "It wasn't a sin to make love to you, was it?"

My eyes pleaded with him. "Please stop."

"*Please stop?* That's not what you said in the bedroom."

"You've made your point, Jazz," I said.

"You've gotta admit, it's a good point."

Rocky excused himself. "I should go."

"Yes. You should," my husband said.

Rocky hesitated. "Babe?"

Jazz roared, "Don't. Call. Her. Babe." He lunged at Rocky, but I grabbed him.

"Jazz, no." I stood between them, clinging to my husband's bare chest. "Please, Jazzy. Can you just go into the room?"

"You want me to go somewhere? So you can finish up?"

"Amanda," Rocky whispered. He never called me Amanda.

"Yes, Rocky?"

"I'm the one who should leave." He turned to go. Just before he opened the door, he looked back to me. "Please find another church to go to." He slipped quietly out of my apartment and closed the door behind him.

I looked at my husband. His look burned.

"Go to another church? He aims too high. I say go to hell.
Amanda."

He stormed into the bedroom and slammed the door. I could
hear him cursing and talking to himself. I stood in the middle of
the room, as still as a stone, shivering in the quilt.

A few minutes later, he came out of the room. He threw the
keys to my apartment across the room. They slammed against
the wall and went crashing to the floor. Amos didn't make a
sound.

"Don't you ever come near me again. I don't want a marriage
to you. I don't want a baby with you. And I don't want *you.*"

He looked like he wanted to say more, but he bit his bottom
lip and hurried out of my door. His last words hung in the air.

I don't want you.

I'd known that's what would happen. I'd known it all along.

chapter
twenty-five

MY PHONE RANG all morning as if a national tragedy had struck. My caller ID revealed that all kinds of folks wanted a word with me, including my boss. My mother must have continuously speed-dialed. I didn't want to talk to anyone. I just wanted to stay curled up in a ball under my great-grandmother's Star of Bethlehem quilt, hoping she'd send the magi my way to lead me back to Jesus.

What I got was someone pounding at my door like the police. My heart fluttered. *It's Jazz!* I couldn't decide if that was a good thing or not.

I took the time to throw on my ratty peach pajamas, though the silver gown lay on the chair beside my bed. *Let him suffer a little bit, too,* I rationalized. I unlocked the locks and swung the door open.

"Good heavens!" I said.

Kalaya stood there, looking livid. "Why aren't you answering your phones? I tried your cell, your landline. I paged you on your beeper."

"Come in, Kal. I had a bad night. I didn't want to answer the phone."

She followed me into the living room. "Well, I'm sorry to say that I'm not bearing good news. Literally."

"What's going on?"

"You're in the newspaper."

"In the *Beat*?"

"You know the *City Beat* doesn't come out until Monday. You made the *Metropolitan Daily*, girl."

I sat down, stunned. "Why would I be in the *Daily*?"

She thrust the paper in my hand. The front-page headline screamed, DEATH, DECEIT, AND SOME SMOOTH JAZZ.

"What is this?" I asked.

"It a riveting tale of how Detroit's *finest* weaseled the state's potentially best witness into marrying him so she wouldn't testify in court against him for the murder of his ex-wife."

I scanned the article. "Oh my Lord." I thought about Dr. Fox calling me repeatedly this morning. "I'm going to lose my job. That rabid IAD officer has been chatting up my boss. This is just great." I felt the walls of my self-deception crumble under the consequences of my choices. "This is my fault. This is all because I wanted him."

"What do you mean?"

"I wanted him badly. It was like my sister said. I wanted him so much that I couldn't see what was right in front of me. I let my lust blind me to the truth."

"I know I just got back into your life, so what do I really know? But I can't believe you married him just to have sex."

"Maybe I don't love him at all."

"Amanda Bell Brown, you couldn't convince me if you had a million years that you don't love Jazz."

"Oh, Kal. I don't know why I married him. Maybe because

I didn't think he'd ask again when this is all over. Do you think he'd pine for me when he's free and clear? He can have whoever he wants."

"Apparently, he wants *you*."

"Or me to bow out of testifying because I'm his wife."

"You don't believe that."

"I don't know what to believe."

She cradled my elbow. "I need to write a story."

I snorted incredulously. "A story? I'm sorry, Kalaya. You missed your scoop. Somebody's already got my story. It looks like they got the whole enchilada. Kate's murder, Jazz charming me right out of my brand-new Victoria's Secret panties, right here for all the world to see."

"You need help. What if you lose your job?"

"There's no way I can afford to live off of what my private practice pays."

"Let me help you."

"How?"

"I'll write another story. Front page of the *Beat*."

"And how is your writing a story going to help me?" I shook my head. Laughed. "You just want what you want, exactly like I did. You never had any interest in me, and I liked you so much. I thought we could be friends." I guessed sheep and the people who fed them weren't meant to pal around.

"Bell Brown, I *am* your friend. You led me back to Christ, and I will be grateful for you for all of eternity. But I also happen to be a journalist and the one person in this world right now who will write a story that won't make you look like the biggest fool in metropolitan Detroit."

"I married a man out on bond for murdering his ex-wife. I *am* the biggest fool in Detroit."

"You're a woman in love."

"I'm an irrational, crazy woman in lust."

She sighed. "You know what I'm getting at. Do you love him?"

I paused. Chewed my lip. "I don't know."

"What do you mean, you don't know? It's been all over you from day one."

"Maybe it's just lust."

Kalaya slapped her hand to her forehead. "Be serious, Bell."

I put my head in my hands. "I think I love him. I don't know. I'm so confused." I looked up at her. "I'm so scared."

Kalaya looked at me in astonishment. "What do you think married love includes? No physical desire for each other? Doesn't a great marriage include great sex?"

"I don't know. My sexual desires have gotten me in trouble in the past."

Kalaya sighed. "Okay. Let's try a different tack. Do you think he played you? Did he marry you to keep you from testifying?"

How well do we know anybody?

The hurt in his eyes. His rage. All that was real. It had nothing to do with court and murder cases. I thought about what Jazz had said about letting God take care of us. Letting God do justice. He had seemed sincere. "I don't think that's why he married me."

"We're going to write us a story, girl."

"I think it's too late for that."

"No, it's not, baby. We're going to write ourselves a love story the likes of which the Big Motor has never seen. It's going to be better than *Romeo and Juliet*."

"*Romeo and Juliet.* Now, that's apropos. A tragedy! Jazz walked out on me when he caught me kissing my pastor last night. He never wants to see me again."

"He caught you doing what?" Kalaya stared at me, the idiot. "Why in the world would you do that?"

I started to answer, but I didn't know why, either. So I jumped to the end of the story. Tears gathered in my chest, behind my eyes. "It's over."

"We'll see about that. Now tell me everything, starting from the moment you met."

I told her everything, sparing no detail. I told her about the red dress and stiletto heels, the one minute of love, his being unavailable, and the call I made from Gabriel's house of horrors to tell him good-bye because I thought that crazy man would kill me. How Jazz came for me and how he'd told me we'd just gotten started. I told her about sugar-glider CPR, Madonna lilies, sweetheart roses, and baby's breath. About Jazz on his knees promising to honor me. About the tearful, angry confrontation when I stood between my two favorite people.

Kalaya and I both cried.

After our sniffles had subsided and I could speak again, I said to her. "I'm going away."

"Where?"

"Far from Detroit. My friend Lisa has a little cabin up north."

"I think that's a good idea. I'm gonna miss you, though. I got a copy of *The Message*. I was hoping we could study together."

"We will. Soon."

She looked a little sheepish. No pun intended. "Look, I know I just asked you *way* too much information about you and Jazz. And I know I'm a Christian now, and I'm so not supposed to ask you this question, but I have to know. And keep in mind that you owe me."

"What?"

"How was the honeymoon, otherwise?"

"It was smokin' hot, girl."

She hit my arm. "Oh, I hate you for that."

We laughed like a couple of girls.

Kalaya rubbed my arm. "God's gonna fix this."

"I don't think so. But thanks. Look out for him, huh?"

"Don't you worry about Jazz. God has his back."

"Kal, look into everybody. The Royal Oak police had pictures of Kate. She'd been strangled by Christine. I need to see them. Either the morgue or Souldier has pictures of Kate postmortem. I need to see the scars on her thighs. Christine said she'd carved the letter *B*. I have to see it. And I need to know if Kate carved the word 'bad' into her abdomen."

"Anything else?"

"Look into any cops in Detroit or Royal Oak with B names. You might want to try politicians, too."

"I'm on it. Hey, that Souldier? Is he the CSI guy with the dreads?"

"He's the one."

"Girl, he's kinda fine."

"He's too fine. And he's a Christian. 'Souldier in the army of the Lord' is what he told me."

"No way!"

"Way, girl."

"Are you doing this on purpose, sending me to him?"

"It's not like you have a boyfriend. But take your time."

"I will. I'll do my thing. He won't know what hit him."

I laughed.

Kalaya squeezed my hand. "He'll be back, Bell."

"No, he won't."

"He married you."

"He married Kate, too."

"But he loved you."

I nodded. The operative word being "loved." Past tense. I stood up and stretched. "You'd better get out of here. You've got some writing and some sleuthing to do. And I've got to get out of town. If I'm estimating things correctly, my mother will be here in half an hour to end my life."

"Stay strong, Bell."

I shook my head. "I'm not strong at all."

chapter twenty-six

THE SMALL VILLAGE where Lisa's cabin was located had turned into a veritable winter wonderland. Christmas was in three days. I'd spend it alone again. Not so alone, actually. I had Amos.

I unpacked us in the cabin, blasted the heat, and settled on the sofa with him. What a mercy. I let him roam all over my chest while I made phone calls. First to my mother, who screamed at me, told me I was trying to kill her, and took me out of her will. Again. I let her convey the news to Carly that I was safely out of sight. Next I called Christine. She'd phoned me that morning with news that she might have a lead on whom Kate had been seeing. She'd said it was just a hunch, but she'd get back to me. I called Kalaya to tell her what Chris had said.

I wanted to call Jazz, but the thought of it pained me. What would I say to him? Worse, what would he say to me? I thought it best that I give Rocky some time. He'd know soon enough Jazz was not just my lover but my husband.

Dear Lord, what a mess.

I picked Amos up, stroking the fur on his back. His big black eyes stared at me. I smiled. Big, silly affecting eyes.

Rocky.

God, I'm sorry I hurt him. I should have just told him. Jazz had prompted me to tell him. Instead, I'd let him think I'd given up everything I'd worked so hard to accomplish spiritually by keeping myself until marriage. And I'd denied my husband like Peter had denied our Lord.

Keep myself? Did I really do that? How hoochie could I get?

I thought of the tantalizingly tight jeans I'd been wearing. Long, sexy braids, teeny-weeny sweaters. Siren-red lipstick. I'd done everything I could to pique Jazz's sexual interest.

He married you.

I know, Lord. But did he rush me to the altar because he wanted to make love as urgently as I did? Or because he wanted the baby? Did he marry me because he loves me, like he said to me so many times last night? Or did he just say that in the passion of the moment?

What made me angry was that I wouldn't get to know the answer to those questions now. I'd let myself get so caught up in the heady rush of wanting him that I hadn't bothered to hear what his heart was saying. Or my own heart. Or what the spirit of God was whispering in my soul.

Read the Song of Solomon.

Don't you hate it when God asks you to do something you know will torment you?

"You've gotta be kidding, right? I'm here to forget about what happened."

You're here to heal.

See what happens when you get into a relationship with the God of the universe? He speaks to you. Tells you things you don't want to hear. Often. How am I supposed to punish myself and wallow in self-pity and self-hatred with God speaking tenderly to me and telling me to read biblical poetry?

I gave Amos a little kiss. He didn't destroy my lips. "I'm going to put you back in the cage, little buddy. It looks like the Lover of my soul is trying to get my attention."

I settled myself onto the sofa sans Amos, with my Bible and a cup of Harney & Sons cinnamon tea. Lisa always had Harney & Sons, the best tea around. They came in silky sachets instead of plain old tea bags. The scent of the Hot Cinnamon Sunset blend inspired worship. And speaking of worship . . .

Jazz's vows came back to me: *With my body I thee worship.*

You vowed the same to him.

So I did.

"Do I have to read this, Lord?"

I opened my sadly neglected Bible and turned to what Jazz called the Song of Songs.

Let him kiss me with the kisses of his mouth—for your love is more delightful than wine.

"Don't make me do this, Lord."

I shut my eyes, recalling with all my senses the sweet nectar of Jazz's kisses. To banish the memory, I read on.

My lover is to me a sachet of myrrh resting between my breasts.

I hugged myself, remembering our lovemaking. Over and over it played in my mind, my heart and body flowering like that last bloom in September. Like I'd blossomed the first time he kissed me.

"I love him. I love him. I love him."

I am a rose of Sharon, a lily of the valleys . . .

I delight to sit in his shade, and his fruit is sweet to my taste . . .

My lover is mine and I am his . . .

"God, why do this to me now?"

You haven't been honest.

"Then help me, Lord."

One last passage jumped out at me: *Do not arouse or awaken love until it so desires.*

"I didn't want to arouse love or anything else in me. I let him go. I let him go because he was too much for me. I've done so many terrible things, God. You know I have. How could someone like him come to me? I don't deserve the love of my life. Jazz thinks he squandered his life being the murder police. I squandered mine living in sin with a man who despised me and caused my baby to die. I don't deserve a good life. Why didn't you just leave me alone? Why did you do this to me?"

Now you're being honest, I heard in my soul. Tears streamed down my cheeks.

A strange sound awakened me. "Greensleeves"? My cell phone. I bolted upright, startled to be in a strange environment, and realized at once where I was.

I felt in the dark for the phone. The number didn't look familiar.

"This is Amanda," I said. My standard greeting, just in case the matter was business.

"This is Chris."

"Who?"

"Christine Webber."

I shook the sleep out of my head. "Chris. How are you?"

"Not too good. I suppose the same could be said of you."

"You saw the story?"

"Yes. I'm sorry about all that."

"It's in God's hands."

At that the woman crumbled. She sobbed for a full five minutes. When she'd calmed herself, she spoke. "I found out something."

"What?"

"She was at a restaurant. She left something behind. It was the diary."

"What? Did you go get it?"

"They called after hours. They said I could pick it up tomorrow."

"Christine, that's great news."

"I don't want to pick it up."

"Why not?"

"Because I don't want to know the truth. I don't want to know. I liked the mystery. It left room for me to fill in the blanks with whatever I wanted."

"I understand, Christine, but we need to know who hurt her so badly. That person needs to be put away."

"I asked the person who called if she was with somebody."

"What did they say?"

"He said she was with a man."

"Go on."

"He described him. He said he was a tall white man with brown hair. They described Jazz."

"Jazz isn't white."

"He looks like he could be white. Anyone could mistake him for white."

Even I hadn't been able to determine his race when I'd first seen him. "Did the person say he was good-looking?"

"He wouldn't say. He started some rant about not wanting to judge how another man looks."

"I understand. Still, it may not be Jazz."

She went on, "Then again, it may be. I told you it could be him. How could any man, any woman, resist a woman as fine as Katie? Maybe he wanted to get back at me."

"Let's not jump to any conclusions. A lot of men fit that description. I'm out of town. I'll come home, and we can go through the diary together. I'll be there for you."

She sniffled. "Okay. You'll be here tomorrow? Promise?"

"I promise."

"I'll see you then."

"Okay, Chris. See you tomorrow."

Before I could set the phone down, "Greensleeves" chirped again. "This is Amanda."

"Bell. Do you have a fax machine there?"

Kalaya.

"I think Lisa has one on her computer. I may have to set it up, but it shouldn't be a problem. What have you got?"

"The pictures. Girl, that Christine is a beast. You should see these."

"That bad?"

"Worse. I think you might want to reconsider your theory after you take a look at these babies."

"Anything else?"

"I got the autopsy pictures and a date for Tuesday night."

"You go, girl."

"On which count?"

"Both. Did you see the *B*?"

"It's hard to see, but I think so."

"What about 'bad' on her belly?"

"Yeah. It looks like what you said."

"Any *B* cops?"

"Two first-name *B*'s and five last-name *B*'s, including your hubby."

"Who looks good?"

"It's anybody's guess. All of these guys are different. The only similarity is that they're male and cops. Their ranks are all over the place."

"I'm coming home."

"Bell, you don't want to do that."

"Why not? There's a restaurant I need to try tomorrow. I'll call you when I get in. Send that fax."

"People are talking. What happened at the station house on Friday? You're, like, public enemy number one with the Detroit boys. You don't want to have enemies like that. It could get very ugly."

"They're cops, Kal."

"Right. Like the cop you think killed Kate. You work with cops. You know they're human beings, and humans have a way of failing, sometimes fatally."

I didn't say anything. The Scripture came to me once again: *The heart is deceitful above all things, and desperately wicked: who can know it?* Gold and silver shields certainly didn't make men, or women, immune to wickedness.

Kal went on, "Girl, you're threatening to expose a killer among them, and people are getting nervous. Just stay where you are for a while."

"I'm coming home. Too much is going on. I'll take my chances, God help me."

I gave her the phone number at the house and asked her for ten minutes to set up the fax.

"Be careful, Bell."

"I will."

chapter
twenty-seven

I'D SEEN KATE TOWNSEND'S dead body, but the pictures of a battered, living Kate were just as horrifying. I repented of my jealousy. If she'd gone to Jazz after that beating, I couldn't blame her.

In most domestic disputes, the signs of strangulation are minimal. There may be redness around the neck. Ligature marks if the perpetrator uses something other than his hands or another extremity. But dear Lord, Chris had tried to take Kate's head off. This was way beyond a mutual game of Rock 'Em Sock 'Em Robots. Chris's hand imprint would have bruised terribly in the days that followed the attack. Kate's voice would have been affected. The internal injuries alone could have killed her days later. Especially since she never got them treated.

Poor Kate. And she went back to Chris. I thought about what it must have been like to be Kate Townsend. Her behavior hinted at childhood abuse, most likely sexual. A very pretty girl, though not all targets of sexual abuse were pretty. I felt so sorry for her.

I considered the phone call from Christine. I didn't think she'd sounded insincere. I hadn't been there to see her or watch the clues her body gave. On the other hand, I thought of the tear-

ful court testimonies of the Menendez brothers, who had slaugh-
tered their parents in Southern California. All those tears pouring
out of two stone-hearted murderers.

Was Christine setting me up?

How likely was it that the restaurant called *after* hours to
report they had something Kate had left behind? And nearly a
week after she'd left it?

I needed advice. I couldn't ask Jazz. He'd spit on the ground
if he heard my voice.

Mason. As soon as I got back home, I'd go see Dr. Mason
May. He'd help me make sense of everything.

Mason insisted that I come right to his house, even if it meant
Amos would come with me. When me and my "baby"—who,
after our bonding at the cabin, really *was* my baby—arrived,
Mason met us gracefully, even though it was six in the morning.
He'd made hot mulled cider and had fresh fruit slices at the
ready.

I laughed when I saw the fruit. "Genevia got you on a diet,
Mason?"

"No, pumpkin, Gen thinks I'm just right. Jazz told me *you*
were on a diet. Said you didn't eat real food anymore."

"And just when did he tell you all this?"

"I've talked to him every day this week."

"Mason. How come you didn't tell me you were seeing
Jazz?"

He chuckled. "You act like I cheated on you, pumpkin. He's

a good man. He needed to work through some things, and I was happy to help him, same as I helped you."

I pouted. "I'm jealous. You're *my* spiritual papa. I don't want to share you. Especially with him."

Mason's home was as lovely as his office. More so. Genevia had decorated the dining room with dark ebony woods and a massive dining table that seated twelve. Bone china graced every place, and real silver polished to a high shine. The room reeked of elegance. Artwork by African-American painters, including an Addie Lee I'd given them as an anniversary present, hung on the wall.

I set Amos's cage on the floor and uncovered it. Mason started. "My stars, what is that?"

At least he didn't scream, run, kick, or otherwise assault Amos. "This is the pet you said I should get."

Mason let out an uncharacteristically hearty laugh. "Girl, I don't know what I'm going to do with you. Jazz is going to have his hands full."

"Pop, Jazz is never going to forgive me. I did something terrible."

"I know all about it. His side. Why don't you tell me what happened?"

I sipped my cider, reveling in the priceless camaraderie—completely free of judgment—that my godfather offered. I didn't even cry when I got to the end, after Jazz said he didn't want me.

"He wants you. He's hurt right now."

"He divorced Kate when he caught her with Christine."

"You weren't in bed with Rocky."

"I was kissing him fresh out of bed with Jazz."

"Rocky kissed you, pumpkin."

"I let him."

"Yes, you did. The question is why? You could have stopped him."

The question is why?

I sipped my cider.

"It wasn't rhetorical."

I gave Mason a sassy look. "I'd hoped it was."

"Why didn't you stop that from happening?"

Be honest.

I took a deep breath. "Because at the moment, Rocky's simple, down-to-earth, desperate kiss made more sense to me than Jazz's exquisite lovemaking."

"What do you mean, little Bella?"

"I don't know, Pop. Jazz is just . . . out of my reach."

Pop looked at me thoughtfully. Ran a hand over his springy white afro. "Pumpkin . . ."

"Uh-oh. You're going to give me the talk, aren't you?"

"You need it."

"Okay. Lemme have it."

"When Jazz was confused and unavailable, you were the most aggressive."

"Mason. He kept coming around, and for more than the case."

"But it was you who kissed him every time, wasn't it?"

I felt a bit of shame creeping up my neck. "Yes."

"When he had to make a difficult decision—I saw how he wrestled with it—he chose you. What did you do?"

"I dressed like a video hoochie and tried to captivate him."

"You'd already captivated him: What did you do?"

"I married him."

"What did you do, pumpkin?"

"I resisted him."

Mason finally answered for me: "You broke his heart."

I shook my head. "Impossible."

"D'you think?"

"People like me don't break hearts."

"You broke two in one night."

"I hurt Rocky badly. But not Jazz."

"Why don't you think you hurt Jazz?" Mason leaned forward on the desk, waiting.

"Rocky loves me, so I know I hurt him. But Jazz . . . he . . ."

"He what?"

I gathered the wind behind my words and let them blow out. "Jazz couldn't possibly love me. Couldn't ever love me."

Now I'd hurt Mason. The pain settled in his eyes, between his brow. "What if he did? What if he loves you more than you love him?"

"Mason . . ." Tears sprang to my eyes.

"Why, beloved? Why did you hurt Jazz?"

"I didn't mean to hurt anybody. I was scared. I felt like I loved him too much. Like what I felt for him, I wasn't supposed to feel for anybody but God. I was scared because I thought he'd wake up one day and realize I was not a Kate. I was not a beauty who looked good with him. We weren't a matching set. I didn't think I was good enough for him."

"You weren't ready for him yet. You still needed to heal. You never really believed the two of you could happen. Never thought you'd have to deal with these choices. You lived like you were half dead on the inside until the night you wore that red dress, the color of Jesus' precious blood. The color of passion. You came alive again the moment Jazz saw you for the beauty you are."

I nodded.

"What you feel—that rush of love, of desire—it's not wrong. You walked around like a zombie for seven years, and Jazz awakened you. You'd suppressed any hint of sexuality for so long you forgot it was a gift from God, not something for you to be afraid of. Yes, the Word tells us to flee the act of fornication, but it doesn't tell us not to feel sexual. God gave you and Jazz the gift of each other. You were made to enjoy each other in physical intimacy. You were made for the delights of the Song of Songs. Go to your husband and tell him that you want him and you won't take no for an answer."

"But I messed up. I hurt Rocky, too."

"You used Rocky in a terrible way. He was as safe as animal crackers to you, but he is a human being. You had no right to string him along to bolster your weak ego."

Ouch! But he was right.

"Will he ever forgive me?"

"Both of them will. It will surely come to pass. In God's time."

A prophet had spoken. The only problem? God's time could be awfully long. I hoped I lived long enough.

Mason found the pictures as disturbing as I did. He shook his head gravely at both. "A sin and a shame before God," he said.

"I know. I feel so sorry for her."

"You're probably right about the history of abuse, you know."

"I know. All this time, working through this case, I've been wading through the murky waters of her sinful life. Sometimes it was too much for me. It made me feel dirty just to think about it."

"Sex itself isn't dirty. It's a gift made to share with joy in a marriage. You know that now, pumpkin."

"Yes." I blushed. "But it can be abused and mess you up for life! I know that, too. That's why I ruined my marriage. It can be distorted. And then it can be used as a weapon."

"You didn't ruin your marriage, but I'll get back to that. About Kate. Her murderer showed her who had the power."

"That's what I mean. As brutal as this photo is, I still can't see Chris for this murder. Clearly, she's capable of doing the physical damage. She nearly killed Kate. But is this the aggression of a scorned lover or a misogynist?"

"The pictures, though . . ."

"I know, Mason. But there was a kind of degradation in Kate's murder that I don't see as the kind of power Christine would wield. She'd fight. These pictures make that clear. Obviously, Kate would fight with her. According to her, Kate started the fights most times."

"This is true. One lost battle in the war doesn't mean Kate was never the victor."

"I'm certain a man killed her—a man who wanted her, even in death, to know he had the upper hand."

"Then trust your instincts. But don't go see Christine alone. Get the police to listen to you."

"But if I tell the police about Chris, I may lose her coopera-tion. What if she really is close to finding Kate's mystery man?"

"Tell them."

"What if the mystery man is Jazz?"

Mason smiled at me and gave my hand a reassuring squeeze. "God said no. Of this I'm sure. And your marriage is in His hands."

I smiled the widest, most sincere grin ever to cross my mouth. God may as well have written it in stone. I believed Him, too.

chapter
twenty-eight

I REMEMBERED the words of my great-grandmother, "It ain't courage if you ain't scared. Do it scared," and braved my way inside the Detroit police department to the stunned stares of Detroit's finest and Detective Bobby Maguire. This time I came armed with photos and not just my great-grandmother's but my godfather's courage.

Bobby sat in his pleather chair, surrounded by paperwork. He didn't have any scary food near him, thank God. He was so surprised to see me that he didn't even call me girl Columbo.

"Amanda."

"Hello, Bobby."

He cussed, then whispered, "For Pete's sake, what are you doin'?"

"Did you swallow a cranky pill today?"

"Yes. What do you want? If Archie sees you, he's going to flip from here to West Hades."

I pulled out the photographs and slammed them on his desk. "I want you to keep looking for Kate's real killer."

He picked up the photos. Shot me a look. Stared at them for a moment. "Where'd you get these?"

"The Royal Oak police department."

He shuffled them around. "Who did this?"

"Christine."

He stopped at the morgue picture of Kate's thigh. "And what's this?"

"Kate self-injured. What I want you to note is the letter *B* she carved on her thigh. The next picture is of her lower abdomen. She carved the word 'bad' there. The scars are about a month old. She must have put them there around the time she found out she was pregnant."

"And what do you think that means, girl Columbo?"

"I think she carved the man she was seeing into her body, and I think she felt conflicted about the pregnancy."

"*B* stands for Brown."

"It also stands for Bobby."

"It could also stand for Big Bird or even Bell. You don't know what she was thinkin' when she carved this."

"I'm asking you to keep looking. Look at her neck. That was from Christine. Look at the fact that she was posed in a way I know Jazz would never do."

"I know you want to protect your husband."

"Did you tell someone? How did the press find out I'm married?"

"You might want to consider that you came here talking. Loud. You're the one who wore a wedding ring. You never know who's listening. And you didn't make any friends with your drama, which is why you shouldn't be here."

"I'm sorry, Bobby." I meant it.

He paused as if he might actually want to believe me. "You okay?"

"Not really."

"You're a good gal. Get rid of him and move on with your life."

"I can't move on, Bobby. I can't."

"Go home, girl Columbo. I'm not thrilled about it, but I'll look into this."

"You promise?"

"I promise."

"Just one more thing, Bobby."

"You doing your Columbo imitation again?"

"I can't seem to help it. Kate had a diary. Chris knows where it is. She's picking it up today. It could have information about the father of her baby."

"What if it's your hubby?"

"Then I'd definitely want to know that."

"Get out of here before Archie sees you. He's mad at you, you know."

"Thanks, Bobby."

"Scat, Amanda."

I headed down the steps and out the building, feeling like Maguire was finally listening to me. "Thank you, Lord."

Christine had planned to meet me at 5:30 P.M. I'd have to brave rush-hour traffic, but for this I'd gladly sit on U.S. 23. I got to Christine's house around five. Her house, ringed with yellow tape, crawled with police, and two Goliath officers guarded the front door.

I drove by the house once, looking for a parking place. I found one around the corner and ran down the sidewalk to the house. A uniform stopped me.

"What's going on?" I asked.

"This is an active crime scene, ma'am."

"What happened?"

"Ma'am, you should leave."

"Who's in charge here, Officer?"

"Detective Greg Parson."

"I'd like to speak to him. I know the person who lives here." I fished in my purse for my credentials. "I work for the Washtenaw County Jail. I'm involved in an active homicide investigation regarding the death of Christine Webber's partner."

"I'm afraid Ms. Webber is now a homicide victim."

Bobby Maguire walked up to me. I hadn't even seen him coming. "Excuse me, Dr. Brown. You're needed over here."

Dr. Brown?

I'm sure my bewildered look was the reason Bobby took my arm and pulled me away. "You shouldn't be here."

"What are you doing here?"

"This ain't my jurisdiction, but you know I'm going to be here. So is Archie Dandridge. Nobody knows where your husband is, and if you don't want a big production in a few minutes when Archie sees you, you'd better get outta here."

"What happened?"

"We don't know. She's dead. Strangled. Get outta here, will ya? If Archie sees you . . ."

"You're the only one who knew about the diary other than Chris."

"Get outta here."

I glanced at his leather-glove-clad hands. "I hope you've got a good alibi, Bobby with a *B*."

"Find out if your husband has one—that's Brown with a *B*."

"This isn't over. So help me God, Maguire."

He gave me the hardest glare I've ever seen. "You'd better go. And I suggest you watch your back."

"Is that a threat?"

"You've got a threat, lady, and it ain't me."

By the time I got back to the Love Bug, my whole body was trembling. I tried to put together all the facts I had. Chris had been killed right after I'd revealed to Bobby Maguire that she had potentially damaging evidence available to her. According to Bobby with a *B*, Jazz was MIA. I had no idea what the name of the restaurant was—dumb of me not to get it. And the person at the restaurant had, according to Christine, described Jazz to a tee. What did that mean? "Lord, have mercy. Christ, have mercy. Lord, have mercy."

All I could think of was how I wished I could find my husband. I needed the kind of advice only he could give me. He knew all the players in the case. The victim, the cops. He knew Bobby Maguire. He'd likely know, even if via gossip, if Kate and Maguire were ever an item.

God, what do I do? Who do I turn to?

I thought about Ma Brown's Star of Bethlehem quilt. When

I was a girl, she'd called the quilts that the slaves used as code to lead runaways to freedom "show ways." *I need a show way. Badly.*

Dear God in heaven, provide one.

I prayed with all my might.

chapter
twenty-nine

T HE REST OF THE WEEKEND passed in a blur. Thoughts of Jazz buffeted my mind. I couldn't stop thinking about our intimacy and fretting over his whereabouts. Most of my doubts about his innocence had been dispelled by Mason's confirmation. I may not have trusted myself, but I trusted Mason. I knew that the praying, fasting spiritual giant heard from God. I wanted to talk to Jazz so badly I called his cell phone twenty-three times and hung up before he could answer, all twenty-three times.

He never tried to call me back.

I dreaded Monday, and not because I had to go to work. The fact was I didn't have to go to work at all. One of the phone messages I'd gotten Saturday morning came from my supervisor at the jail, Dr. Eric Fox. Word of the newspaper article in the Detroit *Metropolitan Daily* had reached him, and he had politely asked me to please take several personal days to attend to my "crisis," which meant I'd embarrassed the department, and if I wanted to keep my job, I'd better get my life in order.

So I cried, prayed, called Jazz and hung up, paced the floor, and waited for the calls—regarding the article Kalaya wrote—to

bombard my phones. At exactly nine-twenty I got the first one.
Archie Dandridge.

"Mrs. Brown?"

Mrs. "Yes?"

"This is Officer Archie Dandridge."

"What can I do for you, Officer Dandridge?"

"We need to talk. I've got the information and the photographs. And I'm afraid they didn't come from Maguire. Your sister and Souldier gave them to me. I think you're on to something."

I slowly released the tension I'd been holding. "I'm so relieved. Can I come down and talk about it with you?"

"Bell . . ."

Bell?

"Do you have any idea where your husband is?"

"I haven't spoken to him since Friday night."

"I don't mean to pry, but I think I may be closing in on Kate Townsend's real killer. I think you were right all along. I don't believe it's your husband, and I believe now that her killer is a man."

"That's very interesting."

"Again, I'd like to talk to you, and as you've probably gathered, it's urgent."

"Just let me know what time to meet you, and I'll be right there."

He paused. "You know that's a problem. It's going to take a tremendous effort to change the opinion of the people around here about you. And I'm afraid I have some concerns about Detective Maguire."

I knew it!

"I'd like to talk to you away from the station. Can you meet me at a restaurant or at my home?"

"Of course. Thank you for accommodating me."

"It's no problem. You may not want to mention to anyone that you're meeting me. This is a sensitive matter. You've had some mishaps with the press. I wouldn't want any problems as something new is developing."

"Just tell me where to meet you, Officer Dandridge."

"Call me Archie, Bell."

I let him call me Bell. If he would get Jazz out of this mess, he'd be my new best friend.

He continued, "How 'bout my home? I'm dog-tired. My wife will be there."

I thought it odd that he felt it necessary to say that. He hadn't been in any way unseemly.

Before I left the apartment, I stopped by Amos's cage. He looked at me, and honestly, it looked like he was smiling.

"Mama will be back real soon, Amos."

He made the clicking sound. *Click, click, click, click, click* with his little tongue. The same sound he'd made with Rocky. It didn't sound menacing at all! I opened the cage, boldly now, and Amos climbed onto my hand. *Click, click, click, click, click, click.*

I had a Sally Field moment. "Amos likes me," I said. "He really likes me."

He was going with Mama today.

———————

Mr. and Mrs. Archie Dandridge lived in a palatial art-deco home in Indian Village. This was high living for the east side of Detroit—definitely not the *beast* side. I recognized the house as being designed by none other than the renowned industrial designer and architect Albert Kahn. The home boasted at least twelve thousand square feet. I could have lived quite comfortably in the carriage house.

"Wow," I said to Amos. "Talk about big-city style."

Amos and I—Amos in a sugar-glider Snugli that looked like a fanny pack around my waist—went to the door. I rang the bell. Moments later, it swung open, and Archie Dandridge greeted us.

He grinned. Shook my hand. "Thanks for coming here," he said. He wore a teal-green suit that looked like it would cost a month's worth of salary from both of my jobs. Generally, I hated every variation of teal. Even though it seemed to work for him, it still looked like gangrene to me—just like J. Lo said in *The Wedding Planner*—a creepy visual that I let go of as quickly as possible. I hadn't been thinking straight lately, as it were.

Archie took one look at Amos peeking out of his Snugli, and a look of horror spread across his handsome face.

"That's just Amos," I said. "I'm in the process of bonding with him."

"Bonding?"

"It's complicated. But he's sleeping now. He sleeps most of the day and screeches and bites his cage like a demon spawn at night. All night. But that's another story."

Reluctantly—I believed mostly because of Amos—Archie led me to a sunroom, full of light and scrumptiously warm, with a view of the carriage house and a magnificent arbor. "You have a beautiful home, Archie," I said.

"Thank you, Bell. It's been in my wife's family since the thirties. I'm afraid it's a bit rich for my blood. I'm a lowly Internal Affairs cop."

And speaking of "wife," I glanced at the pictures hanging on the wall. Archie Dandridge was married to none other than Barbara Marlow. Where in the world had I been to miss that detail? She was old money, from one of Michigan's most prestigious families. Rumors were flying that the monarchical, imposing woman would run for the state senate in the next election. She had to be in her fifties, certainly older than Archie. Not pretty, but she had an honest-looking face. I'd voted for her because of that face.

"You did okay for a lowly Internal Affairs cop," I said.

Amos shifted in the Snugli. The movement startled Dandridge. "Is it okay?" he asked.

"He's fine. I hope you don't mind that I brought him."

"Not at all. What is he?"

"He's a sugar glider. Very cute, don't you think?"

Archie shook his head. I didn't take offense.

"Can I offer you anything?" he asked.

"I'd like to get right to what we need to discuss." The loveliness of the trees just beyond the glass enclosing us captivated me. "The view is breathtaking."

"Thank you. I wanted you to know that I'm pleased with what you've come up with. Let me get a bottle of wine. I think we should celebrate."

A bottle of *wine*? What in the world . . .

"I'll be right back," he said. "We've got a wine cellar, and I have a Bordeaux to die for."

To die for? Strange choice of words. Or maybe I was getting too skittish.

But as stressed as I was, I could use a glass of wine. And a bit of fresh air—especially with such a nice view of the city. "Do you mind if I step onto the porch? Your yard seems so nice, I'd like to enjoy it."

"Go right ahead, baby."

Baby? Every part of me recoiled. The word put me on alert. *No,* I told myself. *It was an accident. Unintentional. Archie has never been anything but professional.*

Archie stepped out of the room to get the wine, and I glanced at the wall of pictures once again. He also had his high school diploma hanging there, which I found kinda sweet. Benjamin Archibald Dandridge. That was funny. I thought Benjamin was a much nicer name than Archibald. I thought it was curious that he'd choose to be called Archie instead of Benny.

The outdoors beckoned me to take a closer look. I opened the sunroom door and stepped into the backyard. A sense of foreboding rushed in with the change of temperature.

I tried to push the nagging dread out of my mind: *You're imagining things, Bell.* I took a deep breath of the brisk, refreshing December morning. Tomorrow would be Christmas Eve, my favorite day of the year.

Will my husband be home for Christmas?

Thoughts of Jazz saddened me. I loosened the Snugli to allow Amos a bit more air.

I took a step to walk out farther onto the porch, but my heel caught and stuck in the lattice-pattern doormat. I bent down to free my heel, and as I did, Amos protested my move with a yelp. My hand flew to his carrier to protect him. In that moment my gaze went to the ground. I caught a glimpse of the tiniest sliver of pottery on the mat. I leaned closer for inspection. I dabbed at it with my finger to pick it up. At the edge of the shard, I detected a glimmer of silver—otherworldly beautiful and as familiar as a steaming mug of tea in my living room.

Realization shot through me.

Addie's pottery. The Starry Night mug.

My heart dropped to my shoes. Locard's law. At every crime scene, the perpetrator leaves something or takes something. He'd transferred evidence, probably from the bottom of his shoe.

I stood ramrod straight. Snatched the cell phone out of my jacket pocket. He may not have wanted to talk to me, but I sure needed to hear from him. I punched Jazz's number into the phone, praying that he'd answer. *Oh, God, please, please, please.*

He answered with a gruff "What do you want?"

"Please don't hang up," I whispered. "Did Archie Dandridge ever have a relationship with Kate?"

"What is this all about?"

"Please answer. I don't have much time."

His tone changed to that of concern. "Are you in trouble?"

"I'm always in trouble. Were they involved?"

"I don't know. She didn't mention him to me, but I know he was interested in her around the same we got together."

"Jazz, this is important. When Kate cut herself, if she spelled words, what kind of words would they be?"

"What makes you think I know?"

"Could she have carved her lover's initials on her stomach?"

I could almost hear him shrug. "I really don't know, Bell. She wouldn't talk to me about the cutting. I suppose anything is possible. She was a sick, broken girl."

He called me Bell. I shook my head, trying to stay on track. At that moment my mind shot me a news flash. Benjamin Archibald Dandridge: *BAD* right on her belly. *Yowza! "Bad" wasn't negative self-talk. It was her baby's daddy.* "Archie killed her. It all makes sense now. The political ties. The baby. Even the leather gloves. I should have seen it from the start. It was all right there."

Jazz paused. "Are you sure?"

"God led me by a star, just like He did the wise men. I have to go. I'm going to speed-dial my house so my answering machine will pick up. I'm going to get him to confess."

"Where are you?"

"I'm at his house."

"And you think he *killed* her?"

"I know he did."

"Get out of there. Now!"

"I gotta go, Jazz. I'm sorry about everything, baby. I love you. I do. I just didn't think I deserved you." I hung up the phone, speed-dialed home, and shoved the phone back in my pocket.

I turned, and there was Archie, holding a bottle of wine. He opened the door to the sunroom for me to walk back in. I stepped inside.

Did he hear? How much?

My stomach sank.

The bottle he held hadn't been opened. I thought about

Sasha's lessons: unopened bottles only. And always wear clean underwear in case you end up in the hospital or dead.

I prayed the hospital would be my destination.

I had to get Archie to confess. A piece of pottery wouldn't be enough to put him away. I had to goad him into telling me what had happened. I prayed my phone was sensitive enough to pick up what we said from my coat pocket.

God help me.

I tried not to look like I was terrified.

Easy, girl. You can do this. Just get out of here alive.

He popped the cork on the Bordeaux and poured each of us a glass. He handed one to me, standing too close for propriety's sake. "How'd he get you to marry him? He must be very smooth Jazz." He chuckled at his play of words, as if everyone in Detroit hadn't read that on Saturday.

"You're very clever," I said. "I thought you said your wife would be here."

"You know how women in politics are."

"No, tell me."

"She's gone a great deal. I find other means to entertain myself, as does she when she's . . . *busy.*"

"Really?"

Now, there was a story to tell Kalaya. Detroit would love to hear about the Dandridges' open marriage. Not to mention Barbara Marlow's murdering husband.

"You're a pretty woman, Bell."

Why was it that every nutjob most likely to kill me was inclined to try out his rap on me? I smiled to humor him, rifling through my thoughts as if flipping through a psych journal, trying to land on the best approach that would get me the info *and* save my life. The only thing that came to mind was to see just how far this rivalry between Archie and my hubby went. "You aren't bad yourself. You're not as fine as Jazz, but I guess you'd do in a pinch."

He flinched. I'd taken him by surprise. He put down his glass of wine. "You're quite forthcoming."

"You have no idea."

"I see why Jazz likes you. You're spicy."

"I'm glad you noticed. Of course, you notice everything Jazz has, don't you?"

He laughed. "Look around. I'd say I have a lot more going for me than Jazz."

"You married money. How hard is that?"

He stood closer to me. If I could just bide my time, I assumed that Jazz, despite our estrangement, would be my hero. People may not always be what we think they are, but I hoped to high heaven I'd called him right. *Be my hero, baby.*

"Jazz Brown is no threat to me."

"Who said anything about him being a threat?" I tried not to sound sassy—almost contemplative. "He is, however, different than you. He's more handsome, more intelligent, more charming."

"That's your opinion, Mrs. Brown."

Nothing useful, but I had to keep trying. "It's everybody's opinion. Why do you think Kate left you for him?"

His jaw tightened. His amber eyes turned cold as January in Detroit. I'd touched a nerve, but he didn't say anything. I had to push harder despite the fear creeping up my spine. "Must have really ticked you off when she left. Did you want the baby?"

"What are you talking about, Mrs. Brown?"

I was reaching. I'd either hit the mark or make a complete fool out of myself. I didn't have much pride left. I had a nocturnal creature strapped to my waist. Looking crazy didn't bother me. "I'm talking about the baby she aborted when she married Jazz. I mean, she couldn't just have *your* baby when she was with someone else—someone better than you—now could she?"

"Shut up," he said.

I needed a confession. For Kate. For Jazz. Neither deserved the lot Archie had cast upon them. Anger coursed through me as much as fear. "'Shut up'? How rude are you? No wonder she dumped you. A player like Kate Townsend dumped *you*."

As quickly as he'd turned cold, he tried to unthaw, or at least appear to. "You're quite amusing. You seem to forget that Kate dumped Jazz *for a woman*."

Shoot. Score one for Archie. I shrugged. "Lucky Jazz. He found out it was impossible for Kate to be faithful to anyone, male or female. Her confusion messed with the mind of everyone she became intimate with."

A look crossed Archie's face before he could control it. Score one for Bell.

Now for the big guns. I prayed I wasn't wrong, even if it meant he'd kill me. "So what was this last little close encounter about? Did you still want her, or did you just like the feeling that she wanted you . . . after Jazz?"

He didn't say anything. I wanted to shake him. Force it out of him. *If* he did it. No, I may have questioned my instincts, but I had to be right. He fit the profile: married, upstanding, much to lose, not a gentleman. He even reeked of Lagerfeld. Now the biggest push of all, fueled by my outrage at the lives he'd ruined: "News flash, Archie. Jazz wouldn't have anything to do with her. You were her sloppy seconds—no, thirds, if you count Christine. You just weren't good enough. As usual."

"We loved each other."

"Bah, humbug." That was the best I could come up with. It was the day before Christmas Eve and quite possible that I wouldn't live to see Santa Claus come to town. "She didn't love you. Kate didn't love anyone, including herself. Or maybe she was the only one she loved. It's hard to say. In that way, you were a perfect match. She was just someone to, as you said, entertain you while you waited for your trust-fund-baby political wife to come back home and take care of the bills."

"You don't know what you're talking about."

"Why did you kill her? You didn't want trust-fund baby to find out about your little offspring? Or was it to get back at every-one who has hurt you? You could destroy Kate. She humiliated you—first by choosing your archrival and then a woman for her bed. You could also hurt Christine, who loved her, and Jazz, who stole your rightful place on the force."

"You have quite an imagination."

His voice said one thing, his expression another.

Another point for Bell.

"She called you that night, wanting you to help her devise a plan to get Jazz in trouble, didn't she? Was it then that you decided to kill her? Or once you got to the loft and she wouldn't give you what you really came for?"

He looked at me like I was crazy. Or like I was on to some-thing. I couldn't tell which.

"They'll pull phone records. They'll find out who you are."

"She had a cheap prepaid cell phone. Untraceable. I'm the one who purchased it for her. She called my own prepaid cell phone. There'll be no phone records. I called *you* on that phone, too. They'll never know it was me."

Bingo! My heart rattled rapid-fire as a machine gun. The good news? He had confessed. The bad news? He was probably going to kill me. I made my face a cold mask of calm that belied the terror rising in my throat. *Please send help, Lord.*

Keep talking, Bell.

"You first thought you could just take her in Jazz's loft, but then she resisted. Told you she loved Chris. She was going to keep the baby, and the women would raise it as theirs. But she'd tell everyone the truth—who the baby's daddy was. And then where would you be? You killed her. You killed a pregnant woman."

He lunged at me. I jumped back, but he was fast. He slapped me, hard, across the face. If I hadn't been so scared, I'd have been salty at God. Every time I tried to help some poor, innocent soul, I ended up getting pimp-slapped. And worse.

Archie grabbed a handful of my braids, twisting them around his hands. He banged my head against the wall. Pain exploded in my head and nearly knocked me unconscious.

"Please," I whispered.

He commenced to call me several names that you wouldn't hear in church. He snapped my head back again, and I did a little business with God.

Jesus Christ, son of God, have mercy on me, a sinner.

I'd been here before. Adam nearly killed me. Gabriel nearly killed me. And now I was about to be beaten to death by a different man—if my husband didn't get here soon. Jazz flashed through my mind. God had given that beautiful man to me, exactly whom I wanted, and I had messed it up.

Archie slipped his hands around my neck. Slammed my head against the wall. Tears spilled from my eyes as the onslaught of pain assaulted me again.

I'm so sorry, Lord.

I'd made such a mess of my life, even after I'd come to Christ. Even after I'd gotten through being with Adam and even after I'd survived Gabriel trying to kill me. I still didn't love people as I should—not my friends, not my family, not my husband, and not myself. I still lived my life cut off from the very goodness—the very *Godness*—that makes life worth living. *Relationships.*

Mercy, Jesus.

If Jesus could remember the dying thief in His kingdom, maybe my quick prayer would grant a sinner like me a little space in heaven.

"How did you know?" Archie hissed. His hands went to my braids again. He snatched my head back and pulled my face close to his. "How did you figure it out?"

"You had to prove yourself in the end. You had to show her that she meant nothing to you—that you were in control. That's where you went wrong."

"But you couldn't know it was me."

"You're right, but you know crime scenes: you leave something. You left your hair, but when you realized it, you removed it from the evidence."

"Nobody knew it was my hair. How did you know I killed her?"

"You took something, too. A piece of Jazz's mother's pottery, probably on your shoe. I'm her number one fan. I'd know that glaze anywhere."

He tightened his grip around my neck. "Poor you. This is the best part. I get to kill the woman Jazz really loves. I read Kalaya Naylor's story this morning. Very touching. Too bad it's over for you. For both of you, because no one will know this wonderful tale you've woven. You'll be buried underneath my lake house up north, never to be seen again."

Man, I'd just left up north. I sure didn't want to turn around and go right back. The police hadn't come. Jazz wasn't my hero after all. I took a deep breath and thought, *You're going to have to be your own hero, Bell. God help me. If I could just get more time.*

I yelled out, inasmuch as I could with what was left of my voice, "You won't get away with this."

The clown actually stopped.

I looked at him. "I have to tell you something important before you kill me."

"Haven't you told me enough?"

"What's another thirty seconds? As it is, you're going to kill me."

"What do you want to say, Bell?"

"First of all, don't call me Bell."

"Is that it?"

"No. They're on to you, Dandridge. They know about the gloves." I had made this part up. "Expensive gloves."

"They don't have my gloves."

"No, but they've got trace evidence of the leather. They're not your garden-variety gloves, are they, Archie?" I remembered the gloves he wore. I had mistakenly thought they were fashionably distressed. Kate must have clawed at them. "Was that calfskin?"

I caught the glimmer of fear in his eyes.

"They'll never know."

"They already do, Archie."

"Liar." His hands went back to my neck. The pressure was unbearable. I could hardly breathe. I thought about how long it would take to die. Four eternal minutes. I needed more time.

"Wait," I barely squeaked.

The nightmare waited.

I drank air into my lungs. "Archie," I said, my throat raw from the battering. "God loves you and has a wonderful plan for your life."

It was all I could think of. I didn't happen to have a copy of *This Was Your Life!* on me.

"The Four Spiritual Laws, Bell?"

I coughed. "You know them?"

"We used to give those tracts away at Bible camp in middle school."

I managed to croak out, "You have to know God isn't pleased. Murdering people can really interfere with His wonderful plan for your life. Did you kill Christine? Do you have the diary?"

He sighed. "Yes and yes. Now I'm going to destroy you like I did the diary. Good-bye, Mrs. Brown."

"Wait!" I said.

"What?"

"It really hurts to be choked like that."

He sighed. "Is that what you wanted to say?"

"I just wanted to know if you would like to accept the gift of salvation God has to offer. It's not too late, Archie. You don't have to do this."

God, forgive me, but frankly, I didn't really care if Archie burned in hell or not. He was about to murder me, and let's face it, the idea of my own eternal destiny compelled me more. I just needed more time. If he actually converted, well, that would be cool, too.

"Good-bye, Mrs. Brown."

"Wait!"

"Your time is up, Bell."

I hated that he called me Bell!

Again his vice-grip hands got to work. I tried to wriggle away, but I could hardly breathe. Heat rushed to my face. I could feel blood vessels bursting near my eyes. I couldn't bite him. My kicks were ineffective.

All the commotion forced Amos out of his Snugli. I hoped Archie wouldn't kill my poor sugar glider, too.

Still no police. No Jazz. But I couldn't give up. I grabbed Archie's hands and clawed like a sugar glider. I figured if they ever found my body, I'd give them all the evidence I could.

But Archie kept squeezing. His hard, dead eyes bulged in anger as much as mine did in dying. I closed my eyes as tightly as I could. I didn't want his face to be the last thing I saw before I died. A rush of endorphins flooded my body, and I began to relax. I stopped clawing at Archie's hands. Everything went fuzzy and beautiful, and an odd sense of peace enveloped me. I got ready to meet the Lord.

That is, until a weird screeching sound nearly pierced my eardrums.

I felt Archie let me go. He must have thought I was dead. And by now I was inclined to agree with him. But the pain had returned. It was worse than the time I had strep throat so badly that an abscess formed and almost suffocated me to death.

I slumped in a heap on the floor. I ventured to open my eyes just a slit, and I saw something that utterly amazed me. Amos had made the crazy noise. I hadn't heard that one in his repertoire. From the floor, my sugar-glider baby took a flying leap and went airborne. He looked like he had a furry little superhero cape built right into his body. He sailed right onto Archie's head.

Shazam! as Kalaya would say. I didn't know Amos could fly! The saleslady hadn't said anything about flying. No wonder they were called sugar *gliders.*

Archie Dandridge screamed and started tearing at his head, where Amos hissed, scratched, bit, and made *When Sugar Gliders Attack: The Sequel.*

I didn't have much strength, but Archie was quite engaged in trying to keep Amos from killing him. I knew Amos could be persistent, so I took the opportunity to try to escape. I said a quick prayer, *God, help me get out,* and tried to drag myself out of the room.

I didn't get very far, but I made it to the living room. That was okay. I didn't have to go any farther. The sweet sounds of sirens and a battering ram forcing open the living-room door played like music in my ears.

Bobby Maguire burst into the room. "Girl Columbo," he said as the door flew open.

"It's great to see you, Bobby." I looked around for my husband.

"He's not here," Bobby said. "I told him he'd better not show up. If he did, we'd have to put him in jail for Dandridge's murder. And as you know, Lieutenant Brown ain't no murderer."

"Amen to that, my friend," I said. Then I fainted.

chapter
thirty

CHRISTMAS EVE.

Kalaya and I listened to sappy, incredibly depressing Christmas music while we decorated the tree Jazz had brought me. "I'll Be Home for Christmas" played mournfully on the radio.

All I wanted for Christmas was my husband and his Ricky Ricardo imitation.

The lights twinkled all around the living room. We'd decorated Amos's cage with a sprig of mistletoe, though Kalaya wouldn't kiss him to save her life. I did, thanking Jesus that I was alive. "Kalaya, would you read Matthew 2:10?"

"Yeah, girl," she said. She plopped down on the couch and grabbed my Bible, her long braids swinging across her shoulders.

Kalaya had redone my hair, this time in loose, crinkly "zillions" braids, though my head was still sore. I even got a dye job and sported the same honey-blond mane as Mom Addie's. I looked just as fierce, except for the brace around my neck.

Kal began to read: "'When they saw the star, they were overjoyed. On coming to the house, they saw the child with his mother Mary, and they bowed down and worshiped him. Then they opened their treasures and presented him with gifts of gold and of incense and of myrrh.'"

When they saw the star, they were overjoyed.

"Thanks, Kal," I said. We sat quietly for a few minutes, and I thought about the star that I had asked for, coming as a sliver of my mother-in-law's Starry Night mug. I wondered about the irony of that. What I loved had revealed the truth and ultimately saved me. I wished it were that simple for everyone I loved. Then I felt sad. I didn't love nearly as much as I should. The meager love I doled out wouldn't save anyone, least of all me. I silently promised God that I would change. I'd find my husband and get my friend Rocky back. I'd love in a whole new way. Starting now. "Kalaya?"

It must have been something in my voice. She looked serious. "What's up, girl?"

"Thanks for writing 'In Love and Trouble.'"

She'd named the article aptly, giving a nod to Alice Walker's book of stories of black women by the same title. "In Love and Trouble" had created the biggest buzz in the city, especially since Archie Dandridge was arrested the same day for the murders of Kate Townsend and Christine Webber and for assault on the object of Lieutenant Jazz Brown's "love jones." The story had even gotten mentioned on broadcast news. We watched the anchorwoman gaze starry-eyed at Jazz, who'd said, "My wife makes every moment we have together unforgettable." I couldn't decide if he meant that as a good or bad thing.

North Stars really do lead people to freedom. And love is that North Star.

"I love you, Kalaya," I said.

"I love you, too," she said, her eyes misting. "Thanks for spending Christmas Eve with me."

"You're my friend."

"You're just saying that because I made you famous."

"Hey, go ahead and open your present."

She went over to the tree and unwrapped my elaborately wrapped present. "*What?*" she exclaimed. "You got me a box of Jack Chick tracts!"

I laughed.

"You big kook." She cracked up.

"That's for putting all my business in the streets. I got you several copies of *This Was Your Life!*—in case you want to share the love."

We both laughed.

I heard a knock, not a pounding, at my door. "Who could that be?"

"Maybe Santa Claus came to town," Kalaya joked. "Or maybe somebody will be home for Christmas."

"Cut it out," I said. "It's probably carolers."

But I never got carolers.

I unlocked all three locks and swung open the door. My husband stood there, scowling at me. He didn't give me a chance to be happy to see him. "How many times do I have to tell you to ask who it is before you open the door?"

"Hello, Jazz."

"You didn't have the chain on, either."

Kalaya disappeared into my bedroom.

"Come on in, Jazz." I moved aside for him to enter. "Can I take your coat?"

"I won't be staying," he said, but he unbuttoned the black cashmere coat, revealing suit pants, as usual, and a white button-down shirt.

I smiled at him. I couldn't help it. It was so good to see him. "So, what brings you—"

He exploded. "You're hurt. Badly."

"I noticed, but—"

"You could have been *killed*."

"I know."

"Do you understand the concept of 'dead'? That means you aren't breathing, your vital organs aren't working, your spirit has gone to God, and you decompose with that awful smell."

"I understand dead, Jazz."

"Didn't I tell you not to sleuth?"

"Yes, dear."

"Say this with me: 'Columbo is a television character.'"

We said in unison, "Columbo is a television character."

"Archie Dandridge cannot strangle Columbo to death, Bell."

He'd called me Bell.

"I know."

"I mean it, woman. If you get yourself killed, I'm gonna *kill* you."

"That's a bit redundant."

"You are going to give me a stroke. My blood pressure goes up every time I think about you. You're trying to kill me. I don't know if it was God who sent you to me, or the other guy."

"I think it's hopeful that you're still engaging the question."

He looked at me. "You just have to win the argument, don't you?"

"We weren't arguing. You were just raging."

We stood staring at each other until he looked away. He spoke first, still looking toward the wall. "Thank you. For everything."

"You're welcome."

He looked back, taking me in. "I like your hair. You make a very sexy blonde."

"My mother said I look like Casper the Friendly Ghost."

"My mother would like it."

"I know."

I wanted to tell him how sorry I was, to tell him I loved him, and to tell him everything Mason and I had talked about, but my heart pounded, and I felt afraid and kept it all inside.

"Merry Christmas, Jazz."

"Merry Christmas, Bell."

"Take care of yourself."

His gaze swept my body. "He'd better take care of you."

"Who?"

"You know who."

Rocky.

"There's no he and I."

"There will be."

"No, there won't."

"I thought maybe that was true until Friday."

The hurt in his eyes was too raw and real for me to minimize. I let him hold on to his grief, as I would hold on to mine. I put the matter of *us* in God's hands as we stood facing off once again.

He looked like he was debating with himself, but he finally spoke. "I didn't marry you to keep you from testifying."

"I didn't really think you did."

"I did it for love. I didn't even do it for the baby."

I didn't say anything.

"I'm so mad at you."

"I know you are, Jazzy."

He turned to walk out the door again, not bothering to say good-bye. I didn't say it, either. I couldn't.

I locked the door behind him, then rested my back against the door. "God, that was hard." I closed my eyes. "Please bring him back to me." I took a deep breath.

Maybe God would. Maybe not.

I should have asked for ten million dollars and a Rolls-Royce. Someone knocked at my door. I unlocked all three locks and opened it again.

Jazz said, "You didn't ask who it was."

"I'm sorry."

"You're going to drive me crazy."

"It would seem so."

He sighed. He looked like a sad little boy. "I need to ask you and Rocky to forgive me."

"For what?"

"For this."

That man scooped me into his arms and kissed me to the moon! We nearly singed the carpet. He released me. "Good-bye, Bell." He turned to walk out again.

"Wait!"

He turned back to me.

I had told God I'd do a little better about love. I grabbed that man and put a kiss on him that he'd tell his great-grandchildren about. No love and trouble in that kiss. It was all love, baby. When I let him go, he panted. He shook his head, surprised, but I wasn't through. I snatched the collar of his shirt and ripped it open from neck to navel. Buttons flew like bullets in the air.

"Giiiirl!" he said. "What did you just do?"

"I ripped your bodice."

His mouth dropped, and he laughed like a loon, gathering the fabric together with his fist. He walked out the door, still laughing and shaking his head.

"I'll see you later, baby," I called behind him.

And I would. I'd make sure of that.

what it's like
to own a pet
sugar glider

By Dr. Amanda Bell Brown

PEOPLE ASK ME all the time what it's like to have a sugar glider for a pet, usually following the question "What in the world is that thing?" Let me answer the most compelling question first: "What is a sugar glider?" And no, it's not a kitchen accessory.

This furry little friend is a mammal; infraclass: Marsupialia. Marsupial. Sugar gliders hail from Australia or Indonesia. Adult sugar gliders are ten to fourteen inches long, with six to eight of those inches being their tails. Some people find them awfully cute, with their round black eyes, soft gray fur, and black stripe running down their backs. Others find them bizarre-looking, with their opposable fingers, squirrelly appearance, and the winglike membrane that, when spread, resembles a furry little cape.

You don't expect them to be chatty, but the truth is they make a fascinating range of sounds. They bark, chirp, hiss, and make a particularly frightening noise called "crabbing." After crabbing, your sugar glider may mercilessly attack you. You will find those opposable fingers quite annoying when your beloved pet is trying to murder you with them.

Be aware that sugar gliders need attention. In their natural habitat, they are sociable and tend to live in communities of twenty to forty. You will need to spend time with your sugar glider, holding it, playing with it, and letting it roam freely in your home. Even with this loving attention, it may still try to kill you on occasion. However, a vicious sugar glider is most helpful if a homicidal maniac is choking you to death.

Ignoring your sugar glider's need for time and attention may cause it to become depressed. I could help with that, but you don't want to go there. A depressed sugar glider is worse than a depressed thirty-five-year-old woman whose husband left her on their wedding night after he caught her kissing her pastor and friend because she was confused after having sex for the first time in seven years. That's *very* depressed. So please play with your pet.

Finally, sugar gliders are nocturnal creatures, which means they are up *all night*. If caged, your sugar glider will screech and bang against its cage until you free it to roam about your home, destroying your drapes.

That's what it's like to have a pet sugar glider. It's a wild animal, people! If your need for a baby gets extreme, get a dog or a kitten. Or maybe even a snake.

Then again, your sugar glider may just have your back, as my estranged husband is fond of saying. Who knows? The life he saves may be your own.

discussion
questions

1. Bell repeatedly pondered the Scripture "The heart is deceitful above all things, and desperately wicked: who can know it?" (Jeremiah 17:9 KJV). What do you believe that Scripture is saying? Does it imply that the heart cannot be known? Do you believe you know your own heart? Do you believe you can know someone else's?

2. Bell sees Jazz right before she is called to the crime scene. Do you think her assessment at the scene was influenced by his visit?

3. Has someone you were close to ever gotten into serious trouble? How did it affect your relationship?

4. Bell ended up sharing a passionate kiss with Jazz, even after she left the crime scene. How would you explain her behavior? How would you explain Jazz's?

5. Do you believe Bell and Jazz went too far physically? Did they sin? What is acceptable physical contact between a man and woman in love if they are not married?

6. Bell and Carly argue at the morgue. After Carly asks Bell if she slept with Jazz, Bell angrily tells her that if she had, it would be her, not Carly's, business. Is Bell's sex life her sister's business? Is sex outside of marriage a private matter?

7. Bell reminds Carly of her own involvement in sexual sin with her boyfriend, Tim. If you had a friend or family member professing Christian faith and you knew they were in sexual sin, how would you deal with the situation?

8. *Death, Deceit & Some Smooth Jazz* deals with real, difficult struggles with sexual temptation. Was it uncomfortable for you to read of Bell and Jazz's struggle? Why or why not?

9. Why do you think Bell married Jazz? Should she have?

10. Jazz caught Rocky kissing Bell. What should she have done immediately in that situation?

11. Bell decided to allow both Rocky and Jazz some "space." Should she have done that? How do you think she should have reconciled with her friend? With her husband?

12. Bell realizes that she wasn't as self-aware as she believed herself to be. Her experiences showed her that she was not as loving in relationships as she could be. What steps do you believe she should take to change this painful aspect of her life?

the show way

I GREW UP HEARING SLAVE STORIES. Instead of reading them in books, they came riding on the voices of my mother and aunts. Some stories were horrifying, some inspiring, but all of them were *personal*. They were about the people in my family—people whose names I've memorized, who suffered in ways I can only imagine. The oral tradition of my family was a deep wellspring from which to draw strength and courage. I feel blessed to be a keeper of those tales.

My great-grandmother was named Amanda Bell Brown. I loaned her spirit and name to my main character, Bell, because she needed a loving guide. I also gave Bell something I no longer have: my great-grandmother's quilt. I miss that quilt nearly as much as I miss my great-grandmother.

Quilts played a vital role in our country's painful history. They were something to keep the slaves warm—needful in the harsh, cruel environments they were forced to live in. The quilts were a beautiful and expressive testimony of the creativity of people who were literally considered subhuman. These quilts were often called "show ways" because a secret language hidden within their designs could point a slave to freedom.

Show ways were often employed in the Underground Railroad. Rebel seamstresses, black and white, stitched specific directions in the quilts' patterns. A monkey-wrench pattern was a call to pull the tools together to make the perilous journey. A sailboat pattern indicated that boats were available. The drunken path warned sojourners to travel east to west. The variations of the star pattern always reminded travelers to follow the North Star, Polaris.

It's estimated that 60,000 to 100,000 people made their way north to freedom using the Underground Railroad. While we are fortunate in America to now enjoy the freedom my slave ancestors were willing to die for, many of us still need a show way every now and then. As frail human beings, we are prone to the bondage that sin entangles us in. We need directions when our lives are blown off course. And when the world seems cruel and cold, we could surely use something to keep us warm.

May Jesus be our North Star, and may love wrap itself around us and lead us on a sure path to Him.

Saints, Suspicions &
a ticking clock

**an amanda bell brown mystery
book three**

excerpt from chapter one . . .

ROCKY SHOWED UP at my door with an offer that, in his words, I "no coulda refuse." Or maybe those were Marlon Brando's words. I couldn't be sure. My blond, dreadlocked former pastor/ex-boyfriend locked me in a stare with those big brown puppy eyes. He'd puffed his jowls out to utter the Godfather's most famous line while grazing his cheek with the backs of his fingers—an excruciatingly amiss imitation. I'd seen newborn babies smile more intimidatingly...

Rocky had on a typical Rockyesque uniform underneath his white down jacket—khaki pants and a long-sleeved Batman T-shirt. On that awful December night six weeks ago when I'd last seen him, he'd been wearing Napolean Dynamite moon boots. Now he sported a pair of hunter green Birkenstock clogs and rainbow-colored organic cotton socks he got at Whole Foods.

A cupid earring dangled from Rocky's right ear—a tormenting herald that Valentine's Day was coming soon. I'd celebrated it every year with our church, the Rock House. When I was still a member, my attendance left a lot to be desired, but I never missed our Valentine's Day feast. It assured that I wouldn't be alone and lonely, and I could actually give out some love from my meager supply.

That and we always had a chocolate fountain.

I tried not to think about the sting of Rocky kicking me out of his church. I didn't want to think about anything that had happened six weeks ago. Still, I figured whatever had brought him to my door had an olive branch attached to it, and whatever he asked of me, short of sin, I'd be willing to do to reconcile with him.

Rocky hung up his jacket, kicked out of his Birks, walked over to my rose red velvet sofa, and sat. I followed him, plopping down right beside him.

"So, what's the offer, Godfather?"

He stared at me. "Did you gain weight?"

Because I know it's rude to kill your loved ones, I let that one slide and gave him a polite smile.

"What's the offer, Rocky?"

I grabbed a mud-cloth throw pillow and cuddled it to my obviously expanding waistline. I waited for his answer.

"I want you to go to a meeting with me. It's only going to be the way coolest event you've been to in forever," Rocky gushed in a most *un*-Godfatherly way.

"Can you be a little more specific?" I had a feeling he didn't mean the Valentine's Day feast as the way cool event.

He didn't answer, just reached out and touched my hand, rubbing his thumb across my knuckles. "I really missed you."

Oh, man. That small gesture—him touching the hand nobody held anymore—that tiny movement had the effect of a pebble in a pond, creating ripples of unexpected sadness that circled out of my soul. *Lord, have mercy.* I didn't want to fling myself at him, begging like a rhythm-and-blues singer to keep loving me, to not give up on me, but something in me wished I could.

I didn't want to *marry* Rocky. I didn't want to couple with him at all. He had never been the love of my life. In that moment, I simply wanted to banish the nearly incarnate loneliness dogging my heels—my solemn, maddening companion, shuffling me through all those days without my best friend Rocky.

Without my husband, Jazz.

I gazed up at him with my own version of puppy eyes. "I missed you, too, Rocky."

We let a bit of silence sit between us on the sofa like a third and very quiet presence. Our heads hung low. Apparently we were both still smarting over the pain of separation.

Minutes passed, our hands still clasped together, while Rocky's merciful presence soothed the dry patches of my soul like olive oil.

Thank God. Thank God for every kind soul I don't deserve in my life who loves me anyway.

"Rocky." I made my voice as soft and small as a baby's blankie. He turned to me, his face as open and vulnerable as that blankie's little owner. I squeezed his hand. "I'm so sorry I hurt you."

Those puppy eyes shone with the compassion I knew like the backs of my freckled hands.

"I'm sorry for the things I did, too, babe. For the things I said that night."

"Don't call me babe."

He chuckled. "Some things never change." Again, those gentle peepers bored into me. "Why didn't you tell me you'd married Jazz?"

"At the time I didn't seem too clear on it myself. Things happened pretty fast, and the next thing I knew, I was a wife." I paused, the weight of that statement shifting just a bit since Rocky had shown up to help bear my burden. "He's mad at me."

"Duh-uh. You were kissing your blond boy toy." He nudged me with his tattooed arm. "What's going on with the two of you now?"

"I've seen corpses on Carly's autopsy table more involved than our marriage." I wondered if I'd ever get over Jazz. "I can only imagine what his parents think of me. I guess they'd say I'm the nightmare that took his ex Kate's place."

He regarded me with the care and concern I'd seen him lavish on the fortunate souls he counseled as a pastor. Rocky was only twenty-eight years old, but he'd been a pastor for two years. Two good years. He didn't have the life experience an older pastor would have, but God had given him an extraordinary shepherd's heart.

"You're not a nightmare," he said. "You jumped into a marriage with no spiritual or emotional preparation."

Like I, the stupid clinician, needed him to tell me that.

I sighed. "Yet another psychologist-heal-thyself thing." I looked away from him, guilt gnawed at me. "Maybe Jazz and I just aren't meant to be."

"Have you talked to him?"

I shrugged. "Just once. He came over for a few minutes on Christmas Eve. I let him know I wanted him in a way I knew he'd understand. And then I waited. He never came back."

"Why didn't you go to him?"

"The same reason I didn't come to *you*. I wanted to give

him some space to feel whatever he felt, and then decide on his own."

"But maybe he's not like me, babe."

"Ya *think*? And don't call me babe."

"Maybe he needs you to help him decide. Like some extra reassurance or something."

"That's crazy, Rock."

"It's not so crazy, babe."

In my mind I took back every nice thing I'd just thought about him. What did he know? Yes, he pastors a church of more than two hundred members. He did missions work. He had a shepherd's heart. He took pastoral counseling classes in seminary, but honestly! His voice sounded just like Patrick's on SpongeBob.

Rocky glared at me. "Babe . . ."

"Don't call me babe."

"Babe! You gotta go to him."

"But he yells. Sometimes he cusses like a fishwife."

"What's a fishwife?"

"I don't know, but my great-grandmother used to say that, and it stuck with me. Maybe only females cuss like fishwives. Maybe he cusses like the fish." Now *I* sounded like Patrick!

"Fish don't cuss."

"Okay. I know I should have reassured him."

He sighed. Looked at me with those eyes. Squeezed my hand. "Will you ever let anyone love you?"

"People love me, Rocky. My sister. My secretary. Sasha."

"I have doubts about Sasha."

I thought about that and chuckled with him. "You may be

right. My mother has done a few things that make me wonder. Now I'm really depressed."

"I want to see you happy."

"I want to see you happy, too. Speaking of which, how are you and Elisa?"

He reddened, grinned, looked away.

"What? Did you marry her in six weeks? My goodness!" For the first time, I didn't feel jealous that someone was interested in Rocky. Well, not much.

"No. I'm not married. I'm . . ."

"You're what?"

"She's really special, but it hasn't been that long since she left creepy cult dude. I'm not sure I should be involved."

"How involved are you?"

"I'm involved, babe."

"You're in love?"

He wouldn't say anything, but his goofy grin spoke for him.

"Rocky?"

He nudged me. "Cut it out, babe."

So Rocky really was in love. Wow. I always knew it would happen, but I didn't realize I'd still have the teensiest bit of pain knowing he'd moved on from me for good. I had seen a flower of astonishing beauty blossoming between Rocky and Elisa when I saw them together, even though it nearly killed me at the moment. But God knows Rocky deserved the biggest, juiciest love he could find. He needed to look beyond the nonexistent us. And he *still* calls me babe.

"Just take it slow, Rock. Trust me. The cost of moving too fast is astronomical, even if you are in love."

I could tell he didn't feel comfortable talking to me about Elisa. I decided to let their love blossom without my tending, pruning, or pulling up weeds. I got back to the business at hand. "Are you ever going to tell me what your offer is?" I eased into my sofa's lush upholstery.

Rocky's face lit up. Honestly, if that guy had a tail to go with those puppy eyes, it'd be thumping my sofa with joy.

"It's gonna be awesome, ba—I mean, Bell."

Apparently our little chat about Elisa had made him correct himself.

"You think everything is awesome, Rocky."

"I don't think *everything* is awesome."

"You said my Love Bug was awesome. You said Switchfoot's new CD was awesome. You said my new zillions braids were awesome, and you said the ice cream at Cold Stone Creamery was awesome." Okay, the ice cream at Cold Stone happened to be awesome for real. Lately I'd been craving it like the blind crave sight.

"But, babe." There he goes again. A holy war couldn't make that man stop calling me babe. "Those things *are* awesome."

"God is awesome, Rock. 'Awesome' meaning the subject inspires awe, as in reverence, respect, dread."

"You *reverence* your tricked-out VW Beetle," he said. "And I *respect* Switchfoot, especially Jon Foreman, and your way cool, African-goddess hair *inspired* me to get dreads."

I stared at him. Comments like these coming from Rocky rendered me temporarily speechless.

He filled the silence with his proposal. "I want you to go see Ezekiel Thunder with me."

WANT TO READ MORE?

Then check out *Murder, Mayhem & a Fine Man*.

Amanda Bell Brown is a forensic psychologist who needs a night out on the town. Depressed and knowing that her career isn't nearly as cool as prime-time television makes it out to be, she sets out to celebrate her recent birthday alone and winds up at the scene of a murder.

Believing she knows who the killer is, Amanda must collect all her wits to investigate the death, but it doesn't help that she would love to be asked out by the lead detective on the case.

As the mystery deepens and whole closets of skeletons come to light, Amanda realizes she may be the next target for the murderer. All Amanda wanted was to keep her faith strong, find a fine man, and enjoy another year of her life. Is that too much to ask without getting killed for it?

HOWARD BOOKS
A DIVISION OF SIMON & SCHUSTER